THE BOND

THE SECRET TALES, BOOK 1

SANNA BRAND

Afterworld
Publishing

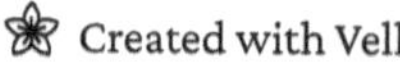 Created with Vellum

To Monica Enderle Pierce ~
A superb writer and an even better friend

The bond that links your true family is not one of blood, but of respect and joy in each other's life.
—Richard Bach

An Impossible Choice...

Lady Rosamund Fielding hides a secret so terrible it could ruin her, her family, and Major General Lord Rhys Lansdowne, the man she loves. Rose and Rhys were inseparable in childhood—their friendship was the one shining light in Rose's dark upbringing.

Yet when Rhys proposes, Rose refuses, for he can never know her shameful truth.

Returned from the Napoleonic wars and now the Marquess of Ravenscroft, Rhys is determined to uncover the reason behind Rose's rejection and win her hand and her heart once and for all.

Yet Rose's father, Earl Fielding, is demanding Rose accept Brigadier Viscount Pennworth's marriage proposal, threatening dire consequences if she does not obey.

Time is of the essence as Rose faces this difficult crossroad, where she is forced to confront past demons and choose a path.

Should she marry Rhys, deceiving him, and forever be branded a liar in his eyes? She cannot.

Wed Pennworth? Never.

Or flee? Away from Rhys, away from her father, and away from all she holds dear.

Rose has faced many dangerous choices in her life. Will this final one destroy her?

PROLOGUE

1802, ENGLAND

The click of a cocked shotgun, and fear shot down Rosamund's spine.

Holding Tessa's lead in a fierce grip, she froze. The person holding the gun stood by the copse, a youth, for he was smaller than Papa. At eight, Rose was tall for her age, but he looked a lot bigger.

Any minute, he might point the barrel in her direction. He wore a huge, wide-brimmed leather hat, so she couldn't see his face. Maybe he was a stable hand with those thick boots and that rough barn jacket that came to his knees. He uncocked and broke the gun, then hefted it onto his shoulder, walking toward her with confident strides.

Rosamund had come to Ravenscroft to give them Tessa. Papa once said with scorn they "cosset their animals," so this would be a good home for Tessa and her pups.

The youth was almost upon her when he spoke in a husky voice. "Who might you be, and what are you doing on our land?"

Rose knew she would have to speak to the Ravenscroft people, and she had dressed appropriately and practiced lowering her voice, so they would think she was a boy. "I am here to see your stable master."

"What are you doing with that dog?"

"She is *my* dog, Tessa."

"Where are you from?" he said.

Tessa's belly moved in and out, and the young man tilted his head as if not understanding.

Hadn't he ever seen animals having babies? Rose pointed in the vague direction of their estate.

"Fielding. I see," he said. "How did you get here?"

Boys could be so dumb. "We walked." Obviously.

He said nothing for a long time. What was wrong with him? She should just start down the hill towards the stables. He wouldn't shoot her. Probably.

"I will give you a ride home in our gig," he said.

No. Rose would not turn back now. "I *need* to see your stable master."

The rain had eased, but a chill breeze started her shivering again from the earlier downpour's soaking. Oh, how she wanted to be in her bed, nestled beside Tessa who would lick her face.

"I won't go home until I see the stable master." She crossed her arms like Papa did when he was angry.

The villain chuckled. "Come with me, then."

Rhys could not believe that the scrawny girl with her pregnant dog had walked from the Fielding estate to theirs on a miserable rainy day like this one. Her thinking was not sound, not at all. The odds she would be injured were high. Or the dog could have gone into labor. Or crossing the log bridge, the girl might have fallen into the river below. Ridiculous child.

He'd been in the woods on one of his survey missions, for he must be canny and sharp when he joined the cavalry in a few years. Surveying the estate was one of his self-appointed tasks, which was where he'd found the girl and her pregnant dog, her disguise as a boy not fooling him in the least.

He would get the pair to the barn and drive them home in the trap.

When they neared the stables, Fergus stepped from beneath an archway, skepticism writ large on his face. Ravenscroft's stable master was a canny one and shot Rhys a look that said the girl's disguise also failed to fool him.

She ran up to Fergus and stretched out her fisted hand holding the rope. "Please take Tessa. Please."

Fergus' gray eyes bored down onto her. "And why would I do that, young sir?"

For some reason, Fergus was going along with her playacting at being a boy. Odd. Rhys shrugged. It didn't matter.

Leading Tessa, the child inched closer to Fergus and petted her dog's head. "She is a purebred English setter. She got herself in the family way." A flush brushed the child's cheeks, but she didn't seem to care. "You must take her. You must." The girl notched her chin as she stared at the six-foot-tall, grizzled stable master who brooked no nonsense. Many a time, that steel gaze had sliced Rhys to ribbons. The girl did not flinch, determination taut in every fiber of her being.

"And what am I to do with the pups?" Fergus said. "We would have to feed and house the litter. That costs quite a few farthings."

The chit smiled. "I can help with that. I get a monthly gift of pence from my papa, and I will give it all to you if you will take Tessa and raise her puppies. You could give some away if you wanted. Only to good homes, though."

Rhys bit back the laugh about to explode. "You have a lot of demands, child."

"My Lord," Fergus interrupted. "I would suggest returning to the house before your father notices you are in possession of the shotgun and prowling the home wood on your own. You may be tall for your age, but you are only half-grown."

Rhys puffed up. At twelve, he was nearly a man. Boys of fourteen went off to war and that was but two years away. But Fergus had cut him down like a hatchet to a sapling.

The girl twirled to stare at him. "You are only a boy, too. Look at you acting like a grown-up, like someone in charge."

Rhys gave her teeth, but Fergus's eyes warned him not to overstep. He had almost blurted he was a courtesy earl. Patrick, his sarcastic younger brother, wouldn't hesitate with a set-down. But Rhys admired her pluck. Hard not to.

Which was when it struck him that she was Earl Fielding's daughter. How strange he had not met her before this. The girl was something special, and nothing like he imagined an earl's daughter to be.

She thrust the dog's rope toward Rhys. "Take her. Please, take her. If you do not, she will die."

The desperation in those big green eyes gave him pause. She was terrified, that was plain. Rumors filtered through his mind, ones about Earl Fielding. Nasty ones.

He held out his hand for the rope, and the girl's eyes morphed into a mixture of joy and sorrow.

With tight lips she handed it to him, got down on her knees, and hugged the soggy setter, burying her face in the dog's wet fur. She inhaled deeply, then whispered in the pup's ear. He could imagine her words, for he knew well the loss of parting from a beloved animal.

The girl rose, her expressive face calm. She did not weep. But those eyes, those damned eyes drew him in with a look of tragedy he'd long remember.

"Thank you." She turned and thanked Fergus, as well, then strode back toward the hill.

"Wait!" Rhys handed Fergus the dog's rope and ran after her. "Hold up." She patiently waited with her soggy clothes and sad eyes. "I will give you a ride home."

She shook her head. "No thank you, my lord."

Stubborn, too. "I will take you in the cart and pretend I'm delivering an order to the kitchens. No one at the house need ever know you were gone."

She assessed him as if determining whether or not he was worthy. The girl must have seen something acceptable, because she nodded. "All right. Thank you."

Rhys readied the trap and began harnessing the pony.

"What a beautiful Welsh Mountain Pony," the chit said.

He grinned as he slung on the saddle and put the breeching around the pony's body, fastening the crupper about his tail. Few adults in this locale knew the breed. Impressive for a little squirt. "He is that."

She scratched the pony's head. "Did you know they were here before the Romans came?"

"I did." That *she* knew came as another surprise. He finished harnessing the pony and climbed onto the seat. "Come on up. What is your name? And I already know you're a girl, so don't bother giving me something fake."

She scrambled up to the seat. "Rosamund."

"Lady Rosamund. Rose. But you're not exactly a Rose, though you are prickly enough for one. No, with that shade of hair—"

She scrunched her little face and wagged a finger. "Do not say carrot. Don't you *dare*."

He grinned. "I was about to say Rosie."

"Rosie? No one calls me that!"

Such a fierce child, determined and curious. "That is why I shall. Get on the floor in front of my legs."

Rosamund climbed into the small space before him. "What is your name?"

"Lansdowne."

"Your *full* name?" she said, lying down. "I need to know, my lord."

He placed a basket of vegetables beside her head and flung a blanket atop the pile of girl and produce. He had already learned people saw what they expected or wished to see.

Rhys inwardly groaned. "Griffin George Rhys Alistair Lansdowne. My tutor calls me Talbot, as I am currently Earl Talbot."

"Talbot? But you're a Ravenscroft, aren't you?"

"Of course I'm a Ravenscroft. Someday, I will be marquess. But my father, along with being a marquess, is also Earl Talbot, and that became my courtesy title at birth."

"Oh. Well, as I see it, if you are giving me the nickname Rosie, then I can call you Rhys, which is my favorite of your names."

It was his favorite, too, what his mother had called him. He laughed. "Understood. I expect we will become friends after this."

Rosie grinned. "Friends."

Rhys flicked the reins, and off they went.

CHAPTER

ONE

1816, 14 YEARS LATER

The soirée was intimate by *haute ton* standards, though exclusive was more apt when describing Almack's assembly rooms. But Rosamund, with her dislike of crowds, found it a crush. To dodge the raptor gaze of Almack's patronesses, she'd positioned herself behind a palm frond and indulged in reading her book.

Though off-season, Almack's patronesses were hosting several assemblies to celebrate the war's end. Lady Fielding wished her girls, Charlotte and Claire, to attend them, so the entire family had made the journey to town from Fielding Manor.

Rose sighed and turned the page in *Emma*, the newest book "By a Lady." At times, she wished for Emma's petite frame, pale complexion, and blonde hair. But only sometimes, for Rose's tall, spare frame worked well atop a horse, though she didn't love the multiplicity of freckles she gained from her hours spent outdoors. And while her eyes were a startling green, rather than the popular limpid blue, the color complemented her auburn hair, even if blonde locks were the fashion.

Ah, well. The more she imagined looking like Emma Woodhouse, the more she was content. For Emma could not permit the sun to splash across her face as Rose did. Nor could she leap atop a horse without the aid of a mounting block. And of course, were she a perfectly beautiful woman, annoying suitors would plague her even more, hungry for her dowry.

Rose turned the page. She had loved the writer's earlier works, and *Emma* was becoming a favorite, as perfect Emma was deliciously un-self-aware and quite amusing.

A burst of laughter, the chatter of the cotillion intruding. The voices, the sounds, the smells—all familiar. And tiresome. Clinking glasses, tittering laughs, and swooshing gowns were accompanied by the occasional shriek when a celebrated person entered the room.

Rose used her finger as a placeholder, her mind growing chaotic. She swallowed, the insipid ratafia punch taste lingering on her tongue. *He* might come.

Cedric, her cousin, said it was a possibility. Ceddie might be a terrible gossip, the ton chatter his meat and drink, but another acquaintance had echoed his words. Her stepsisters were giddy with the possibility of "our neighbor, the famous war hero's, return." They were young, twenty and twenty-two, and in their first and second seasons. Rose smiled. She adored them and their sweet enthusiasm.

He never used to enjoy Town, but still... He might appear.

To all of England's great relief, the war with Napoleon had finally ended, with the Little General now ensconced on Saint Helena. Rose hoped he stayed put this time. British troops had flooded home, and Lord Griffin George Rhys Alistair Lansdowne, Marquess of Ravenscroft was one of them, laden with honors and medals, and the youngest major general on Wellington's staff. Knowing Rhys, he would disdain the gilt and kudos.

Rhys was safe now, which was all that mattered, but the prospect of seeing him made Rose waver between elation and terror, for she had not seen her best friend in eight long years.

Ahhhs and sighs rippled through the room. Every fiber of Rose's being stood on high alert.

Rose craned her neck and sighed. The newest arrival was the Prince Regent. The prince wasn't a bad fellow, but he wasn't a particularly good one, either.

Nearby, her sire, Lord Fielding shoved his way toward the prince, her stepsisters and Lady Beatrice in tow, determined to introduce them. His lordship always found the lures of prestige and royalty irresistible.

Rose sat back, repositioning the palm leaf. Each wallflower beside her was high born, enough so that the patronesses offered them vouchers. Each was lovely in her own fashion, which happened to be out of fashion with most of the *ton*. Consideration of character sat on a much lower rung than beauty or money. Rose's bluestocking tendencies were anathema, as well, and her broaching of intellectual topics put off many a gentleman, as intended.

Oh, dear. She set her book aside and stood as the earl and her stepmother approached. Rose's anxiety, unusually high, made her reflexively pat her leather-lined pocket where her knife always rested.

"Your Lordship, Lady Fielding." She smiled and curtsied. "Are you enjoying the evening?"

His lordship wore a concerned frown. "Why aren't you dancing, sweeting?"

Revulsion shivered through Rose as she stared at the handsome man who had sired her, at his artfully styled auburn hair, with its wings of white. His imperious nose stared down at her, his mean eyes calculating.

She held his gaze, fighting the terrible dread that always accompanied his presence. "But I have danced, sir, with Lord Atherton and Sir Kingsley. As you know, I prefer to read."

His eyes laughed, but his tone remained smooth and earnest. "Lovely Rosamund, reading is a waste of good—"

"Now, Cornelius," Lady Bea said. The tall, curvaceous woman whom Rose adored patted her husband's arm. "Your daughter is where she wishes to be."

The earl's mouth thinned, but the orchestra struck up a waltz, a dance newly permitted at the assembly rooms. Bea took his arm, eyes sparkling, and suggested they take a turn.

The earl relented and off they went, though Rose caught his spark of fury directed at her.

Rose gave a relieved sigh and leaned back in her chair. Encounters with that maggot pie were exhausting. Some days, she felt as a will-o'-the-wisp, tossed this way and that by the earl's edicts and demands.

Renewed murmurs, more titters, and a shriek. Ah, a handsome male had entered. Rose couldn't quite see the entrance, but she would not stand up. That wasn't at all the thing.

More oohs and ahhs as the important someone approached the marble landing to be announced. She half-rose, pretending to straighten her skirts, gasped, and thumped back on the seat.

Rhys was *here*. Her heart nearly stopped, her joy so full.

He had led his share of cavalry charges on the Peninsula, but his acumen at strategy had gained him his position with Wellington's staff. Rhys saw far beyond what others perceived. He had always been brilliant, Rose knew that, of course. But he was also funny and wise and kind, traits not mentioned in the dispatches from the front.

Rose began to tremble. *Drat!* Though she'd seen him a few times while he'd attended the Royal Military Academy, more than a decade had passed since they'd spent much time together. Nonetheless, she knew him—she always would—and his and his sister Susannah's letters enabled Rosamund to keep him close during the wars.

But war changed a man. She had seen it herself in Fielding's returning staff, most of whom the earl had turned away due to their injuries, much to Rose's sorrow and horror.

Her breath stuttered out. Terror at seeing Rhys was winning over elation.

Was she perspiring? Dear heavens, don't let her be perspiring.

Should she reopen *Emma* and pretend to read? Perhaps leave it closed and chatter with a lady seated nearby. Maybe she should stand? *No. No.*

She wanted Rhys to seek her out, needed him to want to see her. Their letters during the war indicated he did. And yet…

Perhaps he had moved beyond their old friendship, after all, progressed so far from her reach that he no longer felt as she did.

Rosamund reopened her book and sank into the narrative. Or at least pretended to do so.

A presence approached.

She wasn't a coward. Yet she could not look up. With her nose buried in *Emma,* all she saw were white dress breeches, stockings, and black slippers.

Rosamund raised her face, and breath ceased to exist.

He wore his smart red dress uniform jacket, complete with medals and gold braiding, a sash wrapped around his waist. His ravens-wing hair, now clipped short, had turned white as snow.

Susannah had written about Rhys' hair changing color and how he often removed his hat so the enemy could spot him first. Idiotic, high-minded man.

The color change nonetheless startled her, though she knew of it. But those eyes, the color of a bluebird's wing, had not changed. Rose stared into them, shocked by their unfathomable sorrow mingled with an incandescent joy, the coupled emotions seemingly impossible.

He loomed larger than she remembered, but leaner, too, and it hurt that war had worn him down.

Rosamund dipped her head, her cheeks on fire, while her blood seemed to rush to her toes.

A white-gloved hand appeared, palm up, and he leaned forward. He was warm, his breath a balm on her cheek.

"Come dance with me, Rosie?" he said, his voice a rough whisper.

Tears threatened, eyes aching to spill. No one but *he* called her Rosie.

"Lady Rosamund?" he said.

Without raising her face, she placed her gloved hand in his, his grip confident.

He was here. The man she had loved forever. Also the man forbidden to her by her own sense of fairness and justice.

"Lord Ravenscroft." She stood, tipping her head to peer up at his great height. His face was stark and drawn and weathered, with fresh lines absent from the boy who had left for military college when he was sixteen and she twelve. And yet, the humor and delight in those eyes shined bright, too.

He leaned forward again, his breath brushing her ear. "You look quite lovely, Rosie mine."

"Thank you, my lord." Why had her voice trembled like a chit just out of the schoolroom? "I am no fashion plate. Nor do I aspire to be one. Rather, I am a mature woman long on the shelf."

He laughed as he walked her toward the dance floor. "Absurd. You are but six-and-twenty."

Rosamund pursed her lips.

"Then am I an old codger at thirty?"

Rose's lips twitched, but she somehow managed to keep her solemn air. "I often assist Lady Fielding as a chaperone, Lord Ravenscroft." She nodded toward her stepmother and sisters.

Grinning, he glanced their way, then fastened his gaze on her. "If they knew the real you and all your misdeeds, they would not let you chaperone a pony."

She sniffed. "I am a different person now than when you left."

"I should hope so, considering the last occasion we spent any time together, you were but twelve. But your letters tell the tale."

True, they had written many letters to each other via her friend Lucy, though their frequency had diminished after the Peninsula campaign.

"In fact," he said. "I would bet Ravenscroft Manor that you tumbled into as many scrapes as you did when we were children."

She laughed. "I believe you would lose your estate, sir."

"And *I* believe you are bamming me. Come, Lady Rosamund. Let us dance."

Rhys was back, and Rose had never been so happy. Or so sad.

CHAPTER

TWO

Rhys could not believe his Rosie was here, twirling the room in his arms. Rosamund was the fiercest girl he had ever met. Had she been on the battlefield, they would've won the war that much sooner. Yet she was a deeply compassionate soul, as well, caring for all wounded people and creatures. And him.

That day they had met at Ravenscroft when she had brought Tessa to them, their friendship had bloomed until they could finish each other's sentences.

She'd been quixotic as a child, impetuous and exuberant. Now she took his breath away, her uncommon grace exquisite.

Through the blood and the battles, the cries of the wounded, and the silence of the dead, her letters had warmed his soul. Those missives had also allowed him to see her grow from child to adult.

Ever since he'd met her, Rose was his stay, his warmth, and his delight, of which there was little to be had at Ravenscroft after his mother's passing. His Rosie would write him notes, send birthday cards, and gift him shells or pebbles, all telling him he mattered. She brought a wild joy to his life, and that was but one of the many reasons he loved her dearly.

Yet something had profoundly affected his Rosie. He could not explain it, for her letters remained enthusiastic, a joy to read. But between the lines, he sensed a hovering cloud that had darkened with each passing year.

Not once had she hinted of anything amiss, even when he'd queried her. Now that they were together again, he was determined to find out what exactly was plaguing the woman he adored.

Rose was stunned—all her dreams had come true. Well, most of them.

Rhys had not been seriously injured in the war, thank all the stars in the sky. He was whole, albeit thin. And they were dancing. Oh, how often she had imagined them waltzing, and it was splendid, even better than her fantasies. His grip on her hand and waist was gentle, but firm and authoritative.

But her thoughts trod a dark path, one dangerous both to herself and her dear friend. She would not, could not allow him inside.

Ah. It seemed she had become as unaware as most of the *ton.* Rhys was already inside, and he always would be. Heavens forfend her feelings showed. That would be disastrous, perhaps deadly, for both of them.

"How are your siblings, Rhys? From Susannah's letters, she and Thomasina are fixed at Woodbine."

"They are, and doing well."

"Susannah says Thomasina is a wonder with the horses you breed and raise there."

"All true."

"What of Patrick? I know of his prominence in the victory at Trafalgar."

"He continues his obsession with the sea."

"And the Royal Navy?"

Rhys chuckled. "Same obsession."

"Your cavalry compulsion I understood, given you talked about it *ad nauseam.* Yet I would swear Patrick, but a year younger, fixated on the sea to outdo you, in his mind at least. And your father, of course."

"That he did, Rosie, but his passion for the sea is quite real."

"Are you enjoying your stay in London?" she asked.

He raised a single black-winged brow, the one that bore a small scar from the time they had climbed the forbidden oak tree.

"All right." Rose chuckled. "I shall assume you still loathe town and all its accouterments."

"'Accoutrements?'" he said, grinning. "That's one way to put it."

If she could keep the questions coming, he couldn't question her. "Hermes is faring well, I hope."

"Dead." Clouds of sorrow darkened his eyes.

Horrified, she began to tear up *again.* Dear heavens, don't let this become a habit. But she had known his war horse as a foal, watched Hermes grow into a sweet and intelligent stallion with a brave attitude. "I'm so—"

"Forgive my abruptness, Rosie. I did not write about his recent passing as the wound is still fresh. Hermes had many injuries, yet held on until we defeated the French at Waterloo. Then, in a matter of days, my old friend simply faded away."

"He was a grand, stalwart boy."

"That he was. What of Lightning Bug's foal, Firefly? How is she?"

If she thought too hard about Bug, she would scream. The Earl had sold her beloved stallion when he'd turned twenty, saying Rose was too attached. "Firefly is wonderful and my particular mount."

Rhys nodded, his pupils contracting, but he said nothing. He loved horses as much as she, and he had loved her first stallion. When she'd written her sad tale of Bug's departure, Rhys had been appalled. "I am sure Firefly is a goer."

"That she is."

A man walked by and winked at Rose. She nodded back.

"A suitor?" Rhys said, plainly disgruntled.

A laugh burbled up. "Certainly not. As I mentioned in my letters, the earl calls me his horsemaster, stud master being too risqué." She lowered her voice. "I bred the man's mare to Diablo and their get has won several races."

"You mentioned few remarked on your youth or gender at your equine abilities in your letters."

Rose laughed aloud as they turned about the room, then peered beneath heavy lids at the gawking crowd. Within the circle of Rhys' arms, she cared not a whit. "Though my status at Fielding is unacknowledged, the owners seem pleased enough."

"I don't doubt they are, given your obsessions with horse breeding and husbandry. Since you were ten, as I recall."

"Nine, actually."

"Horsemaster." His crooked smile appeared. "The unconventional term suits you."

"Thank you! The earl enthuses over the profits I add to his coffers."

"As expected."

"Yes, well, no client speaks aloud of my position. Hence the wink. In truth, I collaborate with Fitz—"

"Fitz is still your stable master? He must be a hundred years old."

"Nearly!"

The music's tempo picked up, and they ceased talking as they twirled around the room.

Rhys' letters had been her salvation, his descriptions of the landscape, animals, and people vivid and filled with beauty and even humor, though he did not sidestep the battles. She had appreciated that, appreciated, too, when he shared his thoughts and feelings on the war.

But the war had taken a toll, his eyes weary with lines scoring his cheeks and furrows across his brow.

The battles must have been horrific things where men and horses were slaughtered right and left...

"Still with me, Rosie?"

Rose met Rhys' solemn blue eyes. She must say *something*. "Your hair. Susannah wrote me about the color change, but not why it occurred."

Rhys' amused smile made her heart flutter.

"A consequence of battle, or so I've been told. At the end of a particularly brutal campaign, my hair began falling out in clumps, so I shaved my head. I assumed it would never grow back."

A campaign so horrific his hair had fallen out. "Were you the only one this happened to?"

"I'm afraid so, at least in our company. I was the butt of many a joke."

"How awful."

He grinned. "I didn't mind. My men had a pool on whether or not it would grow back." He nodded, his white hair on full display. "It kept them occupied, always a good thing during a lull."

"It's quite surprising," she said. "Yet your brows remain black."

"Fortunately, or I would look like a ghost!" He shook his head. "At times, I feel like one."

Troubling words. "Your hair is striking and handsome." They both smiled, but Rose wondered what sight would make a man's hair fall out.

"Are you upset it took my sister to tell you about it in her letters, Rosie?"

She shook her head, eyes focused on his chest. "I'm simply thankful for my Miss Lucy acting as a conduit for our letter exchanges, but..."

Rhys must have read her grief at his suffering. "I am well, dear girl. All is well."

"Of course it is." She pasted on a bright smile.

"You are a horrible liar. You always were."

"Perhaps to you, but I am otherwise *good* at it."

He grinned. "Yes. I can see that."

A smirk escaped. "No need to lash me with your famous sarcasm."

The music came to a rousing end, and Rose resented it greatly.

Would that she could remain forever in his arms, where she was safe and cared for. Where she could keep him safe and care for him. But all things came to an end. She knew that truth too well.

Rhys released her waist and kissed her gloved hand. "I anticipate many more dances with you, my lady."

A thrill bloomed inside her, and she was about to reply when a hush filled the room. At the entrance stood the great man himself, the Duke of Wellington, flanked by two officers.

Rhys hissed.

"What prompted that?" she asked just as Lady Jersey announced the Duke of Wellington along with his two titled aides. Rhys laid her hand on his forearm and walked them toward the refreshments table.

"Ravenscroft!" bellowed the commanding voice.

His forearm tensed. "It appears I am summoned. Join me and meet the Iron Duke?"

Flummoxed, she could only nod.

Rhys eyed the three men, narrowing them on the striking officer standing to Wellington's right. He, too, wore enough medals to sink a ship. Rhys steered her toward the trio, now hidden amidst the crowd of well-wishers, but his height and breadth and, yes, those medals, easily cleared the path to his commander.

To her surprise, Wellington was not above average height, as was one of his military companions. The other matched Rhys, a tall man, elegant in bearing.

The commander eyed Rhys but slid his gaze to Rose. Oh, those bedroom eyes—a bright blue, they radiated admiration and appreciation, as if the great man had singled her out as unique. How fascinating. Her heart fluttered just a bit. Perhaps those rumored affairs were, in fact, truth.

"You wished to speak with me, sir?" Rhys wore a faint smile as he neared Wellington.

"That I did, Ravenscroft." Wellington whispered something in Rhys' ear, and Rose stole a good look at the other tall officer, a man

Rhys disliked. She wondered why. The officer was handsome, in a bronze-god sort of way, but his looks were not to her taste.

Wellington straightened.

"Always, sir," Rhys said.

"Ravenscroft," said the bronze-god officer. "Do introduce me to the fair lady at your side."

Rose nearly snorted as she found herself unexceptional looking.

"Lady Rosamund Fielding," Rhys said. "May I present you to Field Marshal Wellington, Brigadier Sir Jeffers, and Brigadier Lord Pennworth."

Rose executed her deepest curtsy before Wellington, then lesser ones before Jeffers and Pennworth.

Wellington took her hand and bowed over it. "A true pleasure, my lady. Ravenscroft spoke often of you."

The expected embarrassing flush burned her cheeks, but she donned her "my lady" face and smiled demurely. "As children, we had many adventures together, Your Grace."

"Perhaps my favorite tale was the one about your Tessa." Wellington raised searing eyes to Earl Fielding, who hovered mere steps away, the earl paling at the great man's scrutiny.

Her sire wore a smile—Fielding smiled a great deal—but she knew it for the lie it was. He was furious she had been introduced to the fabled duke before he had. After all, he was an earl.

She cared not one whit. Long ago, Rose had severed his stranglehold on her. Mostly severed, for he was endlessly concocting schemes for her to marry, which she had so far managed to thwart.

The orchestra struck up another waltz, and Pennworth held out a hand, his eyes boring into her like cold gray marbles. "My lady Rosamund, would you do me the honor of a dance?"

Rhys said nothing, but his one eye twitched in displeasure, a tell she recalled from their many poker games.

"I would," she said.

When Pennworth winged out an arm, Rose rested her hand

lightly atop it. Once on the floor, he bowed over her hand, a lock of bronze hair falling forward. "My lady."

Something about the man made her shoulders itch.

As they waltzed around the now-stuffy room, he held her gently, no tighter than was proper, his long, lean frame graceful. He wore his hair in the forward-combed Brutus fashion, the style emphasizing his oval face, so unlike Rhys' more angular one. Though Rhys disliked him, and he did not suffer fools, Rose would make her own appraisal.

"Major General Ravenscroft omitted my full name," he said. "I am Brigadier Lord Pennworth and Viscount Pennworth, as well."

Well, the man thought highly of himself, that was certain. Perhaps he should, but Rose never admired boasting. She nodded and smiled. "And which do you prefer, sir, Viscount Pennworth, or Brigadier Lord Pennworth?"

"Pennworth will do."

Rose tittered, a laugh crafted for just such an occasion. "But I barely know you, sir, and that is much too familiar."

"Then we must become better acquainted," he said in a jovial tone.

"How lovely."

See, she wanted to tell Rhys she could lie with the best of them.

CHAPTER

THREE

Days later, after their return to Fielding, Rose practiced her *kalari* forms, then took her breakfast in the light-filled morning conservatory, where beyond the glass windows, the early September heat had already begun to simmer. Nightmares about her father had troubled her sleep, tiring her, but cheerful birds plucked fruit from the chokeberry bush as vivid butterflies danced from flower to flower. A breeze rustled the beech leaves, and while she had sat in the same seat for days on end, Rose never grew weary of the soothing garden view.

She took another bite of toast topped with Scottish blaeberry jam, a favorite sent down by her Scots relatives, and lifted her knitting, while she returned to scanning *The Times*.

Soldiers continued to pour into the British Isles, many bearing brutal injuries both physical and mental. Yet there was little work available to these exhausted and battle-weary men.

Several returning locals, as well as former servants, had come to Fielding seeking work. The earl had turned them all away, much to her sorrow. But yesterday she'd had a bit of luck. She had spotted Billy Broad, a blond giant who had lost an arm at Waterloo, his posture stooped and dejected. Rose had snuck outside to talk with Billy, reminding him that Ravenscroft's marquess had fought and returned, as well.

Billy balked at approaching such a high-ranking and lauded peer, but she'd said the marquess donned his pantaloons one leg at a time, just as he. Billy had laughed, and Rose had quickly penned a note for Rhys, giving it to the former soldier. With a tip of his hat, Billy headed back up the drive, whistling, until his straight, determined figure had vanished beyond the rise.

Her tea had grown cold with her musings, and she hadn't knit more than a row on Bea's shawl. She replenished her tea from the pot, thankful the staff knew she often ruminated over breakfast and always supplied her with extra.

Amidst completing another row, Lucy bustled in. Her former maid, governess, and now factotum-cum-companion had been with Rose for near twenty years, a fierce protector and true friend. Lucy had nicknamed Rose *Minnu*, which meant "full of light" in Hindi. She was a beautiful soul and a constant in Rose's topsy-turvy world.

Rose's debts to Lucy could never be repaid. Her friend had taught her *kalari*, which enabled Rose to defend herself. Given her correspondence with Rhys was socially unacceptable, Lucy had been the one to mail Rose's letters to Rhys and to receive missives from him intended for Rose. Her friend had done much more, yet today, worry crinkled Lucy's lined face.

Rose set her knitting aside. "What is wrong?"

Her friend crossed her arms over her belly and harrumphed, a sure sign of her displeasure. "Your father has requested you honor him with your presence at the barns."

Of all places... The stables held no interest for the earl.

Rose's talent with horses had come from Maman, yet no matter his faults, His Lordship wasn't a stupid man and took advantage of Rose's gifts, though the earl seldom bothered with the equine beasts. His Lordship disliked their smells, their sounds, their largeness—all qualities which delighted Rose.

His request was an order, of course. "Thank you, Lucy. I'll attend to it." Rosamund picked up her knitting and began another row.

"You know as well as I, *Minnu*," Lucy said. "Keeping the earl waiting is never good."

Rose inwardly sighed. As the years passed, Lucy had become more and more distraught by Rose's tortured relationship with the earl. Through artifice and daring, Rose had managed to keep it in hand, but Lucy still fretted.

One last sip of tea and she stood with a smile and pressed her hands over Lucy's crossed arms. "It will be all right, Lucy."

"I do not trust him," Lucy said.

"Nor do I." She held the smaller woman's eyes, hers softening with affection. "Please do not worry."

Lucy's jaw bunched, her chocolate eyes deep swirls of concern, but she nodded.

"Would you brush out my blue plaid riding costume, please?"

Lucy rolled her eyes. "The one with the split skirt."

Rose laughed, she couldn't help it, having chosen the outfit to irritate the earl. What agency she had with His Lordship was eternally precarious, her clothes but one of the small ways she asserted herself.

"The one with the split skirt," Rose said.

Lucy sniffed, then departed.

Having displeased her friend and expecting to vex her father even more, Rose girded herself for the sparring match to come.

Rose's mood lightened as she climbed the familiar hill to the barns. It always did when horses surrounded her. They nickered from their pastures as she passed, and she returned their greetings, calling their names and telling each they were fine fellows or gals. These magnificent beasts had been her surcease during the troubled years where each day was agony and each night worse.

Up ahead, the earl stood beside Fitz, deep in conversation with their stable master. Hard to imagine what the two had to discuss. Though a bruising rider, the earl cared little for the animals other than the gold guineas they fetched or the quality of the foals they produced. Rose often wondered what drove His Lordship to become a horse breeder. Then again, his motivations often eluded her.

It had been Maman, a Scottish earl's and a French countess' daughter, who had taught Rosamund all she knew of horses and beyond. The earl had loved her mother, in his own way, she supposed, or perhaps he merely appreciated Maman as a possession, as someone on his arm who complemented his good looks with her sparkle and beauty? With Maman's death, Rosamund experienced a deep loneliness. But that was long ago.

Today, the earl was dressed to the nines, per usual, while she had donned her breeches and boots.

"How can I be of assistance, Lord Fielding?" Rosamund stepped before the earl and curtsied, one in direct contrast to her apparel. As expected, the earl reacted.

"Dear Rosamund, what horror are you wearing?"

Fitz drifted away as her father stepped near. Disgust filled her to the brim, but she presented the calm and composed demeanor of a respectful daughter.

Both of them knew it for the fakery it was, yet neither uttered a word about their permanent estrangement.

Around them, stable hands bustled, pointedly ignoring them. The world closed in, as if she and the earl were alone in this universe, a silent conversation threading beneath their verbal one.

"I looked at that mare of yours. She is quite gravid."

"Yes. Ravenscroft's stallion took. Firefly is getting larger by the minute. Soon, I'll have to choose another mount."

"I don't recall the stud's name."

"Enbarr."

"Never heard of him."

Unsurprising. "He returned from overseas several months ago. A swift and sturdy war horse."

"Let's hope their get is profitable."

"Let's." Horses meant two things to the earl—profit and transportation. Little did he know she had no plans to sell Firefly or Enbarr's foal.

The earl headed toward the barn and walked down the aisle, Rose following, and for each wicker she received, she paused to give that horse her attention. She scratched behind its ears or beneath its chin or kissed its nose, the velvet muzzles irresistible.

"Come along, sweeting," the earl said.

Her stomach lurched at the endearment, but Percival, a Belgian-Thoroughbred cross, nipped at her hat, a common occurrence that left many scars on her headgear. She tapped his nose, trying in vain to keep the laughter out of her voice. "Stop it, you beast."

Percival's response was to pull the bonnet from her head, hair pins and all.

"Beastie!" She rapped his nose harder. "Let go."

He did, and Rose noted the small tear in the hat's jaunty brim. Nothing a good needle couldn't cure. She punched it back on her head, her hair now falling in disarray around her shoulders.

"Enough of your deflections, daughter," His Lordship said in his jolly way as he halted. "I have news."

The man hovered like a fat black tick, bloated on his own importance. "And what might that be, my lord?"

He clasped his hands behind his back. How he remained lean and fit with his excessive drinking she did not know, but he bristled with confidence. Rose never underestimated him.

"I have received three requests from gentlemen wishing to court you." An unctuous smile rippled across the earl's face.

The requests were not new. As an heiress and a lady, she had been deluged with courtship requests after her come-out. She had rejected them all, and soon her reputation for turning away suitors made her pursuers cease, other than the occasional request by a deluded gentleman.

Initially, His Lordship had harangued her to accept someone, *anyone.* But as he saw his equine profits mount, his diatribes had tapered off, then ceased.

These fresh requests surprised her, and the earl knew it, though neither by word nor gesture did she reveal her feelings. Her mind raced to Rhys, but she swiftly doused that absurd dream. "I see. I can only wonder what has brought this about."

His Lordship's self-deprecating chuff was as false as his heart. "I may have mentioned to one or two friends that you were open to courtship."

"But I am not—"

"No?" he said. "But, dear daughter, you have so much to offer."

Not *her,* but the Scottish lands and inherited pounds she possessed. Thirty thousand was a tidy bundle, indeed. Couple that with the Scottish estates that became hers at eighteen, and she was prime pickings.

His Lordship had jockeyed to acquire the land. A futile attempt. Her settlements included a guardianship, not the earl, but the Chieftain of Clan Murray and the fourth Duke of Atholl, a Scottish title, though he possessed an English peerage as well. The earl was most wary of the duke.

Her lands and monies had been bound in an ironclad trust by her mother, which made His Lordship both livid and avaricious.

"Your husband would be the proud possessor of your lands and those many gold guineas," His Lordship said.

He would, and Rose would lose all control. Irrelevant. Rosamund would never marry. She had vowed that long ago. "I have no interest in marriage, my lord."

"Interest or not, I have given permission for you to be courted."

She rolled her eyes, allowing that slight movement to break through her stoic facade. "And who, might I ask, are these three paragons?"

They stepped into the light, the welcome barn scents mingling with air perfumed by nicotiana and gladiolus. She inhaled while watching the turning maple leaves dance in the autumn breeze, then walked toward the house, the earl keeping pace.

"First," he said. "We have the Reverend Sir Abernathy, who looks to rise in stature. He is, after all, the second son of an earl."

"I'm shocked you would even consider a second son," Rose said.

The reverend was a decent enough man, though she had little in common with him. As if that would influence her father in any way.

The earl smiled, eyes dancing with one of his schemes. "Continue."

He ran a finger down her cheek.

She froze, then forced herself not to back away.

"Brigadier Lord John Pennworth," he continued. "He is greatly attracted to you, daughter."

She knew exactly what attracted him, and it wasn't her. That touch of animosity between Pennworth and Rhys sparked her curiosity. She must ask Rhys what lay between the two when she next saw him.

Rose spotted Petals, the barn goat, a funny creature who wandered the aisles often entering stalls to keep various horses company. She called, and Petals pranced over to receive the head scratches she was due, while Rose took care the goat didn't mistake her breeches for luncheon and begin to gnaw.

"The third is Ravenscroft," Fielding said, his expression sour. "Though I wished to decline his suit, he had the gall to have Wellington pen me a note touting his praises, which made it impossible for me to refuse him."

His disdain was unusual, for Rhys was a wealthy marquess. "Why wish to decline his suit?"

There was that nasty smile again. "I have my reasons."

The thought of Rhys courting her...her heart sang. As it always had.

Rose had fallen in love with Rhys when she was ten or maybe nine. A child's version of love, true, but love nonetheless. They had been dear friends, comrades in everything since she was eight, and when he would arrive home from boarding school in summers or holidays, her heart would go all aflutter. At twelve, she hadn't understood what those flutters meant. But they proved to be an awakening of seeds planted throughout their friendship, which had grown and blossomed into much more.

One sunny day in May of her eleventh birthday, Papa away on some jaunt or other, she peeked out her bedroom window to see Rhys walking the drive carrying a large basket that swayed with each step.

Maman had recently moved Rose from the nursery to her own grown-up girl's room, Maman having deemed her old enough. At the time, Rosamund had not understood why her mother waited so long for the move. One year later, given the earl's actions, she did.

That day, Maman was out with the horses and Rose flew downstairs, dying to see her friend. Did Rhys intend they have a picnic? What fun!

Rhys stood in the front hall, the basket at his feet. That funny flutter hit her again. He had grown taller and more gangly than ever, his features all boyish determination. Rose's heart thumped.

She rushed into the hall, her face splitting into a smile. He smiled back in a way that made her feel...special. Maman made her feel the same way, and she had hoped one day Papa would, too. The curtsy she executed was almost perfect, though she did not dip as low as her mother required. She had to get it right, for Rhys would be a marquess someday. Not that either of them cared about such things.

His returned bow was perfection, but at fifteen he knew his way around courtly manners.

Miss Lucy had followed at a more stately pace. Born in India, Miss Lucy had taught her many exotic things and Rose loved her. Now, she observed them with warm eyes.

"Hello, Rhys. What a nice surprise." Rose was pleased her calm tone held none of the quivers she was feeling.

"Rosie." His smile was broad and a little bit devilish. He winked at Lucy, who showed her teeth, which said he was being too cheeky by half.

"Today is your birthday," Rhys said. "I brought you a gift."

She clapped, too excited to hold it inside. "What? What? Tell me!"

He gestured to the basket. The *moving* basket. She knelt and flipped the lid.

Out pounced a puppy!

She scooped it up, nuzzling its soft fur. "Oh, he's beautiful."

"He's a purebred, as your papa dislikes mixed breeds, a Cocker Spaniel. I hoped that with you turning eleven and his being a pure-bred, you would be allowed."

As gently as possible, Rose placed the pup on the floor where he began to sniff at her and Rhys, who crouched beside her. The pup moved to Lucy, then to a chair, and lifted his leg. Rose scooped him up and bustled outside where the little fellow christened a marble pillar. Back inside they went.

"My lord!" Maman breezed into the hall, smiling with delight. "Welcome! What is this?"

Rhys sketched a bow. "Good day, my lady. I've brought Rosamund a puppy."

Her mother's smile faltered. "A thoughtful gift, your lordship, but..." Maman peered first at Lucy, then down at Rose, again holding the pup who nuzzled her neck.

"Isn't he wonderful?" Rose said. "He's a purebred, Maman!"

"He is, *petite chou.*" Maman sniffed and straightened. Her mother might be half-French and half-Scottish, but her French side always won. "But I am afraid you must not keep him."

Rose set the pup on the floor with care, eyes burning. "Why ever not, Maman?"

Maman bit her lip. "You know why, *mon rayon de soleil.*"

Rose *did* know—Papa.

Tessa had almost been lost to her, and a year ago, her papa disapproved of her pony, Patches. The sweet pony disappeared without a word to be replaced by a horse. Even worse was the injured rabbit she had rescued in the wood and was nursing back to health. One evening, when Cook served coney for dinner, her father casually thanked Rose for fattening up such a fine meal.

No, she could not keep the pup. She lifted him once more and handed him to Rhys. "Thank you, but I cannot accept."

"Very well." Rhys frowned, then brightened. "I know. I will keep him for you, and when you come visit, he shall be as yours." Rhys was a canny one, and in his pretty blue eyes, she saw sadness and understanding. "Someday, I will gift you a pup you *can* accept, Lady Rosamund."

The blacksmith's chime of metal on metal returned Rose's attention to the earl. "I see. Those men are quite a triumvirate, though none will succeed."

He slapped his hands together. "One will, and within the month."

She whirled on him, the time for playacting ended. "I will not marry, my lord."

"Oh, you will, sweeting." He winked, his smile widening. "Or your sisters will suffer."

Even if she wed, her sisters could not accompany her, as Charlotte and Claire would never leave their mother. Her stepmother

Beatrice was a kind woman attached to an evil man, their relationship mystifying.

His call to battle rang loud and clear, but she must be clever about this. "We have discussed this. You will never get the land, for it will belong to my husband."

"But I will," the earl said. "For those Scottish lands will be attached to the dower contract. Once wed, your husband will hand them over to me, you see. He will get the money, after all."

Rhys would never accept such an arrangement, but Pennworth or Abernathy... Rose would bet he had made bargains with one or both men. "You will *never* gain control of my lands."

"Think on it, and on what your sisters will experience. Just the three of us, Charlotte, Claire...and me."

He well knew she loved her stepsisters. Curse him. She would find a way out of this newest conundrum.

"With your marriage," he continued, pacing near a grassy paddock. "I will vow your sisters will remain intact, don't you see?"

She saw. But if he broke his vow, no matter what happened to her, she would cut his cock from his body and stuff it into his mouth. *Contain the fury, Rose.* "That option has its appeal."

"I thought it might. Abernathy arrives at two o'clock to accompany you on a ride. My suggestion."

Rose nodded, though her anger rose again.

"Do go change." The earl's gaze moved from her toes, up her body, to the top of her head, his expression one of amusement. But she noted the heat behind those eyes, the avarice, and speculation.

The smile she offered him was a dulcet one. "I plan to do just that, my lord. Do excuse me."

"Of course, my dear." He brushed the back of one hand across her cheek.

She slapped it away, cursing herself for allowing him to provoke her fury.

Her father just chuckled and sauntered off.

Rose hurried down the path, mind a-whirl, heart thumping.

The earl desperately wanted her land, which contained a profitable whisky brewery. He always had. Yet Maman had willed them to her.

Thoughts of a forced marriage, threats against her sisters, and her feelings for Rhys made her frantic. With Rhys courting her...

She must remain strong. She must refuse.

Her chuffed breath was a bitter one. Her trials with the earl had made her strong, her mind and heart wrapped in bands of iron. Except when it came to Rhys and others she loved.

Rosamund bustled through the conservatory door.

Lottie, seated on the sofa, looked up from her sketchbook, and her charcoal stilled. "Where are you off to in such a hurry, sister?"

"I'm riding out with the Reverend Abernathy and I must change."

"I see." Lottie rolled her eyes. "Isn't he rather...bland?"

"A milquetoast."

"Not for you." Lottie began sketching again. "Most definitely not for you."

Upstairs, Lucy had laid out a pale ochre riding habit with a full skirt. A subtle message of what a lady *should* wear and how a lady *should* behave. Which was absurd, given Lucy had taught Rose *kalari*, a most unladylike practice. And yet she persisted.

Not today, dear friend. Rose stalked to the larger armoire and flung open the door. She *was* unladylike for a woman of the peerage. The idea delighted her.

She chose the red habit, with its gold braid details, and she pulled out the jacket and split skirt. Her riding astride should quite horrify the reverend. Annoying wrinkles covered both.

A soft knock, and in breezed Lucy, who took one look at the habit Rose held and said, "Bah!"

Rose explained the earl's demands and the habit's purpose, and she slumped onto the bed.

"It's back to the same old thing, Lucy—what I'm worth." Lucy slid up beside her, wrapping an arm around her waist.

"How many times have I asked your permission to kill him?" Lucy said.

A watery laugh bubbled out. "I wish I'd kept count."

"Once again, *Minnu*, you are not the source of the rot."

A deep breath later, Rose said, "I know. Yet I can't help but feel worthless. A creature reduced to pounds and land."

"Recall your value as a human being," Lucy said. "How you have protected those who serve your father from his wrath. How you make your sisters and stepmama feel cherished. How you care for the people and animals on the estate. All love *you*."

"You forgot how I allowed Maman to die a useless death."

"Stop this!"

Rose startled.

"You did not allow your mother to die, *Minnu*," Lucy said. "You did all you could to bring her out of her sorrow."

"My resentment—"

"Was natural. She surrendered to the earl, to her fate, rather than help you. Do not discount how much you helped her, Rosamund, particularly that final year. No, you must remember your strength, which is bounteous."

Rose straightened. "You're right, Lucy. I will do my best."

Hours later, Rose donned the red habit, then sat at her secretary to write Rhys a note. Her hand stilled.

Her dear friend. Her dearest friend, who was about to come courting. If she sent him notes, even ones railing against the earl, he might feel Rose encouraged his suit.

She lay down her pen, her heart tightening. Did he know he had been her surcease and comfort during the worst time of her life? The year he had completed boarding school before advancing to the Royal Military Academy, she had used his warmth and kindness as a balm to escape her horrors.

Maman began to fade that twelfth year, the earl... Soon, Maman was unreachable by her or anyone else. Rhys had been both her rock and shelter, though she had never revealed to him what plagued her.

Over the course of that year, Rhys had enabled her to survive and to grow strong, and when he left for the academy, she stood straight and proud, sending him off with a smile.

No, she could not write Rhys a note. Rosamund brushed off her skirts and prepared for battle.

CHAPTER
FIVE

The Rev. Abernathy was an average-sized man with sandy hair and an overbite. He was not unkind, but Rose could not call him kind, either. He was a neutral person, near invisible at times, but she had always sensed an underlying current of entitlement within his pastoral breast. While the Good Book stressed humility, she suspected the reverend had failed to read those specific passages.

And there he was, costumed in his usual clerical garb riding a nervous bay stallion. The beast wasn't a bad sort. She had met him a time or two, but in Abernathy's too-busy hands, the horse was devolving into a near-unmanageable ride.

The reverend nodded a hello, and Rose responded with a weary smile. She forced herself to brighten as he cantered up to her in the stable courtyard where Firefly was saddled and happily eating grass near the paddock rails.

"You really should tie that horse, Lady Rosamund," Abernathy blustered. "If you plan to ride that one, you really must change her tack to an appropriate sidesaddle."

Rose did not laugh, though it was hard not to. She might rule the stables, but male condescension was both typical and tiresome. The wish to flee to Scotland appealed, to live a less fraught life. But Charlotte or Claire could not be left to His Lordship's tender mercies.

"Thank you for that advice, Reverend Abernathy, but Firefly is fine as is." She clucked, and the mare walked to stand in front of her, knowing perfectly well of the treats in her habit's pocket. Rose handed over a carrot, then kissed the mare's impossibly soft nose.

"Shall I walk your mare to the mounting block, my lady?" he said from atop his stallion. "Or can I fetch a stableboy to change your saddle?"

She often used the block when wearing her split skirts, but today she wished to make a point.

"Thank you, but neither will be necessary."

Rose walked to Firefly, hiked her split skirts, fingers in the loop of her train, and bounced, lifting her foot into Firefly's left stirrup and swinging her right leg over the mare's back and into the saddle.

Abernathy's horror felt rewarding, and she chided herself for being so pleased.

Surprising her, the reverend said not a word.

Claire bustled up the hill in her bright blue habit. "Sorry I'm late!"

A groom brought Claire's side-saddled gelding, and Claire mounted.

"Lady Claire is joining us?" The reverend said. "How, er, delightful."

Rose inwardly smiled. She had asked Claire to join them, and her sister was late, a frequent occurrence, for she was often deep into one of her archaeology treatises or books. "It would be most improper were I to go off alone on a jaunt with a gentleman, sir."

"Might I join you as well, Lady Rosamund, Lady Claire?"

A new voice and Firefly danced at her shocked reaction to Rhys' arrival. Rose got herself and her horse under control, enough to answer in a well-modulated voice.

"How delightful to see you, Lord Ravenscroft," she said. "Please do join us."

Abernathy sputtered but said not a word.

"I see your horse has a foal in her future," Rhys said.

"How indelicate, my lord," Abernathy quipped.

"Nothing but the truth, Abernathy," he said in reply.

"She is showing quite well," Rose said. "Soon, no more riding." She patted Firefly's neck.

Rhys wore a broad smile, and when Abernathy adjusted his stirrup, Rhys winked. *Winked!* Rhys had never winked at her in his life, and though he had a fine sense of humor, it tended to be dry as dirt.

"I have arranged a ride with Lady Rosamund," Abernathy said, puffing out his chest.

"I see that," Rhys said. "And Lady Claire?"

Abernathy puffed up. "Well, of course I am delighted with her presence."

Rosamund bit her cheek. Devil it, Abernathy was a stuffed shirt.

Rhys nodded. "Yet you object to *my* presence because...?"

"No, of course not," Abernathy said. "Not really. I just..."

Rhys grinned, and merciful heavens, he was handsome. When he smiled like that, a dimple appeared on his left cheek. A *dimple*.

She felt the dreaded red creeping into her cheeks and knew her freckles would shine like beacons. Her mouth dried. The urge to touch Rhys made her fist her hand. This situation would not do.

"Ours was a private outing, you see, Lord Ravenscroft," Abernathy said. "Private."

Rhys patted his horse's withers. She knew the stallion well, given he'd sired Firefly's foal. He was a striking liver chestnut over seventeen hands high, but under Rhys' hand was well-behaved even in the presence of Abernathy's stallion, whose delicate frame was dwarfed by the war horse.

"Private, you say?" Rhys' words held a low growl that startled the reverend. "My, my."

Through gritted teeth, Abernathy said, "Lady Rosamund, what is your opinion on the matter?"

Her opinion was that Abernathy should leave, but manners prevented her from voicing the words. "That our quartet shall have a grand time!"

Rose cantered off, and the remaining trio followed suit, Rhys catching up and riding alongside until she slowed to a walk. They entered the home wood, a sun-dappled path with showy autumn leaves, to halt on a promontory overlooking Fielding's hills and valleys.

Rhys and Claire looked relaxed, while Abernathy visibly sweated beneath his collar and heavy coat. The day had warmed to uncomfortable levels, and though her habit was the lightest of wools, she had begun to sweat, too. Rose began to undo her jacket buttons.

Claire mirrored her actions. "We had that awful, wet, cold summer, and now this divine heat. I love the heat. Do you not, Rose?"

"I do, though I'm not dressed for it. It's rather surprising this time of year."

"That it is," Rhys said.

"Is there a problem, Lady Rosamund?" Abernathy pointed to her jacket resting before her saddle.

"No problem. We're on home ground, and everyone's warmer than a baked muffin. Feel free to remove your coat, as well, Reverend. On a jaunt such as this, we practice a bit of informality."

"Well, if you say so." Abernathy unbuttoned his coat, though did not remove it, while Rhys tossed off his jacket and cravat.

She and Rhys had no compunctions about doffing clothes as children. When the earl and Maman were away, which was often, they loved to sneak off for a swim, her in her chemise and him in his smalls. A blissful time.

"My Lord Ravenscroft!" Abernathy said in a shocked tone.

The man was both tiresome and predictable. "Reverend," she

said. "Do loosen up a bit on our ride. We are here to enjoy ourselves, do you not agree?"

Abernathy's long face stiffened, though his words were jovial enough. "We are, my lady."

A wave of nostalgia overcame her. She and Rhys had stood on this same promontory atop Lightning Bug and Hermes many, many times. Devil it, she was becoming a sentimental fool.

"You ride Enbarr," she said. "Lugh's horse of the Tuatha Dé Danann. Do you not, Lord Ravenscroft?"

"Yes," Rhys said, surprise lighting his eyes. "You recognize him."

"I do."

"Irish mythology?" Abernathy said. "An unusual choice."

Rhys stared across the valley spread before them. "Lugh's horse could traverse both land and sea and was swifter than the wind. I have great hopes for this fellow."

"He is magnificent," Rose said. "Of Hermes' get, is he not?"

"That he is. With both Portuguese Andalusian and Hanoverian in the mix." The look he gave her was one of devilry, and she knew exactly what it meant—a race!

Rose leaned forward, gripped her, and squeezed her legs against Firefly's sides. "Beat you to the chestnut tree!"

They galloped, and Rose thrilled at the wind across her face, the world blurring to nothing but her horse and herself, and that magical suspended moment when all four hooves left the ground and she was flying. Rose laughed upon their arrival at the tree, panting as hard as Firefly. Rhys gave her another devilish look. Though he had won by a hair, he knew she would insist on a rematch soon. Sides heaving, Firefly pranced, enormously proud of herself even though they had lost.

In better spirits, Abernathy had joined the race, and though he had come in third, he had acquitted himself well, while Claire cantered sedately up to them.

"You did well, Reverend. Come," she said as she dismounted. "Have some refreshment."

That morning, Rose had Cook put up food in a large wicker basket to be left by the chestnut tree. Unfortunately, she had not counted on four participants, two of them men.

They tethered their mounts and as it turned out, Cook had packed heaps of food. They drank lemonade and ate sandwiches of ham and cheese, watching the breath of wind play with the fading wildflowers. Rose always had a hearty appetite, yet she found it difficult to keep weight on her bones. She must eat a substantial amount or she would start resembling the scarecrows dotting the fields.

"I ate too much," Claire said with a delicate sigh.

"So did I." Rose leaned back against the tree.

"You could use it, Lady Rosamund," Rhys said with a frown.

The reverend puffed up. "How dare you speak to the lady thus?"

Rose waved a hand. "His Lordship is often indelicate with me as we are old and dear friends, sir."

"Well!" Abernathy said.

"You know what I mean, Rose," Rhys said, frowning.

"It's true," Claire said. "You could use a bit more flesh on those sturdy bones of yours."

"Sturdy, are they?" Rose thought about it for a minute. "I'll take that as a compliment, sister."

They chattered on, both Rose and Claire attempting to include the reverend, who watched Rhys with narrowed eyes, their banter seeming to make him uncomfortable. In exaggerated motions, he checked his timepiece.

"I must be going." Abernathy bowed to both Rose and Claire, nodded to Rhys, and gathered his horse's reins. "I will call on you another time, Lady Rosamund. I hope then we can be more private."

She knew what that meant, and she would make certain never to allow that to happen.

The reverend trotted off, and Rose finally relaxed.

Moments later, Claire said, "I'll be off, too, if that's all right, Rose. We *are* on home ground."

"Of course," Rose said.

As Claire went to stand, Rhys assisted her. "Pray tell, why are you leaving us, my lady?"

Claire's face took on a far-away look Rose recognized. "In truth, I was reading a fascinating passage on the Parthenon, my lord. I am somewhat desperate to return to it."

Rose had written to Rhys about the girls' various interests and passions.

"Ah!" he said.

Claire gave Rose a wink before mounting her gelding with Rhys' aid and trotting off.

Now, it was just Rhys and her sitting beneath the chestnut with their horses grazing nearby, as they had done many times before. Rose glanced at Rhys. While many years had passed, their being together felt comfortable and familiar.

"Tell me," Rhys said, nibbling on a bit of cheese. "What made you breed Firefly to Enbarr?"

"He is impressive," Rose said, eyes a-twinkle.

"That he is."

Rose couldn't hide her grin. "When I went to breed Firefly, I visited Ravenscroft. You have a fine herd of cattle."

"That we do," he said.

"Enbarr was easy to spot. He stands out. His conformation is perfect, and for a stallion, he is a good and kind boy. I knew he would make a perfect sire for Firefly's foal. I said nothing because I wanted to surprise you." There was that cursed blush again.

Rhys' grin was broad, his eyes warm. "You have, vixen!"

"You brought him home early."

"Once the fighting ended, I wanted him safe, so I sent him to Ravenscroft long before I left the continent."

"You're pleased?" she said. "About the breeding, I mean."

He spared a pride-filled glance at Enbarr, then surveyed Firefly. "She is a fine mare. I'd like Thomasina to see her."

"Do you travel to Woodbine soon?"

"Soon! Sina and Susannah are plaguing me for a visit, and I am just as eager to see them."

"And Patrick?"

"He is a most annoying correspondent, Rosie. But I believe he will be home soon."

"I hope he's mended his prickly ways."

Rhys' laughter boomed. "I seriously doubt it."

"With the war's conclusion, it will be lovely for all of you to be together again."

"That it will. I saw the girls briefly on my return, but it wasn't nearly enough."

Long minutes of silence ensued, and she wanted to say something, anything, but for some reason could think of not one thing.

"It was bad, Rosie." Rhys held her eyes with his, and she read a wealth of pain and suffering, along with a hint of regret. "You haven't asked, and I appreciate that."

Rose cleared her throat, gone dry as dirt. "The fighting must have been horrible. The papers were almost too descriptive."

He nodded, but the words expressed in his eyes were never voiced.

"I pictured you at the front." Rose shivered. "On the peninsula at Roliça and Vimeiro, and at Waterloo, too."

He shrugged, lips thin, then shook his head.

The noise alone...Rose could imagine it. The rifles and cannons, men's shouts and horses' screams must have been cacophonous, the smell horrific, too, with blood and excrement everywhere. Comrades and friends injured, dying, and...

"What are you hiding, Rosie?" he said, resting a hand on hers.

Rose inwardly jerked. "Why, nothing at all, Rhys."

"All is well?" He handed her a wedge of pear.

"All is well." Time to steer their conversation in a different direction. She bit down on the pear, sweet and juicy. A dribble escaped, and he wiped it away with his index finger, licking it afterward.

"You are one of the youngest major generals in Wellington's army," she said. "A fine accomplishment."

He snorted. "It was a field promotion. One which I appreciate, though I question its merit. Wellington said my strategies made a difference. Who knows? But I accepted the rank, though the last thing I need is medals and ribbons."

"Where is your next posting?" she asked.

"There will be no posting, Rosie. I am resigning my commission. Forgive me for not noting that in my letters. The decision was a fraught one."

Rhys had startled her, shocked her, really. He might be a marquess, but for as long as she could remember, he had wanted to be an officer. And yet, as she stared at him, a profound grief bled from his eyes, and she thought she understood. "I see."

He ground his teeth, nostrils flared as if he were battling powerful demons. "I felt too much."

"I know." Rose nodded, plucking a clover and twirling it. "You always have, dear friend. But no one masks those feelings better than you."

"Let us talk about horses, shall we?" he said.

The shift did not surprise Rose. "You've chosen to keep breeding war horses, then? Enbarr is certainly a prime example."

He spared his horse an affectionate glance. "I plan to breed battle mounts, along with the hacks and racehorses we currently breed at Woodbine."

The Ravenscroft stables in Devonshire. "I immediately liked the looks of your new boy." When she had bred Enbarr with Firefly, they'd naturally given her his full lineage. "It's rather odd that none of your grooms or stable boys mentioned he was your personal mount."

"I requested they not. I want stud fees for the horse himself, not the title attached to him."

He unwrapped a cigar he'd removed from his pocket and lit it, not bothering to ask if she minded. He knew she would not. By the time he was fifteen, he had regularly sneaked the smelly things from his father's study.

"You haven't mentioned my courtship," he said.

Oh, dear, here we go. "Your obvious dislike of Lord Pennworth leads me to suspect your 'courtship' has more to do with keeping me from his clutches than it does with marrying me." She glanced at him then, though it was fleeting. "Why do you hate him so? That's quite unlike your nature."

"My *nature* was revolted by his dishonorable actions. His cruelty to his subordinates. His claiming glory for actions others had performed. Pennworth has no honor. His bullying, his abuse of his mount, his use, or should I say *misuse* of the camp women. Though he took their favors, he was not kind to them."

She peered at him, eyes wide. "Were... Were *you* kind to them, Rhys?"

He started, then grinned. "I was, but not in the way you imply, Rosie. Never that way."

"So it is true," Rose said. "You are courting me because of your disdain for Pennworth."

"Not the only reason," he said.

She waited, hoping he would expand on his words. Heavens, she didn't want to ask what they were.

"I care for you, Rosie."

Damned with faint praise. "Care" was such a bland word compared to what she felt for Rhys.

He stared at her, the famous stare known throughout the kingdom, or at least the county. The Stare didn't affect Rosamund, for she had seen it many a time, designed to make its receivers spill all of their secrets.

She giggled.

"What in blazes...?"

"I am sorry, Rhys, but The Stare always makes me laugh."

Rhys rolled his eyes. "That is absurd. No one laughs when I glare at them and all are terrified of me." He grinned, a charming one. "I swear I become another person when I am with you."

"Do you?"

He frowned. "Yes, for that man allows himself to be twisted about your pinky with little effort, as you have always done."

"That's not so!" Her back stiffened. "In any case, your courtship is unnecessary. I do not plan to marry anyone."

He blinked. "Why ever not?"

Rosamund began to repack the picnic basket with the detritus of their meal.

"Rose?"

"I am just...not. Even though I have an exceptional estate manager, I hold my Scottish lands, servants, and tenants in my hands. At present, I have a wonderful steward, a member of my clan. I cannot trust the man I marry to do the appropriate thing for my people and their holdings without my guardianship."

"How could you not trust me, Rosie?"

"I do. Of course, I do. It is not about me, but others."

Rose longed to tell Rhys the true reason, to tell him all. She could not.

Rhys narrowed his eyes, his male brain working overtime. "As you know, I have money and lands aplenty, and I have no desire to usurp what is yours."

Hero worship had been a part of her devotion to Rhys all those years ago. That hadn't changed, though her love had deepened and matured. He had always sided with her, taken her thoughts and feelings into account, and spoken with her as an equal and not a mere child. Losing his friendship would devastate her.

She must choose her words with care, or he would hear her lies.

As Rhys' wife, Rose would have a greater means of protecting her stepsisters than in her unmarried state. His marchioness could take Lottie and Claire under her wing and chaperone them around London until they found husbands of their own. They could visit, where they would be away from the earl. Where they would be safe.

Point of fact, Rhys' influence and connections might keep the earl on a tight leash. Perhaps she could even exact revenge.

Rose would have freedom, security, her beloved horses, a home that was a true sanctuary, and the ability to protect the people she loved. Rhys might even give her his love.

But to do all of that, Rhys must know the truth. Impossible.

"You are no usurper, Rhys," she said. "You were never a greedy person. I am fraught with indecision, I..."

"Tell me, Rosie."

"It is nothing."

Rhys leapt to his feet. "I see."

His dour expression made it clear she had hurt him.

Her belly squeezed and her heart faltered. She never wanted that.

Rhys offered her a hand, and she stood as well. She felt uncomfortable in her skin, as if it were a dress bound too tight to contain the feelings whirring through her, his very touch making her wish to lean toward him, to hold him, to *tell* him all.

As children, they had never lied to one another, and now she was peppering her words with falsehoods. It made her ashamed.

Rhys lifted the picnic basket. "And what about your father's insistence on you marrying within the month?"

"I will manage him until I have reached a decision."

He stood straight and tall, an imposing man. "Will you or will you not consider my suit?"

His strong face reflected his stalwart character. She could not hurt him further. This could be disastrous, but... "I am honored by your courtship and I shall *consider* it, Rhys. That is all I will say at present." Courtships and engagements could take months or years. She could draw the prospect out until she could leave for Scotland.

The irony of the situation almost made her laugh. Rose should be leaping into marriage with the man she loved. Ah, well, here lies to Rhys would fit nicely within the basket of shame she carried with her.

"That is something, at least." Rhys leaned forward and her hands clenched so she did not touch him.

His eyes darkened to stormy with what might be longing and his warm, sweet breath brushed her face. "Rosie."

He kissed her—a slow brush of the lips back and forth that sent her pulse racing, her lips atingle.

When they parted, her fingers rose to her lips. Her first kiss. So often she'd dreamed of Rhys kissing her, but this feeling... Excitement, joy, pleasure. It felt better than any dream she could imagine.

Without thought, Rose placed her hands on his shoulders, stood on tiptoe, and kissed him back. Only a peck, but she'd done it. Of her own volition.

His slow smile made her flush. "That was nice, Rosie."

"We should get back," she said, though she never wanted to leave this meadow or Rhys. "The day is dying."

"Agreed," he said, and he looked as reluctant as she felt.

As they rode across the hills, he carried the basket, while the folded blanket lay across Firefly's withers.

Rhys had grown silent, perhaps because she hadn't fully explained her reticence to marry. Ah, well. She couldn't, and that was that. They exchanged the occasional word, but she knew this Rhys as well. The thinker. A man who traveled internal paths unmapped and mysterious.

If only...

They parted back at the barns.

"Thank you for your consideration of my suit," he said. "Like it or not, I will not see you marry Pennworth."

"Under any circumstance, I do not plan to do so." Hands on her waist, he lifted her from the saddle. "Please know how much I deeply appreciate your offer, Rhys."

Bollocks. She hadn't meant to sound so formal.

He remounted and cantered up the drive, then cut across a field toward Ravenscroft.

Rhys was disturbed as he put Enbarr to the gallop and they flew across a meadow of wildflowers and butterflies. A bucolic scene that only further darkened his mood.

Rosie was making little sense, and there was more to her prevarication than met the eye. He had observed the shadows in her eyes, her disheartened posture, even her distant tone of voice—something deep and dark was troubling her. Yet she would not share it with him.

Though a near decade had passed since they had seen each other, Rose had been forthright and open in the frequent early letters they exchanged. But as the years had passed, he'd noted how she'd revealed less and less of her inner feelings.

An *event* had occurred. What? And why wasn't Rose sharing it with him? She hadn't been a voluble child, but always a courageous, even mischievous one. He admired her spirit greatly. In the past, Rose had been as open with him as he was with her.

He loved her but hesitated to say the words. His Rose preferred actions to speeches. Thus, he determined to unearth the cause of her troubles and eradicate it.

That kiss, *their* first kiss, and her returning one had warmed him to his toes.

His Rosie was joy...or had been.

Rhys suspected the source of her burdens. But as a man who analyzed words and actions with care, he would first learn with certainty the who and the why. Then he would act. Anything else was unacceptable.

Earl Fielding, having traveled to London, sat at a table at White's playing piquet with Pennworth, the air stuffy with smoke in this too-small room. Annoying. He dealt the next hand, staring into the eyes of his future son-in-law. Fielding grimaced.

The top-lofty git thought too much of himself, for beneath that elegant figure, the fine clothes, and copious medals, the man was an unprincipled snake—which was exactly the type of man the earl needed.

Pennworth's affectations attempted to disguise the egoist who had killed dozens upon dozens during the war, not all of them French. Given Pennworth's temperament, the earl would be unsurprised if he hadn't shot a woman or two as well. Perhaps a child.

All of which told Fielding that Pennworth would accept his offer, while neither Abernathy nor Ravenscroft would.

"The chit's monies are far less than I had hoped." Pennworth raised his quizzing glass, his nails buffed to a sheen.

All fussy affectations. Fielding leaned back, folding his hands on his chest. "Do not speak absurdities, Pennworth, or you will find yourself minus a bride. As we both know, while you are desperate for my daughter's pounds sterling, your desire to wed her has more to do with getting your revenge by thwarting Ravenscroft. You *were* engaged to Lady Prudence Hathaway, the wealthy widow, correct?"

Pennworth's eyes sharpened. "I was."

"I understand the lady cried off whilst you fought on the Peninsula."

Pennworth stiffened, but his eyes grew cunning.

Delicious. The intelligence Fielding had gathered appeared legitimate. "I made some…inquiries. It seems your intended received a letter from one of your fellow officers, which contained enough ammunition for her to break the engagement."

"Is that so?" Pennworth's nostrils flared.

He was riled. Good. "*I* know who sent that letter."

Silence, with that pretty visage of his tightened into a white mask. It amused Fielding to speak, to see the other man's reaction. "Ravenscroft. *He* posted the letter."

"None of this is your concern, Fielding." Pennworth signaled for another brandy, his face relaxing into its usual amenable lines.

"I think it is, my lord," Fielding said. "For I've learned your unentailed estates are in peril from your debt. You could lose all but your manor house. Your courtship of Lady Rosamund has little to do with her, per se, but rather your need for money and your hatred of the marquess."

"You are quite the investigator, Fielding," Pennworth said through clenched teeth, then laughed. But the brigadier's eyes weren't smiling.

"Marrying my Lady Rosamund," Fielding said. "Will kill two birds with one stone—you will get the money your estates need and simultaneously take your revenge on Ravenscroft, who is also in pursuit of Lady Rosamund."

Pennworth leaned back in his chair and stretched out a leg, brandy in hand, affecting a disinterested air.

Ah, but the man's indifference hid a corrupt, amoral soul. Fielding liked that. Of all of Rosamund's many suitors, Pennworth was the most greedy, but his lack of a moral compass was the crowning stroke.

In those early days of Rose's come out, both fortune hunters and monied suitors had beaten a path to their door. His willful daughter had rejected one and all.

Fielding wanted Rosamund gone. The woman interfered with his peace and his pastimes. Yet even he—he was her father, for Christ's sake—could not force her to marry. Pressure, yes. But he could only compel her by threatening something or someone she loved. He planned to continue doing exactly that. "You want her."

"As does that pissant Ravenscroft. But *I* shall have her." Pennworth smiled, his eyes hot with hate.

The earl nodded, his sage expression practiced for just such an occasion. "I plan to hold a salon on the twenty-second where you and my daughter can become more familiar with one another. I've also had an idea on how we shall arrange for you and Lady Rosamund to be alone."

"Compromising her," Pennworth said. "A delightful idea. She strikes me as quite biddable. A mouse of a thing, albeit overly tall."

His Rosamund was the antithesis of a mouse, recalling with an inward shiver how she'd nearly unmanned him, but Pennworth need not know that. "And so she is. The perfect vehicle for your revenge." He withdrew a sheaf of paper from his coat. "Here is the contract. As it stipulates and we have discussed, you get the money and I get the lands."

Pennworth smirked. "And the whiskey brewery they contain, one of the finest single-malt distilleries in Scotland."

Fielding laughed. "My dear fellow, I could not agree more. You and Lady Rosamund will be a match made in heaven."

Or hell, as Fielding suspected.

Pennworth retrieved a pen, inkwell, and sand, and began signing the contract. "Your lust for this property... Hum, seems more than the brewery to me, profitable though it is."

Fielding growled. "That is none of your concern."

The bugger was right. Amalie, the first Lady Fielding, knew how much he wanted the land and its brewery. Yet the woman who professed to love him had gifted the chit not only her money but her landholdings as well.

A betrayal. His wife should have left it all to him, her husband, her lord and master who saw to her every need. All that bounty should have been *his*, Amalie's bequest to Rosamund the ultimate insult. He would not stand for it.

Another oddly warm autumn day had sapped Rose's strength and made her sweat, the humidity thick and cloying. Rose gathered Claire, Charlotte, and Lucy along with some bath sheets, and they walked through the home wood to the pond.

Birds sang, oblivious to the heat, while her two sisters moaned and groaned about it. She didn't blame them.

Once at the pond's sylvan glen, they doffed their clothes down to their chemises, lying them on the bench, the one she'd had carved with roses in memory of her mother who loved to swim. Lucy took a seat and began to weave a basket using the jute and dried grasses she had brought.

Soon, their trio was crossing the pond with long even strokes, the water blissfully cool. Refreshed, Rose swam to the bank, resting her arms and cheek on its grassy pillow.

Lottie swam up beside her on her left, with Claire on her right.

"How I love to swim," Lottie said. "Though I prefer the sea with its crashing waves!"

"I do, too," Rose said.

"We are finally alone," Lottie said. "Without those nasty footmen listening to each word we speak, only to report all to Lord Fielding."

"I agree," Claire said. "Just yesterday, one of those burly fellows followed me to my room. When I left an hour later, he leapt aside as I opened my door. I said, 'How can I help you, sir?' And he said, "Just protecting you, my lady.' Bollocks!"

Lottie grinned. "My dear sister, you present such an angelic persona. I do so love it when you swear."

Claire grinned back at her. "I enjoy swearing. I wish I could do it all the time."

Rose laughed. "I do too."

They giggled, their arms on the bank, their legs drifting this way and that as the gentle stream that flowed into the pond pushed and pulled at them.

"Tell us about your trio of men, Rose," Lottie said.

"Why should I?" she said, hiding a grin.

"Because you look about to burst with it." Clare's amber eyes filled with laughter.

"I most certainly am not about to burst," Rose said. "How indelicate! You two are ganging up on me."

"Of course we are," Charlotte said. "It's what we do!"

Rose so enjoyed their banter. "The Reverend Abernathy bores me silly. He will prose on and he is such a high stickler. Even if he remains silent, you can feel his disapproval beneath your skin."

"Sort of an odd man, is he not?" Charlotte said. "Word has it, he is hiding things."

"Oh, Lottie, you and your gossip-mongering. He's simply boring, is all."

"I cannot say I care for him," Claire said. "But I confess I dislike Lord Pennworth even more."

"He is very handsome," Lottie said. "Commanding, even."

"He is that," Claire said. "And he is as greedy for Rose's land and money as Abernathy is. Have you noticed his heavy lizard eyes? Always calculating. I cannot trust him."

Nor did Rose, but she couldn't help an inner smile, for it appeared she need not say a word when her sisters would do all the talking for her.

"He is up to something with your papa," Claire said.

Which was when two pairs of eyes swiveled toward her.

"Well?" they both said.

"Well, what?" Rose plucked a blade of grass, cupped her hands with her thumbs holding the grass, and blew. A satisfying whistle erupted.

"I wish I could do that," Claire said, failing in her attempt.

A soft breeze brushed Rose's skin. Would forever be too long to stay here?

"On several occasions," Claire said. "I have seen your papa and Lord Pennworth deep in conversation. Yet when I enter the room, silence."

"They are scheming!" Charlotte said. "Did you hear anything, sister?"

"Snippets." Claire tossed the blade of grass away and tried another. "About money and land and Scotland. I saw them shake hands as if making a pact."

Claire's imagination leaned toward the fantastic, but in this instance, her suspicions were feasible.

"Tell us about Lord Ravenscroft," Lottie said with glee. "He's another matter altogether. Your feelings blaze each time he enters a room."

"Do not be absurd," Rose said. "Feelings blaze? Come now." Rose mentally stumbled. Was she that obvious? But if Lottie saw, the earl must as well.

Claire gave her a gimlet eye. "He is handsome as the devil, especially with that pure white hair and those dark brows. And that fierce gaze every time he looks upon you, dear Rose. I believe he is smitten."

"And you are romanticizing, Claire," Rose said, and even to her own ears, she sounded like a prim schoolteacher.

The girls laughed.

"You would take him in a trice, I suspect," Claire said.

"You know I do not plan to marry."

Lottie frowned. "So you say, though why, Rose? I do not understand."

"It is simple." Rose's lips twitched. "I prefer my men with four legs rather than two."

Claire took her hand, her face solemn. "Do be serious, Rose."

"'Four legs?' Ha!" Lottie said. "That is a lie and we know it." Charlotte clambered from the pond and dried off with a bath sheet, Claire following suit.

A shard of ice speared Rose's heart. They could not possibly know what had happened to her. Or could they? Had Claire discovered her secrets and told Lottie? Or vice versa? "You...know?"

"I have observed you and Ravenscroft together," Claire said. "Both your feelings run deep and far beyond friendship."

"I, too, have seen it," Lottie said.

The relief that her secrets were safe made Rose dizzy. "I have set my course, sisters. I am too old to marry, too set in my ways."

They both guffawed.

Lucy tisked, a small perfect basket sitting in her lap.

"Why will you not teach us *kalari*, Lucy?" Charlotte said. "Like Rose."

"Because," Lucy said, drawing out the word. "Lady Rose began her study at the age of six, I believe. Or perhaps eight. Did you know, Parashurama, the sixth among the avatar of the preserver god Vishnu, learned the art from Shiva, our Hindu Supreme Lord? It was Parashurama who taught the art to the original settlers of Kerala shortly after bringing Kerala up from the ocean floor."

Her sisters stared at Lucy, goggle-eyed.

"Oh, my," Claire said.

Shaking her head, Lucy continued. "It would take many hours. Too many hours and too much study for you to begin learning at this stage, I am afraid."

"Could we not learn some of the forms, as you call them?" Charlotte said.

"I will think on it." Lucy stood. "Now, it is time we go, my ladies."

With moans and groans, they left the pond and dressed.

"You do not wish to be late for supper, do you?" Lucy said.

"Never!" Lottie said, laughter in her voice, then pointed a finger at Rose. "We are not done with you yet, sister. I think you love him."

As they walked the path, Claire leaned close. "I think so, too."

CHAPTER

SEVEN

Rose wore a dress of sprigged muslin, with sweet embroidered hummingbirds entwined with ivy, a favorite, the dress the color of new-fallen maple leaves. Not entirely appropriate for unwed ladies, she loved its design, which enhanced her spare frame.

The afternoon's salon at Fielding Manor was His Lordship's favorite form of gathering. True, he had the expenses of food and drink, along with the occasional violinist to provide soothing music, all intended for political and information gathering.

But as a salon, the earl did not have to offer a full orchestra, nor would he have to present the supper routinely available on grand occasions. A cost-saving measure for his miserly soul.

Raven-haired Charlotte rushed into Rose's room.

"What do you think?" Lottie said, twirling before Rose in her pale blue confection, beribboned and bowed.

"It is perfect and you look lovely."

Lottie was aflutter with enthusiasm, as usual, anticipating all the people she would meet, her fascination with the human species vast. Charlotte was an artist, her passion springing from her late father, a baron and a renowned painter. With her insatiable hunger for gleaning gossip, though she disdained to spread any, Lottie was the most outgoing of their trio.

Claire entered via Rose's dressing room door wearing a striking pale green muslin gown that flattered her already-splendid figure, but her beautiful face was wreathed in its usual look of dread. Where Lottie was a social bee, blonde, exquisite Claire was the antithesis, an intensely private girl, one with the heart of a lion. Archaeology and ancient lands consumed Claire, who often lost track of time. While Rose's special pocket always held her knife, Claire had copied the design but slipped a treatise on some dig or other within hers. In case she grew bored at social functions. Which she did. Often.

Both girls looked stunning in their gowns, yet their expressions could not be more different.

Rose took a final glance in the mirror and smoothed a loose curl. That face... Her reflection appeared unchanged, yet she was sure someday her inner ugliness would bloom across her features. Then, everyone would know the truth.

A part of her ached for all to know and to see. Most would turn from her, true, but perhaps this heavy sorrow would dissipate, freeing her.

Lottie peered over her shoulder, pulling a ribbon from the dresser and winding it in her hair. "Are you ready, Rose?"

Rose blinked, as if awakened from a fever dream, then smiled. "I most certainly am."

"Dear Claire," Lottie said. "Get that sour expression off your face. This will be fun."

Claire rolled her eyes. "For you."

"It would be for you, too," Lottie said. "If you wore a more pleasant face and exercised some effort. You look as if you ate a lemon."

Claire winked. "Perhaps I did."

"You two will be the death of me," Rose said, though in truth, the girls' banter delighted her.

"But it will be a fun death," Claire said with a faux-severe face.

Rose hugged them both. "Come, girls. You've done this before. You will know several of the guests, so it won't be as painful as when you entered those ballrooms in London for the first time."

Lottie giggled. "It won't be painful at all. It will be perfectly fascinating."

"Ugh," Claire said as Rose led her sisters downstairs and into the grand salon with its marquetry floor covered in lavish oriental carpets. Seating groups artfully scattered invited conversation, while a grand piano and stately marble pillars added to the room's elegance. All designed by her maman years ago.

The Reverend Abernathy would be in attendance, the earl had assured her, as would Lord Pennworth. Rose hadn't asked about Rhys, but the earl would commit a huge breach of etiquette by not inviting his next-door neighbor to the soirée. Though Fielding's attention to his household, his wife, and his daughters were ramshackle at best, the man never breached manners in public.

They entered a room alive with lords and ladies, gentry and military men, one very puffed-up reverend, and Lord Pennworth, who smiled and nodded at her though he was conversing with the earl.

Rose did not see Rhys, shrugging off a pinch of disappointment, for she feared a conflagration if he encountered Pennworth.

Pennworth strolled to her side and bowed. "Lady Rosamund."

"My lord." She dipped a curtsy.

"A croquet game is being played in the garden. Shall we join them?"

"I am afraid not, Lord Pennworth. But thank you."

A flush of red rose from his neck, turning his face scarlet. He fastened his hand to her elbow and steered her to the French doors. "Of course, my lady."

He looked her up and down, like a fish being scrutinized for the dinner table.

"The style of your gown is quite fetching," he said. "I particularly like how you have done up your hair."

"Why, thank you, my lord."

He lifted his monocle to his eye and smiled. "I might mention something, my lady, if you do not object."

"What is it?"

"That particular shade casts a sallow aspect to your complexion." He smiled. "If you do not mind my saying so. It does you no favors."

How bizarre. Did the man not see the offensive nature of his words?

"I would be more than happy to assist in your color choices," he continued. "My expertise is considered unparalleled when it comes to fashion. Only if you wish for my advice, of course." Another smile.

"Thank you, sir, but I prefer my *own* choices."

He sketched a bow. "My lady."

She returned to her sisters, thinking what an odd conversation she'd just had.

A rustle at the door and the man who often occupied her thoughts entered in all his military splendor, today wearing his white pantaloons and Hessians. His companion wore the uniform of a Royal Navy captain, glittering epaulets and all, and he prowled into the room as if he were a leopard stalking prey. Rhys' brother, Captain Patrick Lansdowne, had returned home and appeared unscathed by war, which pleased her for Rhys' sake. At the same time, she and Patrick always had a fractious relationship, and as a child, she had often been the butt of his mocking tongue.

"Who is that with Lord Ravenscroft?" Charlotte said.

"The marquess' brother, Patrick," Rose said. "He is a naval captain and served during the wars, which is why you've never met him. It seems he is as medaled as the marquess. Do note the dress sword he wears. His Royal Highness gave it to him in recognition of his bravery." Rhys had written about how thrilled he was with his brother's honor.

Charlotte said nothing, though her blue eyes narrowed with an assessing glare.

"What is it, Lottie?" Rose said.

Charlotte tilted her head. "The look of that man is one of arrogance and entitlement."

"How judgmental, dear sister," Claire said.

"Whether or not Patrick has changed, I do not know," Rose said. "Though he was an arrogant boy, I have never seen him behave in an entitled manner."

Claire nodded. "I suspect in the years since you last saw these men, they have changed, as have you, Rosamund."

"Be that as it may," Rose said. "He was a decent boy and I hope you both will give him your courtesy."

"Naturally we will," Claire said.

But Rose didn't miss Lottie's sly glance, as if she were arming herself with verbal volleys to decimate him.

Just what Rose needed.

Worse, Pennworth ambled over *again*, and Rose busied herself introducing him to Claire and Charlotte. He oohed and ahhed over her sisters while sliding covert glances at her.

The introductions ended, Rose girded her loins.

"I'm glad you have foregone your lace cap today, Lady Rose," Lord Pennworth said.

"And why is that, sir?" He had seen her wear a cap *once*.

"I am afraid it created a dowdy effect."

He actually raised a quizzing glass to inspect her again. Unbelievable.

"Were your eyes damaged in the war, my lord?" she said, unable to resist.

"This?" He held up the eyepiece. "No, but my quizzing glass helps me see more clearly. Its rim is of tortoiseshell, you know."

Poor tortoise. "I believed a military man's eyesight needed to be acute."

Rhys and Patrick approached the earl and her stepmother, doing the pretty.

Pennworth's laugh was high pitched. "Well, look who has

deigned to join us. The major general along with some naval sycophant."

"Captain Patrick Lansdowne," she said in a dry voice. "The marquess' brother."

Rhys' focus locked on her and she flushed. Pennworth jabbered on to Lottie, while Claire had taken Abernathy's attention as Rhys and his brother approached. Rhys walked with the air of a man who knew his place in the world—he always had—and he looked grand in his uniform. Her heart soared, then squeezed. He could never be hers and never was a *very* long time.

Rhys studiously avoided Pennworth's gaze. Not quite the cut direct, but close. The Lansdowne men bowed, and the women curtsied. Patrick, unreserved as usual, first took her hand in his, and then her sisters'. He lingered over Lottie's, a mischievous glint in his eye.

Oh, dear. "Lord Ravenscroft, Lord Patrick," Rose said with enthusiasm just as Charlotte opened her mouth. "Might I introduce my sisters, Lady Charlotte Halafair and Lady Claire Halafair."

"A pleasure, Lady Claire, Lady Charlotte," Patrick said, Rhys echoing him.

Claire drew Abernathy away to the refreshment table.

Rhys turned his back on Pennworth. "I see Lady Claire is occupying your reverend."

Rose fought not to roll her eyes. He was baiting her. *Your reverend* indeed. "Claire is engaging with our guests."

"Sodding prig," Patrick said, not bothering to whisper. "I heard one of his sermons, an experience I pray I never relive."

Rhys' jaw bunched, though he looked as if holding in his laughter might make him explode.

"Do you often call people sodding prigs, Lord Patrick?" Lottie said.

Patrick's eyes shot to hers. "Only when called for, Lady Charlotte. Is that not one of your father's paintings?" He pointed to a large landscape on the far wall.

"Yes," Lottie said. "You recognize his work."

"Indeed, I do," Patrick said.

Pennworth turned to face Rhys. "Do you not greet a fellow officer, Ravenscroft?"

Rhys scored the man with disdain. "Not if you are that man, Pennworth."

"How unkind," Pennworth drawled. "May I get you some punch, ladies?"

Lottie, always sensitive to the surrounding currents, hooked her arm through Pennworth's. "I would be delighted."

"You ladyship?" he said to Rose.

"I shall procure my own, thank you."

Pennworth and Lottie ambled off, their remaining trio following to the refreshments table, where Rhys frowned at the punch bowl. He sniffed, then leaned close.

His breath warmed her cheek, the scents of sandalwood and Rhys teasing her senses. "I see your father continues to provide the same swill as always."

"Oh, yes," Rose said. "His Lordship is a traditionalist, if nothing else."

"Pity," Patrick said, turning to Lottie. "And what are your thoughts on the punch, Lady Charlotte?"

"Oh, la, the punch is—"

A man flew into the salon, hat askew, face dusted with soot.

"Barn one is on fire!" he shouted and raced out again.

CHAPTER

EIGHT

The screams of terrified horses and frantic men made Rose's heart pound as she raced up the hill to the horse barns. Nothing was more feared than barn fires. Sparks shot into the late afternoon sky, the air thick with acrid smoke, accompanied by the screams of horses and shouts of men.

She reached the crest to see stable boys and Fitz leading horses from the inferno at a rapid clip, and paused, for she could barely breathe, her fear for their horses making her dizzy.

The roof of barn one, where they stabled most of their horses, was aflame. Men with ladders and others with buckets swinging from yokes climbed the barn's sides in an attempt to quench the fire.

Rose ran again, ducking beneath the barn entrance. Smoke enveloped her, as did the fire's crackle, the panicked horses' screams, and the desperate shouts of men trying to save them. She dashed down the aisle.

Someone grabbed her from behind and swung her over their shoulder, slamming her head against a support post.

Stabbing pain, with spots dancing before her eyes. Her stomach roiled.

Her abductor ran out the barn's far end.

"No!" she said, her voice faint. Her vision pulsed in and out, her head throbbing.

The man pounded up the hillside and into the trees. Poplar and pine whizzed by as he kept running, each thudding step agitating her stomach more.

He finally stopped and heaved deep breaths.

Bile filled her mouth, and Rose vomited down his back.

"Bollocks!" He flung her to her feet, holding her waist so she didn't topple.

The soot-blackened face of John Pennworth stared back at her.

Rose coughed, teetered, breathing hard, trying to clear her throbbing head. "Why in all that's holy did you do that?"

His hands moved from her waist to her shoulders. "To save you, my dear Rosamund."

"Save me?" The world still spun, and she staggered, bracing herself on a tree.

"From the fire, of course." His hand roved from her shoulder toward her collarbone, his thumb brushing back and forth.

"Stop that!" She slapped his hand away, her head beginning to clear.

"I am caring for the woman I intend to make my wife."

She pushed away from him, or tried to, but he failed to release her, his hand on her shoulder drifting toward her breast.

Never.

Her *kalari* training rose to the surface. Her right hand struck away his roving one, her left thwacked his face, and she followed with an elbow strike.

Pennworth reeled.

"Never, *ever* touch me like that again."

"But my lady, you are to be mine," he said.

"How dare you be so grasping? As of yet, I have not chosen."

He reached for her, and she danced out of his way.

"I was trying to save you!" he hollered.

"Thank you," she said. "But I shall save myself!"

Rose raced back to the burning barn.

Inside, Rose could barely see for the smoke, but she needed no eyes to know which stall held which horse. The nearest stall doors stood open, and she ran down the barn aisle toward the end.

She had almost reached Firefly's stall when a man slammed into her shoulder, landing her on her bum, trampling feet everywhere. A boot kicked her hip, but she pushed to a stand and scrambled to free Perseus from his stall. The gelding's eyes rolled, and he reared, crashed down, then backed away.

Like a ghost, Rhys appeared and flipped a cloth over Perseus' eyes, then slinging a rope around his neck. He raced the gelding toward the barn's exit, while Fitz did the same for Grandy, a nervous chestnut with a ride hard as rocks. Sparks rained down onto her dress, and she swatted them out until finally reaching Firefly's stall.

When she jerked open the door, the massive horse charged.

Rose flung up her arms, waving, shouting, "Firefly, it's me!" The pregnant mare's forelegs thudded to the ground to stop her forward momentum.

Coughing, eyes burning, Rose tore the fichue from her neck and wrapped it over the mare's eyes, holding on to both ends.

"Shush, pretty girl. Let's get you out of here."

A loud crack from above. A roof timber.

Too many horses remained trapped in their stalls.

Rose ran, Firefly trotting beside her. Sighting the light at the end of the barn, she slapped the mare's rump and watched her gallop from the building. Rose ran back towards the inferno. Strong arms gripped hers.

"What are—"

"Do not go further, Lady Rosamund," Pennworth said.

Dratted man! "Let go!" she screeched while wriggling in his arms. "There are horses still trapped. They will die!"

"They are doomed," he said. "And so are you if you go any farther."

"Doomed? I think not." The fool would not learn. An elbow to his gut relaxed his grip, and she ran down the aisle, passing men leading horses, with Lottie leading a fractious Grimoire. Rose couldn't see well, but she could feel, and she checked the stalls after Firefly's until she came to a latched one. Diablo's, an elderly former stud and a sweet boy who had served them faithfully and well. Rose ripped a sleeve from her shoulder and bound it around his eyes, holding the halves together to lead him outside.

On an inhale of smoke, a coughing jag bent her in two, while Diablo gave a furious scream and tried to rear. Rose was losing her grip.

Someone tossed a rope over the horse's neck and caught it.

"Time to go, Rosie," Rhys said.

"There are more—"

"Diablo is the last of them. Come."

Another thunderous crack from above. Timbers breaking loose. Smoke billowed and sparks flew as a cascade of wooden beams plummeted toward them.

Arms clamped around her waist, and Rose was flung into the air.

She screamed, landing hard, then a heavy body covered hers, while a cascade of death rained down.

Coughing, Rose blinked. Above, blue sky peeked through the wreckage of the barn's roof. Behind them, a pile of beams, stable doors, and timbers smoldered.

But they were all right. Singed, but not crushed. Of course it had been Rhys who'd thrown her to safety.

"Go!" he barked, his voice harsh.

He lay sprawled atop her, and she crawled from beneath him, her aches telling her she lived. She stood, then offered Rhys a hand up. He took it and went to rise. But his foot was stuck.

"Damnation," he growled.

Above, a timber cracked, then gave. Chunks of wood flew, one slamming into his head. Rhys collapsed, blood dripping down one side of his face.

Rose tugged at the beam holding Rhys' foot. Others poured into the space and began to pull at her.

"Stop it!" She shrugged them off.

Fitz and Tom Barker appeared and lifted the beam enough for her to slip Rhys' foot from beneath the timber. The two men slung the unconscious Rhys' arms over their shoulders and dragged him down the burning aisle.

Rose staggered after them. Outside, the air was not much fresher than in the barn. Tom and Fitz lay Rhys down on the ground. Fitz was spent, and he leaned heavily on Tom.

Patrick strode through the smoke like a determined wraith.

"Help me with him, please," Rose said.

Patrick hoisted his brother up, swinging Rhys' arm around his shoulder and clutching his waist. Charlotte eased Rose away, tucked her shoulder beneath Rhys' other arm, and they walked Rhys toward the house.

"He's fine," Patrick called back. "We Lansdownes have thick heads."

Rose wished to accompany them, but her responsibilities came first, ones that insisted she stay until all humans and animals were tended and safe.

A blast of sound.

Rose whirled.

With a tragic finality, the remaining beams collapsed to the ground in a burst of sparks.

Rose scraped her singed hair back to survey the courtyard. Whinnies, neighs, and screams continued as Rose began to review horses and people to confirm all had escaped.

Everyone was out, everyone but Diablo.

Exhaustion bit at her, and her skin pinched where the sparks had winnowed beneath her clothing to her flesh. Aches throbbed, her throat afire. But others were hurt worse than she.

For the next hour she made sure each horse's and human's injuries were tended to, and that the displaced horses were settled, either pastured out or fixed in barn two. She did not work alone. Stable boys, farmhands, footmen, maids, and even guests pitched in. Patrick had returned to the fray and set up a triage station for both horses and humans, Lottie and Beatrice assisting. Claire was tending to wounds while the reverend and Fitz talked to the local constable.

Pennworth and the earl ambled toward the manor house, aiding no one.

After what seemed like hours, the chaos began to subside. Rose staggered to Patrick.

"He's all right?" Her heart was a metronome beating triple time.

Patrick shot her a cocky grin. "He'll be fine, though he'll grouse about his aches and pains and sprained ankle."

She doubted that. "Thank you for the help." Rose trotted toward the manor, to Rhys.

If Pennworth... Merciful heavens, she was furious at his high-handed tactics. When he next crossed her path, she just might plant him a facer.

As she walked, her ire cooled. Pennworth's actions had been strange in the extreme. Perhaps he intended something nefarious. She recalled his eyes from when he'd reached for her breast. Not gleaming with lust or desire, but rather triumph.

Telling the earl would be imprudent, for he would light on her and Pennworth being alone together, would say she had been compromised, and that she must marry the viscount. A perfect excuse.

Rose would keep the incident to herself, as well as make very sure Pennworth never got her alone again.

Fielding, red-faced, wheeled on Pennworth when they reached his study. "You said a trifling fire. Nothing concerning, you said."

Pennworth peered out the window through his monocle, then waved it at the earl. "I admit the fire got out of hand. Think on the bright side, Fielding, you will get a new barn out of it."

"A new barn!" Fielding sputtered.

Pennworth raised a brow. "You have insurance?"

"Not for the damned horses, all of which could have died!" Fielding wished to throttle the arrogant prick and would have done if he didn't need him. "Bollocks!"

"Yes, well," Pennworth said, affecting a languorous tone.

Fielding wagged a finger. "You didn't even get my daughter alone to compromise her!"

The viscount cleared his throat. "But I did. Sadly, she escaped before anyone saw us. I had instructed my valet to do exactly that. The man failed to appear and will be replaced."

"This disaster—"

"If you recall," Pennworth said through gritted teeth. "The fire proposal was yours, and I mentioned at the time I thought it an imprudent idea."

"Keep your place, my lord, or I will rip up our contract!"

"Would you?" Pennworth leaned forward. "I very much doubt that."

Jesus Christ. Jesus Christ.

Rhys awakened to a cacophony of pounding, severing thought. Down slammed a blood-red curtain, swarms of hornets surrounding him. Buzzing, asking questions, *touching* him.

"Leave off!" he bellowed. "I have an ostrich-egg size bump on my head, a blasted headache, and a throbbing ankle."

He swatted at those hands like hornets, beating and batting at them to leave him be. "Piss off!"

What would make them go away?

Rose flew into the drawing room. Rhys. He lay on the settee, filthy, bloody, arms flailing, swatting at the doctor as Abernathy and other guests watched wide-eyed.

Rose strode into the room, aches and pains forgotten, to stand by Rhys, who lay pale and distraught, his eyes glassy.

The doctor signaled, and Abernathy and a guest pressed down on his shoulders, restraining him.

Oh, fustian! That was the worst thing they could do.

When he was fourteen and she ten, she'd seen that same glassy expression. Homer, a favorite pup of his, had been killed by an adder, and Rhys had gone into a trance-like state, grief blinding him. He'd struck out, cuffing Rose on the face, until she began speaking. When he realized he'd hit her, he'd been devastated.

The boy she'd known was so expert at stuffing his emotions into a locked chest that when they overtook him, he journeyed to some internal place of horrors. She'd only seen that reaction once, but she would never forget it.

"Get away, my lady!" the doctor barked.

Rose fell to her knees and took Rhys' hand, though the men continued to restrain him, and leaned close. "It's me Rhys, Rosie. Come back. Please come back."

He cuffed her ear, but those haunted eyes broke her heart.

"Leave!" she said. "All of you. Get out."

Hands at her shoulders, pulling at her. Why were people always pulling at her? Curse them!

"You will be injured, Lady Rosamund," Abernathy said. "He is not fit for a lady's company."

She gritted her teeth. The reverend was a carbuncle on her arse.

Rhys' fisted hand met Sir Abernathy's nose. Blood spurted as the reverend stumbled backward, clutching his beak.

"Leave! Out gentlemen!," she said, desperate to bring Rhys back to himself. "Now!"

Muttering and a huff, then footsteps. The room quieted.

"Come back, Rhys," she said. "Come back to me, to your Rosie. You are safe. We saved the horses. The barn can be rebuilt. You did your best and rescued so many."

"What the hell are you doing, Rose Fielding?" Patrick said, his quick temper aflame.

She spared him not a glance. Rose was used to the brothers' berserker tendencies. "Don't be a buffoon, Patrick, and help me here."

He stopped short. "A buffoon? You're the termagant in the room, my lady."

"I'm not 'my lady' to you, and you know it well. I've done this before."

"Aren't we the nursing wonder?"

His surly tongue was in fine fettle as he reached for her.

Rose glared. "Touch me, and I'll bite you!" For no sane reason, she stuck her tongue out.

Patrick laughed as Rose turned back to Rhys, whose eyes were clear.

"Rosie?" He blinked.

"Yes, it's me, somewhat dirty and disheveled, I admit."

His eyes shuttered, but not before she glimpsed terrible pain. "I hit you. I—"

"You had a reaction, like when the adder struck Homer," she said. "Nothing harmed, truly, though you did give the reverend a bloody nose."

That garnered a twitch of his lips.

"Brother," Patrick said, taking a knee.

Rhys raised a singular brow. "Yes, we've been brothers for a very long time, pest."

Patrick grinned. "I see you're on the mend. Might I bring you some wine?"

"Scotch," Rhys said. "A double. With some headache powder."

Patrick snorted, gave a swift nod, and disappeared.

"Did Diablo make it?" Rhys said.

Rose shook her head. "But all the other horses are safe, their burns relatively minor."

"Christ! At the front, I would lose myself, as well. I do apologize."

She could imagine him mowing down opponents while in its thrall. Rose shivered. "Truly, there is no need."

He nodded, brow furrowed. "You remember Angus. He became my batman and grew skilled at returning me to myself. Wellington did as well, much to my chagrin. But those incidents were few and since my return home... I believed I was done with them." He whooshed out a sigh and closed his eyes.

Rose sat back on her heels, relief amplifying her exhaustion. "The conflagration sent you there." To relive his own personal nightmares. Unable to stop herself, she brushed a lock of hair from his forehead, the white covered in soot.

He was so dear, so strong and stalwart. She had counted on the boy, and he had never failed her. The man would never fail her, either. Or so she suspected. She admired him so.

A dry chuckle. "In future, I'll make a note to avoid conflagrations."

"A fine plan," she said, brightening.

"You are shivering." He ran a hand up her sleeveless arm.

"Oh?"

Oh, no. Everything went black.

CHAPTER

NINE

Something cold and wet and delicious touched Rose's lips, and she opened them to swallow a sip. *Oh my, that felt good.* She took another and then another until the glass disappeared.

"Not too much, my dear Rosamund," Bea said. "Or it will disturb your digestion."

Dear Bea. She scrunched her eyes tight, reluctant to open them because the world would come crashing back. Diablo's death, the horrific fire, and her love for Rhys which must be denied.

Rose cracked her eyes to see Bea's sweet smile.

"Is she awake yet?" the earl said with a grumble.

"Just this minute," Bea said in a soft voice.

"Good," he said, looming over her. "Well, daughter, that is quite a mess we have in the stables."

"A mess," she repeated, voice faint. The terrible fire could be called many things, but "a mess" was not one of them. She pushed herself to a seated position, a bit dizzy, and gave her father a baleful glare. "Where were you when we were racing down the aisles freeing the horses?"

"Coordinating the efforts, naturally!" he said on a jovial note, the kind that made her want to vomit.

Bea looked at him askance, and Rose suspected her stepmother had grown weary of the earl's posturing. Rose was beyond weary, but if she called him to account, he would slither his way to another excuse and then another, all the while masking his lack of courage.

"I must go to the stables," she said to Bea. "To see about the horses, the stable hands. I need to talk to Fitz, too, and check the tack room."

"My dear," Bea said. "The fire is out, the horses and the hands have all been attended to, and Fitz is resting."

Fitz was old, Fielding's stable master since her childhood, and growing too frail to shoulder all his duties. Tom Barker had a way with horses, and Rose hired him as Fitz's assistant. By bringing him on now, Tom could ease into the stable-master position when the time was right without bruising Fitz's feelings.

"The doctor is here to see to your burns," Bea said.

Their doctor was older than Fitz and stuck in ways from the eighteenth century.

Where was Rhys? Was he all right? "The girls?"

Bea flushed with pleasure. "My girls have not seen that much excitement in years. Did you know Charlotte put on Firefly's halter herself and led her to the second barn? Even I could not believe she had done so, her fear of horses seeming to dissipate during the conflagration." Bea smiled. "She will become a horsewoman yet."

When Beatrice had married Earl Fielding, Lottie was a timid rider, her terror of horses renowned. Over the years, Rose had worked with her in slow, gentle increments, and little by little Lottie had begun to relax around them. True, they were huge, but really much like pups.

"The doctor may tend to me, but after that, I'm going to the stables. I need to see the wreckage and examine everyone."

Bea frowned. "But no—"

"Be my guest, Rosamund," Fielding said. "That way you can land flat on your back with no settee available to cushion your fall."

She brushed off her skirts. They were filthy, filled with holes, and horribly wrinkled. Rose bit back a curse. She didn't have many favorite dresses, but this one she had liked very much, no matter what Pennworth thought of it.

His lordship threw up his hands and stomped out while the doctor fussed over Rose. Afterward, Bea helped her stand. She swayed a bit but found her equilibrium along with her confidence. How much time had passed since she had fainted, a first for her?

She wished to see Rhys, to know how he fared, but she could not ask Bea with the doctor and a footman in the room.

Rose entered the kitchen to retrieve her barn boots in a niche by the door. Out the window, a man cantered away. Rhys.

"M'lady?" Cook came up beside her and held out her hand.

A pebble lay on Cook's palm, perfectly round and smooth, and black as midnight, with a white band encircling the stone.

Rose's heart hitched. "Yes?"

"Lord Ravenscroft bid me give you this when you returned to the kitchens," Cook said, her expression rife with curiosity.

Rose seldom entered the kitchens except for her boots, but was unsurprised Rhys had known where she stored them. As a strategist for Wellington, he absorbed details most men missed. He must have noted the boots, identified them as hers, and known she would retrieve them at some point. Which was why he had left the pebble in Cook's competent hands.

She took the cool stone and clutched it tight. A gesture from their childhood, one they continued through their letters, where they would exchange pebbles for various reasons, some as a blessing or a request for forgiveness or even an "I told you so" when one of them won a game.

"A strange man, if you don't mind my saying so." Cook bobbed her head.

Whether or not Rose minded, Cook always said her piece. "Strange? How so?"

"I suggested His Lordship wait in the parlor, as what's suitable for his rank and station, but he insisted on staying here for news of your awakening."

Rose tucked the pebble into her pocket and sat on the bench by the door, removing her slippers and lifting a boot. Rhys had always been most comfortable in the kitchens, stables, or rookeries of Ravenscroft, and was not much given to formal occasions. As he had ascended the military ranks, he must have hated the formalities attending his elevated position.

Rhys had waited, but had left without a farewell.

How much she wished to talk with him now.

The day after the fire, Rhys avoided the Fielding manor house on his way to its stables, spotting Pennworth's stallion being led away by a groom. Bloody bugger.

The stables were abuzz with workmen clearing the wreckage from the burned barn, much to his annoyance.

His time in the army had taught him many things, including how to assess a disaster scene. A massacre, an exploded building, a pillaged town. He wished the workers had let the barn be, at least for a day. They may have moved a piece of crucial evidence or damaged a delicate clue. Damn.

Wisps of smoke from the disastrous fire swirled skyward, the smell noxious. Rhys tethered Enbarr to a pear tree laden with fruit, dismounted, and released his cane from its sheath. He limped up the rise to find Fitz perched on a log supervising the men. When he spotted Rhys, the old man's frown softened to a smiling grimace.

"Good morn, m'lord." Fitz doffed his cap but did not rise. The weary man looked near broken.

"Hello Fitz," Rhys said, joining him on the log. "How do you fare?"

"I be good. Been better, though." Fitz's hand fisted on his heart. "I've cause for celebration, as most of our stock was rescued. Cause for sorrow, for the fine barn and...."

Fitz paused, seeming to battle his powerful emotions.

"Diablo," Rhys said.

"Aye. A good boy who served the earl long and well. He din't deserve his fate."

"No, he did not. I am going to look around, as I wish to understand where the fire began and, if possible, how and why."

Fitz nodded. "I'd be a mite careful around them timbers and such."

"Duly noted."

Rhys rose, placing a hand on Fitz's shoulder. "Good man."

The right words often failed him and it was beyond him to comfort a man who had lost a beloved horse and the barn where he had labored for the past forty years. There was no consolation to be found.

The crumpled barn teetered before him, and he used his cane to push away any detritus in his path as he walked closer. From perhaps ten yards away, he paused, to see and to assess.

The roof—now caved in atop fallen timbers, horse tack, and feed—made a V shape. They had managed to quench the fire before the entire structure had become ash. The men working had only just begun on the edges of the wreckage, and Rhys stalked the perimeter noting nails and other unburnt leavings.

He sucked in a deep breath, nostrils flaring. The fire had begun on the roof, according to many, and he carefully lifted a scorched saddle and brushed aside a partially burned feed bucket. He walked on, continuing his reconnaissance. At the barn's north end, by a corner, the light caught a glint, an oddity poking from beneath a flattened stall door. Rhys heaved the door aside to discover a gold medal, its ribbons singed from the fire. An Army Gold Medal, a match to one of his. Also known as the Peninsular Gold Medal, it was awarded to officers whose status was no less than that of battalion commander or equivalent. In other words, rare.

Many at the salon had been in uniform—himself, Patrick, and several others. Few would possess such a medal.

Pennworth came to mind, in part because he wore such a medal, and in part, because Rhys so thoroughly despised the viscount, a man possessed of no honor and vast cruelty.

Motive was the problem. Rhys saw no possible gain for the viscount to set the blaze. From his inner pocket, he withdrew his pencil and daybook and noted the medal, pocketing the piece.

He moved on.

A beam's unburned end poked skyward, rising a good foot above his head, so he fetched a nearby bucket, turned it over, and stepped up to get a closer look.

"Be careful there, my lord!" Fitz hollered. "You don't want to slip and re-injure that bad ankle."

"Will do, Fitz," Rhys said, though his eyes remained on the beam. The rafter would have held up the roof, but the end revealed a neat three-quarter cut across the rafter's face, spikes from the break on the remaining quarter.

A deliberate cut that had held until the fire.

He stepped down from the bucket, carrying it as he continued around the barn's perimeter. Most of the rafters were split or charred, a few still smoldering. He felt faintly sick as he imagined the Ravenscroft stables afire. How pitifully easy barns burned, practically made for mischief.

A single cut. Was that enough? Coupled with the medal, it was.

But arson was no mere mischief. With his boot, he sifted through harness rings and iron bolts, all that was left of the many halters and latches at each horse's stall. He turned, only to spot a hoof peeking from beneath a burnt barn door.

Rhys leaned heavily on his cane. He should be used to this by now, used to not just the rubble of things but of life. He'd seen the same often enough. In truth, he had witnessed worse. Yet those scraps of life never failed to move him.

When he wound back to the barn's collapsed entrance, Fitz rose, standing with hands on his hips. "Well?"

"Have you any idea," Rhys said. "Why someone would set your barn ablaze?"

The old man's barrel chest contracted with a whoosh. "I can't imagine. Fielding has rivals, of course, as does Ravenscroft. Hard to see why any man, or woman for that matter, would do such a heinous deed."

"Nor can I."

TEN

In the two weeks since the fire, Rose could not remember when she'd been as tired. They had erected temporary shelters for the overflow of mares and geldings from barn one, their stallions, Romulus and Padishah, housed in a barn distant enough to remain untouched by the blaze.

Fielding's estate manager had brought on extra men to clear the debris, while Rose had hired an architect, along with carpenters, masons, and others to begin the laborious process of redesigning and rebuilding the barn. With never a blink, the earl had approved all Rose's upgrades and expenses, and she begrudgingly gave the man his due for his ready acceptance of her improvements. For all his faults, the earl was not stupid. He understood her improvements would save the earldom many pounds.

But Rose's exhaustion had little to do with the barn or the horses and everything to do with the three men courting her. After years of circumventing courtships and proposals, to be the focus of such attention was beyond wearisome.

Rhys was easy to be around, their time both a joy and sorrow and a constant longing for what could not be. Abernathy was a gnat who buzzed and flitted around her. All she wanted to do was swat him away. Pennworth, on the other hand, was both controlling and conciliatory, and unceasing in his pursuit. His back and forths were like the pounding of ocean waves she had experienced on holiday in Scarborough with the Lansdowne family long ago. Though Pennworth's pestering was far less enjoyable than those holidays.

And those were delicious days. Maman had been a dear friend to Lady Ravenscroft and continued to nurture her friendship with the family long after her ladyship had passed away.

They'd taken many trips together, delighting Rose, and she'd seen the sights and larked about with Rhys, Susannah, and even the caustic Patrick, though she often wondered about the missing sister, Thomasina, a child she had never met and one seldom spoken of.

Their quartet had swum in the sea, a grand experience, and she often ventured out from the bathing machines girls and women were forced to use. Her bathing costume was weighty enough to sink a clipper. Thus she swam into the ocean with a rope around her waist, another frustrating addition to her costume, and battled the mighty waves. The best part was when she caught a wave just right and could roll atop it toward shore.

Sweet, sweet memories.

Today, the hill to the stables felt longer and steeper. She'd taken to wearing a raggedy pinafore above her day dress, as ash from the fire was everywhere. She hastened her steps to see how Fitz fared. The fire had taken much out of him, Diablo's death hitting him hard. Fortunately, Tom had stepped into the breach, taking on more of Fitz's duties. Yet Fitz soldiered on.

Inside barn two, she found her stable master calming a fractious Petunia, while Tom laid a poultice on the mare's leg and wrapped it.

"She had a hard workout?" Rose asked Tom.

"That she did, m'lady. This'll take the heat right out of that swelling."

Hunkering down, she was pleased to see how Tom had dealt

with the leg. They hoped to breed Petunia in the spring, but only if she was sound.

"Well done, Fitz and Tom," she said, peering up at the men.

"I agree," Lord Pennworth chimed in.

Odious man.

Pennworth had snuck up on them. Typical.

"Good afternoon, my lord," she said, rising to her full height.

"And to you, Lady Rosamund." He gave her a bow, she curtsied, and from behind his back produced an enormous bouquet.

Beautiful, yet his attentions were so very tiresome. He acted as if he'd never accosted her in the wood. Of course, he did, for he knew if she told the earl, he would jump on the impropriety as an impetus for their marriage.

The thought of marriage to Pennworth gave her hives.

Rose hesitated to take the awkward bouquet. "How lovely."

"Yes," Pennworth said. "Lovelies for my lovely."

"I thank you, sir."

"Once you are my viscountess, you will no longer need raggedy pinafores like that wretched one you have on."

"Indeed?" His arrogant, indelicate comment made her wonder if he were tipsy.

"You will be dressed in only the finest." He chuckled. "Not working in the stables like a low-bred peasant."

A sharp rejoinder almost burst from Rose's lips when the bouquet's odd familiarity struck her. The flowers were all from Fielding's gardens. The nerve. She slipped her hand into her pocket to rub Rhys' pebble.

Petunia twitched her tail, Fitz stumbled, and the mare's back leg shot out, connecting with Pennworth's midsection. Thank heavens it was a halfhearted kick and Petunia unshod.

Nonetheless, Pennworth flew into the air, the floral bundle soaring like fireworks before he landed on the straw in a shower of blooms.

Rose clenched her jaw. She would not laugh. Fitz and Tom were not so considerate, their guffaws ringing the stall.

Unkind, as Pennworth could have been badly hurt. Certainly, his dignity was. She bit her cheek.

Rose held out a hand to assist him. "I am so sorry, my lord. Are you hurt? Here, let me help you."

His lordship slapped her hand away and leapt to his feet.

"Lord Pennworth, are you—"

"Devil take you!" he barked at the men.

Fitz doffed his hat and made a bow. "Forgive us, m'lord. Petunia, here, can be a mite bit nervous."

"Cantankerous even," Tom echoed.

Pennworth would sport a bad bruise, and she hoped nothing was broken. The last thing she needed was an invalid Pennworth in the house.

"I'm fine," he ground out. "That horse should be properly trained."

Tom rushed over to brush off the back of His Lordship's coat.

Pennworth batted at him. "Get off me, fool."

"My lord," Rose said, intervening. "Petunia is a perfectly amiable girl who usually never kicks out."

"She did at me." He looked in pain and much the worse for wear.

"Tom, Fitz, finish up here while I send a message to the doctor."

"I have been to war, Lady Rosamund," Lord Pennworth said, chest puffing. "I do not need a doctor."

His constant posturing wearied her, and she bit back, *Men at war need no doctoring?* Instead, she kept her tone serene. "You could have cracked something, a chest bone or a rib."

"I did not, or I would feel it." He stared down at her, his Roman nose assertive.

"Come, lean on me, and we'll walk to the house."

"I need not lean on anyone." His jaw tightened. "If you will excuse me." The man strode down the path.

She had to admit Petunia was an excellent judge of character.

• • •

A serene two days passed as the earl prepared for the trip to his Scottish hunting lodge. He appeared in the morning room carrying one of his fly rods and handed it to a footman.

"See to its repair," the earl said.

Rose watched in awe as the footman stood awkwardly holding the fly rod. Poor man, he had no idea what to do with the thing. His lordship strode from the room without addressing her and the air cleared. She returned to her knitting and her book, *A General System of Horsemanship* by the Duke of Newcastle. Though she'd read it many times, its wise pages often revealed more on additional perusals.

Yet today, her focus was nil. Dust motes absorbed her attention as they danced through her perch in the window's nook. What was Rhys doing? She hadn't seen him since the fire.

Rose set aside the book, completed another row on Bea's shawl, and held it up to the light. The pretty thing was taking shape, a lovely peach color, with leaf greens for the hem, perfect colors for her stepmama. Rose had dyed the yarn herself using Fielding's merino, the descendants of sheep smuggled into Britain by King George III himself. Though she hadn't spun the wool, a craft she'd like to learn. As it was, her father derided her knitting, as "peasants' work, not fit for a lady." His opinion rankled, but she cared little. Fitz's wife had taught her, and she found the pastime soothing. She needed it now, as she was in the glums and wished they'd be gone.

As if her thoughts had conjured him, the butler announced Rhys, who strode into the morning room in his usual commanding manner.

"My lady." He bowed.

Rosamund stood, smoothed her skirts, and made a curtsy. "My lord, you look something like a ghost covered in all that dust." Ash dotted his white hair, his clothes sooty as well. "What have you been up to? Here, have a seat and I'll ring for refreshments."

"Are you sure? The dust..."

"Of course. Sit."

"I could use a coffee. My throat is dryer than the Tabernas Desert."

Rosamund rang the bell, then waved him to a chair and took the opposite one before the fireplace burning with a small but happy blaze, the September heat having abated its odd hold on the month.

Rhys eased into a chair, his ankle obviously still paining him.

They said little until a maid appeared and took Rose's request for tea, coffee, and scones. Once alone again, she said, "What is it?"

"I have been up to the barn twice since the fire. Talked to the workmen, the assistant stable master, and Fitz, thus coming to a conclusion I dislike immensely. I fear the fire was deliberately set."

Her eyes widened. "We all assumed, I assumed an oil lamp had broken or someone had been careless with a cheroot."

"I do not believe that to be the case." He scraped a hand over his weary features. "I found this in a corner of the barn."

He handed her the gold medal.

"Oh!" she said, turning the medal over in her hand. "But this could have been lost while helping douse the blaze."

"Perhaps. But it bothers me—"

"Is this not the Peninsular Gold Medal?" she said, her mind arrowing to a certain viscount.

"It is. More disturbing, I noted a cut made to a supporting rafter. A clean, deliberate one."

A deliberate cut. Rose stared at the drifting oak leaves as they were buffeted by a chill wind. She thought of Diablo and his miserable death, and of the many deaths that could have been.

Rose could think of no reason for Pennworth to burn their barn. Though his bungled abduction... No, that would be too much, even for him.

"Rose?"

"What?" she said, annoyed at her chaotic thoughts.

His eyes probed hers. "I am concerned. A man who would intentionally set a barn afire is evil. Have you no idea who might have a reason to do such a thing?"

She almost blurted Pennworth's name, but the idea was too horrible. "I cannot believe—"

"Yet someone did so, Rosie. Penn—"

"Do not say it, Rhys. That conclusion comes from our mutual dislike of the man, nothing else."

"He possesses such a medal," Rhys said, rising just as the maid returned with the tea tray.

"As does the general you introduced me to."

"True. And yet... I must go." He bowed and left without even a decent farewell.

The following day, Rose went for a walk, needing to think away from the manor's hubbub. Not without sustenance, of course. She'd plucked a Pitmaston pineapple, a favorite, though why they called it a pineapple when the fruit was an apple, she didn't know. She added bread, cheese, and a jar of lemonade from the larder to her basket, all for a picnic by the river. Her dress was an old one, but conformed to convention, though she'd rather have worn her breeches or pantaloons.

Who would sabotage their barn? *Why* would someone sabotage their barn?

No matter how she dwelled on those questions, turned them this way and that, the name that always sprang to mind was Pennworth's. Though a second, the earl's hovered in the background, considering the insurance money came to a large sum.

But, no. That could not be.

They'd had little rain, and the river far below the path was a languorous drift, unusual for this time of year. She watched small eddies dance until she came to the log spanning the Fielding and Ravenscroft properties. A familiar place where a lovely grove of beech trees made the perfect picnic spot, from where she could watch the river amble on its course down the stream and think.

Rose set down her satchel and sat on the grass beneath a sturdy beech, then removed her boots and stockings, curling her bare toes into the cool earth. Lovely. A sense of freedom unfurled, away from the manor's bustle and the earl's demands.

Abernathy and Pennworth battered her daily, though Rhys seemed to have drawn back. Perhaps that was for the good.

Rose unwrapped her food, then lifted the jar of lemonade to her mouth. Her throat tightened like a noose about her neck.

Years earlier, she had formed an escape plan. Yet she wished there was some other way to solve the marriage problem.

She bit off a crunchy chunk of apple, the fruit sweet and tart, just the way she liked. No matter which way she turned the matter over, the end result remained the same—she must leave Fielding Manor. The question was when.

Heaven forfend, she didn't *want* to go. Yet she could find no other way.

"Ho there! My Lady Rosamund."

Rose started, then peered across the river. Rhys stood on the opposite bank in buckskin breeches, a loose shirt, and an open waistcoat.

She moved toward the bank, shading her eyes with her hand. "What are you doing here?"

"I could ask you the same thing," he said with a grin. "I've been out walking, thinking."

"Thinking, eh?" she said. "And have you solved any problems? Come up with something brilliant? Discovered who burned the barn?"

"Not one damn thing, Rosie."

Her hand flew to her chest as he began to cross a log barely wider than his feet.

"Bloody hell, Rhys!"

He leapt his last step to stand beside her. "Pray tell, why are you in such a taking, Rose?"

She was furious. "I cannot believe you walked across that skinny log. You could have fallen, been killed!"

He raised a brow. "What's put you in a dander?"
"You!"

CHAPTER

ELEVEN

Rose was acting strange, and Rhys wasn't sure why. "My lady, you have crossed that log just as I did many a time."

"I remember it well. But I was a child, and it has been years."

Now it was his turn to be surprised at her reluctance. He took her elbow. "Come, shall we sit in the shade?"

They moved to the beech and sat. "Any victuals for a poor starving fellow?"

She rolled her eyes. "One thing has not changed since your departure at sixteen. Your ravenous appetite!"

"I confess that is true," he said with faux sorrow, leaning forward to brush a hand down her cheek.

It pinked to a delicious peach, so delicious Rhys kissed it, then leaned back. *"Shall I compare thee to a summer's day? Thou art more lovely and more temperate."*

"A sonnet." She laughed. "But *'temperate'*? I?"

He grinned. "Perhaps not. What have you there?" He eyed the food with avarice.

Rose unwrapped the wedge of cheese and loaf of bread, broke off a hunk of each, and handed them to him.

"As I recall, Rosie," he said between bites. "You had quite a hearty appetite, as well."

Rose flushed. "Gentlemen should not say such things."

"When we are alone, have I ever behaved the gentleman?"

She ripped off a hunk of bread with her teeth and chewed. "I take your point."

"Why this reluctance to cross the bridge?"

Rose shook her head, then slipped a piece of cheese between her lips. Lips he'd very much like to kiss again. "Rose?"

She chewed, her eyes on the river, then reached for the jar. "Lemonade?"

"Thank you." He took a swig. "Talk to me, Rosie. I distinctly remember a girl crossing the log with her pregnant dog. I believe you were eight at the time."

She laughed. "Oh, God, yes. But much has happened since, Rhys."

"Indeed? Such as?" Her words disturbed him. Rose had been fearless. Exactly what had happened?

"I worry about my balance, is all," she said.

"If anything, given your passion for riding, I would suggest your balance has improved, not diminished with time."

The bread and cheese disappeared, and she shared the apple with him as well.

"Come," he said, holding out a hand. "Cross with me."

"I daren't."

"You will not fall."

"How can you say that?"

"Because I know you. I have seen you. Your balance is the best of anyone of my acquaintance."

"Fustian! Abject flattery."

"Not in the least." His brow furrowed. "I speak the truth to you, Rose. I always have."

Her eyes grew liquid with fear. "I cannot."

He would not push her, for if she were too timid, she would fall. "It is all right, Rosie." The fear he saw in her eyes was layered as if the bridge were some sort of symbol. Rather than stress her further, he took her hand and kissed her palm. Her eyes became saucer wide.

"I must be off." He waved his farewell and crossed the log in a trice, waving to her from the opposite bank and blowing her a kiss.

Rose dangled her legs over the bank beside the log.

Unlike when they were children, Rhys hadn't pressed her. She was thankful for that.

When she'd been twelve, after Rhys had left for the military academy, the fears had begun...then amplified. She knew the root cause, yet found her reaction odd, especially when it sprang up at unexpected moments, like a lurking beast.

Rose filled her lungs with the fresh autumn air.

How had she become such a coward? She had crossed this log a thousand times.

But would her feet remember the feel of it beneath them? The way her toes had clung to the bark? Or would she tumble down and down?

Well, then. What was she going to do?

She knew before she had even asked the question.

Rose put the tip of one bare foot onto the log. It didn't move, didn't shimmy. The other foot followed, and her toes curled into the rough bark. Though it was chilly, the sun blazed down, and far below the river sparkled, its soft burbling accompanied by a crow's squawk and the warble of a collared dove.

Rose squared her shoulders, further hiked up her skirts, and found her balance. She stepped forward.

She put one foot in front of the other, counting to avoid distraction.

At thirty, she reached Ravenscroft land and stepped onto the grassy bank. Her lips twitched, then widened into a broad smile.

"I was sure you could." Rhys emerged from the screen of trees.

"You watched!" she said.

"Because I knew you would try and succeed."

"I did succeed. Yes, I did."

The following day, Rose had a bounce in her step and a smile in her heart. She felt freer than she had in ages. Near triumphant. Crossing that log had somehow unlocked a sense of self-determination she so often lacked.

"M'lady?" called Fitz.

"Coming!" Rose backed Astonished up near the teasing board where Padishah would appear on the other side. Padishah was a stud from the Byerley Turk Line of the modern thoroughbred, nearly seventeen hands high, a black horse with a fierce attitude and a will to win.

Astonished, though a sweet and gentle bay mare, burned with fire. The mare kept that fire banked, mostly, but if you asked for speed, Astonished always delivered. "You're a fine girl, aren't you?" Rose stroked the mare's muzzle, softer than velvet, her affection running deep for the delicate horse.

Fitz exited the stud barn beside Tom, who led a prancing Padishah. The black knew what was coming, and he was mighty interested.

Tom's muscular arms and keen abilities kept Padishah in check as Fitz opened the gate to the breeding corral. It took a great deal of power to hold a fiery stallion about to breed, and the air was thick with Padishah's fervor. It was their good fortune Tom knew the proper techniques and had the strength for them, though in a pinch, Rose or Fitz could control the stallions.

Astonished and Padishah would make a beautiful foal.

Tom let Padishah prance around the paddock on the lead line to burn off some energy, then he trotted the stud over to the teasing board, Fitz standing back but observing every movement.

Astonished nickered, a good sign, but as Padishah neared the board, a shout came from down the hill.

"Yer father is asking for ya, Lady Rose!"

Well, drat. "Tell the earl I'm busy!" she hollered.

She backed Astonished closer, Padishah's nose pressed against the opening between the boards.

Jeremy crested the rise, hands shoved deep in his pockets. "He's powerful worked up, Lady Rose. He said immediately."

Rose wanted to scream. If she didn't respond, it would be Jeremy who suffered, not her. She sighed. Fitz, aware as always, came around and took the mare. Once done, she brushed off her breeches and accompanied Jeremy down the hill.

Her father was climbing it when he spotted her and halted. Dressed in a brocade coat, satin breeches, stockings, and top hat, he looked utterly out of place.

She nodded as she approached him, patting the pocket where her knife rested to reassure herself, to battle this innate fear his presence triggered. "My Lord, you wished to see me?"

Jeremy peeled off, and she was alone with the one person in the world she despised.

"Pennworth has a bruise on his chest the size of my fist," His Lordship said, shaking his head and fuming. "From one of your damned horses."

She sniffed. "That 'damned horse' has garnered you substantial money, my lord."

"Lord Pennworth said you continue to refuse his proposal." Fury pulsed from the earl's eyes.

"And that surprises you because...?" she said.

"We cannot have that, my dear. No, we cannot. You *will* marry Pennworth."

She modulated her voice to hold its usual composed tones when all she wanted to do was scream at him. "I will not, my lord.

Nothing will make me marry that puffed up, pretentious, shallow lordling."

The earl sighed. "How unfortunate. It appears Charlotte and Claire are distractions, muddling your mind, and that saddens me. So I shall accompany those two adorable chits to the country, to my hunting lodge, in fact. Unless you choose Pennworth, of course."

That same threat a powerful one. Very little hunting went on at the earl's lodge, a fact she knew well from the servants who traveled with him, pouring out their shocking tales to Lucy, who of course told Rose.

Gaming, brawling, excessive drinking, and welcoming professional women to service himself and his friends were all the "hunting" that took place. Imagining Claire and Lottie there, alone with the earl, horrified her. And well he knew it.

In truth, Fielding was attempting to manipulate her, for she doubted he could pull off such a scheme, given Charlotte and Claire were daughters of a peer of the realm, Lord Halafair. And yet she wondered if he was mad enough to try it. Staring into those pale, evil eyes, he just might. So much for self-determination.

"Lady Fielding will never stand for it." She prayed this time the man was blustering.

The earl's sigh was sorrowful. "How wrong you are my dear." Then he grinned, the predatory one with many teeth. "Lady Fielding trusts me implicitly."

Did she? Rose had begun to question his assertion.

Fielding's genial gaze transformed into chips of granite. "I have done with your threats and manipulations."

Rose gathered herself, unable to let his words pass. "Threats? Manipulations? Is not the reverse true, my lord?"

He looked away before affixing that insincere smile once again. "The girls' season will end, but they will experience a great many adventures with me at the lodge."

At times, the earl did not act on his threats. But regarding this, where he would get pleasure from both the girls' and Rose's torment, she believed he would. He had no feelings for his stepdaughters, other than using them as leverage. Rose was truly in terror for them.

She must remove Charlotte and Claire from the equation, though at the moment she could not imagine how.

Rose smiled, nodded, and offered him a morsel. "I will consider Pennworth." To drive it home, to make it feel true, she continued. "Abernathy is out of the question. Period. Understood?"

"Of course, of course, my dear," His Lordship said. "Good. It's settled."

She had convinced him she would consider his plan, implying she would follow it, but her bad angel demanded she tweak the earl. "Funny you haven't mentioned the Marquess of Ravenscroft. His title is grander than Pennworth's."

The earl spat onto the dirt. "He is out of the question. I cannot abide the man, as you know."

"Along with being a marquess, Lord Ravenscroft is quite rich, or had you forgotten? But you are correct, I will not marry him."

He squeezed her upper arm, as someone would a friend. Her stomach roiled, bile coating her throat. Alarm rose. The man who had sired her was no friend, and he well knew how much she loathed his touch. But now was not the time for a missish display, though she imagined sticking a knife into him where it would hurt most.

"If that will be all," Rose said. "I will get back to breeding Astonished."

Fielding winked. "I expect you will shortly be doing the same. Do make your wishes known soon, girl. I grow weary of all this fuss." He raised his hat in farewell and walked off, his pleasure obvious.

CHAPTER

TWELVE

In a foul mood, Rose wished to do something radical.

Now there was no question she must run away.

But the girls... They were older now, wiser. Perhaps she could tell them the truth. Tell Bea the truth.

She could not, at least not to the girls. Imagining their horror made her grow cold. But perhaps this was the moment for Beatrice to learn of the monster who lived inside her husband.

There must be another way. Rose raked her fingers through her scalp, wishing to scatter the pins and free her locks from their bindings.

If Rose was off to Scotland, the earl could no longer use Charlotte and Claire as leverage. Mayhap she need not tell anyone. Ever.

Except, with Rose gone, the earl would be free to do with them as he chose.

What a hideous conundrum.

Rhys called not long after the earl had rendered his edict. When he entered the drawing room, they made their bows and curtsies, which felt especially meaningless today.

His face was bronzed and lined, too lined for a man of his years, yet he was even more beautiful to her eyes. When Rhys was absent, she could dampen her yearnings. With him standing before her?

Impossible.

Rose served tea and coffee, Rhys preferring the bitter brew, and he pounced on the seed cakes. But their chit-chat was desultory, her fault she supposed.

"How is your ankle?" she said.

"Near recovered." He devoured another cake. "These are excellent."

"Cook has a way with them."

"How is Firefly?" Rhys said.

That brought a smile. "Broody and wonderful. I always have the worst problem with horse gestation."

"In what way?" he said.

She flung her arms wide. "It takes too long! Eleven or so months is an age!"

He bellowed a laugh. "I see your point. You wish to see that foal today, don't you?"

"I do. So much." But as she sipped her tea and nibbled a dainty cucumber sandwich, the black cloud of reality descended again.

"Rosie?"

"Yes, my lord." With great care, she set her cup on its saucer. Everything tasted like ash.

"Now that you will consider my suit, I wish to make certain aspects clear. Rest assured your lands and monies will be safe and always in your control. In addition, I will care for you, partner with you."

Everything Rose had wished for. The irony of Rhys' courtship only exacerbated her pain. "I understand. But it is far too soon for me to make a decision, Rhys."

"Why? Just tell me why."

Rose remained silent, explanations eluding her.

"What is troubling you, Rosamund?" he said, with a thread of irritation.

Rose shrugged, hesitant to lie...again.

"You have always met challenges head-on," he continued. "God's blood, you just ran into a burning barn! You braved all for puppies! I was the one who often hesitated, pondering as is my wont, while your decisions were usually made with a joyful or determined spontaneity."

"You are remembering a child, Rhys. I am a woman grown."

"I know that. You've always held me in affection. Been open and honest with me. I have the letters to prove it. Why prevaricate now? Have I changed so much? Have you?"

"The girl you remember," Rose said. "I remember her, too. Faintly. But rest assured that 'joyful spontaneity' is now quite absent from my character."

"I don't believe that." He raked a hand through his hair. "I cannot."

"Do be patient, Lord Ravenscroft."

He leaped to his feet. "I hate when you call me that. You always insisted on calling me Rhys. What the hell has changed, Rosie?"

Rose's eyes burned, her face flushing. "Everything."

He went down on one knee before Rose and took her ice-cold hands in his. "What is 'everything', Rosie?"

His sweet girl pasted on a fake smile, but it wobbled, her secrets smothering the child who was game for anything, any adventure, any joy to be had—with him.

Though she dove into burning barns easily enough, when it came to Rhys, she appeared fraught with indecision. The torment in her eyes slayed him, yet she would not share her troubles. He wanted to help. To ease her pain. To take her away from all that was hurting her.

Yet she would not let him in, this woman with whom he'd shared worlds. They'd explored each other's fears and hopes, his desire for the cavalry, her passion for animals. His abysmal sketching and her dreadful needlework. His lack of interest in birds, his father's obsession. Her indifference in polishing herself to her mother's sheen. All touchstones of their childhood—a million moments that mattered. To him, at least. And to her. Yes, they had mattered to her.

Rose had laughed often, with a tiny snort bursting out now and again. Back then, she wasn't embarrassed, didn't care. Had so much altered?

She had no taste for Abernathy's attentions, that was obvious, and her disdain for Pennworth was even more apparent. What if…

"Have you formed a dislike of me, Rose, now that I'm fully grown?"

"Piffle, you odious man! Naturally, I have not!"

"Then do you not consider me suitable husband material?"

"I can think of no…"

"No…what?" Still holding her hands, he took a seat beside her on the sofa. "What? No worse man? Or no one better?"

Rose closed her eyes, squeezing them tight. "I admire no one more. But I hesitate to wed you, my lord."

Rhys stood, nodding, two vertical lines scoring the bridge of his nose. "Are you angry or displeased with me for some reason?"

"I am not."

He snorted. "If you do not marry me—and I do not consider Pennworth or Abernathy viable suitors—"

"They are not viable in the least!"

"Then what will you do if we do not marry?"

Rose folded her hands in her lap and sat up very straight, and he recognized her battle pose. "I have a plan. I shall leave this place and go to Scotland to live with my clan there. I plan to breed and raise horses, just as I do here."

"You could do that just as well at Ravenscroft."

"But I hesitate to give up my independent life, and because of my mother's planning and my lairdship in Scotland, I can retain my freedom."

His temper rose, always a bad sign, and he cast it to Hades where it belonged. "I wish you would not. I wish you would marry me."

Rose walked to the mantle, and with reverent hands lifted the figurine of a woman riding sidesaddle.

Rhys recalled the silly trifle purchased on one of their trips to the seaside. An item that, for some reason, Rose thoroughly enjoyed. Perhaps it was the rider's expression of great glee. But, no, it must be the porcelain horse who resembled Lightning Bug, her long-gone stallion.

"I am considering it, Rhys," she said, though she did not look at him.

He flung himself into a chair, air whooshing from his lungs. "Good."

"I need to think deeply on the subject. It is a lifelong commitment, after all."

Rhys leaned forward, forearm braced on a knee. "You are harboring secrets, Rosie. When we were children, you told me all. Why not now?"

"These are secrets I cannot share."

"You mean, will not."

A small smile touched her lips. "Perhaps someday I shall."

The following afternoon, Rose was giving Lottie a riding lesson on Amble, a gelding who did just that. No speed was too slow for the horse, making him the perfect mount for her tentative sister.

Observing Lottie in the ring, Rose noted the strong placement of her hands and her straight back. She had insisted Lottie wear boys' pantaloons, so Rose could observe how she positioned her legs while riding sidesaddle.

"Good, Lottie!" she said. "You're doing well and you look fine on Amble!"

Lottie shot her a sharp glance. "I don't feel fine. I feel as if at any moment I will take a tumble."

Damn the sidesaddle. Lottie would find her balance swifter astride, but as a lady, a sidesaddle must be used in company. The girl had insisted on using it to improve her seat. Probably wise, but Rose loathed the awkward saddle, one so insecure it tumbled many a woman from her seat.

"Take some deep breaths," Rose said. "The kind we talked about."

Lottie complied.

"Now raise your arms straight into the air."

"What!"

Lottie had startled, and so had the placid Amble, who merely sidestepped. Now her student teetered precariously.

"Collect yourself, dear Lottie. There you go."

Soon Lottie and Amble were soon in accord.

"Now raise your arms up high! Yes! Now arms out to the sides. Good! All right, gather your reins, and let's try the trot, shall we?"

"Of course," Lottie said, though her face paled.

"There you go," Rose said. "Good!"

A tap on her shoulder and Rose turned to see Beatrice beside her.

"You two were so caught up," Bea said. "I did not wish to startle either of you."

"How long have you been standing there?"

"Five minutes," Bea said with a serene smile. "Charlotte is doing well at the trot."

"She is."

"A canter?" Beatrice said.

"Soon," Rose said. "Bring him down to a walk, Lottie!"

Lottie's body relaxed, the relief on her face palpable.

"We must speak," Bea said.

"Of course. But let's get Lottie safe off Amble first."

Once accomplished, with Lottie blushing at Rose's praise, Lottie walked Amble until the groom took the reins, then she and Beatrice drifted to the barn.

Rose had insisted Charlotte learn to saddle and bridle a horse, as well as to feed and groom them. The more Lottie interacted with the beasties, the more she began to relax, both in and out of the saddle.

Bea slipped an arm through Rose's and walked to a darkened corner of the barn. She frowned. "His Lordship has suggested taking the girls on his next hunting excursion to his lodge in the north."

"Has he?" Dear heavens, he'd spoken to Bea.

"You have been there?" Bea said.

"Yes, but not for many years. I... Excuse me." Rose exited the barn on the far side, and into the sunshine, the subject so dark she needed the day's fine rays on her face.

Bea had followed. "Are you well, my dear?"

Rose shook her head. "Sorry, but the barn became too close, too dark."

"I see," Bea said. "Is His Lordship's lodge a suitable venue for my girls?"

Rose bit her lip. "Well..." She meandered to a clump of daisies and brushed her hand across their soft blooms.

"Rosamund?" Bea, a bright woman, knew Rose was prevaricating. "What has gotten into you?"

Rose closed her eyes and sighed, then took Bea's hand and led her to a bench beneath a towering maple with a view of the gardens. She turned to face her, clasping both her hands.

Out spilled Rose's entire sordid tale, and all the while she hoped Bea's spine was stiffer than Maman's had been.

Beatrice stayed silent for long moments, seemingly focused on a pasture where several horses pranced.

Rose withdrew her hands, terrified in every way. Of being rejected. Of being disbelieved. Of being unsuitable for proper company.

Of losing the three women she loved fiercely.

Beatrice turned her face to Rose, her complexion streaked with tears. "My dear girl." She folded Rose into her arms and wept.

Rose's tears had long ago been spent.

When they parted, Bea sniffed. "Using my girls as bargaining chips does not bear consideration."

"I agree."

"I will send the girls away," Bea said.

"Would that we could," Rose said. "I fear the earl will grow suspicious."

Bea shrugged. "Perhaps." She slapped her thighs. "But we must."

Humiliation and self-disgust had wrung Rose out, but even so, telling Bea had been worth the shame if it saved Lottie and Claire. Nonetheless, Rose wished for a dark abyss where she could curl into a ball and disappear.

"My cousin," Bea said. "She has an estate near Bath. She is always asking for a visit from the girls, as she has no children of her own. I shall say she invited Charlotte and Claire for a visit, one with an indefinite end date, I might add."

A good plan, except... "What if His Lordship says no?"

Bea shuddered a breath. "He may very well. Thus, we shall see them off when Lord Fielding is away from home."

"He will be livid." Rose knew too well the consequences of his fury.

Bea straightened, her eyes blazing with a cold light. "I shall handle His Lordship. He has never struck me, nor do I expect him to do so. I have the wherewithal to sustain a verbal barrage."

Rose squeezed Bea's hand. "Sooner, Bea, rather than later."

"Agreed."

THIRTEEN

Supper the following night was torturous. Cook had overdone the first pheasant of the season and underdone the beans. Hard as a rock, they were. An "event" must have distracted the woman, not an uncommon occurrence at Fielding Manor. A mouse in the kitchen. A stolen pie. A brusk chimney sweep. One never knew.

But Rose was nervous for reasons unrelated to food—Beatrice would introduce the idea of the girls visiting her Bath cousin.

"The fish is quite good, is it not?" the earl said.

"Especially," Claire said, shooting Rose a quizzical glance.

Rose shook her head, hoping Claire would not cause trouble.

"I find it dry," Lottie said.

Oh, dear.

The earl cut her a mean look. "You must have your palate recalibrated, dear stepdaughter, for the fish is succulent and fresh."

Lottie shrugged.

"Dear ones!" Bea exclaimed, cutting off the argument that would inevitably ensue. The sisters' penchant for tweaking the earl inevitably led to some dust-up or other.

Bea cleared her throat. "I was about to say I received a letter from my Bath cousin."

"Who?" Claire said.

"My darling cousin whose estate lays just outside the town."

"Oh," Claire said. "Of course."

Claire had no idea to whom her mother referred, but understood the gist of her tone, which was to close her mouth and listen.

"She's invited you both for a visit to Bath!"

"Out of the question," the earl said.

"She is unwell, Cornelius," Beatrice said. "She wishes for the girls to lift her spirits. Why do you object?"

"Unless the woman is dying, I see no reason for Claire and Charlotte to venture to Bath, especially with winter's approach."

"I see," Bea said. "As you will."

This seemed to sail over the girls' heads, for they continued to eat, disinterested in the earl's or their mother's discussion, knowing His Lordship's word was law.

"Another time, perhaps," Bea said.

"Perhaps." The earl dug into his fish with redoubled gusto.

The following day, the earl left for the north wood to hunt a huge roe deer buck, so rare the species hadn't been seen in southern England for fifty years.

Their head gamekeeper had spotted the unique deer and told the earl of it with great enthusiasm. Fielding galloped off accompanied by his gun and several gamekeepers.

Now it was Beatrice's turn in the plan.

Rose sat in the morning room, marking time with a game of whist with the girls, whilst praying their plan might still succeed.

"I would have liked to go to Bath," Claire said.

Charlotte drew a card. "Why? Other than the sea, which is glorious, it is chilly there now."

"So what?" Claire grinned. "The Roman Baths are well-preserved *thermae* in Bath. A temple was constructed on the site and its presence led to the development of the small Roman settlement known as Aquae Sulis. The baths were designed for public bathing, and I should very much like to investigate them."

"Oh," Lottie said as she played another card. "I understand your interest. But in autumn?"

"An excellent time," Claire said. "The crowds will have thinned to a trickle."

"My trick!" Rose said.

Their trio often played Widow's Whist, comprised of three people. A cunning game, but they were clever players and found it great fun.

Beatrice sailed into the room, frowning. "Morning all."

"What's wrong, Mama?" Lottie stood.

Bea let out a sigh. "I've received a second letter from my cousin! She is dying. You both must immediately go to Bath before her condition worsens."

Bea had clever depths and had written both letters. But Rose suspected she had bribed their head gamekeeper, who held Bea in affection, to craft that faraddidle about the roebuck. A perfect means to get the earl out of the manor.

Lottie rolled her eyes. "It will take hours to pack."

"Not at all." Bea approached her eldest daughter and kissed her forehead. "My maid and I have packed for you!"

Claire narrowed her eyes. "What about my archeological toolbox?"

"All set, dear one." Bea bussed Claire's cheek, then clapped her hands. "Now hasten!"

The girls stared at each other, shook their heads, and rose.

"This is some scheme of yours, Mama," Claire said. "Isn't it?"

Bea only smiled and sped away with her girls.

An hour later, Rose kissed Lottie and Claire farewell as they climbed into the Fielding carriage, the one minus the crest, Bea having given them a letter for her cousin.

Rose's chest was tight with anticipation, nerves a-shiver.

Yet in a brief silent moment amidst their hullabaloo, the clip-clop of hooves sounded.

A footman noticed, for he headed up the drive.

Rose outpaced the footman's more stately progress to spot the earl returning, no deer carcass in sight. She began to trot. "My lord!" she hollered, waving an arm. "How was the hunt?"

Reaching the earl, Rose stood before him.

He halted his mount and grimaced. "The whole thing was a waste of time. Roe deer indeed." He gathered his reins as if to move on.

Rose remained fixed on the road. "What about a red deer? Did you spot any?"

Sounds of the carriage pulling out, heading for the east drive and avoiding the earl.

Fielding chuffed. "Only a doe and I was mighty tempted."

In other words, he had missed. "A shame."

The footman reached them and bowed.

"What is it?" the earl said to the man.

Rose raised a brow at the footman. If he told the earl of the girls' departure, Fielding would ask why he had not stopped the carriage. Since he had not, the possibility the earl would fire the footman was very real.

The footman wasn't stupid, and though he shot her a nasty look, he only said, "I wished to see if your lordship needed anything."

Fielding peered down at the man. "I do not."

The footman bowed, turning toward the house.

"Wait up, man!" the earl said. "Have Cook prepare me a cold repast. Will you join me, Rosamund?"

The last thing she wanted to do, but time spent with him would add a cushion to the girls' escape. "I would like that."

The earl gave her a queer look of incredulity combined with pleasure.

Rose released the breath she'd been holding. By the time he noticed the girls' departure, it would be too late to call them back.

Hours later, Beatrice had told the earl, having shown him the letter from her cousin. No explosion, at least no audible one, but later that day, Rose noted fingerprint bruises on Bea's arm.

A flame ignited inside her. Thank the stars the girls were safe away.

The following day, Rhys readied the gig with the raisable hood, the air's heavy scent and the darkening clouds implying rain. Rain or no, he would call on Rose.

He'd spent a good deal of time over the past days imagining different motives for Rose's resistance to their marriage. No insights had been forthcoming.

When he'd kissed Rose at the picnic, she had leaned into him, her lips warm and pliable, her sigh soft. At other times, most times, if he was truthful, she was reserved, as if restrained while she worked through some inner conflict.

For all the original Lady Fielding had the manners and elegance of a queen, she always encouraged Rosamund's passions and individuality.

How could she not, when Rose knew no other girls her age? The earl preferred to keep Rosie isolated, her few allies Fitz's son, Susannah, Patrick, and himself.

Though Rose attended church, his youngest sister had never seen her at a town social. Nor had she been to finishing school, and Rose herself had described her come out as "meager."

During her childhood, her parents often journeyed to town, while Rosamund remaining at Fielding Manor. Those large gaps in time were when Lucy taught Rose the strange art of *kalari*, the fighting method that fascinated Rhys. The moves she had shown him were quite incredible.

Lucy was an oddity herself, an educated woman who was also

skilled in a tribal fighting style. Impossible not to like the woman, for she was very good to his Rosie, her protector, along with Rhys. Her *only* protector once Rhys had left for college and the army, her mother having succumbed to the fevered dreams of laudanum.

Rose must have felt so alone.

He owed Lucy a great debt, for she had facilitated their letter exchange. A forbidden activity. Corresponding with a person of the opposite sex when unrelated, nor engaged or wed, was anathema to the *ton*.

Without those letters sustaining him at the front, Rhys would not have survived.

Now, Rose was running hot, then cold, her conflict confounding him.

Once he discovered the conflict's source, he believed his questions would be answered, her secrets revealed. He longed for that, longed for Rose herself in every way imaginable—physically, mentally, emotionally. She was the one woman he wanted as his marchioness.

Christ, she was inside him, tethered to him in some beautiful way since the day they'd met. He'd believed it was the same for her.

A thought ghosted through his mind, a specter of dread. What if Rose's affections were engaged elsewhere?

Bugger! He couldn't accept that.

His horse nuzzled him, and he gave him a peppermint.

But what if that was true? What if she loved another?

Perhaps she hesitated to speak of her feelings for another so as not to hurt him. The man could be someone unsuitable, a gamekeeper or stable hand, perhaps, and *that* was why she held off. Or she simply wished to remain mere friends.

No. When he'd kissed her, she had responded.

Devil it, his desire for Rosie, and his unanswered questions had altered his logical brain into a chaotic muddle.

He leapt into the gig and slapped the reins, determined to learn the truth.

. . .

That afternoon, as Rosamund descended the stairs, Lucy trailing behind her, the earl's and Pennworth's voices came from the small salon. She breathed deep, inhaling courage as she felt her deportment slipping away, her sleep having been consumed by familiar nightmares.

That the two were plotting something was expected, and though she didn't know their exact plans, Rose was certain it regarded her, her money, and her Scottish holdings.

Her clan was fierce, but many outsiders failed to comprehend the clan structure and where she stood in the scheme of things. Since she owned land, she was one of her clan's lairds. But she was no chieftain, the man or woman who governed her clan. Their chieftain held much power, and hers was a good man.

Rose believed both the earl and Pennworth comfortably fixed, with extensive monies and landholdings. Their desire to entrap her in marriage confounded her. True, she would be out of the earl's hair, giving him access to Lottie and Claire, or so he thought.

She wished the world knew of his perfidy. Ha! Were that to happen, she would be the one vilified, no matter that she'd been twelve when it all began.

Rose paused before the arched entryway. "Stay with me, Lucy, if you would. Knowing the earl, I am convinced he will leave me alone with Pennworth to compromise me."

"Of course." Lucy rested a hand on Rose's shoulder. "You are strong."

"I am," Rose said as she breezed into the salon. "Good afternoon, gentlemen."

After their curtsies and bows, she sat across from Pennworth, her chair mirroring the earl's. Lucy stationed herself apart from them in a nook by the window.

"Daughter," the earl said.

"My lord." She nodded to him. "Lord Pennworth, how do you fare on this day?" In the distance, thunderheads loomed on the horizon, the day darkening. She must check on that new foal before the downpour.

"I am well, dear lady Rosamund," Pennworth said. "Or should I call you Rosie?"

She tittered, masking the fury that boiled within. "I think not, sir, for it is an annoying childhood nickname."

"Did I not hear Lord Ravenscroft refer to you that way?"

"His Lordship meant it as a joke, I assure you." No one would call her that but Rhys. *Ever.*

Molly arrived pushing a tea cart with two pots of tea and a mixture of savory and sweet tidbits.

"Thank you, Molly," Rosamund said. "Do bring another cup for Miss Lucy if you would." She began to pour.

Pennworth raised his monocle, disdain dripping from his pores. "Your *maid* is taking tea with us?"

Rose put on a bright smile. "Of course! Lucy often does as my companion." She turned to the earl. "Tea?"

The earl stood. "None for me, daughter. I am to meet Lady Beatrice in the yellow salon. Come along, Lucy, as we will leave the pair along to discuss their impending nuptials."

"My lord," Rose said. "Lord Pennworth has yet to formally propose, nor have I yet to accept. Your assumption is precipitous, I fear. Miss Lucy must stay for propriety's sake."

The earl scowled, his eyes sharp pools of annoyance. She wanted to squirm. "As you wish, my dear. I am very much looking forward to visiting my hunting lodge. Do remember, Rosamund? The small delay with your sisters off in Bath means little. They will soon return, and we will jaunt off on a great adventure."

His lordship thought her a fool, as well as a victim.

The door knocker boomed, startling Pennworth. "You are expecting more visitors, Fielding?"

"No," the earl said. "I shall see who has come calling." He stepped from the salon and she heard, "Lord Ravenscroft, what a surprise."

CHAPTER

FOURTEEN

Rose always felt the same response to the name Ravenscroft —a thrill and a sorrow.

But Fielding's false joviality made her smile. In truth, Rhys found the earl as insufferable as Rose did, though in deference to her family, he couched his comments in gentler terms.

"Did you not get my note?" Rhys said as he strode into the room.

Rose's heart danced at the sight of him. He stood tall and relaxed before taking a seat on the couch beside the furious viscount. Unlike the two other men, both dressed to the nines, Rhys wore his buckskins and boots beneath a casual waistcoat and jacket, his cravat styled in elegant simplicity.

"I seemed to have joined a party," Rhys said in his most amenable voice. "How delightful. Good day Lady Rosamund, Pennworth, Miss Lucy."

Though dressed casually, Rhys' manners had been polished to a high sheen, a varnish gained in Wellington's elite company, she assumed. He certainly hadn't learned them at home, his mother long dead and his father an eccentric, or so the ton called him.

"How do you fare today, Lady Rosamund?" Rhys said.

114

"Well. And yourself, Lord Ravenscroft?"

"Particularly well now that I am in your lovely presence." He grinned.

Dear heavens. She choked back her laugh with a sip of tea.

"To come calling wearing thus," Pennworth said in a light voice, as he raised his monocle up and down Rhys' attire. "I am quite, well, frankly astonished, my lord."

"I live to astonish, Pennworth."

Rhys' sly answer set up Pennworth's back. The man visibly puffed.

Oh, dear. Rose leaned forward. "I am not looking forward to this thunderstorm bearing down on us."

"Did you and Lord Pennworth ride out today?" Rhys asked Rose.

"We did not," Pennworth said, interrupting her response.

"Lord Pennworth rode over, but we did not have the time, sadly. I always love a bruising ride. Do you not feel the same, gentlemen?" She was babbling.

"You will get a good drenching on your return trip, Pennworth," Rhys said. "Noting the impending storm, I drove the gig."

"The one with the hood, I hope," Rose said, and took a sip of tea.

He winked. "Of course."

Pennworth saw the wink, just as Rhys intended. Damn all men for their games.

She wished the viscount were less reactive to Rhys' gambits, the room's currents thickening.

The earl breezed in, taking his previous seat, only making things worse, given he stared daggers at Rhys as if that would make the marquess leave.

Rosamund addressed the earl. "You said you were to meet Lady Beatrice, sir."

The earl returned a vacuous smile. "With the addition of Lord Ravenscroft, I told Lady Ravenscroft propriety demanded I return."

What a bacon-faced lie.

For the next fifteen minutes, the four of them made small talk, the men trying to outdo each other with sneers and jibes. Exhausting, but for the glimmers of laughter in Rhys' eyes when Pennworth looked uncomfortable or made a particularly insipid comment.

Rhys, full of the devil, loved upsetting the apple cart.

He wasn't alone in that desire, for the earl's eyes glittered with malice. "I was curious, Ravenscroft, if you knew Lady Prudence Hathaway?"

Rhys tilted his head. "I do not."

"Really?" the earl said with obvious skepticism. "I believe she is Baron Whiting's daughter."

Rose understood. At least in part. Pennworth had been engaged to the lady, and His Lordship was brewing trouble.

"You do not know her?" the earl said.

"No," Rhys said. "Nor do I know a Baron Whiting. Why bring up this lady, Fielding?"

The earl shrugged. "I was sure you had a connection with the gel."

Pennworth sat as a man cloaked in marble, but his eyes snapped with ire.

"My lord," Rose said to Fielding. "Might I pour you more tea?"

"No, no!" he said, chuckling. "Come to think, I believe Lord Pennworth knows Lady Prudence." He gave the viscount a pointed smile. "Am I not correct?"

"I did. Once." Pennworth lips had thinned to a mean, white line.

"La," Fielding said. "It is unimportant. Just making conversation, though I did hear the lady is about to wed."

Outside, thunder cracked. The black clouds sailed closer, flickers of lightning warning of the storm to come.

Pennworth rose. "I fear I must depart as my mount becomes fractious in storms."

Rhys and the earl rose as well, as did Rose.

"Thank you for your visit, my lord," she said.

Pennworth approached and took her hand, raising it to his mouth for a kiss.

A convenient burst of thunder allowed her to jump back, avoiding his lips. Ants marching across her skin would be more pleasant.

"Will you not accompany me to the door?" Pennworth said.

"I shall, my lord."

He offered his arm, which Rose took as they walked toward the front hall.

"Lady Rosamund," Pennworth said, halting. "I feel you favor Lord Ravenscroft."

"I am considering your suit, sir, just as I am considering Lord Ravenscroft's."

The viscount glared. "According to your father, you have agreed to my proposal."

"I told him I would *consider* it, my lord."

"You are such a reluctant puss." His features took on a convivial mien. "Let me put myself forward to you."

The day had been a long one, and now this. "Of course."

Pennworth rubbed the back of his neck. "I own I am not as wealthy as Ravenscroft, nor is my title as elevated."

"Neither matters to me in the way you imply, my lord."

He beamed, though his smile failed to reach his eyes. His booted feet rang on the marble floor as they slowly proceeded again toward the entrance.

"That pleases me," he said. "Penn Manor may not be as grand as Ravenscroft, but it is a fine seat, with many fertile acres."

"I am sure it is, Lord Pennworth."

He took her hand. "I also have fine horses for you to ride, my dear." Grinning when he'd emphasized "ride," a word she suspected wasn't only referring to horses.

Rose dipped her head, mortified by the image. "I do not doubt your lands and estate are quite beautiful."

"What a lovely blush, my lady." He leaned closer and brushed a hand across her cheek, an intimate and tactless move.

"Lord Pennworth!"

"Forgive my impropriety, but I worry about your skin. Do wear a bonnet outdoors, my dear, as you are beginning to brown and your freckles are quite abundant. Other than that, your complexion is exquisite."

Trying to unwrap that backhanded compliment was more than she could manage. Rose simply wished to be rid of him. Another burst of thunder.

"You must hasten before the storm is upon us, sir," she said.

"Pfft! I have been to battle in worse storms."

"I am sure you have, sir, but it is no fun getting drenched."

"Good point, Lady Rose." Having arrived at the front hall, he donned his hat, while their butler, Dunston, placed Pennworth's cape over his shoulders.

"Thank you again for your visit," Rose said.

She dipped a curtsy and fled.

Re-entering the drawing room, Rose found His Lordship deep in conversation with Rhys.

"Wait here, Ravenscroft," the earl said. "While I escort my daughter to her room. I wish to speak with you further."

"All right," Rhys said, concerned eyes locked on her.

"Come, my dear." The earl took her arm, and Rose did not object, well aware of the lengths he would go to control her.

Scheming was second nature to him, and today he wore that hungry expression she had often seen in the darkness. She swallowed hard and lifted her knitting bag, but managed a pleasant smile.

Tension thickened as he escorted her to her suite, halting by her door. "Tomorrow, you will accept Pennworth's proposal. I have acquired a special license."

He released her, and Rosamund took a step back. "I see."

"It is for the best, my dear. Pennworth will take good care of you."

Frustration geysered up. Pennworth would offer her horrid care. The earl knew it, as did she.

Even with all that had passed between them, they continued to toss verbal fripperies back and forth like bonbons, always clothing the truth in a more-agreeable confection of lies.

The earl continued. "I will also inform Ravenscroft you are promised to another."

"I have not accepted Lord Pennworth."

"But you will." He grinned and winked. "Remember your beloved sisters. You do not wish them to suffer, do you?"

Her protest would be expected, so she supplied one. "Except—"

"No exceptions."

She nodded, offering him a final look of defeat before entering her bedroom.

The lock clicked behind her.

Frightened as she was, and disturbed by his pronouncements, she wanted nothing more than to laugh aloud. At this stage in their game, his notion that a lock would make any difference to her was as hilarious as it was absurd.

Rosamund sighed. If he imagined she would flee, he was not far off.

She leaned against the door, eyes closed, and clutched her brocade knitting bag as if it were salvation itself. His Lordship acted as if nothing were amiss. Nothing was ever amiss, as if he'd never begun their terrible game. As if it had never happened.

Often, their past felt like a fevered dream—the musings of an overwrought mind, where all that had occurred with the earl was a fabrication.

Rose sagged. This fight had gone on too long and cost her too much.

But then she thought of Rhys, of what he had endured at the front. Was her spine so weak as to crumble?

Never.

Once more unto the breach, dear friends, once more!

That well-loved play's extravagant phrase suited her mood, for she would *never* wish to erase her past. As well as expunging the earl, she would lose Rhys and Maman, Lucy and Fitz, and so many others who had brought her comfort and joy.

Moreover, she would lose herself.

Rose laid the brocade bag on her bed and surveyed the rooms where she had spent her entire life—the painting by Stubbs of their founding stallion commissioned by her grandfather. The bed she had slept in for twenty-six years. The alcove overlooking the gardens where she loved to read, and beyond that, the stables and horses she adored.

She brushed her fingers across the Florentine lamp her mother had given her and the hand-carved Kondapalli toys from Lucy's home in India.

All cherished. All she must leave behind.

Of course, thinking about the people—Lucy, the girls, Beatrice, Fitz—was worse.

Rose shook her head, breathed deep, and got on with it.

From the larger of her two wardrobes, she retrieved her *Otta* sword and *Kataara* dagger, leaving her *cheru vadi* sticks and other weapons behind.

The sticks were smooth, strong, and well used—a reminder of Rose's sixth year when Lucy had arrived from India to be her nurse-maid-governess and had begun Rose's *kalari* training.

From the first, Rose had loved the martial art, how it strengthened her body and mind, and how it had given her the tools to triumph over her terrible situation.

Another crossroads. Merciful heavens, she was tired of them.

But there was no better time. For now, Lottie and Claire were safe from the earl. Once Rose was settled, Lucy would join her in Scotland.

Time to go.

FIFTEEN

Rose sat at her secretary, dipped her pen, and lifted it over a fresh sheet of foolscap. She wrote the girls, telling them they and their mother would always have a place with her, no matter where. Brief notes to Bea and Fitz. Poor Bea. Rose's revelations had devastated the woman. Yet she had stiffened her spine and done what needed doing. A remarkable person who, Rose suspected, would not remain long beneath the earl's thumb. Next, she wrote to her Scottish chieftain to alert him of her pending arrival. A good man whose moral code never wavered, he would welcome her with a quirky comment and open arms.

Her hand hovered over a blank sheet. No. She could not write Rhys. Not yet.

Rose sealed her letters and left them on the desk for Lucy to distribute.

Unearthing her coat pistol, all of six inches, she set it beside her dagger on the bed. Inside her second wardrobe, Rose removed the buckskin breeches, top boots, shirt, waistcoat, and topcoat she'd prepared for her deception. Two cravats, pairs of stockings, and underthings later, Rose looked with longing at her knitting bag, knowing it was too large and bulky to fit in her pack, Bea's shawl too delicate to include on its own.

As it was, her carry case held her money, tooth powder, soap, flint, tinder, and several spills. If she must camp out, she was prepared.

Last, she slipped the amethyst thistle pin from her jewel box onto the coat's lapel.

She looked forward to arriving at her Scottish lands and being with her grandmother's people.

But Rhys... No point in stewing on what couldn't be.

An envelope slid beneath her door, her name written in an elegant hand. One she recognized. Slicing the seal, she pulled out the note and unfolded it.

Dearest Rosamund -

The girls are away and safe. Soon, I plan to travel to my cousin as well, and from there, meet with the lawyers of my late husband, Lord Halafair, guardians of our estate in Somerset. I will then assess how to remove myself from this marriage. I suspect a separation will work, for as you know, Fielding despises public displays and a divorce would be just that!

With your revelations, I can no longer maintain a life with him. Thank you, sweet Rose, for sharing your most terrible secret with me.

Be heartened that I will watch over Claire and Charlotte. They will be safe. You be safe, too, dear one. Know you are always welcome at Halafair for as long as you wish.

With deep love and affection, Beatrice

With a sniffle, then swift efficiency, she placed Bea's letter and the remaining carry items into the small bag, to which she'd sewn straps so it could ride on her back. Lucy's suggestion.

The woman in her thoughts scurried into the room, locks a mere trifle in Lucy's hands. Lock-picking was yet another skill Lucy had taught Rose.

"I told Lady Beatrice," Rose said in a stiff voice.

Lucy took her hands. "A good thing."

"I was ashamed."

"There *is* shame, but it is not yours," Lucy said. "We have discussed this."

"Then why do I still feel so...unclean?"

"Perhaps, *Minnu*, you should accept those feelings."

"Accept them? They're horrible."

Lucy nodded. "They are. They are also fictions in your mind. Accept them, then move past them, for they no longer have any bearing on who you are now."

"How can you say that?" Rose said.

"Move beyond what was. Move to the *now*."

"But the past matters, Lucy. I keep wondering if I acted in some way to make him..."

"You were twelve, *Minnu*. A child." Lucy folded Rose into her arms, patting Rose's back. "You know the truth of this. You did *not*."

She had wanted no one to learn of her shame. With Lucy, it had been unavoidable. Yet having told Beatrice, her stepmother still loved her. How was that possible?

"As the years pass," Lucy said. "You will find the happiness you deserve and the feelings will fade to a tattered memory that holds no sway over you."

Rose leaned back, unable to even imagine happiness. "I will never feel clean again."

"Fustian," Lucy said in a stern voice. "Though I am no Buddhist, they have some good tales to tell. I particularly like this one."

"Two monks were once traveling down a road. The rain was torrential and as the two men trudged along, they encountered a beautiful girl dressed in silk. She looked distressed and unable to cross the road.

"'Let me help you,'" said the older monk. He picked the girl up and carried her across the road to the other side.

That night at the temple, the younger monk said, "'We monks do not touch females; it is too tempting for us and can create a bad outcome.'"

The older monk looked into the eyes of the younger monk. "'I left the girl behind on the road. Are you still carrying her?'"

Rose's eyes widened. "Oh, my."

"Someday, dearest, you will leave that wounded girl back on the road, where she belongs."

Could she? "I depart this afternoon."

Lucy's beloved face peered up at her. Age had shrunk her companion, for when she had arrived from India, Rose but six, Lucy was tall and strong as a mighty oak, or so she had seemed. Over the years, while Rosamund had grown, Lucy had shrunk. Now, she barely reached Rose's shoulder.

Rose's lips slid into a smile. Lucy was still strong as an oak.

When Lucy discovered Rose's secret, she had vowed to kill the earl. Rose had imagined Lucy doing just that. It held such appeal. In the end, Rose insisted Lucy refrain, the outcome not worth the risk.

Now, only Lucy and Beatrice knew, and it must remain that way until Rose left this world for the unknown. She had doubts about heaven, with all those cherubs fluttering about. She had doubts about many things. But not about leaving. Not that.

"You could marry the big one." Lucy removed a cravat from her bag and refolded it.

"I cannot," Rose bustled around the room, checking that she'd packed everything.

"That one has a large heart, *Minnu.*" Lucy examined the weapons Rose had laid out and lifted the sword. "Such a well-balanced weapon." She replaced it in the wardrobe.

"Why put it away?" Rose said.

"I think you will not be needing it, as you are fighting a different kind of battle. The big one favors you greatly. Your troubles will not make him turn from you."

Perhaps. Rose fingered a fichu embroidered by Maman and lifted it to her nose, wishing for her mother's familiar scent, knowing it was long gone. Maman had turned from her in spirit when Rose was twelve, dying in body when she was sixteen, unable to reconcile her two great loves—that for her daughter and for her husband.

Lucy's love held true, and though she was a pragmatist, she wore blinders when it came to Rose.

If Rose told him, Rhys would recoil. She could not bear to see his warm eyes turn to revulsion, his face tighten, and his lips compress. No longer would his heart be open to her.

Nor could she hold the lie close and marry Rhys. That would be a base betrayal.

And yet she wished to hold him, to wed him, to have his children, to laugh and cry with him, to spend her days and nights with him.

Rose sighed. "I cannot tell him, Lucy."

A brow peppered with gray rose. "Is that so?" Lucy pulled out a handkerchief. "Take an extra."

Rose stuffed it into her bag. She wished this discussion over. "I must check on the new foal. He was born late in the season and I worry."

"Take care they do not see you."

"They" were her father's flunkies, the footmen. "They will not."

Rose returned to her suite, the new foal thriving, to find Lucy had neatly repacked her carry bag.

She sighed, her fingers bunching in the coverlet. Time to go. Swiftly changing into her costume, she placed her weapons in her carry bag, strapped her sheathed knife to her leg, and shoved her pistol in her coat's inner pocket.

The earl was on alert, the footmen his eyes and ears. Escape through the house was dangerous, as she knew it would be, and she dragged the rope she had prepared from beneath her bed.

Rose slid its slip-knotted loop over top of the bedpost and pushed it down, snugging it tight. Then she dragged the thick rope to the window, heavy and awkward from the knots she'd tied to ease her descent. Rose peered out the window overlooking the gardens, a window not visible from the drive.

Finally, she bound her hair tight to her head and donned her cap. Night wasn't far off, and the earl would assume any escape she devised would take place after dark.

The rain had paused. A good omen. She must leave now.

Once gone, Rosamund suspected the earl would want to murder her. But if she died before she married, her Scottish lands would revert to her chieftain, and her thirty-thousand pounds would be dispersed to Lucy, the girls, and Beatrice, with small bequests for Fitz and other servants at Fielding. Firefly would go to Rhys.

She had arranged it all, just as Maman had planned wisely, plans she suspected devised long before her decline. Her mother must have known the secret. Some days Rose believed so, others not.

Her chest a vise, Rose lifted the well-oiled window and hefted the rope outside, testing it for the thousandth time, then slipped her carry bag onto her back.

Rosamund clambered over the sill and out the window.

A chill wind slapped her face, thunder booming, and she hugged the rope tight, hanging suspended, to battle fear and the immensity of her actions. The storm was closer now, lightning darting through the sky, reminding her of that long-ago day when she and Tessa had crossed the log.

The day she met Rhys. The day it all began.

Her legs wrapped around the rope in a death grip, she began her descent to the next knot, and then the next.

Some wickers from the paddock. Dear Firefly. She'd wished to bring her, but her pregnancy made that impossible. Rose's fault. If she'd only waited to breed her...

In retrospect, Rose had made many mistakes in her planning, Fielding surprising her with his insistence she marry. She'd thought her plans rock solid. Instead, they were more jellied aspic.

Any minute, the skies would open up. Rhys would leave soon, and if she timed it right, she could catch him, the manor's circuitous drive through the forested estate making it possible.

Halfway down, she spotted Rhys' gig being brought around front.

Rose descended faster, her gloves heating with friction, then dropped to the ground. She peeked around the corner to see the gig disappear around a curve.

Rose ran, darting behind bushes, boulders, and trees, careful of watchful eyes. Some would be alarmed by an unknown boy running from the manor. Others might try to catch her.

Her route took her to the edge of the burned stable, and she paused, panting, her carry bag gaining a pound for each yard she traversed.

"And where might you be off to, m'lady?"

Bollocks!

As she put a finger to her lips, it began to rain. "You did not see me, did you?"

"You're hard to miss, m'lady," Fitz said.

"Please."

For long minutes he stared at her, eyes damp, then he shoved his hands deep into his buckskin's pockets and turned away, whistling "Auld Lang Syne."

That made *her* tear up.

Fitz would keep his silence, of that, she was sure.

On a thunderous boom, the rain pounded down in earnest, accompanied by flashes of lightning. She raced to the top of the hill and crouched by the stallion barn. The downpour would slow Rhys and she stood a chance of reaching him before he made the main road, where she could wait for him. One more sprint in the open, and the screen of trees would hide her.

Rose ran.

"Hey you, stop!"

One of the stable hands, Jeremy. A terrible shot.

She pushed her body harder, faster.

A shot rang out, the sleeve of her left arm singed. *Lud!* Jeremy *was* an awful shot, for he'd never intentionally hurt anyone. The bullet had ripped her coat, one Jeremy himself had lent her.

Making it to the trees, Rose zigzagged until she found the trail, a shortcut to the main road.

Go. Go!

Her thighs burned, her back aching, and she could barely see, but Rose pushed harder, knowing this was her one chance. She jerked to a halt at the road's edge, panting, then slipped behind a sodden oak. She looked right, then left. Empty.

Had she missed him?

Above the pounding rain, the creak of approaching wheels. Still farther, the thrumming of hooves. Many hooves.

The earl had discovered her escape.

Rose dashed into the road, running and waiving at Rhys' gig.

His horse startled, rearing, but he instantly regained control. "What the devil, Rosie?" he said, leaning toward her.

"Hide me in the gig." The approaching hooves grew louder.

"Get in."

Rose took his proffered hand, braced herself, and leapt into the seat beside him.

"On the floor, quick."

Between bouts of terror, Rose wanted to laugh. They'd done this same dance the day they'd met, when Rhys had returned her to Fielding.

He flung a blanket over her, clucking his horse into a trot. Rose held her breath. The sky had darkened to near twilight, which was good. The rain would help, too.

"Hold up there!" came a shout.

Rhys kept going.

"Hold up!" came again.

The earl himself.

Rhys eased the gig to a halt.

"Are you all right?" he whispered.

"Fine, as long as the earl does not find me." Beneath the blanket, the air was close, the scratchy covering tickling her nose for a sneeze.

The pounding of horses neared.

"Have you seen my daughter?" the earl yelled over the pouring rain.

"As you know," Rhys said, his voice bone dry. "I saw her briefly at your home."

"Since then!" the earl barked. "The chit has gone off."

"Gone off?" Rhys said. "In this storm?"

"The girl is to marry Pennworth in four days. She is nervous. Bridal jitters and all that. She may have done something stupid."

"I see," Rhys said. "If I spot her, I will take her up in the gig and bring her home."

Rosamund froze, squeezing her eyes tight.

The earl cleared his throat. "She may be dressed as a boy."

A pause, then, "Why would she do that?" Rhys said.

"Who knows? She is a disobedient child."

Rosamund heard the snap of the reins, and the gig moved forward.

"Hold up," said the earl. "I'm not done with you yet, Ravenscroft."

"I'm afraid *I* am done with *you*, sir, for though my gig has a hood, I am nonetheless getting soaked. If you wish to discuss this further, come to Ravenscroft. I am weary and so is my horse."

They trotted forward, and Rosamund listened as the earl's troop thundered into the distance.

CHAPTER

SIXTEEN

Rhys flung off her covering once he stopped the gig, and Rose felt like a mole suddenly exposed to light. Lanterns glowed within the small barn, an outer one where they kept tack and a few of the older horses.

"Are you well?" Rhys said. "That tear on your sleeve looks like a bullet hole to me."

"It is, but I am unhurt. Jeremy is a dreadful shot. I think he was trying for a warning shot and missed. Help me up, please. I feel as if I have frozen in this position."

Rhys gripped her under the arms and hoisted her onto the seat. "Better?"

"Much. Everything aches, but I will be fine in a minute."

He jumped down and unhitched the horse, leading him to one of the empty stalls. Returning to the gig, Rhys raised his arms to help her to the ground.

"One of the boys will wipe down Horace," Rhys said. "They will bring him fresh mash and water, and take care of the gig."

"You know me so well."

"You worry more about horses than humans."

"Quite true."

He lifted her from the seat and set her on the ground, but her legs buckled. He caught her before she fell.

"Just give me a moment," Rosamund said.

Rhys hefted her bag and slung a strap over his shoulder, then winged out an arm. "Shall we go inside and get you warm?"

She took his proffered arm, grateful for the support and that he hadn't barraged her with questions.

She had made it to Ravenscroft. To safety. No one and nothing would stop her now.

Rose sipped hot tea before a raging fire in the Ravenscroft family parlor. Once Rhys had settled her and ordered the tea and bannocks, the latter her favorite, he'd disappeared.

The door opened and in popped Patrick. "Ah, the penitent child."

"Come in then, barnacle!"

"Barnacle!" he said, striding into the room. "I would have you know, I am now a viscount, having been ennobled by the king!"

She wiggled her brows. "Rumor has it the man is delusional."

Patrick snorted. "Sadly, most true." His face grew serious. "Are you well?"

She gave him a smile. "Now that I am here. Yes."

"Excellent." He patted her head.

"Stop that!"

"I'll see you in the morning, pest." He blew out as swiftly as he had come.

The warm, sweet brew relaxed her, and she removed her damp stockings, curling her bare toes before the fire's warmth.

She was safe, away from the earl. And all she held dear.

No time to get maudlin. That could wait for Scotland, where she would have hours to ruminate on who and what she had left behind. Maman always said to never look back.

How could she not?

The enormity of her actions hit hard.

Of course the earl would try to reclaim her. After all, she was a valuable asset. But her clan and its chieftain would protect her, he had reassured as much in their exchanged letters. That he was also a titled lord would give the earl pause.

"How are you, Rose?" Rhys said as he entered carrying a lap blanket that he placed over her.

She smiled up at him. "Better. Much better now that I'm no longer beneath the earl's roof. I will never go back."

He took the matching chair across from the roaring blaze. "A room has been made up for you."

"But your servants..."

"Are loyal to me and our family. Rest assured, not a one will speak of your presence."

She leaned back, hands trembling, tea sloshing onto the saucer.

"Come." He placed her cup and saucer on the tray and helped her stand, the blanket pooling at her feet. "I expect a visit from the earl sooner rather than later. I want you safe in your room by then."

"All right." As she took Rhys' arm, her bones felt as if they were melting, she was that weary.

A brush of wings above her head and she squeaked. "What..."

"Damned parrot," Rhys said. "Are you well?"

"Of course." She straightened, hating how she'd startled. Under normal circumstances, she was not a nervous woman. "I recall birds flying around Ravenscroft as a child, but...?"

Rhys' gaze flicked upward. "Yes, well, all were liberated or given to aviaries. Except for Percy."

The multi-colored bird observed them from the mantle.

"The infernal parrot will not be caught," Rhys said.

"He must be ancient."

"The damned birds can live sixty to seventy years."

Rhys' frustration was so clear, she couldn't help but laugh. "I must make friends with him."

He cast an evil eye at the bird, who glided to a chair back and perched. "The blasted thing is friend to no one!"

The third-floor room Rhys had chosen pleased her, for she had used the same on the many nights she'd spent at Ravenscroft as a child. Nothing had changed, the bright yellow wallpaper and stately bed evoking happy memories.

A nightrail lay across the bed, along with a robe and slippers, and in a corner of the room sat a steaming tub.

"I will ring for a maid to help with your bath." He tested the water and nodded. "The clothes belong to Susannah."

"You must miss her, with her fixed at Woodbine."

"I do, but she and Thomasina prefer our Devon estate."

The former marquess had banished Thomasina around her fourth birthday to be raised by the stable master and his wife, the Lansdowne family forbidden to speak of her.

Rhys was eight at the time, but he often spoke of his eldest sister, his anger and worry troubling him for years. He had never forgotten her. As the three remaining siblings grew, they would sneak in visits to Thomasina, but her expulsion infuriated him.

A silver-domed tray sat on the bedside table, and Rhys lifted the lid. "I thought soup might warm you up." He inspected the room, hands clasped behind his back.

"I doubt I can eat a thing."

"Try."

He returned to the bed, staring down at her, as if he could see beneath her skin, beneath her muscle and bone, to her very soul. Whether Rhys understood the whys and wherefores of her leaving Fielding or not, he would battle her father or Satan himself for Rose. She knew this to be true.

She loved him so fiercely that a pain squeezed her chest. "I'll see you in the morning."

He rang for a maid. "In the morning."

As he was leaving, a knock came at the door, and Angus walked in.

Rose had met the tall, heavy-boned man often when they were children. He was somehow related to Rhys, an unusual man with a Scottish burr, dark complexion, and poker-straight black hair.

When she had been a child, an adult had referred to his father as an Iroquois, not that she knew what that meant. But she was a curious girl and had looked it up.

It seemed England had established alliances with the American Native tribes due to Britain's competition with France in the Americas. Quite a few American Natives willingly traveled to England to learn English and for trade purposes. They were presented with fine clothes and gifts, the English wishing to gain their loyalty over the French and Spanish. They'd toured Britain, including Ireland, Wales, and Scotland, which was where an Iroquois chieftain encountered Angus' Scottish mother.

Angus had accompanied Rhys to war and served as Rhys' batman, but he was far more than a personal servant, their friendship much resembling Rose's with Lucy. They treated each other as equals and companions, though in public, Angus called Rhys "my lord."

"My lady." Angus gave her a brief bow and turned to Rhys. "Lord Fielding has arrived with two of his minions, and he demands to see you."

The earl. Right downstairs. Rose shivered.

"Don't fret, Rosie," Rhys said, giving her hand a squeeze.

He laid a hand on Angus' shoulder. "Demands does he?"

"Aye," Angus said. "Shall I put him in the formal salon?"

"No. Leave him standing in the front hall and do not offer refreshment."

Angus grinned, then vanished.

Rhys set his hands on her shoulders. "All will be well, Rosie."

"I know I am in the best of hands."

"*Being your slave, what should I do but tend*

Upon the hours and times of your desire?"

"The Bard." Rose's anxiety melted away. "Your one true love."

He laughed as a maid bustled in, a dark-haired girl she didn't recognize, who curtsied to both of them.

"This is Sally," Rhys said. "She will take good care of you, my lady."

"Thank you, sir."

Rhys lifted her hand to his lips and pressed a kiss, lingering a bit. "Until tomorrow."

Patrick joined Rhys as he strode down the hall towards the staircase where the earl and his flunkies awaited below. Rhys wore fresh clothes, as the earl would find his damp ones odd, and he explained the situation to Patrick as they walked. His brother might be a caustic arse at times, but he was loyal to a fault. He knew how much Rosie meant to Rhys.

"Care to explain, brother?"

"Rosie's despicable father is hunting her." Rhys knew Patrick cared for Rose a great deal. "The shit-sack himself told me she was to wed Pennworth in four days."

"That would make anyone run," Patrick said.

"Yes, but I believe there is more."

"Have you spoken of it to her?"

"She is exhausted and afraid. I do not need to know the details."

"Why has she not considered your suit more seriously?" Patrick said. "The woman obviously adores you. She always has."

"Lady Rosamund hesitates to renounce her lands and monies to a husband. Or so she claims."

"Knowing the pest, that rings true," Patrick said.

"Do not call my intended a pest. Rose is well aware I would never usurp either, but leave her in control."

As they walked, Patrick slipped a cheroot from its case, took one, and offered another to Rhys. "Perhaps she does not care for men in general, if you get my drift."

Rhys slipped the cheroot between his lips but declined a light. Their kiss, that spark of desire in her eyes. "No. That is not the case."

"Has she taken you in dislike?" Patrick said.

"I do not believe so, though her assent to my courtship was not terribly convincing. Rose says she does not wish to marry anyone, though why that is so remains elusive."

"A mystery."

Rhys clasped his hands behind his back. "If I knew the answer to that... That is not the issue at the moment."

"I take your point."

Patrick matched Rhys' strides, and they soon stood in the grand hall before a pacing earl, two Fielding footmen carrying pistols, and three of Ravenscroft's burly men, including the powerful Billy Broad —all former soldiers. Angus hovered out of sight, rifle in hand.

Though his men held no pistols, Rhys knew firearms, knives, and perhaps even a garrote or two were secreted on their persons.

"My lord," Rhys said, nodding to the earl. "To what do I owe this honor?"

Fielding, rain-soaked, but wearing his most haughty face, offered a slight bow. "My daughter is still missing, Ravenscroft."

Though his and Patrick's height forced the earl to look up at them, the earl was at his most formidable.

"Unfortunate," Rhys said. "But I fail to see how that has earned me a visit from your esteemed self."

Fury blazed in the earl's eyes, to be erased by his ubiquitous genial façade. "Given the chit's past exploits, Ravenscroft is the logical place where she would flee."

Rhys grinned and shook his head. "We were but children then. I doubt Lady Rosamund would come here."

"Nonetheless, I insist on searching the manor and its grounds. This pile has many nooks and crannies, places where she might hide. For all I know, your servants are aiding her."

"My lord," Patrick chimed in. "Did you say 'insist'? You sound desperate indeed."

"The foolish child thinks she knows her own mind."

"That *child*," Rhys said, finding it increasingly hard to rein in his temper, "is some six-and-twenty years."

"I have chosen. Pennworth will make my daughter an admirable husband."

Rhys tightened his jaw rather than unleash a diatribe on Pennworth's undesirable qualities. Fielding was winding up to full-blown fury, the last thing Rhys wanted to encourage.

"The viscount is an interesting choice," Patrick said. "But if Lady Rosamund is so averse to the man, choose another. If not me, my brother, perhaps."

The earl spread his arms wide. "She is hesitant, is all, as women often are. She will soon see the advantages of the match."

"Advantages?" Rhys said.

"The man's a viscount, a decorated soldier."

"Whereas I am a marquess," Rhys said.

"True! But Pennworth plans to expand his horse-breeding operation for *her*. What could be better?"

"Indeed." Patrick's arid tone sailed above the earl's head.

"She is headstrong." The earl smirked at Rhys. "As I recall, you can attest to her contrary behavior. In truth, you often aided and abetted her."

A well-placed fist would wipe away that smirk. "As I noted earlier, we were children then. We are children no more, and the idea of you searching Ravenscroft strikes me as both precipitous and absurd. Her ladyship is not here, for I would know if she were. Let that be the end of it."

The earl's gimlet stare slid between Rhys and his brother, his lips thinning until he tilted them into a smile. "We must agree to see things from differing perspectives. Know that I *will* find that troublesome girl and return her to Fielding where she will see the light."

"Best of luck," Rhys said, turning away.

Fielding grabbed his shoulder. "I shall return, Ravenscroft.

Perhaps at that time, you will be more forthcoming. Or trouble shall ensue. I have resources and connections!"

Better men, *far* better men, had threatened Rhys to no avail. "As you will, my lord."

The earl flicked a hand to his men, and they followed him to the door.

The discussion with the earl concerned Rhys enough to speak with Patrick, Angus, and his housekeeper about the preparations. All the while, his gut nagged him about Rosie until he could stand it no more.

Upon returning to her rooms, he found her once more dressed as a man and packing her knapsack.

CHAPTER
SEVENTEEN

"You heard," he said as he stood in the doorway.

Rosamund paused, and he caught a flicker of despair before she busied herself with the dress she shoved into the bag. "I followed you and listened. I must get away now, Rhys."

He leaned his shoulder against the door frame, crossing his arms. "That will only get you caught sooner, my lady."

Rhys did not miss the pistol she tucked into her coat pocket, and he strode toward her with purpose. "See reason. Your father will follow you to Scotland, as you heard. Where else can you go?"

Rosamund whirled on him. "I don't know. But I will find a way. There is *always* a way."

"There is. Marry me. You will be safe from that damned monster who calls himself your father."

She froze, the room's air thick as a brewing storm. "I cannot."

Rhys sat on the bed and tugged her hand until she sat beside him. "You mean, little minx, that you *will* not. I do not understand why. At least give me that much."

Rosie's brow scrunched, thinking deep thoughts. He'd seen that expression many times and chose to wait it out.

"I cannot," she finally said. "Nor can I explain. Can you not just accept it and let this absurd proposal go?"

"In your letters, when I was at school and then the front, you wrote about your mother's fading, a sorrowful situation for such a vibrant woman."

"She was vibrant. Once."

He did not fail to see the tears brimming in her eyes. She scrubbed her hands across her face.

"Has your refusal to do with your mother?" he said.

Rosie burbled a pathetic laugh. "With Maman? No. Those were terrible years, and I confess there were times when I wished she would simply die. How is that for a dutiful daughter?"

"Yet you loved her deeply," Rhys said.

"Yes. She was my magical Maman. But in the later years, I became conflicted as she retreated into the laudanum, as she failed to..."

"What, Rosie?"

A deep breath filled Rose's lungs, her exhale a sigh.

"Watching your mother fade, as you called it, must have been a great burden and sadness."

"She abandoned me, Rhys. Long before she physically perished. Did you know the earl even supplied the drug? A kindness, he called it. It was horrible. When she died, I had few allies but for Fitz and Lucy, and was left to the earl's tender mercies."

She sniffed and stood, rearranging sundry items in her carrysack, refusing to look at him. "But that's neither here nor there. I must leave, for under no circumstances will I marry the viscount."

"I heartily agree."

"I still do not understand why you wish to marry me."

Rhys stood as well and took her hands in his. "As you know, the war..." Rhys cleared his throat. "Combat broadened my perspective in many ways."

"How does that—"

"The truth is really quite simple." His eyes burned from trying to see inside this beautiful, mercurial woman. "I wish you to stay because you make me happy."

Well! After that blasted man had wheedled Rose into staying for the night, she re-donned her nightrail and slid beneath cozy covers, warmed by a comforting brick.

She made him happy. Her chest expanded with an almost painful intensity. *She made him happy.*

How could he say such a thing, then walk out the door? Leaving the decision to stay or leave up to her.

Of course she'd stayed. True, he did not profess his love. That would have been worse. But to make someone happy was a special thing. An important thing.

He made her happy, too.

But her soul was weary, *she* was weary and heartsick from all the years she had battled her father. Even her own secrets turned against her, and she fought them as well, for they sometimes whispered at night saying hateful, terrible things.

She wished to lay down her arms and go to Rhys, marry him, be his wife, his marchioness. That was the intelligent solution. The simplest one, as well.

She would love him and make him proud. The lure of it shined a beacon on her dark thoughts.

And once wed, he would either divine her secrets or she would tell him. Either way, he would be revolted.

Rhys had said escaping to Scotland was no guarantee of surcease. She forced herself to admit he was right. Her chieftain would hold off the earl. But for how long? Weeks? Months? Years?

Fielding would eventually wear him down. Or the king's men would come and pressure her clan.

Only her marriage would end the earl's quest, her monies and lands lost to Fielding forever.

One simple act.

One profound act.

From her pocket, she withdrew the pebble Rhys had left her. Smooth and dull, it was shaped like an egg. A riverstone, a lucky one because of the narrow white band of quartz encircling the stone.

She could always take her mother's path, albeit a swifter one, and plunge into the river with no hope of survival. At last, she would be free of the earl.

Rose often had those thoughts, but she would never act on them, for imagining the desolation she would leave behind made her ill. Lucy, Fitz, others... And Rhys. Of all, he would be the most devastated that she had chosen death over a life with him.

She could not hurt him that way. Not him. Not any of them.

Her eyes grew heavy, exhaustion fogging her brain, and sleep consumed her.

Sounds of clinking china, rushing footsteps, and a farrier's anvil troubled Rosamund's dream. The scents of bannocks and tea brought her to the surface, and she opened her eyes.

The place was a-bustle, and the sounds making her uneasy.

Moments later, Sally tapped on her door and breezed in bearing a pale green gown the color of budded leaves draped over her arms.

"Can I help you put this on, miss?" Sally said.

The dress Sally held was no morning frock but artfully crafted of silk with tiny rosettes of the palest peach dotting the hem and bodice.

"No," she said far too abruptly. "Um, but thank you, Sally!"

Rose headed for the door.

"Miss, you are in your nightrail."

Rose jolted to a halt, then pulled the robe she'd worn the previous night and hastened out the door. She rushed through the hall and down the stairs to find a gaggle of servants filing into the second-floor ballroom. Bypassing the procession, she arrived at the large space now decorated with abundant flowers, a trellis, and a deep blue carpet that formed a center aisle.

Rose spotted Patrick conversing with a footman and walked over. "What is happening?"

Patrick, who apparently hadn't seen her approach, choked. He cleared his throat, then said, "Preparations."

She rolled her eyes. "You have never been obtuse, Patrick. Something is afoot."

"That it is," came his too-jovial reply. "Do excuse me." As if his heels were a-fire, he beelined to Ravenscroft's housekeeper, who carried a large spray of blooms.

"Where is Rhys?" she hollered after him, heedless that ladies did not yell.

"In his study," he said, returning his attention to the housekeeper.

She had her suspicions, of course, but why bother guessing when Rhys would have the answers.

The door to Rhys' study flew open to reveal Rosie in her voluminous dressing gown, hair askew, and eyes alight. She wagged her finger at him as she stomped toward the desk where he sat, doubting a piece of furniture would keep him safe. Thus, he leaned back in his chair, effecting a casual pose, and steeled his nerves.

How much worse could Rose's ire be than Napoleon's troops?

Much, he feared.

"What exactly is going on, Rhys?" Rosie slapped her hands on her hips. "This morning I was presented with a silken dress fit for a duchess, a house bustling with activity, a ballroom decked out like a... a musical evening, well, except for the trellis. And *you*, sitting like a pasha behind your desk with that ridiculous half-smile on your face. Go on, get it off your chest!"

Rhys pursed his lips, unsure how to approach the delicate matter.

"Well?"

"Have you noticed what a beautiful day it is?" He waved at the sunlight pouring in through the window.

Rosie snorted. "So it appears."

"I thought it would be a splendid day to be married."

His clever Rosie didn't even blink. "And just who is to be married?"

He heaved a sigh and pushed to his feet with deep reluctance. "Darling girl, you—"

"You have *never* called me 'darling girl' in your life. I can think of many other things you've called me, most unsuitable for mixed company, but darling girl was never one of them."

Her tongue was an asp, her demeanor overbearing, yet a cloud of sorrow and defeat hovered over her.

Rhys longed for the bright open girl of their childhood, the one who told him her truths with no fear. What secrets lay buried beneath the blanket of unhappiness that had mantled her life? What truths was she unwilling to tell him? *Dammit.* Her distance hurt his soul, as did her lack of faith in him.

"I have thought long and hard on this, Rosie," he said, coming from behind the desk. "Your father will hunt you down and wreak terrible vengeance for your disobedience. I cannot, I *will* not have that. You must marry to keep yourself safe from that man's machinations. I know you are fond of me. So let it be me."

Rose stood as if in a pool of aloneness, her face a haunted mask, unwilling or unable to reach for him. He found that almost too painful to bear.

Rhys reached out and took her hand. "Make me happy, Rosie. Let me be your choice."

Rose inwardly stumbled, though she didn't move an inch. He was right, of course. She had dreamt of her father last night, terrible dreams filled with cruelty and trauma until the familiar nightmare returned to torment her.

She peered into those dear eyes, eyes that said he cared for her, wanted the best for her. Eyes that begged her to allow him inside.

The moment she had dreaded had arrived.

Their past, their letters, their confidences and their truths had all led to this—the moment when there was nowhere to hide.

She *wanted* to wed him. He must know that as well as she and Rhys would dig, nay, explode any secrets preventing the truth from emerging. Nonetheless, she prevaricated, shoving back a truth she never wished him to hear.

"Do you not need a special license?" she said.

He stepped closer. "Already acquired, my lady. Days ago, in fact."

The inevitability crushed her. Not of marriage, but of the telling.

She drew him to the settee. "Please sit, Rhys."

He did so. "Your eyes are troubled. And sad. Is the idea of marrying me so very terrible?"

Sitting beside him, she shucked off years of cowardice, or at least tried to, and wrapped herself in what little courage she possessed. "Not at all."

"Let me help, then." He leaned forward. "How can I help?"

"There is no help to be had." She mapped his beautiful face with her eyes. What a fine man he was, a beautiful one inside and out, the lines carved by years at war making him even more dear. She wished to fold him into her arms and hold him tight, this man who had always defended and protected her.

Her eyes welled up as she pictured the transformation soon to cross that beloved face.

Best get on with it, then.

"I have declined your proposal because I am not pure."

He reared back. "What the Christ does that mean?"

Though she desperately wished to drop her gaze to her lap, she fixed her eyes. "A man has been with me, intimately."

He sat rigid as a statue. "Who?"

Of course, he would ask *that*. Anyone would during a confession such as hers. "The who matters little. What matters is that the deed is done. Don't you see? I cannot be your marchioness."

"Do you love him?"

Rose shook her head, a thrill of revulsion rippling through her.

His face tightened, his jaw bunching. "If we are telling truths, I am not pure either, as I have had congress with a woman."

Rose refused to picture it, and though not unexpected, she hated the thought. *Hated* it. "You are a man. That is different."

He blinked. "All that changes from my perspective is that our marriage bed will not be painful for you."

The marriage bed. Heaven's mercies, she could not contemplate that, not even with Rhys.

"You were saying...?" he said.

"Do you not despise me?"

"How could I, when I have done the same myself? None of us are perfect, Rosie, and I certainly never expected you to be so."

Well! "Why not?"

A twinkle in those devilish eyes. "Come now. This from the girl who dared me to steal my father's prime hunter for a jaunt?"

"Hum. I did, did I not? You are correct. I am most imperfect."

"We all are, or have you not noticed?" he said.

She had noticed. More than noticed, since it appeared he would continue to insist on marriage.

Rose could say the man was dead. Or gone, fled with another woman. Or...

No. She could say none of those things.

She had begun. Now to complete the tale, though her next salvo would devastate him.

"Promise you will harm no one involved in this tale."

"How can I possibly do that, Rosie?"

"Because you must. Because I asked it of you. Either that, or I will remain mute."

Rhys leapt to his feet and paced a circle around the room. "No."

Rose shrugged. "All right. I will leave for Scotl—"

"You will *not*. Pennworth is desperate for your money, and his weak scruples would not prevent him from kidnapping you, or worse. Then there is your beloved sire's determination to see you under his thumb once again."

"I know, Rhys." She rose, brushing out the dressing gown's heavy brocade skirts.

He stormed over and rested his hands on her shoulders. "Rosie, do not make me promise."

Her hand cupped his cheek. "I know you and your vigorous sense of justice. Without the promise, you will be unable to stop yourself. Vow that you will neither maim nor kill the man, and I will confess all."

He leaned into her hand for just a moment, then took it, and seated them again on the settee. "All right. I do swear and promise not to harm the man."

Her gaze fell to her hands, clutching the dressing gown's folds. She could not look at him, simply could not.

"The man who took my virginity was Fielding."

CHAPTER

EIGHTEEN

Rage flowed over Rhys like a boiling shroud, burning him to his core, his breath coming fast and hard, like a bellows being stoked hotter and hotter.

All the war years he'd pictured Rose safe and happy in the bosom of her family. While that bloody monster had been...

Spikes speared his brain, his heart, his soul, blood frothing to the surface as the furious red tide rose.

He drew back, struggling to contain his wrath, afraid it would erupt over Rosie.

Patrick joked Lansdownes had berserker Viking ancestors. Rhys did not disagree.

Now, today, on the settee that bore the wear of years, the berserker heat was consuming him, blood-red sparks dancing before his eyes. His blood surged, his fingers digging into the satin fabric. It split.

Rage consumed him.

The earl.

Fielding.

Her *father*.

"Rhys?"

Rhys would kill him, eviscerate him, burn her father's entrails until he died an agonizing death.

He laughed, a bitter chuckle. Rosie knew him so well. She had denied him the earl's death, for he must hold true to his promise. *Must.* He would not add yet another betrayal to the mountain of them at his Rosie's feet.

With no outlet for his anger, no shape or form for its release, he took great care when he kissed the backs of her hands.

"Wait for me. I will return." He strode from the room, closing the door gently behind him. "Angus!" he bellowed. "To me, Angus!"

In seconds, his friend stood before him. "Ravenscroft?"

"It is upon me. Rose cannot see this."

"Wait, Rhys!"

"No!"

"Think of her, of Lady Rose."

"I am, curse you. Her ladyship will be terrified." The curtain of crimson unfurled before his eyes, and he tried. Dammitalltohell, he tried.

The bloody curtain descended, snuffing all thought, and he raced for the door.

"Where are you going?" Angus said, racing after him.

"To the camp."

"Stop!"

The man's command halted Rhys, and he hurled an offensive Chinese vase.

Angus ducked. "Ravenscroft, for Christ's sake!"

Rhys ran.

Rosamund sat frozen on the settee. The truth was out. Rhys *knew*.

A knock at the door, which cracked open, Angus poking his head in.

"Are you well, Lady Rose?"

No, she was *not* well. "I am fine, Angus. Thank you."

The man, wiser than most, quietly closed the door behind him.

Rhys' fury was not a new thing, for she had seen it twice during their childhood, once when Homer was accidentally killed and the second time when a guest—riding a horse well beyond his expertise—had trampled a kitten. Rhys had been fourteen, the rider full-grown—bigger and stronger—but that had mattered little as Rhys dragged the man from his saddle and began to pummel him. It took two men to pull him off, and Rhys had scooped up the small creature and disappeared. She had found him weeping over the kitten and its senseless death and soothed him until his tears had dried and he simply held the creature. By the time his father's search party found them hours later, they had buried the kitten and were walking hand in hand back to the house.

Rose could have soothed him today, as well, but he needed time to work through to absorb what she'd said, to process those thoughts and feelings assailing him. To understand them.

Rose simply sat, a bee in amber, while the house prepared a wedding and Rhys battled his monsters.

Perhaps an hour passed, or maybe two. No servants had entered since Angus, nor had she rung for anyone, though she was starving.

Her big secret. Her big lie.

She was despoiled and ashamed.

Yet Lucy's voice rang in her ears, railing against those appellations.

She was not the perpetrator. What His Lordship had done was unconscionable, and she, the coerced participant. Yet society would brand her untouchable—loose, ravished, unwanted, and unmarriageable.

How *dare* they?

Rose ran her fingers along the settee's ripped fabric. It had been eight long years since Fielding had touched her intimately. Yet each time she saw him, it felt as if he was entering her body yet again—a greasy, helpless feeling.

When Rose had turned sixteen, she began to plan. Oh, how she had planned, though most of her stratagems came to naught. With no funds and no transportation, Rose had no way out until her eighteenth birthday.

At first, she had been pleased when Fielding's visits became sporadic, his attacks inconsistent surprises. In time, that felt worse, for they stole any remaining sense of agency she possessed.

When her Scottish lands and Maman's inheritance reverted to her on her eighteenth birthday, Rose had originally planned to leave. Though her father retained legal control over her until she turned twenty-one, she would hide out in the highlands for those three years until she reached her majority.

But all her plans came to naught when dear Charlotte, Claire, and Beatrice had entered the scene. His Lordship wed Beatrice in June of Rosamund's sixteenth year, when Charlotte and Claire were aged ten and eleven, mere children and ripe for His Lordship's pickings. Though she desperately wished to escape, she could not leave them alone in Fielding's gentle hands.

So she prepared. Years earlier, Lucy, her true name Meenakshi, began teaching Rose the Indian *kalaripayattu* or *kalari*, the fighting art more than three-thousand-years old, the styles, rituals, and philosophies inspired by Hinduism. Nowadays, the British banned *kalari* throughout India. Most would call it a heathen art. Rose called it beautiful.

Lucy had said dancers, as well as warriors in her province practiced *kalaripayattu*—and Rose's grace and suppleness were greatly enhanced by the martial art, as Lucy called it.

Rosamund practiced with bows and arrows, poles for spears, the curved sword and dagger, including the two-handled one called a *katara*. Much to her glee, she had an affinity for both the dagger and sword.

On the eve of her eighteenth birthday, she lay in bed, chewing her nails and staring into the darkness. Tomorrow was hers, the day she would receive her inheritance. Everything would change.

But tonight was tonight, and it was time to act.

After donning her boys' clothes, Rose walked to the practice room to retrieve her *kadarta* and *irettakathi* knives, then had padded to His Lordship's rooms. The servants were abed and even the earl's devoted valet had retired for the evening.

Rose had placed her lit candle on his bedside, then positioned her *kadarta* above his penis, while her arm rested lightly across his throat, her smaller *irettakathi* hovering above his eye.

"Lord Fielding," she had said in dulcet tones. "Wake up, sir."

She repeated her words until his eyes fluttered open. He jerked, but she held fast. She then explained how she had snuck up on him as he slept and how easy it would have been to remove those precious jewels or stab him in the eye before he even woke.

He lurched for her again, but her arm across his throat pressed downward, her blade an inch from his eye. "Lie back, sir, or you will impale yourself."

The monster had been terrified, and she recalled her pleasure at his fear, this man who had caused her countless moments of terror.

"Promise that you will never touch Charlotte or Claire, nor any child or unwilling woman in your household again."

Rose wasn't so naïve to think she could bind the earl with a promise. Fielding openly wielded power over her in many legitimate ways. Nor could she be on guard around the clock. Nonetheless... "If you break your oath, I *will* act."

She also promised, in turn, to be a dutiful daughter in all conventional ways.

He'd fussed and fumed and wheedled until...

"I so vow."

Finally.

Nonetheless, Rose kept careful watch, aching to tell Beatrice, but unwilling to crush the woman's spirit, for she appeared to love the man, just as Maman had done.

Fielding never visited her rooms again. And so she became a guardian in the years that came after, always wary, always on watch, always fearful. She'd taken to carrying a small dagger in her pocket and keeping her curved sword beneath her bed, uncaring if the maids tattled on her.

Rose shook off the memories, mobilized her legs, and poured herself a Scotch from the sideboard. The first tentative sip burned through her, making her eyes water and her nose tickle.

On the second sip, Rhys blew into the study, ending her ruminations.

He had bathed and changed into more formal attire, looking handsome as sin as he approached.

"Any left for me?"

A smile rose, and she poured him a glass.

Rhys sipped, then cleared his throat. "Excuse my precipitous departure, Rosie."

She understood, and though she wished to take his hand, she refrained. She couldn't imagine him wanting her touch after her revelations. "It is all right, Rhys."

"You will marry me, yes?"

"How can you even think that after what I told you?"

He took a hefty swig. "My thoughts are no different on that subject. However, I now wish to murder the earl."

Dear heavens, the man was insane. "It feels wrong, Rhys. As if I am deceiving you."

"Have you more revelations, then?" he said.

"Those were not enough? No, there are no more, but… I have been working on leaving the girl back on the road, yet I cannot seem to do so."

"Girl on the road?" He took her elbow and steered her to the settee.

"A story Lucy told me," she said, taking a seat. "My feelings remain blackened as if I lured him in some way."

As Rhys sat beside her, he opened his mouth to speak.

Rose held up a hand. "My mind knows I did not. Yet my heart wanders back to then, back to what I might have done to precipitate his actions. Nonsensical, yet I feel a terrible guilt." She sighed.

He wrapped his arms around her and held her close. "Think on this. Many is the time when a soldier fighting alongside me perished from an enemy blade or gunshot. I often felt guilty that he had died while I remained unscathed."

He leaned back, yet kept his hands in hers. "Nor was I alone in those feelings. Many others felt them, as well, as we watched friends and comrades die while we survived."

"Logically, you had nothing to do with their deaths."

"Not true. Had I moved faster, positioned myself better, I might have saved both of us. An unproductive exercise that still haunts me from time to time. I, too, am learning to move past those feelings. The task is not an easy one."

"No, it is not. I must try harder, mustn't I? But ofttimes I still feel unclean."

Rhys' lips twitched. "I have often seen you unkempt, but you clean up quite well."

A chuckle bubbled up. "Perhaps I find it hard to accept that you, a marquess, wish to take to wife a woman who is not virginal."

"Dear Rosie, I am no marquess, not with you, but simply Rhys, the boy who has always adored you."

She searched his eyes and saw his pain and caring. His affection. Nothing hurtful. No castigation. No disdain.

Rose should act noble, tell him she did not return his affections, that her feelings had changed, that he meant little to her any longer. She could convince him of that and he would let her go. After all, her lies would be for his own good.

Rose discovered she was not noble. She could not voice those falsehoods.

"All those years." He shook his head as if his thoughts were inconceivable. "When I would receive a letter, I would picture you playing with your horses and romping around the countryside. I saw you happy and safe, and that made me happy, a precious commodity at the front. How wrong I was."

"I had moments of happiness, Rhys."

"When your letters became less about feelings and more about detailing events, I wondered if you had found a suitor. Or if you had become bored with me."

"A suitor? Oh, my dearest friend, how could I accept any beaux but you? Bored? With you? Impossible."

"I am glad, curse me. So we shall marry." He rose, pulling her to her feet with him, and sliding an arm around her waist.

Her eyes widened. "No. I am tainted by—"

"The only thing tainted is—"

"Stop interrupting me!"

"You just interrupted *me*! The only tainted thing in all of this is your damned sire!" He tightened his hold on her. "I hold you in great affection, Rose, you must know I do. I always have."

She went all warm and soft inside. "And I, you. But what if someone learns of—"

"We will deal with it at that time."

"What if they told the *ton*? It would spread like wildfire. I would be ostracized and your marquessate would be irreparably damaged."

"We would manage, and as a marquess' wife, you would never be ostracized."

Oh, this frustrating man. "You have always been clear-headed, Rhys. Use your good sense now." She rested a hand on his arm. "I hold you too dear to shackle you to a...a..."

"A what? A wanton woman? You are not that."

"No, but—"

He gritted his teeth. "End this prevarication now. It is pointless."

She had seen that determined look many times, one so decisive as to be made of iron. "But Scotland..."

"Is a lovely fantasy, but your father would follow you, as would I."

He spoke the truth, of course. Her plan, though not exactly foolish, was a bit ill-conceived. But designing her escape had given her hope for all those years, a much-needed commodity. "You would indeed follow me to Scotland?"

"I would dare more than that for your hand."

Knowing Rhys, he would dare a great deal. He was so dear and she loved him so very much. She *wanted* to marry the man, for heaven's sake.

"All right, you stubborn, irritating, irascible man. Yes, I would be honored to marry you this very day."

Triumph and joy shined from his eyes. "I am blessed." Rhys cupped her face, then brushed the sweetest kiss across her lips, once, twice, then deepened it.

Rose wished to be closer, her hands clasping his waist, his lips warm and firm, his tongue licking, her opening to him, their mouths melding in blissful pleasure.

When Rhys ended the kiss, she momentarily felt bereft.

CHAPTER
NINETEEN

"I have contacted your trustee who manages your estate," he said.

"Whatever for?"

"Our marriage settlements." He bussed her cheek, then moved to his desk, retrieving a key from his pocket and unlocking the middle drawer. He removed a sheaf of documents and handed them to her.

"I don't..."

"Please read them."

"All right." Rose sat and trudged through the language of the law. Rhys had addressed it all—her dowry, her pin money, the money and lands she would receive were she to be widowed, and finally her Scottish lands and inheritance from Maman, all of which he had gifted to her upon their marriage, placing it in her control and that of their future children.

Papers signed in Rhys' bold script and that of her chieftain. No permission from Fielding necessary, nor any hidden agendas, only plain and simple truths. All for her benefit.

Rose's eyes burned at the evidence of his care and concern, writ large on the page. She slid her arms around his waist, leaning her cheek on his chest. "Oh, Rhys, this is such a big thing, our marriage."

"It is, one that pleases me excessively."

The ceremony was simple and intimate and filled with tears, the latter having nothing to do with sentimentality.

Rose wore the lovely green dress, her hair styled by Lucy, who was waiting in her rooms as a surprise. Rhys had managed to bring her friend to Ravenscroft, much to Rose's astonishment and joy.

Her dress, her hair, even her dainty shoes—all for naught, as Rose was highly allergic to chrysanthemums, and a positive torrent of the cursed blooms flooded the room. That the early frost hadn't wiped them out boggled her mind.

Upon entering the ballroom, Rose began sniffling, and by the ceremony's end, her cheeks were tear-stained, her nose runny, and her face an inflated balloon. The perfect look for a newly minted bride.

Once alone in Rhys' study, Rhys folded her into an embrace.

"Chrysanthemums," she said, waving a handkerchief.

He grimaced, hugging her tight. "I noticed."

"Hard not to, good sir." Rose blew her nose.

"I am very sorry, Rosie."

She rested against him, his warm, sheltering presence a balm. He was the embodiment of her hopes and dreams. And he was hers. All hers. She clasped him tighter. And sniffed.

"Why on God's green earth," she said. "Did you include them in that, that..." Rose stuttered, waving her arms. "That floral explosion!"

"Patrick arranged for the flowers. He would not have known."

She frowned. "Perhaps. Though I wouldn't put it past that devil of a brother of yours." Impossible to keep the laughter inside, so she let it peal. "I'm sure I look quite ridiculous."

He bellowed a laugh, waggling his brows. "Of all the flowers for Patrick to choose."

"This laughter isn't helping, either. I must look like a swollen turnip."

"I do not believe turnips can swell, sweetheart, but since you are weeping even more tears..." He flourished yet another handkerchief from his pocket and dabbed at her cheeks.

"You have an awful lot of those," Rose said with a smile.

"I confess I expected waterworks from a less floral source."

"As did I," she sniffed. "I resemble a ripened tomato, do I not?"

"Perhaps more a red pepper?"

She stole the handkerchief and flicked it at him. "You are a shameful man."

"I try."

A thunderous pounding resounded through the house.

"Ignore it," he said. "Brimley will see to any visitors." Rhys drew her into his arms again. "Finally. You are well and truly safe, my darling Rosie."

Rose leaned her head against his chest and sighed. What they had just done was monumental, a big thing, and yet all that mattered was resting in the warmth, safety, and joy she found within Rhys' arms.

His words, however, set off a niggle. "What do you mean, safe?"

"Your father has lost all power over you. If anything were to happen to you, your trust and lands now go to me. That fact removes you from harm's way."

Had his primary reason for marriage been to keep her safe? Both a comfort and unsettling. She was safe now, true, though believing that would take time to settle into her bones.

Rhys ran a hand across her hair, and a thought blossomed. Rose wished for more than safety. She desired Rhys' love.

He rested his chin atop her head. "Cook has prepared a lovely wedding breakfast."

Footsteps thudded down the hall, and Angus strode into the

room. "The earl is on our doorstep, with the same two men as earlier, along with that Pennworth cur."

Angus' face revealed no emotion, but his eyes burned.

"One moment," Rhys said. "I will finish my conversation with my marchioness."

Angus stepped away and Rhys took Rosamund's hand. "I have a scheme in mind, Rosie mine, one which will expose the earl as the villainous cretin he is."

Strategies. No surprise there. As children, the man's machinations were legendary. The time they stole the knocker from the church bell. Or when he arranged for his father's study door to creak every time it opened or closed it. Others, too many to recall. She expected this one to be a dandy. "Continue."

"We will not speak of our marriage," he said. "But rather our engagement."

"Why?" Rose disliked the sound of this.

"I fear if the earl or Pennworth knows we are married, either may do something rash."

When Rose was ten, she had watched the earl whip his favorite hunter for throwing him, blaming the horse rather than his faulty seat. It had been horrid, made worse when he sold the beautiful hunter to an abattoir for meat. "You have seen his temper?"

"Once," Rhys said. "That was enough. We will tell him we are engaged and will be holding an announcement ball in five days. Invitations have been sent, and I have invited Prinny and Wellington, as well as other *ton* luminaries. Either Pennworth, Fielding, or both will commit some impetuous act before then."

Rosamund's eyes widened. Setting himself up as a target, was he? Their marriage had obviously addled his brain. "That plan is ridiculous."

He ignored her comment and nodded. Oh, she'd seen that sage face during many an adventure, when he was getting his way.

"You will not get your way this time, my lord."

His wolfish grin appeared the one that must have charmed many a lady. "You always call me 'my lord' when you are annoyed with me."

"I am plenty annoyed, *my lord*. Naturally, Fielding or the viscount will go after you if they think we are but engaged. After all, you have stolen their prize heifer."

"A trap, Rosie," he said.

"A trap! Either you or I will be hurt or killed."

"We will both be perfectly safe."

"Safe!" Famous words, often the last ones a person uttered.

"If I cannot kill the bloody bugger, I will see him snared in his own machinations. Caught and held to account."

"No, Rhys."

"Or perhaps I will gut the monster."

"I mean it, *no*." Rosamund's face heated, but she refused to drop her eyes.

He tucked his fingers beneath her chin and raised her face to his. "Beautiful Rosie, I will not have you suffer his schemes any longer."

Rose straightened her spine and stared him in the eye, just as she would a recalcitrant horse. True, she had to look up, but she did with horses, too. "I am married to you. I *am* safe, as you noted earlier. We will tell my father we are wed, and that is the end of it."

Rhys' face went blank.

Damn the man, for she saw stratagems flitting through that busy brain of his.

"I concede," he said, his tone deferential.

What? Too easy. Oh, dear, now he would dream up an even worse scenario.

Rhys ignored the men waiting in the front hall and led Rose to their wedding breakfast laid out in the small family dining room used for more intimate meals. The flowers had been scaled down, with nary a chrysanthemum in sight, praise heaven.

The table, shaped like a U, seated Rosamund and Rhys at the

head, the officiant to Rhys' right, and Patrick to Rose's left. Angus sat at one wing across from Lucy, who sat at the other. All dug into the sweet and savory fare, though Rose only toyed with her meal, girding herself for Fielding and Pennworth's entrance. It felt like a stage play, with little talking and many looks toward the arched doorway.

Except Rose was starving. She scooped up a forkful of eggs.

"Where the hell is my daughter?" came the shout from the hall, along with thundering feet.

Rose froze.

Their butler, Brinley, and numerous servants crowded the door when the earl shoved past the staff and into the room. He halted. "What is this?"

"Good morning, Lord Fielding," Rhys said, taking a sip of tea. "We are celebrating. Would you care to join in our wedding breakfast?"

Pennworth barged in, his face a mask of fury. "*Wedding* breakfast?"

"Such acute hearing, my lord." Rhys lifted a pear and took a bite. "Indeed, yes."

Rose wanted to shrink or perhaps hide beneath the table, her typical reaction to the earl's thunderous ire. Instead, she set her shoulders and notched her chin. "No happy felicitations, my lords?"

Pennworth turned an interesting shade of purple, while the earl's hue was more beet colored as Fielding's two flunkies pushed their way inside the room.

Like watching a bad pantomime.

"As I noted," Rhys said. "There is ample food, and you are welcome to join us. By the by, who are these two other fellows hovering about you?"

Fielding notched his chin. "Leave." The two flunkies retreated into the hall, while Fielding strode forward, Pennworth passing him and taking the lead.

"You were to be mine, my lady." Pennworth slammed a fist on the table, sending plates clattering.

"I was *never* to be yours, my lord," Rose said.

"I did not give my consent." The earl hovered before Rhys, his hand on the pommel of his sword.

"No," Rhys said, his manner agreeable, "you did not. But you broadcast far and wide that three men were courting your daughter, three men who met with your approval. Now Lady Rosamund is wed to one of them, and yet you refuse your consent?" Rhys tut-tutted. "Speculation will be rife."

"I will dissolve this charade of a marriage," the earl said.

"That will prove difficult." Rhys' eyes slid to the officiant. "The church has sanctioned it and Lady Rosamund is over the age of consent."

"Sanctioned?" Pennworth waved his monocle. "Impossible."

Patrick chimed in. "It is quite possible, Pennworth, given the archbishop signed the special license. I was a witness to the signature." He waved a hand toward the reverend. "It was the archbishop himself who selected the officiant."

Pennworth's eyes changed from hot ire to shuttered and cold, a stare far more disturbing than his ire.

The earl turned sad eyes on Rose. "I am greatly disappointed, daughter."

Fielding hadn't touched her heartstrings since childhood. He didn't now. She shrugged. "It is a *fait accompli.*"

The flock of Ravenscroft staff parted, and the one-armed giant Billy Broad along with another burly servant stepped forward, muskets cradled in their arms, along with Ravenscroft's housekeeper, who held a blunderbuss almost as tall as she.

The earl took stock of the armed men and one woman, Pennworth doing the same.

"Felicitations," Fielding said.

Both men bowed and departed, their eyes glittering with malice.

"That was jolly fun," Patrick said.

Rhys grinned at his brother. "Quite."

For the first time that day, Rose allowed herself to relax and dug into the delicious meal. An hour later, she was stuffed and satisfied. "I'm going to change, Rhys."

"Do that, m'lady, for I wish to show you something at the barns."

"Indeed?" She smiled, and since it felt a bit wan, she brightened it before leaving the two men to their discussion.

Rosamund flew upstairs to find her room empty of all her things. Which made sense when she thought on it. As Ravenscroft's marchioness, her rooms must be somewhere else.

Marchioness—an odd thing. Her mind rolled the word over as she walked down the hall in search of a maid or footman to give her direction. Rose was bound to Rhys for always, a state much longed-for. Yet her wedding felt more dream than reality.

Billy Broad was headed in her direction wearing the black-and-red livery of a Ravenscroft footman, his one empty sleeve pinned to his shoulder.

"I am so pleased you took my suggestion," she said to him as a greeting.

Billy nodded his head. "I did, my lady. And I thank you for that."

She smiled. "You are most welcome, Billy. Have you any idea where my things have gone?"

"If you would follow me, m'lady."

He led her down the hall, across the gallery hung with portraits of Ravenscroft ancestors. Perhaps her portrait would hang there someday alongside Rhys'. A strange thought.

They turned a corner onto yet another long wing. The manor was near double the size of Fielding, yet Billy led her with unerring confidence. Nearing the end of the wing, he stopped before a door and swung it open.

"I believe these are your rooms, Lady Ravenscroft."

She was Lady Ravenscroft now, wasn't she. Yet another change that felt peculiar, though she had dreamt of marriage to Rhys countless times. "Thank you, Billy, and thank you again for your service to England, to all of us."

Thick carpet muffled her steps as she entered the massive suite's sitting room, done up in green with comfortable peach and lime chairs, a flocked chaise, a maple burl secretary, paintings of horses, dogs, and landscapes, and a large hearth set against one wall. Above the hearth... Rose gasped. Her Stubbs painting from home, the one she adored, took pride of place.

That man. Rhys had managed to extract the painting from Fielding Manor. As he had Lucy and even Fitz, for Rhys had said at breakfast Fitz was now Ravenscroft's co-stable manager.

Rhys *always* knew what mattered most to her.

"You are dawdling, m'lady."

Lucy stood at the suite's bedroom door.

Rose raced to her friend, the woman who'd kept the flame of Rose's spirit from being extinguished. "I am so glad you are here!"

Lucy's face remained typically stoic, but her eyes sparked with laughter. "Where else would I be, *Minnu*?"

Rose drew Lucy into a hug, holding her for long moments, the blast of emotion gradually softening.

When Lucy extricated herself, she clapped her hands. "You must change, Minnu. Quick, quick now."

Rose wasn't looking forward to it. She had the day dress belonging to Susannah and the pantaloons from her escape. Men's clothes it was, for she didn't wish to dirty Susannah's gown.

She followed Lucy into the loveliest bedroom one could imagine, done up is the same peaches and greens where a satin coverlet with swooping birds draped the enormous bed, a canopy in the same fabric arcing above it. On the bed lay her brocade knitting bag that held the shawl she was knitting for Bea, Rhys, touching her heart yet again. "This is all very grand."

"That it is." Lucy preceded her into the dressing room, nearly the size of her old bedroom. "And what you deserve."

Myriad gowns hung from the racks. *Her* gowns. Her riding habits, hats, stockings, pelisses, and more. All her things were here.

"I have wed a magician," Rose said.

Her jewelry chest sat on a low shelf, her precious thistle pin atop it. When she was seven, she and Maman had visited her mother's Scottish clan. They'd walked Maman's fertile land, and Rose had gathered wildflowers, a bouquet for the chieftain. He was a kind elderly man, and though no longer hale and hearty, he had walked beside them with a vigor and authority matched by few.

When Rose presented her bouquet, her chieftain had gifted her the thistle pin, telling her it had belonged to his brother. He'd said she would be laird someday, so the gift was fitting. She'd asked if it was because she was prickly and he had laughed, his large belly shaking.

That holiday had been one of the few times Rosamund and Maman had journeyed anywhere together, and they had remained in Scotland for eight blissful weeks.

CHAPTER

TWENTY

The pin was priceless, made of sterling and set with tiny cabochon amethysts. She clutched it close, a perfect marriage gift for Rhys, for he now owned the courtesy title of laird for having wed her, while she retained the true title as their marriage contract stated.

After changing into the red riding habit she had worn the day of their picnic, she donned her boots and pinned the thistle in her lapel.

"Rhys is to show me something at the barns."

Lucy wore a small smile, a knowing one.

"You know what it is!" Rose said. "Tell me, Lucy. Please." Whining was very unladylike, but she was dying to know.

"I do," Lucy said, wearing that cursed inscrutable face.

"You will not tell, will you?"

"That fact should be no surprise, *memsahib*."

Rose snorted. Memsahib, her arse.

It was again Billy who escorted Rose down the lane to the barns, all the while Rose hoping the surprise was Firefly. Rhys had managed miracles, extracting Lucy, Fitz, and Rose's things from Fielding. Perhaps he had success with Firefly, too.

She shaded her eyes with her hand to see Rhys not far distant, looking impossibly handsome in a shirt, buckskins, a waistcoat, and boots, his hair windblown. He was carrying a basket.

Her heart stopped.

Oh, but how that basket evoked memories of that long-ago day when he'd brought her a puppy.

He walked toward her wearing that devilish smile, and her heart soared. Rose began to run. When they reached each other, he leaned forward and bussed her cheek.

She flushed. Had the man any idea how his touch affected her? "Another picnic?"

"Many years ago, I tried to give you a puppy of Tessa's. I failed that day, though she lived a long and fruitful life and her descendants still populate Ravenscroft. This gift is not of her get, but I suspect you shall find him acceptable."

He laid the basket on the ground, and Rose crouched down, vibrating with excitement as he undid the latch.

A black nose peeked out, and she reached inside and lifted the tiny pup from the basket. "Oh, my, he is so small!" Joy frothed inside her, overflowing into laughter. "He looks like a wee bramble bush!"

"A gift from your clan."

"He's perfect," she said, grinning while her face got a puppy bath.

"A Cairn Terrier," Rhys said. "Scottish, naturally. They gifted me with a female, one of a different line than this little fellow, so we can breed them."

"How marvelous. These beasties will be wondrous watchdogs and ratters."

"That they will."

She held the puppy up, staring into his eyes. "What shall I name you?"

"Mine is called Lady Isla," Rhys said. "I named her after the river in Strathisla where I had great luck fishing."

"Well then," she said. "I shall name this sweet darling Bram, for he mightily resembles a thicket of gorse. Do you not think so?"

Rhys winked, smiling. "He does, doesn't he?"

Rose carried the pup as they walked toward the barns, a freedom she had never felt coursing through her when an amusing thought tilted her lips to a smile. "We married today, Rhys, rather spontaneously"

"That we did," he said as they ambled on.

"Mmmm. So how is it my clan knew to send bridal gifts?" Rose near chuckled at his abashed face. Bram, having fallen asleep in her arms, snored on.

"Upon my return from Waterloo, I *may* have written your chieftain with hopes to court you."

"Did you?"

"He is, I believe, the cousin of the chieftain you met as a child. A canny man."

Rose nodded. "His cousin was, as well. Did he thoroughly grill you?"

His sheepish look made her laugh.

"I may have mentioned," Rhys continued. "My hope to marry you in the near future."

"I see," she said, her tone deliberately somber. But soon, she couldn't restrain her joy any longer, and she laughed until her belly ached, waking her pup. How typical of Rhys to have planned everything down to the nonce.

"You need not continue laughing, my dear. It was the logical thing to do."

"Oh yes, extremely logical."

Billy reappeared, a seemingly frequent occurrence. "M'lady, I thought to take the pup into the house and feed him while you continue to the barns."

She nuzzled sweet Bram and handed him over. "Be careful. He is very wee." And Billy was very large.

The man cradled Bram with his good arm, sketched a bow, and

left, whistling an old English jig.

"Come." Rhys took her hand. "Billy will take good care of Isla and Bram. Time for my gift now."

"Wait a moment."

"You are not eager? Most unlike you, Rosie."

"Oh, I am eager, all right, but..." Her hands trembled as she unlatched the pin from her lapel and fastened it to his waistcoat. "My chieftain gave me this when I was seven. I want you to have it."

His smile was crooked and so dear. "I am honored and delighted."

"I hoped you would like it."

"How could I not?" He took her hand again and squeezed. "It belonged to you, and like you, it is a treasure."

Inside barn three, the air was dark and cool and musty with horse smells. He led her down the center aisle to one of the larger stalls, though the upper and lower doors were both closed.

A nicker.

"Do open the door, Rosie," he said.

She swung the door wide, expecting to see Firefly.

Rose's breath vanished, her heart thudding.

"Go on," Rhys said.

She approached the huge bay, one whose muzzle now sported many gray hairs, though she couldn't see so well through the sheen of tears. The horse, recognizing her, walked forward, and she wound her arms around his neck, hugging him tight.

Her Lightning Bug.

It seemed the day was meant for tears, for she leaned against her dear horse's neck and wept.

Finally composing herself, Rose opened her eyes to a white handkerchief dangling before her.

"Thank you." She wiped her eyes and blew her nose, sniffling.

"Shall we turn Bug out to pasture?"

"Yes!"

"What do you say we turn Firefly out with him?"

"She is here, too?" Rose turned to her husband and hugged him tight. "Oh, Rhys, I am rather overset. I haven't felt such bountiful joy in...well, never."

He bussed her cheek. "And that, my dear marchioness, gladdens me greatly."

Rather than wait for a stable boy, Rose fit the halter to Lightning Bug's head, while Rhys collected her beautiful, pregnant mare, and she stroked Firefly in greeting, kissing her velvet nose. They led the pair toward the pasture, Bug prancing like a yearling and not nearing thirty years.

The breeze was gentle and sweet, hinting at a chill, just enough to herald winter's approach, as leaves fluttered down from the trees.

Rhys led them to a grassy fenced pasture above the barn, empty but for a rabbit nibbling on sweet greens.

Ravenscroft unfurled before her, its rolling hills and green pastures sparkling in the sun. A glorious place, a beloved one. Now one where she belonged.

It was as if she were living another's dream, filled with joy and an absence of fear.

Rhys swung open the pasture gate, they removed the horses' halters, and Bug cantered away, Firefly following her sire. They raced across the large enclosure, both horses prancing and leaping in play.

They hung the halters and leads on the iron hook, and after closing the gate, Rhys leaned against it, his hands clasped on the top board watching the pair of horses romp.

Rose teared up yet again. "Lightning Bug is the most beautiful and valuable gift I have ever received, Rhys."

"He may be old and gelded," Rhys said. "But only look at him. He's magnificent."

"He is." She watched the pair for long moments. "His spirit is undimmed. I was sure he was dead. Fielding said he sold him to the knacker. How did you even think to find him?"

"First," he said with a grin. "I was convinced the earl would never waste good money by selling a valuable horse to an abattoir. I became convinced he was alive, or at least had been when he'd left the manor. I determined to bring this fine fellow home."

"You are a wizard. Thank you." Her words were barely a whisper. "You have always known my thoughts and desires."

"Long ago, perhaps." His eyes remained on the horses racing across the paddock. "But now, I often wonder what you're thinking or feeling."

Rose nodded. "I leashed my emotions around Fielding to become a dissembler, never allowing my thoughts or feelings to leak through. Perhaps I have become too dispassionate?"

"You, Rosie?" He swooped in to kiss her nose. "The girl who braved the world for puppies? Who withstood a groundsman's wrath to rescue an injured rabbit? The one who most recently raced into a burning barn? Dispassionate? Ha! Your ardent nature may be hidden, but never extinguished."

"You are ridiculous and..." She almost said *I love you for it.* For if that spirited girl thrived, it was because of Rhys. She swallowed. "Your letters..."

"Lucy was a trooper as our conduit."

"She was. They were my lifeline. For the words you wrote and the flower or feather or pebble you included in each one." She laughed. "I saved them all, tokens from my best friend, my dear friend who kept me sane during the troubled times." She brushed his cheek with her hand.

He pressed his hand over hers. "Trifles I thought would make you smile."

"They did. Along with your vivid words, they made all the difference."

"I spoke of war." His stare burned into her, a mixture of emotions she failed to untangle.

"I was glad you did," she said. "Because that was what you were experiencing. But you also wrote of Portugal's intense blue sky, of mighty waves crashing against shore, of scents in the air, and birds in the skies. You spoke of cows and pigs and even a strange wild dog.

You wrote what was in your heart, of your grief and the terrible cost to your men and their loved ones."

"I tried not to get too dour," he said, his words brusk.

"You were never dour! Through the years of that man's assaults and my shame and horror, your letters reminded me I was cared for and valued. That I mattered even just a little bit."

He took her hand in his. "You have always mattered far more than a little bit, Rose. You speak of my letters to you, but yours to me were equal salvation. The bleakness, the terror, the fury, and the sorrow—they are a terrible burden for a man to carry alone. But I was not alone. You were always with me, as well."

"Your family must have written, too."

"And so they did. Sina sent me pictures she drew."

"I am eager to meet her."

"You will adore her, and she, you. Along with her acumen with horses, she is quite amazing for her total recall."

"Pardon?"

"Thomasina remembers *everything*. Literally. A rather daunting prospect, in truth, until I became used to it."

"I cannot imagine what that must be like."

"Sina calls them mind pictures, saying they appear willy-nilly, though if she seeks a particular memory, it will manifest in its totality—from her first steps to our mother to paintings that hung at Ravenscroft before Sina was spirited away. She remembers in toto our father taking her to live with Woodbine's stable master, his wife, and family. That always disturbed me, his separating our sister from her family."

"I know. In many respects, your father was a kind man. I never understood his expulsion of Thomasina."

His smile was feral. "She is away from us no more. When word reached me at Waterloo that my father had died, Susannah joined Sina at Woodbine and moved them both into the manor house, for Sina could not be parted from her beloved horses. I look forward to our journey to Woodbine so you can visit with both my sisters."

"I wish to do that very much." She bit her lip.

He moved impossibly closer, eyes lit with an ardent fire. "I would kiss you, Rosie."

Rose startled, then leaned forward, both embarrassed and eager. "I would like that."

His smile warmed as he slid his arms around her waist and drew her close.

For an instant, she feared revulsion, for the earl often dragged her close with cruel hands. Yet Rhys' arms were gentle, her cheek and waist tingling in the most delightful way where Rhys touched her.

She rested her hands on his shoulders and leaned in, her eyes rising to his questioning ones, unsure of what to expect, yet longing for more.

His face dipped closer to hers, his lips brushing hers back and forth.

Rhys was warm and solid, his muscles bunching beneath her hands, and her arms moved to wind around his neck, seemingly of their own volition.

She pecked his cheek, and his hold on her tightened.

Just as the earl had... *Stop.*

Rose refused to succumb to memory. Rather, she melted into his warmth, burying her face in his chest. He placed a finger beneath her chin, lifting her face to his. "You are finally mine, Rosie."

"I am." She always had been.

Their lips met, his filled with an urgency that soon gentled before he kissed her cheek, her brow, her nape. His touch felt unhurried yet desirous at the same time.

"We have the gift of time," he whispered in her ear, nipping her earlobe.

Rose brushed a hand over his hair. "I... I'm not sure what to do next."

"There is no next, Rosie mine. Just this moment between us."

She yearned for...

"Lord Ravenscroft!"

TWENTY-ONE

They parted as a groundskeeper ran up to them with a question about the north field. After answering, Rhys took her hand, his solid and callused, and they ambled back toward the manor. She decided she loved holding her husband's hand. Her husband... Now wasn't that a dear thought.

She peered up at Rhys. "Before all the excitement—"

"Excitement? An interesting slant, Rosie." He laughed, raising their clasped hands to his lips and kissing hers. "Go on."

"I have an appointment in two days at Basking Farms to look at a stallion and two of their mares. Shall I still go? Or should I cancel? Or do you wish to accompany me?"

"Go, of course. I will check my appointment book, but I do not recall a single thing for that day. I would join your excursion."

Rose was thrilled. "That would be lovely."

"Now tell me about these horses you are considering."

Later that day, they romped with their new pups, rascals that Rose already adored, wearing them out until they were snoozing on their backs in the soft grass, their fat bellies facing the azure sky dotted with puffy clouds. When they returned Isla and Bram to the house, the staff surprised them with hearty felicitations and a glorious wedding cake with almond icing.

As they nibbled the confection, Rhys said, "I thought we'd have an intimate dinner, sweetheart. Are you game?"

The word "intimate" shocked her, but Rose nodded and pasted on a smile. "That sounds perfect."

"Fewer prying eyes."

An hour later, Rose took tentative steps as she entered his suite, one that mirrored hers, but done up in blacks and maroons, with mahogany accents.

Candles lit his sitting room, chasing shadows into the corners. The lavish meal sat atop the small dining table spread with a linen cloth and many delicacies to tempt her palate.

Unfortunately, her hunger had fled. Which was absurd. Rhys would not pounce on her like a ravenous beast like...

Rosamund had donned a chemise and dressing gown, both plain cotton and comfortable, and Rhys left his reading chair by the window to seat her, then taking his place across from her.

"When you are unguarded, my dear," Rhys said. "Your face is a map of your emotions."

Rose frowned, embarrassed, lowering her head to stare at the gleaming cutlery.

"Feel no apprehension, sweet Rosie," he continued. "I have thought much about this evening, and I wish to wait for our intimate relations until you desire my attentions."

Rose flicked out her linen napkin and placed it across her lap. She *did* desire him—to touch him, hold him, stroke his hair, and feel his lips on hers—but unfamiliar ones, of which she had little grasp. She could not imagine accepting overtures entailing more than touches or kisses with any sort of eagerness.

Rose knew Rhys' attentions would be unlike the earl's. Her heart knew that. Yet her mind pictured the experience as painful.

She did like his touch a great deal. In fact, he evoked shivers and sent her heart a flutter. Relief that he was such a caring and desirable man should be her primary reaction. Yet Rose did not feel relieved at all.

The idea of him entering her body felt like a mountain she could never scale, impossible and beyond her reach.

But how could she deny him conjugal relations?

That was cowardly, and she was no coward.

Replacing her napkin on the table, she walked around to Rhys, who peered up at her with unasked and unanswered questions.

She ran a hand across his snow-white hair, down his cheek, then leaned down and kissed him.

His tongue slipped out and he ran it across the seam of her lips.

Oh, that felt lovely. And surprising.

A knock made her jerk, and she scurried back to her chair.

"Come!" Rhys barked in a graveled voice.

"Forgive the intrusion, my lord." Billy Broad bustled in carrying a pitcher, which he set on the dining table. "The staff forgot her lady-ship's lemonade."

He was gone in seconds, and Rose stared across at Rhys, wide-eyed.

"I'm not sure what to say, Rhys."

"Say nothing, wife." He reached across the table and brushed her hand with his, offering up a grin. He lifted his fork. "Simply enjoy your supper."

After supper, one where Rose had barely eaten and returned to her rooms, Rhys dismissed Porter for the evening, wishing to be alone.

For the first time in memory, he felt flummoxed and indecisive. In truth, he did not know how to deal with the intimate aspects of their marriage. He longed for Rosie in all ways, but the problem, as he saw it, was his desperate wish for *her* to desire him.

She'd seemed to like his kisses, hadn't she?

He shrugged his shirt over his head and tossed it in the laun-dering bin. What a confounding situation. Never could he have imagined her father's cruelty, and he had witnessed more than enough brutality to last a lifetime. He slipped his banyan on over his breeches, took his book from its bedside table, and sat by the French doors that led to the bedroom's balcony. He reached over and cracked them open.

Chilly air blew inside, the star-spangled sky putting on a marvelous show, while a few lights glowed around the estate. The damp breeze presaged another storm, but the one in his heart was far more grim as his mind's eye conjured his Rosie being abused.

He opened *The Divine Comedy*, a new translation by Cary in blank verse, and sought peace in the poetry of Dante.

In minutes, the words blurred to gibberish, for all he could think of was his Rose and how to make her transition to wife a pleasurable one.

Their adjoining door opened wide, startling him. Rose glided in wearing a thin chemise, feet bare, long auburn hair cascading in wild abandon over her shoulders.

Christ, she stole his breath away. He set the book aside and stood. "Rosamund?"

Like a wraith, she skimmed across the carpeted floor to stand before him, her face ice pale.

"Conjugal relations are a mountain, don't you see, Rhys? I believe the only way to scale the mountain is to put one foot in front of the other with determination and vigor." She snapped him a nod, her chest rising and falling with rapid breaths.

His brave girl. "I imagine it must feel that way, my darling." He brushed a hand across her curls. "Making love should not be a chore to trudge through, but rather a delight to be experienced. I do not know if your fear and your memories will allow you to feel that delight. Not yet, at least. That bruises my soul."

Abject fear radiated from her lovely green eyes.

"I see your apprehension, dear one," he continued. "Let us wait. Our marriage is new and involved much chaos. Your escape from Fielding, the absurd confrontation at our wedding breakfast, reacquainting yourself with your beloved Bug, our new pups. That is more than enough for one day, do you not think?"

She smelled like honey and cinnamon, like spring daisies and summer roses, like a sweet melody and a wistful temptation more delectable than any treat he could imagine. Touching her was heaven. Kissing her…

Her face scrunched into that adorable expression he had often seen, one of determination. She was set on moving forward, whether she liked the outcome or not. Bloody Christ, what a conundrum.

"Let me see you," she said, surprising him. "Please."

Mesmerized, he removed his banyan.

"Your trousers, please. I want to see all of you."

Off came his shoes, stockings, and pantaloons until he stood naked before her, his fierce erection evidence of his desire.

Her eyes fell on his cock.

Blessed saints, he was about to explode.

Rhys stunned her with his beauty, the way his bones knit to his flesh, his taut muscles, and the dark hair on his chest arrowing to…

Rose froze, an icicle about to plummet downward and shatter into a thousand pieces. Her toes were numb, her skin too tight, terror stalking her as it had during the earl's visits.

She *knew* Rhys would take great care with her. In her mind, at least.

The mountain must be scaled, for only the act itself could eradicate her fear.

But from the flesh beneath her nails to her trembling lips to her hair that felt like another's, Rose fizzed with apprehension.

Rhys was her dearest friend, her love.

Her entire being screamed, "Run!"

He was perfection, his skin aglow in the candlelight. Even the scars on his chest and across his left thigh did not mar his beauty, but rather served to highlight his exceptional frame. "You are bewitching, Rhys, like a sculpture or a stallion, only better."

A blush rose on his weathered face.

"May... may I touch you?" she said.

He nodded, and she ran her hands across his smooth shoulders and down his muscled arms, then across his chest, fascinated with his springy hair, her fingers lightly dancing over it.

"Are you sure about this, love?" he said.

"Yes, very." Lie. But seeing him helped.

She had never seen the earl, his doings executed in complete darkness. Rose knew anatomy, of course, though she'd never seen a grown man naked.

He was wondrous lovely, her vague feelings of desire transforming into a warmth in her belly that pulsed through her. In small increments, Rose's muscles began to relax.

"I cannot, Rosie," he said, shaking his head. "I cannot do this."

That proud erection shriveled, and she had never been more mortified.

Rose backed away to the door of their adjoining suites and closed it softly behind her.

My God, he was an idiot. Rhys raked a hand through his hair. A total bumbling idiot.

When Rose had first entered his suite, she had stolen his breath, all thoughts fleeing on wings of lust. His love and the object of his desire was here, in his rooms, coming to him with open arms.

He'd done as she asked, doffed his clothes, which was when his muddled brain saw her. *Really* saw her. She was utterly petrified. And that look when she left the room—her eyes held notes of disappointment and fear and, somewhere in that awful mix, a touch of longing.

He must fix this. If only he knew how.

CHAPTER

TWENTY-TWO

The following day, when he kissed the top of Rose's head as a greeting at breakfast. She startled. Of course she did. The woman had been through hell. They then spoke banalities as they ate until Rhys set down his glass.

"We should talk, my dear," he said.

"Yes," she said. But she didn't look at him, but at the kippers on her plate.

"I..." He took a sip of tea and sighed. "Trouble is, I'm not sure what to say."

Her forkful of eggs paused mid-air. "It is hard to discuss intimacies, is it not?"

"Yes, but perhaps we should."

"What say you to a ride to clear our heads? I always feel more myself atop a horse."

He chuckled. "As do I. How does after luncheon sound? It is my misfortune, but I must attend estate business this morning. Now that I think of it, have you considered a bridal tour, love? Shall we take one?"

"To visit family who did not attend our wedding?"

"And friends. It has become somewhat customary, I believe."

Rose shrugged, lifting a spoonful of berries to her lips. "We could visit Cedric, I suppose."

He waved a strip of bacon. "That awful cousin of yours?"

"He is, isn't he?" Her lips tilted in a fretful smile.

"Do you *wish* to see him?"

"Not in the least. How about you? Any chums you would like to see?"

Rhys shook his head. What he truly wished for was to be alone with Rose away from estates and horses and obligations. All of which would likely make her even more anxious about intimacies. "Perhaps a trip to Woodbine instead?"

Her grin was the only answer he needed.

"Oh, yes!" she said. "Let us plan on it."

"Good. We shall." He stood. "I must be off."

"I plan to play with the pups and see how Lightning Bug and Firefly are faring."

"Excellent." He kissed her cheek, then left to meet with his estate manager.

They took luncheon in a similar fashion, and then rode the hills and dales of Ravenscroft, even raced through a meadow of dying grasses and faded wildflowers. Rose galloped as if bonded to the Norwegian fjord, Ace. An interesting choice, but Rose had formed an attachment to the short, stocky gelding. No matter which animal was her mount, his wife was a bruising rider with skills matched by few.

'Struth, how he adored her.

Dinner was all horse talk, specifically about the stallion and mares they would inspect the following day. Rhys looked forward to the visit and had pleased her with his desire to improve the Ravenscroft stock.

They retired early, Rose to her rooms and he to hers, and he lay in bed reviewing the bloodlines of the Basking Farms' mares and studs so as not to dwell on the woman asleep in the next room. Putting the papers aside, he opened Dante, but snapped it closed soon thereafter. Damn, but his mind was as restless as a caged panther.

After much struggle, he doused the bedside candle, laid back, and imagined Rose naked, her pleasure heightening as he kissed every inch of her soft skin.

How to ease Rose into intimacy without terrifying her? He sighed. At present, he could not think of a one that wouldn't scare her witless.

The following day at Basking Farms, the mares and stallion failed to reach Rosamund's or Rhys' high standards for breeding. Instead, they purchased a pair of Old English goats she'd fallen in love with. Rose claimed the mischievous creatures were ideal companions for their horses, though Rhys had teased they should be served for dinner instead.

He'd made her laugh, her first one since The Night, as he now termed that disastrous evening. Billy Broad and a new stable hand, George, had accompanied them to Basking, and they would follow close behind, taking charge of the goats for the trip home.

Rhys hoped the carriage ride would be relaxed and convivial, yet his nerves were on high alert...for no reason he could explain to Rose.

"You seem fretful, Rhys," Rose said. "Did you sleep poorly last night?"

"I did," he said in a surly voice. "But I do not need much, either. I wish that were the problem."

This Rhys she remembered well, for if something itched beneath the boy's skin, he would worry it until it lurched into the open air.

Their luxurious carriage was well sprung, a good thing because the roads left much to be desired.

"You sense something, correct?" Rose said.

"Yes, dammit, an itch, a feeling." He whooshed out a breath. "Forgive me, Rosie, for snapping at you. But something is—"

"Bothering you."

"Yes." He frowned. "I am bothered. The trouble is, I know not by what."

"When did the feeling start?"

"When we were at Squire Brimley's."

"Was it something he said?"

His lips thinned. "No."

"Something he did, perhaps?" she asked.

"No. It hasn't to do with the squire, and that cursed itch at the back of my neck is worsening."

"I know you will worry this like a sore tooth. I wish I could help, but I am afraid I have no idea what is troubling you."

"A shame you cannot read my subconscious." He chuckled.

In fact, Rose would love that. She gestured toward the window. "What a lovely prospect."

The road hugged the hill, which dropped to verdant pastures below where sheep grazed, a black-and-white dog herding them.

Rhys would figure out the problem in his own time, for the man's mind always made interesting connections, saw nuances others did not. But those feelings also often drove him to distraction.

"The overlook is stunning," she said.

"Pardon? Oh, yes... That is *it!*"

"What?" The sounds of rock shifting, slipping, shrieking drowned out her question.

"Rhys!" she screamed.

"Bollocks!" He leaped for Rose, covering her just as something hit their carriage with tremendous force. The vehicle teetered but didn't topple.

All would have been well had another rock not thundered into their back wheel. The coach overbalanced, sending them both flying as it began to slide down the hill.

Everything tumbled and rumbled, and Rose prayed their coachman had cut the traces and he and their horses were safe.

They bumped and jostled, boxes, cutlery, and dishes from their picnic flying about like missiles until they slammed into something hard. They stopped, her head bouncing off the coach's side, making her dizzy. She'd lost hold of Rhys, who'd been thrown backward, an unmoored coach lantern bashing his head.

Dust and debris swirled, finally settling. Everything ached, her head ringing.

"Rhys?" she croaked.

He failed to answer.

"Rhys!"

The coach lay on its side, Rose pressed against a corner. In front of her, the door and window remained unbroken, but Rose reclined amidst shattered glass from the other windows.

She craned her neck to peer outside. The coach pressed against the huge tree that had halted their downward trajectory. Rhys lay sprawled at an odd angle, blood trickling from his temple across his face.

Rhys' left arm lay at an odd angle, his right one limp above his head, his legs trapped beneath the seat that had detached in their tumble. Heaven above. From her awkward position, Rose leaned forward to stretch out her arms, trying to move the seat atop him and raise it enough for Rhys to pull his legs out.

"Rhys!"

Silence.

Her arms shook as she gently lowered the seat, rather than have it collapse back with a thud and injure him further.

Anxiety buzzed around her head.

He could not be dead. *Could not.*

Gravity was no friend when she tried to move, and she noted more places that were sore and would bruise, all minor and dismissible. She thanked the heavens that the tree had stopped their downward plunge. Now, she needed to be near Rhys.

Rose crawled sideways and pressed her face close to his. Warm breath brushed her cheek, and relief spun through her.

Faint but discernible, the clop of horses neared at a trot. A cough. Someone clearing their throat.

Perhaps rescue was at hand. Maybe Billy or George had caught up with them. She opened her mouth to call.

"Will they be dead?" came the guttural voice outside the carriage.

"I expect so." This voice was higher, with a note of irony.

"His high and mighty said the girl had to be alive."

"Then why did *you* tumble that rock, fool?" came the first voice, filled with annoyance. "You most likely killed 'em both!"

"Look at that thing."

"A right wreck, it is."

Merciful heaven. Those boulders had been no accident, Rhys' troubling feeling come home to roost.

Now what?

Deadly to wait for further disaster. Rose squirmed back into the coach's far corner, a sliver of glass slicing her forearm in the process. Rhys looked dead, and that was a good thing. She wiggled her right hand into her pocket where her small *kathi* knife rested and pulled it from its leather lining, wishing she'd brought the larger *kadara* dagger. Her eyes searched the wreckage for her reticule. There. She crawled her fingers toward it, dragging it to her, and pulled out her pistol. All right.

The horses had neared, the duo laughing at some joke or other.

Rhys had shown her where he stowed weapons beneath her seat. Pressing her feet against the carriage side, she inched upward to find the latch and lifted the lid, thanking heaven for the well-oiled hinges.

"What was that?" said one man.

"Just the wreckage settling," said a deep bass voice.

A third voice. *Three* of them.

"If they ain't dead, we kill the toff and take the girl."

Lord above. Her hand snaked into the compartment, her fingers searching.

A musket, far too large for this confined space. Even as she pictured the ambushers nearing the carriage, her fingers scoured the chest. Where was the damned pistol? Rhys said they carried one.

The horses were almost upon them, and while she was an excellent shot with her pistol and good with her knife, they wouldn't be enough to hold off three brigands.

"You go look, Hammy," one man barked.

"Why me? You know I hates blood."

The men were almost upon them.

As Rose withdrew her hand, it grazed the smooth wood of what might be a pistol. Her fingers stretched and she clutched it tight, lifting it from the chest. Hoorah, a Newland Dragoon Flintlock!

In quick order, Rose checked that it was loaded and primed. Merciful heavens, it was. Clutching the pistol in two hands, Rose shoved herself back into the corner, her pocket pistol and knife in her lap. From here, she'd have a fine view of anyone who appeared at the window.

Stones tumbling from above. Someone was coming down the hillside.

Rose lifted the flintlock.

She glanced at Rhys, still unconscious. The dearest face in the world.

A very different face appeared at the window.

"The girl's—"

She pulled the trigger.

Blood and brains splattered outward as the face vanished from sight.

Her body shook. She had killed a man, taken a life. God in heaven.

Not now, Rosie! Rhys' voice in her head. Right. Two more men were coming for them.

Impossible to search for more shot to reload, so she lifted her small pistol, then withdrew two of her lethal hairpins, ones specially crafted to her specifications. She listened.

Silence.

The buggers had grown wary.

Surprising her from behind was difficult, as one side of the coach pressed against the tree. No, she would see them coming. A good thing. Drawing her handkerchief from her sleeve, Rose wiped the sweat from her neck, then her face. *Focus, girl. Focus.*

Forcing herself to remain perfectly still, she heard a weapon being cocked.

She flattened to the carriage floor just in time.

Boom! A hole ripped through the coach door.

Idiots! If they wanted her alive, randomly shooting was an absurd way to go about it. Whoever had hired them had not chosen the brightest candles in the chandelier.

Boom! That one sailed above her head.

Rose clenched her jaw, beads of sweat dampening her face.

Boom! Splinters tore through the carriage, one nicking her beneath her eye, and blood seeped across her cheek.

Footsteps.

Rose levered back to a seated position and scraped a forearm across her bloody face, then unbuttoned her jacket to reveal her white bodice, smearing the blood across it. She narrowed her eyes to slits, feigning unconsciousness.

A ginger-haired man's face appeared at the door's now-glassless window, resting a gun pointed at her on its frame. "Zeke's dead, and the girl's all bloody!"

Without raising her arm, she angled the pistol upward and shot him.

He vanished on a satisfying scream. Perhaps not a killing shot, but a disabling one. She *must* believe that because one villain remained, and he would be enraged.

Sounds—slipping, sliding, cursing. The third man would not peer into that same window where his two compatriots lay. No, he would come around back, but unless he pressed against the coach, he couldn't see her. If she were lucky, if fate gave her one more chance, she could stab him with her dagger.

Or he could shoot Rhys and then her. Or maybe the other way around. Yes, that would make more sense.

A hat appeared to her right, and she froze. The hat wobbled, and Rose suspected he'd raised it on a stick. A villain smarter than the other two. Probably the leader.

The barrel of a gun appeared in the window. "Move an inch and you die."

No face, no hands, just the gun's muzzle pointing directly at her. She held her breath. What to do?

Her eyes frantically searched for something to throw, the interior a jumble of broken wood, glass, and twisted metal.

A head materialized through the broken window. Bearded, dirty, and too far to reach with her knife.

Say something, idiot. Talk. Explain. Anything for more time.

His pockmarked face grimaced with hate as he cocked his pistol. "Bloody toff who hired us. I'm done with that cocksucker. You killed me cousin."

Rose spared Rhys a glance.

His eyes flickered, though they remained barely discernible slits.

The brigand smiled at Rose, then spat a wad of tobacco that landed on her face. "Ain't got nothing left, has ya?"

Time slowed.

Rhys grimaced.

The brigand's finger tightened on the trigger.

Boom!

CHAPTER

TWENTY-THREE

Rose patted her chest, not quite believing she was alive.

Rhys had fired with accuracy, and the brigand's blood, brains, and bone had followed the tobacco's path. Warm, sticky, and disgusting.

Rose's heart fluttered, while lights pulsed and black encroached. She cast up her accounts, wiping her mouth with the handkerchief. "Rhys?"

"Let's lift this thing." He pushed at the carriage seat atop his legs with his right hand. "I believe my left wrist is broken and my shoulder dislocated."

Rose strained to lift the seat off Rhys just enough so...

He scooted his legs from beneath it and began to pull himself forward.

"Wait. Can you sit up?"

He did, though in obvious pain. Rose wanted to weep. Instead, she sliced her petticoats with her knife, then got on her knees to bind Rhys' dislocated arm and broken wrist to his body. He kicked open the door, panting with the effort, and she helped him crawl up the floor to the door and out of the coach, over the two dead men, and onto the damp earth.

They lay gasping from the effort.

"We must go," he said.

They inched up the hill in small increments, normally an easy climb, until they reached level ground and the road.

Rhys flopped onto his back, eyes closed, teeth gritted.

Rose finally exhaled.

They were free, not severely injured, and their killers were dead.

Rose cupped her hands to his cheeks and peppered kisses across his face, her tears bathing them both. "I'm so happy you're alive." She had shocked herself, kissing him that way, something she had never done before.

His eyes cracked open, a quirk of a smile on his bloody lips. "You look rather dreadful, my love."

"What a way to greet your lady!" she said with mock disdain. "You look awful yourself."

He chuckled. "Are you badly injured?"

"I am not."

"Christ, what a pair, lying here awaiting who knows what to come along. I suggest we rise."

"A fine idea." Her aches and pains shrieked as Rosamund pushed to her feet, swaying until she found her bearings.

Rhys raised his good arm, and she helped him get vertical, neither of them very ambulatory.

He grew serious. "Truly, Rosie. How badly are you hurt?"

Rose puffed an errant lock of hair from her face. "I feel like I've been tumbled inside a box of rocks."

"An apt description."

"How much pain are you in?" she asked.

"Enough that my eyes are crossing."

"All right. We have been in situations like this before."

"You mean that fawn retrieval when you were ten?"

"Exactly." She sniffled, clutching Rhys as an anchor.

"One foot in front of the other and all that. Where the blazes have Jeffrey Coachman and the horses got off to, and where are Billy and George?"

A puff of dust in the distance moved in their direction.

"Someone's coming on fast," he said. "Whoever plotted our demise could be that dust whirl." Rhys peered around and pointed. "That will make a good cover."

They hobbled to the large oak, the brush proving a fine screen from where they could watch the road. The horseman neared.

"Do you have a weapon?" he said.

"Only this." She held up her knife.

"That will do." He produced a pistol from inside his boot.

"You are full of surprises, husband," she said in a whisper.

"I try." He sighed.

Around the bend came the strangest sight Rose had ever seen. Billy, atop his horse, with a pair of baby goats sprawled in front of him across the saddle. They were bleating their heads off.

Rose stumbled from the brush as fast as her sore body would take her, waving her arms.

Billy reined in his horse and stared. "M'lady?"

"We had a bit of a commotion," she said.

He leapt from the saddle. "The marquess?"

"The marquess is injured and needs assistance. Where is George?"

"On his way, ma'am. His girth snapped, and he stayed behind to repair it."

Rhys stumbled onto the road. My word, but her husband looked like he'd been through the wars. Poor analogy, that, and tears sprang to her eyes. Rose stomped her foot, sniffling. Now was not the time.

From the opposite direction, around the bend, came the thunder of many hooves.

"Rhys!" Rose's heart sped up yet again.

Billy had slung the marquess' good arm over his shoulder, his one arm banding Rhys' waist.

"I believe the author of our little 'accident' would be a lone man," Rhys said.

Rose wished she could see who approached, but the bend and the trees obscured the view. She glanced at their wrecked carriage, then at the two men she had killed. Her nerves clenched with that same horrible feeling of dread.

Around the bend rode Patrick and Angus, followed by a half-dozen Ravenscroft staff, including Fitz.

Rhys' people. *Their* people.

Black crowded her vision, gold motes dancing before her eyes. She rested a hand on Billy's saddle to steady herself. A goat began to lick her face.

"Gods above, what happened to you?" Patrick flung himself from the saddle and ran to Rhys.

"That's a rather sorry tale," Rhys said. "We survived thanks to my lady."

"And to my lord," Rose said, her voice unnaturally faint.

"Where's Johnny Coachman?" Rhys said. "Did you see him, the horses?"

"It was he who alerted us," Patrick said. "By the time he got the team under control and had mounted one of the geldings, he was almost to the manor house and continued on."

"Get us on a horse and home," Rhys said.

After much effort, Rhys sat winded in the saddle, rivulets of sweat running down his face. Rosamund stared up at him.

"Ride with Angus, darling," he said. "He will be stronger and safer."

She shook her head, and damn if she couldn't stop her lips from trembling. She bit the upper one. "I will only ride with you." Her voice was small, wobbly, and mortifying. Rhys stared at her for a moment, then nodded, so Angus hefted her onto the horse in front of Rhys and offered her the reins.

She shook her head, a cascade of feelings stealing her breath.

Her husband took the reins in his good hand and urged the horse forward, and Rose pressed her cheek to his chest. She could do nothing but weep.

A day later, with their bruises and cuts attended to and Rhys' wrist and shoulder reset, he felt much better. True, he'd had a bad night, nightmares plaguing him, but nonetheless had caught several hours of rest.

Now he sat facing his desk on a comfortable wing chair, that rascal, Isla, begging for his lap, paws on his shins, eyes imploring. He lifted her one-handed, and once she settled, he began stroking her fur.

Rhys let out a sigh. His sweet, brave Rosie was resting, and not wishing to disturb her, he summoned Patrick and Angus to his study.

Rose had never killed a man. Now, having dispatched two, her reaction to those deeds had set in. She had been brave. So brave. His Rosie would be fine, he knew that, but feelings of fury lingered, his temper near the boiling point.

Angus and Patrick entered, Angus pouring Scotches for the three of them. Rhys accepted a glass and savored the smoky taste.

His and Rose's deaths had been so close, an abhorrent feeling he recalled too well. Either of them could have died, or he would have taken a bullet while thugs carried off Rosie. That they came away relatively unscathed was due to Rosamund's bravery, coupled with the sheer luck that he had roused in time to shoot the cur.

The question was, who organized the attempt? Pennworth was his top candidate, with the earl not far behind, for the attack was vicious rather than well imagined.

"Is Lady Rose well?" Patrick swirled his drink and sipped.

"As well as can be expected after such an ordeal," Rhys said. "My lady will be fine, but that she had to experience such infuriates me."

Angus slammed his glass on the table, droplets of Scotch flecking the wood. "The question is who, and two viable candidates come to mind."

"That they do," Patrick said.

Rhys set Isla on the floor, stood, and began to pace. With his arm in a sling, his shoulder pain dulled, he could not stay still. Pacing helped him think. "My bet is on Pennworth." The medal from the fire nagged him.

"Mine is on the earl," Angus said. "Patrick?"

"I am with Rhys."

"Pennworth is a vengeful man," Rhys said. "I have seen it in action."

"The man was a soldier," Patrick said. "A brigadier, no less. You must admit the attempt was rather ramshackle."

"That it was." Rhys took a sip of his drink. "Those men were not locals."

"Ramshackle," Patrick reiterated. "What was to say both of you would not have died? Pennworth would have nothing then."

"Nor would the earl," Angus said.

"Her ladyship overheard bits of the men's conversation," Rhys said. "They spoke of 'taking the gel.' The avalanche was ill-conceived, the man who orchestrated the attack dressed down by the leader, according to Rose."

"Fools," Angus said. "That both of you are not dead is a miracle."

"Just so," Rhys said. "The viscount was infamous for his fits and starts on the battlefield, much to the detriment of his troops. Too often his temper took command of his reason."

"Patrick," Angus said. "Have the magistrates identified any of the dead men?"

"Unfortunately, no." Patrick smelled, then lit a cigar. "From what I saw of the dead villains, they could easily be former soldiers."

"Which signifies nothing." Rhys refilled his glass. "There are legions of them in England."

Out the bay window, the clouds had dissipated, the day turned bright and cheerful. Too cheerful for his thoughts. "Or they were brigands or cutpurses from London. It matters little. Over the past twenty-four hours, I have given this much thought, and I see only one solution. They want me dead, words overheard by Rosamund. Therefore, I shall offer them an opportunity to do just that."

"Using yourself as bait?" Patrick said, puffing his cigar. "Risky. Though I regretfully agree that appears the best solution for flushing out the perpetrator."

"I must agree," Angus said.

Patrick rested a hand on Rhys' good shoulder. "Stay close to home while you heal. Once you are fit, we shall catch the bugger who planned this."

Rhys raised a glass, and the three men clinked.

Isla yipped, making him laugh, but his smile soon dimmed. "He will pay."

"What about the wedding ball?" Angus said. "Shall you cancel it?"

"Perhaps, as Lady Ravenscroft is unavailable for—"

The study door opened and in glided Rose, Bram at her heels. Her smile was warm, though lines of strain bracketed her mouth. "I am quite available, my lord."

"My lady!" he said, walking toward her.

Patrick and Angus sketched bows, appearing as surprised as he to see his marchioness.

"Does not the ball seem out of place after these trying events?" Patrick said.

"Does it?" She raised a brow. "I believe it is exactly what we need."

Rhys reached her, wrapping an arm around her waist, and she stared up at him, eyes soft. He noted her mixture of anger and sorrow, as well as a determination to hold fast to her course. His magnificent valkyrie. How he adored her.

"So let us get a move on, gentlemen, shall we?" she said. "We have much to prepare."

CHAPTER
TWENTY-FOUR

Rhys hovered at the ballroom's entrance with Rosie on his arm. His wife looked magnificent in her gown of emerald silk overlaid with bronze gauze and embellished by an embroidered hem. A matching fan hung from her wrist, her auburn hair confined by the Ravenscroft tiara.

The tiara's matching parure—a diamond and emerald necklace, bracelets, and earrings—adorned her throat and wrists, and she shone in the candlelight like a star, far brighter than the gems at her throat. Rose looked every inch the quintessential marchioness.

His costume was propriety itself—black satin knee-breeches, white waistcoat, clocked stockings, and a black tailcoat.

They made a fine pair as they took their place at the head of the receiving line beside Patrick, his youngest sister Susannah, and his eldest, Thomasina, the two having come up from Woodbine as a surprise. Susannah stood with her arm linked through Thomasina's, elegant in her pale blue and silver gown, while Sina's golden confection dotted with lily of the valley looked equally fetching.

Many months had passed since they had all been together, and having them at Ravenscroft was a joy.

The Woodbine carriage had lost a wheel on its way to Raven-scroft, thus Rose had only a few brief minutes with Sina and Susannah before the ball commenced. Rose had embraced both, yet Susannah's reserve had surprised his wife, for she noted how her letters had been bubbly and filled with descriptive tales and amusing anecdotes. Once the subject turned to horses, Thomasina took charge, speaking of them as friends with much infectious laughter. Sina was both different and unique, a woman whom much of society would shun. They had best not at the ball.

The crush of gravel, wheels creaking, and doors opening signaled their guests' arrival. Soon, the queue for the receiving line stretched outward. Rhys took sharp notice of the stares and whispers as the guests approached Thomasina, some so uncomfortable as to avoid her altogether. Their loss.

A hullabaloo at the entrance heralded His Royal Highness the Prince Regent's arrival, and Prinny soon stepped into the hall. God's blood, the prince had brought Wellington.

Rhys leaned toward Rose. "Wellington is here with Prinny."

"I thought the duke declined."

"Indeed, he did. His appearance means he and the prince have an agenda. They will renew their attempts to inveigle me back into service."

"I sincerely hope not!"

"I would wager pounds on it, my dear," he said. "Wellington was greatly displeased by my retirement. I cannot go back, Rosie. I simply cannot."

Her husband's adamance startled Rose. Rhys always chose his words with care, a hallmark of his personality, and his fervent denial of his return unsettled her, as if something terrible would occur were he to rejoin. That would not happen, Rose vowed.

The prince neared, returning Patrick's bow.

Would that Charlotte and Claire were here, Lady Bea, too. But Bea's letter said the girls had left their cousin's home for the Halafair family seat, unbeknownst to Fielding. Nor could Rose invite Bea without the earl. That she would never do.

More chatter, as the prince moved on to Rhys' sisters. How would he react to Thomasina, whose eyes held an instantaneous warmth, as if Sina had opened her arms wide to hold Rose close?

Sina's face was rounded, unlike her siblings' more angular ones, her eyes tilted upward, yet she retained the Lansdowne look of her siblings, particularly her smile, which appeared often. Her speech could be a challenge, as she spoke quickly, her enunciation often unclear. But if one paid attention, Sina could expound on a variety of topics. When introduced, Sina had said little until Rose asked her about her horses. The memory evoked a smile, for Thomasina had expounded on "her beauties," her infectious enthusiasm making Rose even more eager to visit Woodbine's stables.

The prince bowed over Susannah's hand, and Rose held her breath, for Thomasina was next. She prayed the man wouldn't cut her.

When the prince stood before her, Thomasina performed a lovely deep curtsy, saying, "I am honored, Your Royal Highness."

To Rose's relief, the prince nodded in return.

"I hear you have a way with the cattle at Woodbine," the prince said. "I visited once."

"I remember, Your Royal Highness," Sina said.

The prince chuckled. "Do you? You were but ten, as I recall."

"No," Sina said. "I was eleven, and you wore a blue coat with big brass buttons, fawn breeches, and tall black boots. Your cravat had come undone. Your man in a brown coat fixed it for you."

The prince's eyes held surprise and not a little awe. "I do recall. How remarkable, Lady Thomasina."

"Thank you, Your Royal Highness."

"Pon rep, I must visit Woodbine again."

"An honor, Your Royal Highness."

The prince moved on to greet Rosamund, and she dipped a curtsy. "We are honored you have chosen to join us at Ravenscroft, Your Royal Highness."

"My, my, Ravenscroft has done himself and the marquessate proud. You are enchanting, my dear."

She flushed. "I am honored, Your Royal Highness."

"Do stop with the royal business and call me Prinny. Everyone does."

"Of course..." Rose smiled, swallowing hard. "Prinny."

"Might you save me a dance, my dear lady?"

"I would be honored."

"Excellent!" The prince moved to Rhys and she was confronted by the Duke of Wellington's stern visage, except for those heavy-lidded eyes that again spoke of appreciation.

Rose curtsied. "We are honored by your presence, Your Grace."

Wellington bowed, took Rose's gloved hand, and brushed his lips over it. "I am the one who is honored, my dear, and quite delighted to see you again."

The assembly at Almack's was months ago, and Rose was shocked he recalled her. She could not help but be flattered.

"I very much hope," he said, his eyes warming, "to steal a dance later this evening."

Goosebumps pricked her arms. Those eyes said he would like to dance her to bed, his reputation with bedding married women legendary. She must take great care.

This sober-faced war hero wanted her husband. He could not have him. "I would be most honored and delighted to accept a dance with Your Grace."

Wellington winked. Heavens above, had he truly just done that with Rhys looking on?

After greeting Rhys, Wellington joined the prince, who had begun meandering through the guests, accepting greetings and accolades amid much jocularity.

"Good Lord, Rhys," she said with a sigh. "I felt like a trout on the end of Wellington's hook."

"Have no fear, love." He kissed her palm. "As much as your charms draw the duke, and I know they do, the fish at the end of this particular hook is me."

Rhys clasped her hand and turned to their guests, all eyes locking on them.

"It is my honor to welcome you all to Ravenscroft, in celebration of my marriage to the Lady Rosamund, now Marchioness of Ravenscroft. Enjoy the ball!"

Over the applause, Rhys signaled the orchestra to begin, and the notes of a quadrille sounded. The Prince Regent stepped forward and raised his hand to Rose. "M'lady?"

Rose took it, glad her gloves hid her sweating palms.

Though one-armed with his sling, Rhys was to open the ball with her.

"I think not, Prinny!" Rhys said with a laugh.

"You caught me out, Ravenscroft," the prince said, acting abashed, but for the twinkle in his eye. "I wondered if you would rise to the bait and hoped you would forgo dancing with that wing in a sling. Ha! I made a rhyme!"

Amidst much laughter, Rhys led Rose onto the dance floor.

Every eye was on them. Every single eye. Drat. But their dance was pure heaven, for waltzing in Rhys' arms was a dream come true. At Almack's, when they'd last waltzed, Rose never believed they would dance together again.

So much had happened since then.

At the dance's conclusion, Rhys led her to the refreshment table.

"I will send Patrick over."

"You need not bother," she said.

Rhys bussed her cheek. "Yes, I do." He then strode off to dance with Susannah.

Rose was content, preferring to watch, and when he escorted his sister to the floor, Rose concluded he was the handsomest man in the room. Nay, all of England.

From behind, an arm snaked around her waist.

Patrick, that devil.

But when the fellow slipped her arm through his, grasping it too tight, he began to drag her toward a pair of French doors leading to the balcony.

Pennworth. Who had *not* been sent an invitation.

"Unhand me, sir!" she said, pulling her arm.

But her arm didn't budge, as he covered her hand with his own, larger one in a punishing grip.

"Let us not repeat that scene in the woods," she said. "You know well I can escape your hold."

He smiled down at her, his pasty face mean and vicious, his eyes puffy, bespeaking sleepless nights. Good. "Ah, yes. But will you wish to make such a rumpus at your wedding ball, Lady Rose?"

"That is Lady Ravenscroft to you, sir." But he was correct. Rose would not cause a scene in the ballroom, but once they were on the balcony alone, however...

"Now that you are breached." Pennworth bent close, his breath hot on her face. "I thought we should get to know one another *better.*"

That utter prick. As they neared the balcony doors, Rose pictured the moves needed to break his hold.

A rustle at the ballroom entrance.

"His Lordship, the Earl of Fielding and her Ladyship Evaline Mortenson."

Pennworth grinned down at her. "Ah. More guests."

More uninvited ones.

"I have much to discuss with my compatriots. *Do* excuse me." With a broad smile, he said, "I truly loathe you and that bugger Ravenscroft. Someday, I will see you both ended." The viscount released her and sauntered toward the earl and Lady Whatshername.

Odious cretin. Rose cut her eyes to Rhys, who stared at them showing not an iota of emotion. She, on the other hand, did not conceal her fury.

That Pennworth and the earl had crashed the ball said they were bent on sowing trouble. The woman was the unknown, but whoever she was, it boded ill. Pennworth was a carbuncle on her arse— impossible to be rid of.

How dare they intrude? Rose masked her fury with a serene expression. She'd dissembled enough around Fielding to know what was needed.

Susannah and Thomasina joined her.

"You invited your father, Rose?" Susannah said.

"Indeed, I did not."

The unwelcome trio swanned by Rhys to hover before the prince, the interlopers executing deep bows and a curtsy.

Rose walked to Rhys, and they joined the group surrounding the prince.

"It is an honor and a privilege to see you, Your Royal Highness and Your Grace," Fielding said.

Pennworth and the woman mimicked the earl like parrots, and for once she wished Percy was here to harry them.

The trio turned, and Lady Whatshername placed a hand on Rhys' chest. "So very good to see you, my lord."

Rhys stared at her hand as if it were a leech, and the woman removed it. "A pleasure to meet you, your ladyship."

The woman tittered, reminding Rose of Christmas bells. Who was she?

Her raven hair was done up in an elegant style, parted in the middle, with a few ringlets and a fringe of bangs. Her gown was impeccable, as well, made of satin with highlights of navy blue to match her eyes.

Her familiarity with Rhys made Rose wish to rake her nails down that beautiful face, those sly eyes hiding secrets. And they were sly, even if Rose had to admit they were stunning as well.

"Lady Evaline..." the earl said in his most solicitous voice. "How to put this, for it is most indelicate? Her ladyship was Lord Ravenscroft's fiancée."

Impossible. More chicanery from Fielding to discredit their marriage.

"The nerve," Susannah whispered in her ear.

Thomasina patted her forearm. "It will be all right."

Rose squeezed Sina's hand. "Thank you, my dear."

But Lady Evaline was striking, and Rose could see any man wishing to engage her affections.

Rhys snorted. "I have never seen this woman before in my life."

"Oh!" Lady Evaline's hand flew to her mouth. "My lord, how can you say thus, for we knew each other well on the continent?"

"If I met you casually," Rhys said. "I fail to recall the occasion."

The ballroom had gone preternaturally quiet, the prince and Wellington near goggle-eyed, and Rose steeled herself.

"We knew each other between the conflicts," Lady Evaline continued, her voice dropping. "Between the Peninsula and Waterloo, while the Little General was ensconced on Corsica."

Around that time, Rhys had become adjunct to the Duke of Cambridge, remaining on the continent between the conflicts.

The earl had done himself proud this time.

"Pray, dear sirs, m'lady," Rose said. "Let us repair to my lord's study, shall we?"

"I think not," the earl said, his handsome face turned to a frown.

Lady Evaline's head tilted attractively. "And who might you be, my dear?"

"Lady Ravenscroft is my wife." Rhys' voice would cut steel. "The Marchioness of Ravenscroft."

"But how is that possible, Rhys?" Lady Evaline said in a wan voice.

"Quite simple, m'lady," he said. "We wed four days ago."

The woman swayed, and Pennworth caught her elbow to prevent her fall.

Rose despised the theatrics and gestured toward the seats at the ballroom's edge. "Do let us move so we are no longer quite the circus."

Pennworth peered down as if to devour her. "Of course."

Rose stumbled, his avaricious perusal so like the gaze Fielding used to pin on her. Then she took Rhys' arm, signaled to Sina and Susannah, and they walked to the room's perimeter.

Pennworth, the earl, and *that woman* followed.

"My dear," Lady Evaline said to Rhys in a honeyed voice. "I see your injury. Shall I bring you some refreshment to sustain you?"

"No, Lady Evaline, you may not," he said. "Let us complete this rather sordid business, for I grow weary of it."

Rhys' eyes flashed to Rose. He was furious, though not at her, but humor lurked there as well. She saw nothing funny about the situation, least of all *that woman.*

The prince and Wellington had not joined them but stood conversing nearby. Rhys indicated the orchestra should strike up a tune, which they did, and gradually couples joined in La Boulangere.

"By Jove, this is a shocking occurrence," His Royal Highness said.

Lord Wellington, a keen assessor of character, narrowed his eyes as he perused the earl and his party, his focus quickly returned to the earl.

"There is something discomforting about Fielding," Prinny said. "Do you not think?"

"I could not agree more, my friend," Wellington said. "It is all in the eyes, you know. I have faced men like him on the battlefield, and they seldom fought with honor. I am equally disturbed by Brigadier Pennworth's disagreeable behavior and aligning himself with Fielding. The man is usually a stickler for fine deportment, with all the proper social graces."

"Shall we see how it plays out?" Prinny said.

"Let's do." Wellington believed this a ruse cooked up by Fielding, though he could not imagine why. A part of him wished the "fiancée" part was true, for he found Lady Ravenscroft a most compelling woman. "We can always rescue the pup if he needs assistance."

"Knowing Ravenscroft," Prinny said. "He will need none."

CHAPTER

TWENTY-FIVE

Staring at the unpleasant trio, Rosamund recalled their accident, and her anger escalated. Pennworth or Fielding was the perpetrator of their near-deadly coach ride. Each was a vile scoundrel, and she wished to... She wasn't sure what she wished to do, but was comforted by the weight of her knife resting in her gown's pocket.

"Do have a seat." Rose waved to the awful trio. She was doing all the talking while Rhys observed, which was odd. Strategizing, she supposed. Too incensed for strategy, Rose wished to wring each of their necks, especially that woman's.

The trio, with theatrical reluctance, sat, the woman taking the chair beside Rhys. Lady Evaline again lifted a hand toward Rose's husband.

Rhys' quelling look saw the lady maneuver that hand to her lap, the first sensible move Rose had seen from her.

"Pray," she said to Lady Evaline. "Do tell us where you met my husband?" She had emphasized the last two words.

The woman's lashes fluttered like butterflies. "Oh my, I would be delighted to do so. We met after the battle of Bordeaux at the field hospital where I volunteered."

"Oh!" Rose said. "How admirable that you offered your services at the front."

The woman's lids dropped, a modest pose. "It was the least I could do. You see, my brother was fighting, and we are very close. I could not send him off to war without helping."

Doing it up brown, indeed. "And what hospital might that have been?" Rose inquired

"Near Bordeaux. His Lordship was brought in one day, terribly wounded, but we saw him through, the field surgeons and myself, did we not, my lord?"

Rhys stared at Lady Evaline and remained mute, while Rosamund filled the breach. "And when might that have been, my lady?"

"His Lordship was there for a good month's time, his recovery gradual. I believe it was February if my memory holds true."

Rose's ballgown felt too tight, while her hairpins stabbed her skull. "I see. What had wounded him so grievously?"

Without even a pause, her ladyship answered. "A bayonet wound to his thigh, an awful thing."

During their aborted intimacy, Rose had seen such a scar, giving some veracity to the woman's words. But Rose was certain much was amiss. "February of that year, you say?"

"Indeed." Lady Evaline nodded most emphatically. "The more I think on it, the more I'm certain that His Lordship was discharged from the hospital early in March."

Thomasina shook her head. "She is wrong."

The girl was serious, with an assurance impossible to miss. "Ah. Well..." Rose slapped her lap. "It seems you are incorrect, my lady."

"I am not." Her ladyship looked at Rhys with limpid eyes. "I thought you loved me, my lord. I believed the promises we made to one another would hold true."

Through gritted teeth, Rhys said, "Nothing about you is true, madam."

"Oh, Rhys, how can you say such?" Her voice was so plaintive, angels would weep.

Pennworth cleared his throat, then pulled a folded sheaf of papers from his coat's inner pocket. He handed them to Rhys. "These should clear the matter up."

Rhys raised a brow, then perused the pages, Rose peering over his shoulder.

A marriage contract.

Rhys flipped the page. At the bottom of the second page, Rhys' bold signature was dated March 23 of that year.

Though she knew the document to be false, chills ran down her spine.

Sina sat with her hands on her lap, shaking her head.

"What is it, sister?" Rhys said.

"You were not near Bordeaux in March."

Lady Evaline's eyes narrowed and she sniffed, dismissing Sina. "These papers are proof he was."

The earl leaned forward, his forearm resting on his knee. "Lady Thomasina... You are Lady Thomasina, correct?"

"Yes," Sina said.

"Best to stay out of the grownups' doings, my dear, lest you overtax your brain."

Rose was livid. Thomasina was no child, but a woman grown to twenty-six.

Susannah laughed. "Overtax her brain, my lord? Lady Thomasina's brain holds far more than any of ours combined."

The earl stared at her, incredulous.

"It is true," Susannah continued. "Lady Thomasina remembers everything precisely, my lord. A rather remarkable gift, do you not think?"

"Not *everything*, Susannah," Thomasina said with solemnity.

"Just about, dear sister. Tell us about your chart and why you know your brother was not at Bordeaux in March."

Thomasina grinned. "My chart. I made it when I lived with the Grimes. I had permission to put it in the dining room, and I pinned it to the wall."

"I cannot see what any of this," Pennworth said, flinging his arms wide. "Has to do with Lady Evaline's marriage contract."

"You are Lord Pennworth, are you not?" Susannah said. "Though we have not been formally introduced, I am Lady Susannah. You are not a patient man, I take it."

Oh, good heavens. Susannah had pricked Pennworth if his narrowed eyes were any indication.

"Allow Lady Thomasina to continue, Pennworth," Rhys said in a stern voice. "Without interruption."

Pennworth rolled his eyes. "She's an idio—"

Rhys bared his teeth. "Take good care, sir, that you say nothing regrettable."

Pennworth clamped his jaw tight.

"Do continue, Lady Thomasina," Rhys said.

"Yes. Brother was riding to Brussels then." Sina sat back and smiled.

"Ah," Rose said, picturing her own map, not that she remembered the details as Sina had done. "He traveled to become adjunct to the Duke of Cambridge."

"Absurdities," the earl said. "How could Lady Thomasina possibly remember such?"

"I am curious as well," Lady Evaline said, her tone languid.

Rose sat straighter, her eyes boring into Lady Evaline's.

Sina continued to smile. "I can tell you my brother's movements from when he went to war until he returned."

"Ridiculous," the earl said.

Sina closed her eyes. "He left for the Peninsula on the RMS Hastings, landing in Portugal on the twenty-sixth at the port. He traveled to Lisbon on Hermes, then—"

"Pray do not continue!" The earl said. "We are here about Lady Evaline's betrothal, not a litany of Ravenscroft's movements during the war."

"That is quite a prodigious memory, Lady Thomasina." The woman's smile was poignant, as if Sina's words were folderol.

"Memory can often play us false," Pennworth said.

A small smile hovered on Rhys' lips. Gods above, this was embarrassing, mortifying actually, and made worse by Rhys' laughing eyes.

"I could not agree more, my lord," Rose said. "Memory is often a trickster. But you see, Lady Thomasina's memory differs from ours. She sees events as pictures."

"Pictures?" Pennworth said.

"What Lady Ravenscroft is trying to clarify, my lord," Susannah said. "Is that Lady Thomasina remembers everything from when she was about eighteen months old. Point of fact, we can show you the chart her ladyship made. It is quite detailed."

Wellington and His Royal Highness had moved near, enough so that Rose witnessed the duke's eyes dancing with mirth.

"The contract is obviously falsified," Rhys said.

Sina pointed to Rhys' signature. "See the 't'? Rhys never crosses his 't's like that." She grinned. "Rhys wrote me many letters and I have them all and he does not cross his 't's that way."

"Why not ask the duke?" Susannah said.

Now the duke strode forward. "Indeed," Wellington said. "I would be pleased to assist." He examined the contract. "I fear I must agree with Lady Thomasina, for I recall Major General Ravenscroft's arrival in Brussels on the twentieth of March. Do you question my memory, Brigadier Pennworth?"

"I do not, Commander," Pennworth said.

Fielding shot Pennworth a viperous stare before drawing back in a flurry of indignation. "Lady Evaline, you have deceived us!"

The woman began to weep. "I could not help it, for having met Lord Ravenscroft, I fell hopelessly in love with him."

Wherever they had found "her ladyship," Rose must give the woman credit for a fine performance.

Pennworth stood, cutting Rhys a vicious look. He winged out his arm to Lady Evaline, who took it, leaning heavily on the viscount as the trio proceeded from the room with exceptional dignity.

After the uproar, the ball continued as if the appalling incident had never occurred, though word would slither through the *haute ton* like a venomous snake.

Prinny chatted up guests and danced with Rose. Wellington asked her hand for a waltz, and she obliged, their conversation focused on horses rather than the abominable incident.

Inevitably, Rhys took her hand for a waltz, and though she was most embarrassed, she allowed him to lead her to the center of the ballroom.

His clasp was warm and firm as he took her hand in his, and she rested hers on his shoulder. The sling might prevent him from wrapping his arm around her waist, but his eyes were warm with good humor. Rose had revealed too much during that odious discussion, and rather than revisit her words—embarrassing in the extreme— she fervently hoped he would light on horses or the manor or the pups rather than...

"How is it you remembered my dispatch to the Duke of Cambridge, Rosie?" he said, whirling her around the room. "It lasted but a minute."

Mortification hit, and her eyes dropped to his shoulder. "I may have kept a journal of your movements."

"Not a map, as Thomasina had done?" he said, the glee in his voice plain.

"Perhaps a small map, too."

His voice deepened to husky. "I knew you held my boyhood self in affection, but nonetheless you surprise me, love."

Rose cleared her throat and gave him a tremulous smile. "Just as you do, my lord, I live to surprise."

"Without fail, you always do, my darling girl."

When the waltz ended, his wolfish grin said the subject was not closed, but Wellington greeted them as they stepped off the dance floor.

"A word, Major General?" Wellington said to Rhys.

"Of course, sir." Rhys led Rose to Susannah and Thomasina, bowed to the ladies, and departed with the duke, His Royal Highness joining them.

As the ball wound down, Rose had a mission—to talk with Rhys alone, a challenge since he had returned from his tête-à-tête with Wellington and the prince.

She watched him, now dancing with Susannah, his face placid as they performed the quadrille. When the set ended, Rose made a beeline for Rhys, who had escorted Susannah to the refreshments table.

"Might we speak, Rhys?" she said as she reached the siblings.

He nodded, and without a word, placed her hand in the crook of his elbow just as Patrick arrived with Thomasina.

The notes of a quadrille began.

"Shall we?" he said.

Rose shook her head. "Rather, let us find a cozy nook."

His frown signaled his reluctance, but he led her to an alcove flanked by palms.

"What is it, Rosamund?"

She took his hands in hers. "What did the prince and Wellington say to you?"

His lips thinned to a white slash. "Conflict is brewing again between the cursed East India Company and the Maratha Empire. They wish me to go to India to support Governor General Hastings."

"The Earl of Moira, yes?"

"Yes, and a good friend of the Prince of Wales. It was Prinny's influence which got him the post of Governor General."

"He oversaw the victory in the Gurkha War, did he not?" Rose said.

"Yes." Rhys nodded. "Now the Pindaris have increased their raids, Wellington believes war with Maratha is inevitable. He and the prince insist I am the only man to manage the strategy for combating the Maratha. I would not be involved in active fighting."

"I see." She squeezed his hands, then released them. "I could go with you."

He nodded. "You could."

"But...?"

"I will think on it, as I told them."

A new tune was struck, another waltz. Rhys shook his head, the way Bram often did when getting a bath. "Dance with me, Rosie?"

"I would be delighted."

As they swept through the steps, the taste of their troubling discussion lingered like a sip of turned wine.

TWENTY-SIX

A sound awakened Rose in what felt like the dead of night, but glancing out the window, faint streaks of dawn painted the sky. Morning neared.

The ball had kept them up until the wee hours, and she should be sleeping like a babe.

What had roused her?

Beyond the door, a board creaked, then shuffling footsteps.

Rose slid from the bed and donned her wrapper, cracking the door to her rooms.

Rhys and his valet, Porter, were heading toward the staircase.

Odd. Rhys was no morning devotee and seldom rose before eight.

Rose eased the door closed. Their departure was probably nothing. And yet the stealth... She threw on her oldest riding habit, the dark green with the split skirt, and followed. Out a hall window, the pair loped toward the barns, their movements covert.

Concealing herself behind trees and bushes, Rose hastened to the stables.

This was ridiculous. Yet having gone to bed at four, only a vital task would cause Rhys to rise at such an early hour.

She crouched beside the first barn and soon watched Rhys and Porter depart at a swift trot. She ran inside, barely greeted by the half-awake stable boys. Firefly was too pregnant to ride, so she saddled Ace herself. Outdoors, she put him to a healthy trot following the path the two men had taken. After about a mile, Rose spied them cross a meadow, then head up a narrow path to disappear at the hill's crest. Beyond lay a forest of spruce and pine and not much else.

Stranger and stranger, indeed.

The path was fairly treacherous and, in this light, not a comfortable climb, but nothing the sure-footed Ace couldn't handle with ease. By the time she reached the first switchback, she understood their destination—the top of the hill.

Dawn's gray light smeared the world as a gentle rain began to fall. Without her cloak, she would be a soggy mess by the time she reached home, the return trip awkward on the slick trail. Rose crested the hill, surprised to see two men, a footman and a stable hand, standing before her. They held muskets, of all things, and when they saw her approach, they stood at attention.

"Gentlemen, how fare you today?" she said.

Guilt splashed across the footman's face as he bowed, the stable hand raising his cap and mimicking his companion. "M'lady. We are well."

"What brings you out on this damp morning?" she said.

"Duty!" said the stable hand, only to be elbowed by his companion.

"Duty?" she said.

"Don't you listen to Peter, m'lady," the footman said. "He ain't never at his best in the morning."

"The marquess and Porter passed this way, did they not?" she said.

The footman pulled his collar as if it were too tight. "That is correct, m'lady."

"Thank you."

She urged Ace onward, but the two men moved to stand together, the footman raising a hand. "I am afraid you cannot proceed, Lady Ravenscroft."

A surprising turn of events. Intriguing, in fact. "Pardon?"

"I am afraid we are here to prevent anyone from proceeding," the footman said.

Rose smiled. "And I am afraid you will not prevent me, gentlemen."

"We must!" blurted the stable hand.

Time to think. As a boy, Rhys would go on secret jaunts, as he called them, but he was a man now. Whatever Rhys was doing, he did not wish to be disturbed. She *could* barrel onward. They obviously wouldn't shoot her. Or she could bide her time to see if Rhys mentioned his morning excursion.

"I see." These men would tell Rhys of her attempt, but that might be a good thing. "Do allow me to turn Ace on level ground, gentlemen."

"Of course, m'lady," the footman said, and they moved aside.

The perilous downward trek took all her attention, but Ace held rock steady. Arriving back at the stable, Rose handed off the fjord to a groom as she pondered the odd scenario on the hilltop. Even her imagination, which Rhys said was overly fertile, could not conjure a single idea of what Rhys was doing.

Two days later, her focus turned to a more serious situation, but her mind was never far from Rhys' odd excursion. She had remained silent in hopes he would broach the subject. He did not.

The new foal's birth should have been routine, a simple labor. But what had begun as easy evolved into something far more worrisome. Rose had sent a footman for the vet, but he was across the county on another case. As one of the few men who had studied at the recently established Royal Veterinary College, the man was much in demand.

Rose assumed his duties and soon saw the foal was presenting in a posterior position.

She summoned Rhys.

Rhys found Rose in the barn washing the mare's genital area, the horse's tail already wrapped. She was aided by Fitz, who stood at the mare's head.

"You sent for me?" He walked to stand beside Rose.

"I did," she said. "I need your help."

"Where is our other stable master?"

"In town retrieving supplies."

Rhys ran a hand down the mare's side. "Damn. It looks as if we are in trouble."

She put on a bright smile. "We are, but Fitz and I have dealt with these situations before."

"I sent a second footman after the vet," Rhys said. "Curse him for not being on call for Rapunzel's foaling. He assured me his presence would not be an issue."

"Enbarr is a big boy and this will be his first foal," Rhys continued. "A year ago, I received word Enbarr was to cover a small mare owned by the squire with assurances she had given birth twice before with no complications."

"That is not holding true today," Rose said, clearing her throat. "But Enbarr's size is not the problem. The mare is tired and straining because the foal is backward, its hind leg thrust forward."

"Bloody hell." Rhys raked a hand through his hair. "I haven't done something like this in years, more than a decade, really. Rose?"

"You will be fine." His sweet girl smiled up at him. "You see, we are going to pull the foal out."

Devil it. Rhys doffed his jacket and waistcoat. "I will get a stable hand to assist us."

"Yes, but allow me to direct the proceedings." Rose looked at Fitz, who nodded.

"Of course." Rhys was back in minutes with a large stable hand built like a bull, but a boy of no more than fourteen.

"What is your name, young sir?" Rose asked the boy.

"Charlie." The boy blushed to the roots of his blond hair.

"Well, gentlemen," Rose said, pointing at Charlie and Rhys. "Fitz will stay at the mare's head to keep her as calm as possible while you two do the hard work." Rose gave Charlie her attention. "Do exactly as I say. Understood?"

"Yes, m'lady."

"I am going to put straps above the fetlock joints of the mare's hind legs. When she strains during a contraction, you will pull with all your might."

Rhys and the boy nodded their assent, both looking a bit green about the gills.

With straps in hand, Rose buried her arms inside the mare's nether regions, clutching two straps. She waited a moment or two for the mare to calm from the invasion, then tied the first strap to the foal's hock, and doing the same with the second. Extracting her arms, she handed Rhys and Charlie each a strap.

By now, the mare was heaving with exhaustion and wished to lie down.

"Keep her standing, Fitz!"

"Aye!" Fitz said.

"The mare will stop to rest," Rose said, standing behind the mare to catch the foal, if necessary. "Ignore it. You must keep pulling. We go on my command. Ready?"

Rhys nodded, bracing himself, and hoped this disaster didn't result in the mare's death. Fitz and the boy stood fast, as well. "Ready."

"All set, Fitz?" Rose said.

"As good as it's gonna to get, m'lady."

A contraction came. "Pull!"

God's blood, Rhys wanted this foal to live, and he strained pulling on the foal.

"Keep pulling," Rose hollered amidst the mare's screams of pain.

Hips emerged.

"Pull harder!" Rose yelled.

They did, and in a whoosh of liquid and foal, the small creature fell onto the bed of fresh straw.

"Hurry," she said, as the mare turned her head to see her foal, nickering for her little one.

Rhys lifted the limp foal onto another clean straw bed, the poor creature unconscious or dead, and she kneeled beside him. She reached for a clean, dry towel and cleared the mucus from the foal's nose, then took a piece of clean straw and tickled inside a nostril.

The foal remained lifeless.

She slapped his ribcage and leaned back.

Nothing.

With the foal on his side, Rose extended his neck and head. "Pinch one nostril, Rhys. Charlie, you hold his mouth shut."

Rose blew into the open nostril, the foal's chest wall rising. After allowing the air to exhale, she repeated the process again and again.

Minutes ticked by. No response.

Then a hoof twitched, a whoosh of breath, and Rose leaned back on her heels.

The three of them watched the newborn's chest rise and fall on its own. After a few more twitches, the foal raised his head, then got his feet beneath him and stood, Rose steadying him. Soon, the bay colt staggered over to his dam, where he searched for a teat and latched on.

God, that was a thrill to see. Fitz laughed and Charlie clapped, then Fitz pulled a silver flask from his shirt pocket and handed it to Rose.

"Ye did mighty fine, my lady," Fitz said. "Mighty fine!"

"We all did." With a tremulous smile, Rose accepted the flask, took a sip, and passed it to Rhys. Then his brave girl covered her face and wept.

· · ·

The morning following the foal's birth, Rose awoke early and waited. But no sounds came of Rhys sneaking outside. Three mornings later, she was rewarded with the same furtive footsteps in the corridor, this time made by a single pair.

Dawn had yet to break, but Rose had prepared, and she slid from bed making sure not to awaken Bram, who had taken to sleeping with her. She dressed quickly in her male clothes, her own boots, and a cap purloined from an unknowing stable hand. One she would return, of course. Lightning Bug nickered as she ran down the barn aisle, and she paused to scratch behind his ears. Waving off the sleepy stable boys, she saddled Ace and followed the same path up the hill.

Near the hill's crest, but beyond sight of the sentries, she looped Ace's reins around a bush by a sweet patch of grass where he could graze and continued on foot. She evaded the two sentries, her green and brown togs blending with the trees, and climbed through the forest, one familiar to her since childhood.

Shafts of dawn shined atop the hill, peppered with boulders, trees, and scrub. No sign of Rhys. She inhaled, and smoke tickled her nose. Was that meat cooking?

Rose couldn't imagine what Rhys was doing up here in this semi-wilderness and headed further into the wood, following the scent of smoke until she came to a large boulder partially covered with moss. Beyond it was a grassy verge backed by large rocks and a few scrub trees, while a grayish-brown piece of cloth held up by a center pole flapped in the breeze. A tent.

She patted her pocket, reassured her *kalari* blade rested there, then hugged the boulders and trees until she reached the verge, where she hid behind a large tree.

Indeed, it was a tent, a camp chair resting beside it. How strange. Stranger still was seeing Rhys exit the flap to throw his jacket over the chair back, then hunker down before the campfire to turn a rabbit on a makeshift spit.

What was going on?

Rhys froze and scanned the tree line, his eyes boring into where she stood.

He couldn't see her, but there was no point avoiding him any longer, and she walked toward her husband with a touch of swagger, as if her appearance was an everyday occurrence.

CHAPTER

TWENTY-SEVEN

Rhys stood, hands on hips, staring as if she were a mirage.

A clear look at him only increased her bewilderment.

His pantaloons were military, the jacket he'd flung over the chair, blue-and-red. As a major general, he wore a long blue coat, but this short jacket was worn by officers of the light dragoons. The same as he wore on the Peninsula campaign.

His jaw was set, his eyes wary as she neared. "Hello, Rhys."

"My lady." He offered a nod.

"Forgive me for appearing so covertly, but I was worried. I heard you leave and... Whoever tried to end our lives with the carriage attack is still out and about. I fear for you."

His lips twitched into an almost smile, but his eyes remained troubled. The sky began to drizzle, plinking leaves with icy drops.

"Come," he said. "Join me in the tent. The coney is well cooked."

"All right." Rose found the whole scheme disturbing. Rhys hidden away on a mountaintop. A military camp and chairs. The uniform from his cavalry days. She did not understand.

She ducked beneath the half-open tent flap and entered as Rhys lifted the spit. When he joined her, he slid the rabbit onto a tin plate and began carving it with his sword. "Sit, please."

"It smells good." She took one of the camp chairs and doffed her cap.

"This is typical fare from my campaign days."

"I see."

He peered over his shoulder at her. "You must think me foxed or crazed."

"You are not foxed," she said. "Nor have I met anyone more sane than you, husband."

He cleaned his hands in a bowl of water, dried them on his pantaloons, and forked several pieces of meat onto a plate, handing it to her. He took another one, filled it with rabbit, then sat on a stool and began to eat.

Though not a particular fan of rabbit, Rose nibbled, admitting the coney was quite tasty. Which nonetheless left her many questions begging for answers.

Silence permeated the tent, Rhys acting as if all was as it should be.

Her throat thick with anxiety, she set her plate aside, and with a shrug, wiped her hands on her breeches. "Why?"

"Ah," he said, looking up from his meal. "We get to the heart of it, do we?"

She nodded in hopes he would continue.

"Waterloo, in particular, changed me, Rosamund," he said. "My many campaigns on the Peninsula were up close, my maniacal tendencies—"

"Maniacal? You are not."

He waved a hand. "Whatever you wish to call it, then. They suited the situation, but by Waterloo, Wellington had brought me onto his staff. I was honored. Felt privileged, point of fact, to stand beside the great man. My stratagems pleased him and succeeded often enough for Wellington to promote me to major general. A great honor, I assure you. Or so I thought."

She nodded but stayed silent, hanging on his every word. The drizzle increased, and she shivered. Rhys fetched his jacket, laying it across her shoulders.

When Rose took his hands, they were ice cold, and she pressed them against her cheeks to warm them. "You take good care of those you love, Rhys."

"I try. As do you."

"Tell me about Waterloo."

"Ah, yes. Of course," he said and paused. "Waterloo was a battle for the history books. A triumph to end all triumphs. A close run one, at that."

His voice had become hard, his tone sarcastic.

"I see," she said.

"With the battle complete, the victory ours, I surveyed the scene alongside Wellington. Wreckage and bodies despoiled the once bucolic fields, now blackened with devastation. The dead and wounded... Thousands of men and boys, children really, and women, too, and horses, dogs, and pigs, for Christ's sake. They lay in heaps atop that field, their lives gone. Thousands of humans and animals lay moaning in pain or grief, with little hope of medical aid. All reduced to cannon fodder, to meat, even as the scavengers and grave robbers plucked at their remains like so many hyenas."

He scrubbed his face, his eyes burning with a terrible light. "I find it difficult, the role I played in those deaths. I dream of walking amongst the dead with a notebook and pencil, noting each one with a number. But then I get confused. I lose track of the numbers, become frantic, and race back to begin all over again. Awake, while I live happily at Ravenscroft with you, my mind flinches at that legion of the dead."

Rose knew not what to say or do.

"When I returned from the front, I resigned my commission. Soon after, Wellington and Prinny began pressuring me to return to the military, saying I was too valuable an asset to lose.

"I cannot return, and when the weight became unbearable, I

built this camp, much like our Peninsula one. It gives me a certain surcease from pain. For all the Peninsula was horrific and bloody, it felt real, visceral. Do you see? At Waterloo, it was as if I were directing mere tin soldiers on the field battle. Send that troop here, that battalion there. You see? They were not human, but rather pieces on a chessboard."

He saw it again, following Wellington around the battlefield as if the duke were a great wave, his staff in his wake. There, a man felled by a bayonet, then another, and another, limp as paper dolls. A head blown off, a horse's leg, a man's arm. A small tear in a jacket stained crimson. That horrible stillness. Over and over and..."

"Rhys?"

He sighed. "I returned here a few days ago, the first time in months."

"The morning after the ball. I followed you."

"I am well aware." His smile was tired.

"Your sentries were most effective, insisting I go no further." She smiled.

"They and my other men are quite enthusiastic in their self-appointed positions."

"Your men?"

His laugh was hollow. "The former soldiers on staff at Ravenscroft hold me in esteem for the killing machine I was."

"That may be so, but that is the least of it. They speak often of your leadership, the care you take with your people, both at the front and here. They admire your treatment of them and the animals, and your management of Ravenscroft. Do you not understand? They revere you far beyond the soldier you once were."

His smile was self-deprecating. "Perhaps. Though my haven here may seem a contradiction, life in the military is no longer for me."

Her heart was breaking, though her pity could only offend. "While you fought your demons alone, I had Lucy."

"Lucy?"

"Yes," Rose said. "She was the only soul who knew about the earl.

We would talk about shame and worthiness. It was she who made me see I bore no blame for his actions. You see, I too know how one can become desperate and ill of mind. If we are speaking truths here, thoughts of ending my life would flit through my brain, imagining relief from the terrible pain."

"Rosie, no!"

She smiled. "I never planned to take action. Never."

"Were you ever happy, my love?"

He'd called her "my love," had often done so. Did that mean he loved her or were his words merely a term of endearment? Rose wished she knew. "After Maman's death, I became very glum, my sense of worth shrinking each time the earl came for a visit. But there were moments of joy, too. This camp allows you some peace, and I applaud that. Would that I could be your Lucy."

"You are, darling, in many ways. Angus was there, as well. Though his presence helped, it was never enough. Do you now understand why I cannot rejoin? India would be the end of me, though I am ashamed to say it."

Her eyes softened, her voice husky. "There is no shame, Rhys. You fought well and hard for your country."

"My one wish as a boy was for the military life." He shook his head. "The irony."

Rose stood and kissed his cheek. "You are a good man, Rhys Lansdowne. Thank you for your honesty. I will leave you to it, then."

Rhys rose as well.

More than anything, she wished to hold him, to cup his cheeks and tell him all would be fine. But there was no simple solution for his mental anguish.

Rose turned to leave when impetuosity overcame her reserve, and she reached for her husband, clutching him to her.

His arms wound tight around her and long moments passed where they breathed each other in.

"Touching you is bliss." He kissed her neck, a fluttering of butterflies that set her heart pounding.

"You battle your demons here, in this camp," she whispered, tucking her head into the cradle of his shoulder. "I wish to battle mine as well."

He brushed a hand down her cheek, amused. "I doubt a mountaintop tent would produce the desired effect."

"Oh, you ridiculous man! You know very well that is not what I meant."

Laughing, he pulled her close while his hand rubbed circles on her back.

"I will always adore and protect you, my love," he said. "You are my one and only."

"Please recall you are mine as well, husband. We are partners, are we not? We always have been. Upon your return to the manor, perhaps we can work on my demons."

He nuzzled her and in a dark whisper said, "Perhaps we can."

Rhys insisted on accompanying her home, and upon their arrival, Rose requested two baths, one for each of them, though thoughts of watching Rhys bathe intrigued her.

After her bath, a swift one so she did not lose her courage, Lucy arranged her hair. Bram rubbed her leg, and Rose handed the pup to Lucy.

"Take charge of him, would you?"

Lucy took the pup with a smile, and Rose lifted her dressing gown and hesitated, gnawing her lip. She must do this. She wanted to do this. She was terrified of doing this. She slipped her robe over her chemise.

A glance at Lucy, who watched with eyes that held no judgment.

"I must," Rose said.

Lucy shook her head, ever contrary, while wrestling the lively Bram. "You always have a choice, *Minnu*. Feeling compelled is but a trap."

"I do not," Rose said. "Well, I do, but it is not a bad sort of feeling."

"The choice is always yours. You love your marquess. I see that."

"I do," she answered. "Very much."

"The marriage bed can offer many pleasures. But it can be frightening, too, especially to someone who has experienced what you have. Trust is the key."

Rose reached for her knife. Hesitated, laying her palm atop it.

Not tonight. Not with Rhys.

With a deep breath, she crossed the room, resting her hand on the door latch. "I do trust Rhys, Lucy. But... I am afraid."

Her friend came up behind her, the pup sniffing Rose's hair. "Of course you are, *Minnu*. Accept the fear and try to move past it, while knowing there is no rush. You see?"

"No."

"Think on that night you took charge of your fate. Ha! You threatened His Lordship's jewels."

Rose blushed thinking of it. She had become crazed by the years of abuse, revolted by Fielding's easy smiles and jocular words to all and sundry.

That night, Rose had found her courage, even knowing nothing could erase the years of pain and suffering she had endured.

But that was eight years ago. Rose had grown, was a different person, one married to the man she loved.

Rose turned the knob and entered Rhys' bedroom.

CHAPTER

TWENTY-EIGHT

Rhys stood before the window in the soft afternoon light. His large hands were clasped behind his back, his white hair mussed, his broad shoulders straining across the banyan he wore, which failed to hide his naked beauty beneath its folds. He was a glorious man, a lovely man. *Her* lovely man.

She walked forward with no hesitation to stand before him.

"Hello Rosie." He gave her a roguish grin, but she did not miss his flash of concern. "Do you recall I have elected not to touch you until you desire to touch me?"

Shyness cloaked her, and she stared at her hands, white with tension. "Can we close the drapes?"

Rhys did as asked. "May we keep a candle lit?"

"Yes. I wish to see you."

He sat again by the French doors in his reading chair and he reached to pet Isla, asleep in her dog bed. Then he lifted the book from the side table, withdrew a red ribbon, and began to speak.

"When, in disgrace with fortune and men's eyes,
I all alone beweep my outcast state,
And trouble deaf heaven with my bootless cries,

And look upon myself and curse my fate,
Wishing me like to one more rich in hope,
Featured like him, like him with friends possessed,
Desiring this man's art and that man's scope,
With what I most enjoy contented least;
Yet in these thoughts myself almost despising,
Haply I think on thee, and then my state,
(Like to the lark at break of day arising
From sullen earth) sings hymns at heaven's gate;
For thy sweet love remembered such wealth brings
That then I scorn to change my state with kings."

"A beautiful sonnet," she said.

"Come. Sit on my lap, if you will."

Instead, she stepped back until she leaned against the foot of his bed.

"Shall I read another?" he said, eyes serious.

"Do, please."

"All right."

He removed a second ribbon, found his place, and read, his smoky baritone curling a spell around her.

"Let me not to the marriage of true minds
Admit impediments. Love is not love
Which alters when it alteration finds,
Or bends with the remover to remove.
O no! it is an ever-fixed mark
That looks on tempests and is never shaken;
It is the star to every wand'ring bark,
Whose worth's unknown, although his height be taken.
Love's not Time's fool, though rosy lips and cheeks
Within his bending sickle's compass come;
Love alters not with his brief hours and weeks,
But bears it out even to the edge of doom.
If this be error and upon me prov'd,
I never writ, nor no man ever lov'd."

A cocktail of desire and fear churned through Rose. She could almost picture their intimacy as strange sensations assailed her—an unfamiliar heaviness and a powerful longing.

But the fear... Fielding always mounted her from behind, the experience abhorrent. She recalled his thrusting and slapping, the pain, the disgust. The earl would never touch her like that again, memory and Rhys mingling.

Yet other sensations rose, as well, those elicited by the poems, by Rhys' whisky voice, by his very presence. They were the antithesis of pain.

"What comes between, Rhys?"

"Between?"

"In between this...and copulation."

He set the book aside, studying her with gentle intensity.

"For example," she said, her tone crisp and serious. "When we prepare for a breeding, we bring the stallion to the teasing board where he sniffs the mare's vaginal area. That sort of thing."

Rhys laughed. "Though we are not horses, dear Rosie, a man and woman do tease each other into a state of desire and arousal."

Rose huffed. "I simply cannot imagine it being pleasurable." She threw up her hands. "Bonbons are pleasurable. Galloping is pleasurable. But..."

"No need to imagine, dear one. I can show you if you will let me. Do you wish to touch me?"

"I... I do," she said, surprising herself. "I find that very odd."

He chuckled. "I do not. What is stopping you?"

Fear, her old friend who visited often.

"I will not pounce." He leaned forward.

She stiffened. "You certainly will not."

"We will do nothing you dislike. We must communicate what we like and what we dislike, do you see?" He smiled, that glorious one that rose all the way to his eyes.

"I hope you will have many likes," he said, waggling his brows.

Her lips twitched. "I just might, you beast. But I cannot seem to stop clenching my muscles in dread. Remember how I panicked the first time?"

Rhys would never forget, and he believed Rose should not make love with him that day. It was too soon, too strange, too full of abhorrent memories. No, at present intercourse was a poor move, though he longed to be inside her, to move with her, to join with this woman who held his heart.

Rather than rush, the true path to winning Rose's heart and trust was to ease her into the realm of desire and pleasure.

She had yet to touch him, though she admitted wanting to do so. Perhaps if he touched her.

"May I touch you, Rosie?"

Her startled reaction gave him pause.

"Um, yes."

Her face bore both fear and desire, a thorny combination, and he rose, approaching her with gentle eyes. He brushed her collarbone first, then her shoulder, then her neck, whisper touches that she seemed to enjoy. His hand moved to palm one breast, softer than eiderdown, and heat blazed from his hand to his cock.

"Oh!"

He roved to the other breast, her eyes widening. "Does that feel good, Rosie?"

She nodded, biting her lip.

The desire in her eyes made him bold. "Should I remove my banyan?"

"Yes."

He dropped it to the floor.

"You are beautiful," she said, eyes wide. "Shall I remove mine, Rhys?"

"Please do, my lovely girl. I wish to see you, too."

Rose nodded, her jaw tense, and the dressing gown slid to the floor.

Standing there in her thin chemise, she was a rare beauty, tall and ethereal, with delicate bones and a determined demeanor. His daring Rosie who always walked beside him through their youthful adventures, through the harsh schooling that made him an officer, and into the very depths of war.

Night was near, and he lit a candle on each bedside table. "Would you lie down on the bed for me?"

She lay prone, clutching the pillow as if it were a life raft.

"Please turn to face me, Rosie?"

Again, Rosamund complied, terror tightening every inch of her.

Rhys inwardly cringed. "May I lie beside you?"

Her eyes surveyed his body, and she reached a hand toward him. "Yes."

He took her hand, kissing it, as he eased onto his side. He smiled. "You are exquisite, Rosie mine."

Rose stared at him, and he would swear he caught a small relaxing of muscles.

"Where would you like to touch me?" he said.

"Here." Her hand trembled when she brushed it over his shoulder, her pupils dilated and her lips parted.

Rhys was a soldier, a man used to discipline, but he had never been so tested as remaining still beneath his Rosie's touch.

"Do you like how I feel?" he said.

"I do." She stroked his shoulder, moved to his bicep, then brushed delicate fingers across his face.

"May I touch you again?" *Christ*, he hoped she said yes.

Long moments passed, and he tried to relax. Rhys found himself gritting his teeth.

"Yes," she said.

A tremor shook him, but he stroked her shoulder, as she had done his, then gave it a soft kiss. "Shall I stop?"

Her eyes widened, and she shook her head once.

With gentle strokes and soft kisses, he led her to a small awakening, and soon both he and Rose were stroking and kissing one anoth-er's flesh

How fiercely he wanted her.

"I ache to kiss your lips," he said.

She wrapped an arm around his neck and drew him to her, taking his lips with hers, the moment indescribable.

Their passion increased along with their stroking and kissing, her awakened desire a powerful thing.

But he'd vowed not to enter her that night. Instead, he taught her other ways to bring pleasure, ways that pleased them both very much.

That night, Rose fell asleep in his arms, and his world had never been finer.

CHAPTER

TWENTY-NINE

The slant of the sun inching between the closed drapes said it was mid-morning. Rose rubbed her eyes. She had slept well, better than she could remember, and had felt loved and safe wrapped in Rhys' arms. She smiled.

Rose smoothed a hand across the sheets where Rhys had lain. Cool to the touch. He'd gone, and she had drowsed through his departure. Rose retrieved her dressing gown, shrugging it on beneath her naked flesh, and stretched her arms above her head. A few twinges recalled their lovemaking, making her blush. For the first time in her life, she had an exquisite experience that transcended the thrill of galloping on a horse. And when Rhys' mouth had touched the center of her womanhood. *Well.*

She crawled back into bed, where that silly pup Bram licked her hand. Rose nuzzled him, laughing. She recalled Rhys lifting the pup into their bed, his plaintive cries through the door wearing down her husband while Isla slept like a little princess on her doggy cushion.

Rose pushed to a sitting position as Lucy bustled in bearing a tray of hot chocolate, fruit, and seed cakes. She leaped up and took

236

the burden. "Dear one, I have asked you not to carry these heavy things. Someone of lesser years can easily do it."

"Bosh. I am not enfeebled yet."

"You are certainly not." Rose smiled at her aging, beloved Lucy. "But why carry a heavy burden when someone else can and should do it for you?"

Lucy huffed. The woman loved being in charge.

Rose took the tray into the sitting room rather than breakfast in bed. Lucy didn't mention the previous night, though it was obvious Rose's smile pleased her.

"Do you know where His Lordship has gone?" Rose said.

Lucy laid out the dishes, cutlery, and food, and Rose began to eat, famished.

"I do not." Lucy crossed her arms, seemingly annoyed.

"Sit, sit." Rose gestured to the opposing chair. "Tell me what is new with you."

Lucy sat on a "harrumph." "That bird."

"You mean Percy the parrot?"

"Is there any other bird inhabiting this pile of stone? He should be flying around the jungle, not a manor house!"

Rose bit down on a slice of pineapple. Such decadence. "I agree, but he has eluded all attempts to capture him."

"He invades the kitchen and steals what he wants." Lucy nodded sagely. "I suspect he is a demon."

"Very possible."

"Perhaps I shall shoot him. Have you been practicing your kalari forms, *Minnu*?"

"Every day, Lucy, as you know very well."

Lucy nodded in obvious satisfaction.

"How are the staff treating you? Are they friendly? Kind?" Rose said. "I know these are early days, but at Fielding, you felt..."

"I felt fine there. I feel fine here. Let us get on with our day, shall we?"

Rose almost giggled. Today, nothing could dim her sunny outlook. "Would you prepare my tartan riding dress?"

"Finally, you choose to wear something sensible instead of those man pantaloons." Lucy bustled into the dressing room.

"The cakes were delicious," Rosamund hollered after her. "The chocolate is perfect." Rose had seldom felt in such harmony with the world.

Lucy reappeared wearing a frown. "The tartan is not here."

"I'll wear the mauve instead."

With Lucy's help, she donned her mauve riding habit and slippers, and they left in search of Mrs. Dawkins. Perhaps the housekeeper had sent her tartan habit to be cleaned.

As they approached the staircase, she spotted Rhys and Angus headed for the servants' staircase, which was odd. "Your Lordship!" She cleared her throat. "Rhys!"

Rhys whirled, guilt writ large on his face. "Good Christ."

"What an unexpected way to greet your wife."

"Rosie, I—"

Lucy hovered, tsk-tsking.

Rhys approached, while Angus looked everywhere but at her.

"My dear." Rhys kissed her cheek. "I am afraid we are on a bit of a deadline."

He headed for the staircase.

Rose traipsed after him. "I would appreciate you telling me what's going on."

Rhys opened the door, and Angus took the first step.

"Damn you, wait!" she said.

Angus halted with a sigh.

"We must be off, Rosie," Rhys said.

Rose had a bad feeling. A very bad feeling. "You are planning something. What?"

His face turned to stone. "We are going to trap the perpetrator."

"The man behind the carriage accident?" she said.

"Yes. I believe that same man set the Fielding barn afire."

Rose disliked his deception, though he believed it would keep her safe and content. Rather than a partnership, his paternalistic attitude grated, reminding her too much of Fielding's.

"You chose not to discuss this with me?" Did he see her as so feather-headed he would plan a dangerous outing without explaining or even speaking to her about it?

"I did not consult you," he said, "because you would have wished to be included in the plan. That is unacceptable."

Rose crossed her arms. "I see. In other words, it is fine if you or Angus risk your lives, perhaps to be injured or killed."

"I do not anticipate such an outcome."

"How dare you! How dare you value your life less than mine! Or for that matter, Angus' life!"

"Lass," Angus said. "We ha' a plan. We will no' be alone, but flanked on either side by Ravenscroft men."

"Please fetch my cloak," she whispered in Lucy's ear. Rose puffed out her chest, her spine steel. "I will make a much more effective decoy than Angus."

"Angus is not a decoy." Rhys took her hands in his. "Rose, don't do this."

The apprehension in his eyes made her hesitate. "But..."

"In truth, I fear you will be a distraction for myself and the men."

"Why do you even imagine you will come upon this miscreant?"

He raked a hand through his hair, whooshing out a sigh. "The stable boy, George. We believe it was he who alerted our attackers to when and where we would be on the road home from the squire's."

She nodded, harrumphing. "I confess I found that broken saddle girth troubling. Fitz keeps our tack in top condition, so it struck me as unusual."

"We suspect he is in the assassin's pay, Rose," Angus said, rolling his "r"s in that Scots way of his. "We ha' planted some seeds about a wee journey over to Broadlands today and expect he will take the bait."

"I see." She sniffed, holding Rhys' eyes with hers.

All people kept secrets, yet when secrets exploded, they damaged the very foundation of one's belief in the secret keeper. Worse, that knowledge eroded the confidence in one's own judgment and in oneself.

She told herself to not overreact. This was Rhys, and she trusted him. Yet it hurt that he had not shared his plans.

"I understand your desire to trap this man. I do. But that you didn't tell me... Well, it doesn't shine a good light on our partnership, does it? All right. Safe journeys, gentlemen."

She turned and walked away, heartsore.

Rhys was in a devil of a mood when he and Angus set off in the gig. The day was stunning, the air clean and crisp as autumn eased into winter. No need to raise the gig's hood, which worked in their favor, as did the lack of wind.

Leaving Rose out of charity with him had been hard, as if his skin no longer quite fit. He had hoped to escape undetected. A foolish desire. Had he told her his plan... But how could he tell her knowing she would wish to take part?

"Put it out of ye head, Rhys," Angus said.

"Easy for you to say."

"As ye ken, if her ladyship joined us, the men would be troubled. We would lose our focus, and she could be hurt—a far worse outcome than any potential injury of ours."

True. But Rhys had broken Rose's trust, a trust he cherished. Angus was right. This mission could prove deadly with a split second's inattention. Thoughts of Rose's safety must not intrude.

"I will put my discontent in its proper place," he said.

But he had hurt his Rosie. Even worse, it felt as if he'd damaged the bond they shared.

Thirty minutes later, they neared a stretch of road ideal for an ambush, the gig moving along at a measured pace.

The chill of battle coursed through his veins, a preternatural awareness settling over him like a mantle.

They continued on, no hint of being observed, a soft breeze brushing his face, the bare trees clacking.

A flaming arrow streaked through the air, thudding into the back of the gig. The horse tried to bolt, but Rhys had done this dance before and held him in check.

A glint on the nearby hillock.

He slashed the traces as Angus reached to rip out the arrow.

"Jump now!" Rhys hollered, the horse racing off.

The gig exploded.

Rose pictured Rhys and Angus injured, bloodied, or dead, and she left off arranging the flowers atop a table in the manor's grand entryway. She had made a mess of it, her mind far distant.

Out of sorts with worry and frustration, Rose startled when a footman approached bearing a note with the Fielding crest. For a moment, she simply stared at the missive until he handed it to her. With hesitation, she slipped her finger beneath the flap, opened the envelope, and pulled out the missive.

Dearest Rose - I have returned to Fielding manor for a few days whilst Fielding dallies with his cronies at his hunting lodge. In my earlier haste to leave, numerous treasures I care for were left behind, ones I wish to take to Halafair for myself and the girls.

Do come over. I surely could use the help in collecting them. Mostly, I wish to see and speak with you. I am so happy you have wed!!! Much love, Bea

Dear Bea. She missed her and the girls very much, and the prospect of seeing Beatrice was a fine distraction to take her mind off Rhys and the danger.

She found Lucy in her room. "I am off to Fielding. Do you wish to join me?"

Lucy's face pleated in worry. "The earl..."

"Lady Fielding assured me the man is at his hunting lodge, so we will not encounter him."

"Can you be sure the note is from Lady Bea?" Lucy said.

Rose waved the missive. "I recognize her hand."

Lucy's eyes narrowed. "Why go at all?"

"I miss her. Plus, her ladyship needs my help. Her previous departure was so precipitous, she left behind personal items that she wishes to retrieve. My assistance will move things along that much faster. Also, I am fretting. Lady Bea will take my mind off... We can take the second gig. Or would you rather ride?"

"I would not."

Lucy fetched her cloak, and they were off.

The ride to the manor took mere minutes, with Rose handing the gig off to a groom upon their arrival. She took a moment, a deep breath, before linking her arm with Lucy's and walking the steps to the front door.

Dunston, the earl's surly butler swung the door wide, frowning when he spotted them. She might now be a marchioness, but he still saw the wild child who caused him innumerable problems.

"We are here to see Lady Beatrice," Rose said.

"M'lady is in her boudoir, Lady Ravenscroft. I shall see if she is receiving."

"No need."

She and Lucy breezed by him and up the grand staircase toward the third floor. On the second, Fielding's housekeeper waylaid them, and after a few conversational words, she left Lucy with the woman.

"Come up once you are done, Lucy."

"Of course, Lady Ravenscroft," Lucy said, amidst sharing a recipe for peach pie the housekeeper was mad about.

Rhys thanked the heavens and any deity he could recall that he had recalled Pennworth's tactics during the war, how the brigadier would initiate a distraction, followed by a cannonball, blasting everyone to smithereens.

He rolled into the gorse alongside the road, thorns pricking, pistol drawn, hoping Angus had followed his command.

Dear God, *please*.

"You are bleeding," came a voice to his right, a welcome one.

A swift glance told him his friend had survived, though Rhys could not say the same for their clothes. They were in tatters.

"I caught shrapnel from the gig," Rhys said. "Nothing major. You?"

"The same," Angus said. "The horse?"

"Took off home."

For a moment, he stared at the gig's remains, still burning, smoke curling skyward.

Up ahead, a second explosion.

"Our men," Angus said.

Rhys briefly closed his eyes, praying no one had been injured or killed. "They are good men, hale and hearty, and hardened soldiers. They know how to look out for themselves." He hoped he spoke the truth.

The hillock above, where Rhys had spotted the musket glint, appeared abandoned. That made sense, given the perpetrator's failure to kill them. He got his feet beneath him, pistol at the ready, and crept through the thick gorse alongside the road, the screen of trees not far distant. A gust of wind blanketed them in a sulfuric smell, like rotten eggs and tar, plunging Rhys back to Waterloo, to its stench and sights, to devastation, to death.

On his right, an enemy, veering toward him with a bayonet. He struck out with his sword.

"Rhys."

A hiss in his ear. A comrade? An enemy?

A rustling. Someone approached through the haze of cannon fire and he readied himself to strike.

"Rhys, confound it," said the harsh whisper. "Remember Lady Rose."

Rose? His Rosie.

He shook his head, the battle upon him. Where would the enemy strike? To his left? His right? Head on? There. He hunkered lower. To his right, the enemy was moving toward him. Close. Closer. Rhys readied himself to spring.

THIRTY

Once on the third floor, Rose turned down the left hall and headed for Lady Bea's rooms that marched beside the earl's own. A shiver coursed down her spine, which was a sad commentary on her family seat. But her memories of the place were a jumble of warmth and chill, and she could not untangle the love from the loathing.

Rose knocked when she reached Bea's sitting-room door. With no answer, Rose assumed her stepmother was in her dressing room and hadn't heard, and she opened the door.

Done up in pale blues and gold, the room was in disarray—several boxes half packed, a shawl on the floor, bedclothes tossed on a chair. Bea must be in a terrible hurry, as eager as Rose to quit this cursed manor house behind.

Rose removed her pelisse and lay it across a chair. "Bea!"

Only silence greeted her, and a pinch of anxiety made her wince. Rosamund rolled her shoulders, trying to loosen her apprehension.

Thick carpet muffled her steps as she walked through the sitting area to Bea's bedroom door and swung it open.

All fell away at the sight. The room was dark, with but a single lamp glowing by the bedside casting light on Bea, who lay naked and bound to the four posts of the bed, her chest mercifully rising and falling. Thank the stars for that.

"Bea!"

Rose raced to the bedside and patted Bea's cheek, speaking her name, willing the woman to awaken.

Beatrice remained still and unresponsive, and Rose wished for a vial of *sal volatile,* which half the women of the ton carried in their reticules. She did not, however, so she withdrew her knife and cut the rope at Bea's left wrist, her arm falling limp to the bed. *Oh, Bea.*

Rose moved swiftly to her left foot, then to the...

Arms wound around her like tentacles, binding her, trapping her own arms in a vise. Fielding, his scent surrounding her like a miasma.

Her knife slipped from her limp hand as memories reared of a pitch-black room, of lying on her belly, of...

Viper fast, a hand gripped her throat, holding a knife to her jugular. The earl's soft laughter echoed through the room.

"I have waited patiently for an opportunity to take you one more time, daughter. But not here, I think. No, it will be more delicious, more familiar in your old rooms, where we once dallied so pleasurably. *Move.*"

Dear God! "You are a monster."

Though her back was to him, she could feel his smile, his chest heaving as if he were out of breath, his erection pressing into her through her muslin gown.

"A monster, am I?" the earl said. "Perhaps."

Rose could not panic. She *must* not, and though she tried to stand her ground, it was all she could do, alarm rising as he squeezed her throat tighter and pushed her toward the bedroom door. She couldn't breathe, couldn't think. Frantic, she bent an elbow and raked Fielding's hand with her nails.

"Faster!" he gritted out, driving her forward, his stranglehold unrelenting...

As if the world had frozen, time paused, a voice in her head reminding, demanding, insistent...*move, child, move.*

Her *kalari* training surged, and she bent her head, letting it loll as if she were faint, and scrabbled one hand's fingers toward her hat, curling them around the brim.

The earl shoved her closer to the hall door, his knife nicking her throat. Yet the movement eased a bit of pressure on her arms, which was all she needed.

She tugged a pin from her hat, ones crafted for this explicit purpose. She would never again be his victim.

"Walk, girl!" The earl moved her closer to the door, his body pressed tight to her back.

She clutched her hairpin in her palm, but he must have seen what she held, for he bent her wrist at a horrible angle, the pain explosive. Rose bit her cheek to prevent a scream, clutching her weapon tight.

"You will be sorry, bitch," he growled, kneeing her in the back. "I will take you one more time and then I will *destroy* you."

With a mighty effort, Rose relaxed, loosening her limbs as if she was growing dizzy. As hoped, the earl's hold lessened further.

Collecting all her strength, she pushed against him and whirled, powering through the inconceivable wrist pain, to glimpse his hungry, eager face. She stabbed the pin through his ear canal and into his brain.

The earl's face went slack, eyes wide, mouth open as if to speak, then he dropped like an anvil to the floor.

Rose froze. Earl Fielding lay still, his clothes tidy in the extreme, though his pantaloons were half unbuttoned. Preparing for Bea? For her?

His eyes remained open as if in shock, the hairpin jutting from the earl's ear, its black-beaded end dull and bumpy in the lamplight. That bead, given to her by Lucy, was a stonefruit seed from the Rudraksha tree, a powerful symbol of protection, which was why she had used it to adorn her lethal hairpin.

Heaven help her, but it had worked its magic.

She looked away and staggered, thoughts a-jumble, feelings riotous. Teetering, Rose caught herself on the bedside table with her good hand. She took a few breaths, unable to look at the thing on the floor, her injured wrist throbbing to the beat of her too-rapid heart.

Lucy glided into the bedroom and halted with a hand pressed to her heart, taking in the sight of Beatrice on the bed, Rose leaning on the delicate table, and the earl limp on the floor.

Her friend advanced slowly and gathered Rose's hat and scattered hairpins and handed them to her, then she wrapped an arm around Rose's waist. "Are you well, *Minnu?*"

"I am all right." A spurt of adrenaline pumped through her. "Yes. All right."

"Can you stand on your own?" Lucy said.

Rose straightened. "I can."

Lucy crouched down but did not touch the earl. "There is little blood. We will fasten his breeches."

Mother in heaven, Fielding was *dead*. Gone. Poof.

In a fog of shock and pain, Rose dropped to her knees and helped Lucy set the earl to rights—she could think of it no other way or she would have a vaporous fit—and with much tugging and pulling, they fastened his falls and waist buttons.

A thread of black wove through her vision.

"*Minnu!*" Lucy hissed, clutching her arm.

The black dissolved. "Except for my wrist, I am fine."

"I will pull him out into the hall."

"But the pin in his..."

"We will remove it in a moment."

"Wait." Rose found her knife and cut Beatrice's last two bindings. "We cannot just leave Lady Bea like this."

Lucy walked to the bedside and sniffed Bea's breath. "He must have given her a sleeping draught to subdue her. I shall straighten the sitting room and we shall dress her so it appears a natural sleep."

Rose searched the dressing room for a suitable nightrail,

returning with one to the bedroom to find Lucy stuffing Bea's bindings into the pockets of her voluminous cloak. Her friend handed her the pelisse she had left on the chair and Rose slipped it on.

She had murdered Earl Fielding. A lord. A peer of the realm.

"Do not be sick," Lucy said, binding Rose's injured wrist with a handkerchief from her bag.

"Yes... Of course. I understand."

Dressing Beatrice wasn't easy, especially as Rose was one-handed, but they managed, then Lucy pulled the bedcovers up to her chin. "She will be all right."

Rose kissed Bea's warm cheek and emotion surged. "We must claim Lady Bea is unwell, and we will take her to Ravenscroft to be cared for."

"Yes," Lucy said. "Keep that wrist out of sight."

"I will."

"Open the door to the hall, *Minnu*, and check that no one comes."

Rose did as asked, feelings of disembodiment floating through her. "The way is clear."

Lucy wrestled her hands beneath the earl's arms and tugged him out the bedroom and into the hall, continuing to pull until he was nearly at his own suite's door.

Rose ran back into the bedroom, all in order but for the tilted bedside table. She straightened it.

Now all was composed but for a sleeping woman snoring softly in bed.

Rose scooched down beside Lucy, who sat back on her haunches. "Now we remove the pin."

Though she reached for it, Rose was swifter and withdrew the pin, thankful for her gloves that were now stained red. She stuffed pin and gloves into her reticule, white stars on a black firmament pulsing in and out.

A calming breath later, Rose pressed at the blood trickling from the earl's ear to stop its flow, regretting she must use her bluebird handkerchief, one of the few she had embroidered herself, one she would burn. She then spat on the linen and wiped all traces of blood from his ear and neck.

Bile rose in her throat, and she swallowed hard.

"Let us roll him to his other side," Lucy said. "Any remaining blood will drain into his brain. I was careful as I dragged him, and with his death, the flow will soon cease."

Her beloved practical Lucy.

Once accomplished, Lucy straightened the earl's leg, closed the earl's eyes, and stood.

Still on her knees, Rose peered up. "What next?"

"You will scream, for you have just discovered the earl crumpled on the floor. Perhaps he had an apoplectic seizure. A shame, isn't it? Do you see? Come."

Lucy smiled as she helped Rose stand, then dabbed a fresh handkerchief at Rose's tears, unaware she had shed them.

Rose avoided looking at the face that defined her nightmares. *He was gone forever.*

"I will enter the sitting room," Lucy said. "When I hear you scream, I will race into the hall."

Lucy disappeared as Rose leaned against the wall, dizzy. She searched her reticule for her second pair of gloves, ones she always carried in case of accidents. No accident *this*. She pulled on the fresh pair, tugging one over her swelling hand and wrist through the pain, the stars, the rapid breaths. She managed. Then she opened her mouth and screamed.

In seconds, a maid rounded the corner. She took one look at the man on the floor and started screeching her bloody head off.

Around the same corner raced Tussit, the earl's valet, a small man with a smaller heart, one who was complicit in the earl's doings. He took one look at Rose and demanded she move out of the way.

Lucy reappeared as Rose donned her most haughty expression. "Tussit, you are speaking to the Marchioness of Ravenscroft. Watch your tone, sir, and your words."

He fixed her with a gimlet eye. "Of course, my lady."

"Call the doctor. I found the earl collapsed on the floor." She took a step back, and Tussit crouched by the earl.

The valet wore a smirk, eyes piercing, as if he knew what she had done. "His lordship is dead."

Maman's oft-used phrase came to mind. *Dieu ait pitié de moi, mais je suis satisfait!* God have mercy on me, but I am satisfied!

Rhys sprang up, pistol at the ready, listening for the enemy.

"Remember Rose," the demanding voice barked.

Rose? Rose was safe at home. At the manor. Home...

Ravenscroft. Not Waterloo. No.

With brutal effort, Rhys wrenched his mind to the present. To the gorse, the trees, the scent of powder, the pricks of pain.

Angus stood before him. God's teeth, he'd near shot his friend. "Thank you, Angus. Once again."

They flowed like wraiths into the wood and came upon the scene of destruction. Limbs and branches scattered the forest floor, while the trunk of a tree wheezed, then toppled to the ground.

Half-a-dozen men stood in a semi-circle, pistols and swords raised. Upon spotting Rhys and Angus, they lowered their weapons.

"Anyone injured?" he said, unable to voice the words, "Anyone dead?"

"All well and accounted for, Your Lordship," chimed a stablehand.

Relief near felled him.

Angus peeled off to speak to the farrier's apprentice.

"Where's Billy?" Rhys said.

The stable hand shrugged. "He had a hunch and took off."

Billy was no hothead, but Rhys had never seen him in battle.

"Here!" came a cry.

Billy emerged holding an indignant George, his one good arm

around the boy's waist, his pistol pointed upward toward the stable hand's chin.

Two men took George in hand and bound his wrists with a rope.

"Anyone else?" he said to Billy.

"Not anymore, my lord, though I found burnt cloth and fletching up on that ridge." He pointed to where the shooter had positioned himself. That person was not George, a boy but half grown.

Rhys strode to the captive, eyeing him with a combination of fury and sadness, for he couldn't be more than twelve or thirteen. A child. But children his age had seen battle, some fighting as well as grown men. He must remember that.

"You have been busy today, George," he said.

"I ain't done nuthin'!"

The boy's accent niggled. "No?"

George could only hold Rhys' gaze so long before he looked away.

"I would like to see your hands." He lifted them. "Powder burns. As I thought." Rhys softened his voice. "Why, George?"

George shrugged, his eyes suspiciously red.

"Has someone at Ravenscroft hurt you? Offended you? Been cruel?"

The boy shook his head.

That niggle coalesced. "You are London-born, are you not?"

"So you says!" he said with false bravado.

"Who sent you to Ravenscroft, George?"

George stared at his boots.

"If you tell us, we will be far more lenient to you and your family." Rhys had a suspicion.

The dam broke. "My mam and sister needs money. The lord offered me two pounds!"

A fortune in the child's eyes. His family could survive weeks, perhaps months, on that much money.

"I see." Rhys squeezed the boy's shoulder, hoping that gave George the confidence to continue. "A large sum, to be sure. But being involved in a murder plot is a hanging offense."

Panicked, the boy wailed. "I ain't killed no one!"

"But you might have, arranging that gunpowder in our gig, not to mention alerting the lord as to our carriage's whereabouts on the road." Thinking about the risk that incident posed to Rose rekindled his anger. "Lady Ravenscroft could have been killed."

"But she weren't!"

"No. Lucky for you. But my death was the intention, was it not?"

George's expression remained mulish.

"Yet that man left you to suffer the consequences of being caught. He abandoned you, George."

The boy's eyes rose to Rhys' and hardened. "My mam has the money, so I don't care."

"No?"

"No! Even if they hangs me!"

"Why did he leave you?"

George grinned, not a nice one, either. "He said I was ta stall."

"Stall?" Rhys said, his tone light, while panic clenched his heart. "Why do you need to stall, George?"

"Because." George rocked back on his heels wearing a wide smile. "The lord said he could ransom the lady, and he would gives me two more pounds if I did."

Rhys wanted to tear off home, but he had to be certain. "This man's name?"

"Brigadier Lord Pennworth, also known as the Viscount of Pennworth. He said to tells you at the end when you'll be too late to catch 'em!" George spat. "How'd I do?"

CHAPTER

THIRTY-ONE

Rose sat beside the bed in a Ravenscroft guest room, her injured wrist bound in a sling, waiting for Beatrice to awaken. After the hullabaloo of the earl's passing, Rose insisted on bringing Bea to Ravenscroft.

Her stepmother appeared physically unharmed, and Rose very much hoped that was the case. Though her mind was wont to drift back to Fielding Manor, she forced it away from what had occurred to focus on Bea.

Rhys had yet to return, and she worried that fact to a fine nub, resorting to her *kalari* breathing techniques to force her thoughts from all that troubled her, a skill acquired during her years of torment.

Lucy sat on the opposite side of the bed, and they had brought clothes and toiletries so Beatrice could dress. No one ever need know what Fielding had done to Lady Bea.

"*Minnu*, see." Lucy pointed to Bea's right hand, which stirred restlessly on the covers. "Soon."

Under her lids, Beatrice's eyes began to move, as did a second hand, and Bea squeezed the covers into tight fists.

"Beatrice, it is Rosamund. You are alone with myself and Lucy, and we are at Ravenscroft. You are safe."

Bea blinked rapidly, then her lids rose.

"Beatrice?"

Her stepmother stared at Rose, as if unaware of who she was.

"It is Rose." She took Bea's hand and squeezed. "Rosamund.

Beatrice sighed.

Rose lifted the water glass on the bedside table, slipped an arm beneath Bea's neck, and raised her enough so she could drink. When she downed half the glass, Rose eased it away.

"You are safe," Rose said.

A smile, a twinkle making a brief appearance. "You are sure I am not dead? For I never expected to awaken again."

Rose grinned. "You are definitely alive, dear stepmama."

"I would like to sit up."

Rose and Lucy assisted Bea into a sitting position, then Lucy retrieved a small tureen of soup and spooned some into a cup. She steadied Beatrice's hands while she drank.

Husband, where are you? Rose bit her lower lip hard, forcing the terrible worry away.

Fear skated across Bea's face, and she clutched Rose's forearms. "Where?"

"He is dead and will never trouble you again."

Bea's eyes closed, lips trembling, and a tear rolled down her cheek. "I never knew such depravity existed." She reached for the water and took another sip. "I believed him away at his hunting lodge. All a ruse to trap me. He knew I was missing my things and would come after them."

Rose imagined what would have happened had Beatrice not sent her the note or had she not responded. The monster would have done his worst. They were lucky. Very lucky.

Beatrice plucked at the high neck of her nightrail. "Fielding planned to kill me. He said so. He also told me all the things he planned to do to me whilst I was tied to that bed."

Bea wept, and Rose held her, murmuring words of comfort, until the storm passed.

"What happened?" Beatrice said.

Rose merely sat there, speechless, unable to voice the words. She did not want to think about it. Could not.

"Lady Bea," Lucy said. "It appears Lord Fielding had some sort of stroke or apoplexy and died."

Bea looked from Lucy to Rose. "I see. I am glad."

Bold words from her friend, and Rose agreed most heartedly.

"We are as well," Lucy said.

Rose abruptly stood. "I must go." She looked from Lucy to Bea. "You are in safe hands with Lucy. Some of your clothes are here, and you can dress at your leisure or stay as you are and rest. All will be well, dear one. I promise." Rose hugged Beatrice. "But I must go."

Minutes later, Rose stood stick straight in Ravenscroft's grand hall. Rhys had yet to return, and she waited, avoiding all thoughts of what had just passed, what she had just done. Bea was safe. That was all that mattered.

Rhys was tracking a murderer. Where was he? Why was he taking so long?

Sweet little Bram danced around her feet in an effort to play. She wished to lift him into her arms and hug him tight, but if she did so, she couldn't hug Rhys on his return.

Lucy hovered at the hall's edge, her expression concerned.

A knock had Brinley swinging open the door to reveal Viscount Pennworth, of all people. The man muscled by Brinley and paused when he spotted Rose. He flourished a bow.

"My lady," he said, rising.

"Lord Pennworth." Rose dipped a shallow curtsey. Her face felt like a block of ice, her legs wobbly after... "What a surprise."

"Lord Ravenscroft has been injured!"

"No!" Brinley said.

Pennworth rushed forward, but Rose stepped back, holding up her good hand. Her mind might be muddled from recent events, but

Rhys would *never* send Pennworth to deliver a message, not to mention where were Angus and the men?

"I do not believe you, sir. In truth, what is your purpose?"

"My lady, might we speak somewhere private?"

"I am afraid not, sir. I plan to wait for Lord Ravenscroft here. Now, either leave or state your true reason for barging into my home."

Brinley stood beside one of the hall pillars, Lucy nearby. Rose was safe. She was fine. She could handle Pennworth. But terror tightened her throat. *Might* Rhys be injured?

Pennworth reached beneath his coat and withdrew a pistol, the barrel pointed at her.

Ah, a ruse about Rhys' injury, as she had suspected. Thank the stars. Was the viscount truly that big a fool?

"You will come with me, Lady Rose."

"I have no intention of going anywhere with you," she said. "And it is Lady Ravenscroft to you, sir."

Pennworth sniffed. "Quite frankly, I don't give a frig what your name is. I need to speak with you. Now."

She couldn't help but stare, for he had gone mad.

He approached, banding one hand around her upper arm, the pistol pointed at her head. "Now."

His hand was steady on the trigger, but Pennworth's eyes glowed with a savage light. Rose hesitated. She could disarm him, but if the gun went off, Lucy or Brinley could be injured or killed. "All right. Shall we repair to the yellow salon?"

"I think not." His eyes swept the hall. "No, I think we shall depart."

He began dragging her forward.

"Wait." Rose dug in her heels. "At least allow me my cloak."

"Get it for her," he barked at Lucy. "Hurry up!"

Lucy did as bid.

Pennworth tugged her close, his lips bent to her ear. "Though you cheated me out of our marriage, all is not lost. You will make a fine object for ransom. From observing Ravenscroft, the fool will spend many pounds to retrieve you."

They waited in silence, confidence oozing from the viscount's pores, the arrogant sod.

Lucy returned carrying Rose's cloak over her arms, her summer one though it was chilly outside.

Rose prepared as Lucy neared, while Pennworth eyed Brinley with suspicion.

As Lucy stood before them, she dipped Pennworth a curtsy.

Then she leapt, flinging the cloak over his head, while simultaneously thrusting Pennworth's right arm upward. On her downward trajectory, she shot a swift chop to his temple.

Breathtaking moves only her teacher could accomplish. Lucy made it look easy.

The viscount collapsed on the floor, the gun blasting a hole in the portrait of the late marquess.

Rose kicked the gun away, while Lucy struck Pennworth's temple again for good measure.

The door flew wide, and Rhys and Angus barreled in.

"Good Christ!" Rhys took in the viscount as he strode to Rose's side.

Angus gawked, then marshaled a footman to retrieve some rope, while he sent another to the kitchens for a cleanup crew.

Lucy, nonplussed as usual, asked Rose, "Are you well?"

Rose could not answer, for there was blood on Rhys' and Angus' torn coats and cuts scored their faces.

Rhys crushed her to him. "All is fine, Rosie."

She shook her head. "He was going to kidnap and ransom me."

"Cocksucking prick." He framed her face with his hands. "All will be well, love. Trust me."

"I do."

The viscount moaned.

"How will you deal with him?" she said.

Rhys' face hardened. "I shall do what must be done."

Rose pressed a hand to his heart. "Please do not kill him." She'd had enough killing that day.

His lips thinned.

"Promise." She gripped his lapel and, when he said nothing, she continued. "Please. For me. Do not end his life."

He searched her eyes, looking for who knew what.

"I need you here, Rhys, with me. Not carted away to jail for having murdered a viscount."

He released her and walked to Pennworth, where Angus and the footman were tying up the viscount.

Rose wobbled. She could not, *would* not falter. Not now. A deep breath later, several footmen and Brinley carried the unconscious man into Rhys' study.

"Release me!" Pennworth said, his entitlement intact as he squirmed in the chair facing Rhys' desk. "How dare you bind me!"

"Better that than you dead at my hand," Rhys said. "A result I fervently wished for had Lady Ravenscroft not stayed me."

"She should have married me," Pennworth said with a growl.

Rhys sat across from the villain, drew his pistol, and took a bead on the viscount. "I do not understand why you have ruined your life over your obsession with Lady Ravenscroft."

"Obsession with Lady Ravenscroft?" Pennworth said, shrugging a shoulder. "Hardly that."

"The barn fire, the fake fiancée, now this feeble attempt at kidnapping and ransom. Why?"

"You took Lady Hathaway from me."

"Lady Hathaway? I do not know her, sir."

"It was your letter that turned her off me."

"I sent no letter, Pennworth."

"I do not believe you, for you have attempted to outdo me at every turn."

"Outdo you?"

"You, worming your way into Wellington's inner circle. I was there first! You are supposed to be a gentleman. Yet you are no more than a beast in battle."

"I cannot disagree with the latter. Yet how any of that impinges on you, I do not see."

"You interfered with my handling of my men."

"Only to save them from undeserved beatings."

"It is patently obvious you obstructed my courtship of Lady Hathaway. You persist in meddling and bought your way into an elevated post so you would not have to deal with the rabble."

Rhys scoffed. "I admit my wealth cushions life's jolts, but neither my money nor my title defines me. You and I have more in common with the rabble, as you term them, than you could imagine."

"Absurd. In common with the rabble we commanded? Preposterous."

Having fought beside butchers and footmen, farriers and bankers, Rhys found them not so different from himself. War made all men equal—fodder for bullets, sabers, and cannon fire—and had forced him to see truths that, under normal circumstances, never touched a marquess' life. He was glad to have learned those things, though it appeared Pennworth had not.

Pennworth straightened, shoulders back, chin thrust. "At every turn, you put yourself forward to outshine me."

"God's teeth, Pennworth, battle wasn't about shining but surviving. I lived, as did you. That should be ample compensation, as so many did not have that option."

"And what of I, who returned to little money to find myself abandoned by my bride-to-be? The woman could have set my finances to rights!"

"I told you, I have no knowledge of any Lady Hathaway." In truth, Rhys could not recall the woman.

"You may deny knowledge of my fiancée," Pennworth said. "But it was you who told her about Quatre Bras."

Rhys pondered the man's words, failing to recall Pennworth's actions during that particular battle.

"You told my lady how my horse stumbled, taking me out of the conflict."

Illumination, at least regarding Pennworth's misadventure. "I recall the incident and you pushing your mount so hard it collapsed."

Pennworth laughed. "Continue to dissemble about Lady Hathaway. Fielding told me all."

Fielding. Of course. "He spoke lies."

"Naturally you would say such."

The dance had continued too long. "I have a proposition for you, Pennworth."

"Nothing you propose could interest me in the least." Pennworth's mouth firmed.

"You attacked our carriage," Rhys said.

"I did not."

"Regarding the barn fire. Lady Ravenscroft told me of your fake rescue. A cork-brained scheme."

"The woman has no sense. She was dashing into a burning barn."

"I found your Peninsular Gold Medal in that barn, sir."

"Perhaps, as I was helping with the horses. Release me, sir!"

"A lie. Patrick spied you in conversation with Fielding during the conflagration."

Pennworth said nothing.

"Now, shall you hear my proposal?"

"Or what? I assume you plan to bring me up before the House of Lords for some sort of ridiculous trial. You will lose, naturally."

"Will I?" Rhys grinned. "How droll. But you are wide of the mark."

"I have an appointment at Fielding that I do not wish to miss. The earl and I plan to bid on a prime piece of horseflesh and he will note my absence if I do not arrive."

Rhys laughed, a soft one that held all the bitterness and pain this arse-monger had caused himself and his beloved. "Whether he notes it or not, you will miss the auction. Here are your choices: leave the country for the continent or Africa for all I care—"

"I never knew your sense of humor was so keen, Ravenscroft." The viscount guffawed.

"I am quite serious. Leave the country or I will shoot you."

"Shoot me?" The viscount's smile was disingenuous. "You? Here? Not a chance. You are priggishly honorable."

The urge to squeeze the trigger powered over Rhys, the curtain of red beginning to descend. He gripped his desk.

Focus on Rose. Only Rose.

"Two choices, Pennworth. Make them now, for now is your one chance to save your pathetic life. I am aching to shoot you in that duplicitous face."

Pennworth's smile died. Perhaps it was Rhys' stance or he'd seen the berserker in Rhys' eyes. No matter. For the first time, the man believed Rhys might pull the trigger.

"You will have no way to explain my disappearance," Pennworth said with bluster.

"Absolute truth. Then again, why would I even speak of your absence, Lord Pennworth? Why would anyone look to me?"

"Everyone knows we despise each other. The events at the ball. Logically, they would point fingers at—"

"Enough!" Rhys stepped back. "Choose. *Now!*"

"I will not leave my estates, my friends, my station."

Rhys cocked his pistol. His hand itched, literally *itched* to pull the trigger. They could bury the man far from Ravenscroft. The wilderness of the Highlands would suit.

A vision of Rose, blood smeared, the brigand holding a pistol aimed at her head. Rhys' vision bled red.

"Yes." Pennworth's bravado collapsed, his left eye twitching. "All right, yes. I will go, you cretin."

The curtain receded, and Rhys paused for a calming breath. "And you will not return."

Pennworth snorted, arrogant prick that he was.

"Take him." Rhys signaled two footmen. "Get Billy Broad and the farrier's apprentice."

Pennworth huffed. "You plan to leave me in the hands of thugs?"

"Better men by far than the trio you sent after me and my lady." Rhys unlocked a desk drawer and retrieved some pounds, handing them to Billy once he entered the study.

"For the journey," he said to Billy. "Give the viscount ten pounds on his departure." That would see him to Calais and beyond.

"If he gives you trouble en route," Rhys said. "Shoot him dead and bury him."

"I will not stand for this!" Pennworth shouted as a footman led him away, Billy holding a pistol to his head. "I will blow up your home. I will end those you love! I will make you suffer!"

Pennworth's shouts grew distant, then ceased as he and Angus left the study.

CHAPTER

THIRTY-TWO

"You should have killed Pennworth," Angus said.

"Her ladyship requested I not."

"Tha' varmint will be back." Angus shook his head.

"Fool that he is, most likely. I shall change the venue, however. We leave for Woodbine in two days. Let us prepare."

Rhys sped from the room, concern for his lady hastening his steps to find her standing in the front hall. She moved forward on silent feet, and brushed a hand across his hair. "How do you fare, Rhys? You look a bit battered, my lord."

He clasped his hands over hers and gifted her with a brief kiss. "I am fine. Angus is fine. All the men are fine. What is this?"

"My wrist? Um, I injured it earlier today, nothing serious." Tears welled in her eyes. "Let us get you bathed and patched up."

His cuts stung like hornets, nothing he couldn't tolerate, but he was concerned for Rosie. She looked like death itself, her complexion gray, lips white as ice, with bruised circles beneath her eyes. Those eyes—huge pools of emotion he could not discern. Fear? Horror?

"Everyone is fine, Rosie," he reiterated. "Truly fine. What about you, my dear? Are you—"

"Come. We must care for those cuts." She bustled him toward the stairs.

Their steps were measured, not because of his wounds, but because Rose was overset by increased shivers.

His valet greeted them and began to undress him.

"Thank you, Porter, but you are dismissed. Lady Ravenscroft will attend me."

"Of course, my lord." The man bowed himself out.

Though her fingers shook, Rose insisted on unbuttoning Rhys' jacket, taking great care to gently peel it from his shoulders. His shirt was a bloody mess, and he shrugged it over his head and tossed it to the floor.

Rose gasped. "Your wounds! What happened?"

"I am more worried about you, Rosie. Never have I seen you so undone."

"I feared for you."

"As I would have for you. But I am well. What has happened to overset you, my dear?"

Her lips thinned, and she shook her head.

A knock and in trooped footmen carrying the copper tub followed by maids with steaming buckets. While they filled the tub, Rose gathered several bath sheets, a washcloth, and soap, her movements stiff and unnatural.

Rhys removed his boots and stockings, then doffed his trousers and smalls, with Rose walking him to the tub as if he were an invalid. It would take more than cuts and bruises to lay him low, and ordinarily, his wife would know that. Her actions were so out of character, he became deeply concerned.

Wincing as he sank into the water, the warmth soon relaxed his muscles. Rose began to wash him. Devil it, that hurt.

"Tell me," she said.

He rested his wrists on the side of the tub and leaned back, closing his eyes. "Pennworth was the villain all along. We captured George."

"The stableboy," she said.

"Yes. He told us all." Among the child's crimes was his assistance with the Fielding fire, as well as the coach accident and today's explosion. "George mentioned Fielding was involved with some of Pennworth's folderol, but it was Pennworth alone who blew up the gig today. Not the earl."

"I knew that," she said.

"How is that, Rosie mine?"

"Because I saw the earl."

He startled. "Today?"

"Yes."

She'd shocked him. "You visited Fielding Manor while he was in residence?"

"Lady Beatrice said he was at his hunting lodge, so I assumed all would be well. I am afraid she was wrong."

If possible, her complexion grayed further, her eyes unfocused, her lips atremble. Rhys gently gripped her shoulders. "Rosie, please talk to me. Something obviously has happened. What?"

She straightened and stared him in the eye. "I killed my father."

Of all that he could have imagined, *that* was not even a possibility.

Rose continued to wash him as if she had said nothing extraordinary. So he waited. He took the cloth from her to clean his privates while she poured a warm pitcher of water over his hair and worked up a lather, her gentle fingers trembling like leaves in a brisk wind.

"Please explain, my love."

In a mechanical voice at odds with her usual melodic one, she detailed what had occurred. He clenched the rim of the tub, stunned by the terror she must have experienced. He reached up and stilled her hands.

"My dearest girl, I am so sorry."

"I have become the monster I always imagined, Rhys."

"Monster? You are but a woman caught up in a terrible situation, one that you rectified. How is her ladyship?"

"Safe. Well. She is here." A sob bubbled up. "He would have raped his own wife. He did not... He did not complete the act before... I..."

"Good! You acted swiftly and with good sense. You did what had to be done. Even so, I am a bit jealous."

"What?"

"I wished very much to kill the earl myself, you see. You have stolen a march on me, Rosie."

Tears pooled in her eyes. "How can you jest about something so terrible?"

He cupped her cheek. "I am not jesting. Were it not for my promise to you, I would have ended his life weeks ago."

"I was his *daughter*."

"And he abused you unmercifully."

"But..."

"There are no buts, Rose Lansdowne, and I would lay five hundred pounds on it that Lucy agrees with me."

The morning of the funeral, Rose awakened in Rhys' arms, growing accustomed to the joy of his warmth and shelter.

She nuzzled his shoulder, and he squeezed her tight, then kissed the top of her head.

"Morning sleepyhead," he said in a rumbly voice. "How's the wrist?"

She moved it and winced. "Better. Not all better, but better."

"Good."

"Have you been awake long?" she said.

"A bit. I have been reading."

"Still Dante?"

"Coleridge. *A Statesman's Manual*. It deals with political skill and foresight."

"Such dry reading for early morning." She pushed herself to a seated position, though she kept hold of his hand, kissing its back. "I prefer his poems. Have you read "Christabel?" It was recently published and is a delight, though *The Rime of the Ancient Mariner* remains my favorite."

"I have, though I find much of his work too fanciful for my taste."

"This, from a lover of Shakespeare!"

Rose lifted the brocade bag, withdrew her knitting, and began a new row.

"Feeling anxious?" he said, dropping a kiss on her shoulder.

"No, but lately I never seem to have time to knit, and I must finish this for Bea."

A knock and Lucy entered with chocolate for her and coffee for Rhys. Rose took a deep sip of her drink, inhaling its fragrance.

"I'll brush out your gown," Lucy said, disappearing into the dressing room.

The horrible mourning dress was a shroud that shrieked hypocrisy. Her hands began to shake, and Rhys took them in his. "Do not go all glum on me, Rosie mine. We will get through today, and each day thereafter will be a better one."

"Each day a better one. Yes, I like that."

She stared into the chocolate swirling in her cup.

"It will be all right, Rosie," Rhys said.

Would it?

The funeral was a miserable affair, cold and rainy, but thankfully just for family. Her cousin Cedric, the new earl, wanted Fielding's funeral to be executed with fanfare, accolades, and a huge display.

The man in the casket deserved none of it, and though she forebear to give Cedric her reasons, he acceded to her request for a small family send off.

During the funeral, the ever-frivolous Cedric chattered about ton doings as he had all their lives, and he punctuated anything Rose said with an "Eh, wot?" as if echoing the rightness of her words. The man was shallower than a puddle.

Few mourned the late earl, certainly not Beatrice, though she had once loved a man Rosamund found impossible to love.

Before the funeral, Rose had invited Bea and the girls to stay with them at Ravenscroft if they wished while the late earl's affairs were put in order and Cedric moved into the manor house. But though they had returned for the funeral, the girls were fixed at Halafair House, and she doubted neither they, nor Bea, would accept.

Rose and Rhys must wear black, but he agreed there was no call for all of Ravenscroft to go into mourning. She was thankful her new home did not have to bear the weight of the earl's passing.

Some days, what she'd done felt like a dream. Others, the act felt so visceral she could feel her pin thrusting through ear cartilage into the softness of the earl's brain. The only thing saving her sanity was that Beatrice had recovered well and would now leave for Halafair.

Rose's actions were right, and yet they were wrong as well. She wondered what Maman would have thought, though she knew the answer. Rose had the strength to do what her mother had not.

Did doom for her actions lay ahead, like some sword of Damocles? Rose feared it with a sense of inevitability.

Once the earl was entombed in the family crypt alongside her mother, and after Beatrice, Charlotte, and Claire had left for Halafair House, she and Rhys began their journey to Ravenscroft's horse-breeding farm in Devon, a visit Rose eagerly anticipated.

In three months or so, Firefly would give birth, and Rose could imagine no better place than Woodbine. So they loaded baggage, Lucy, Rhys' valet, the pups, and sundry accouterments into two carriages, tethering Firefly, Lightning Bug, and Ace to the servants' carriage, while Percy rode in a cage.

A victory of sorts—Percy the parrot had finally been captured, much to the joy of Ravenscrofts' staff. When Thomasina had visited, she had expressed an interest in him, so he, too, would travel to Woodbine, as would Billy Broad and Angus, accompanying them as outriders. After much chaos and many grumbles, shouts, and expletives, they were off.

Seagulls wheeled above and sea scents wafted inside the carriage, and Rose knew they were nearing their destination. The journey had taken many hours, and she ached to stretch her legs. Soon, they turned onto a drive flanked by tall Sessile oak trees.

Rose heaved a sigh. She must accept her actions, both the wrong and the right of them. Then she *had* to move on, though she doubted the burden of her deed would ever truly leave her.

"Almost there," Rhys said, clasping her good hand.

Rose squeezed his back as she peered out the window at the stately trees, grasses, and shrubs they passed, now asleep for winter. "It is beautiful, Rhys."

"A peaceful place for healing." His gentle smile lit her heart. "And for breeding and raising horses."

"Yes. Firefly will do well here. I cannot wait to meet her foal."

"Nor can I." He grinned. "Enbarr's and Firefly's get will be a symbol of our bond, our unity. We are true partners, Rosie mine."

"We are lucky, are we not, to have found one another?"

"That we are."

Around a curve, the manor came into view. The striking medieval building of whitewashed limestone rose three stories high amidst an expanse of woodland, meadows, and gardens, while a sculpted fountain in the shape of a horse took pride of place in the courtyard. On a small rise to the left of the manor sat a series of barns, three of them low and long, while the fourth was a taller, gambrel-roofed structure comprised of the same stone as the manor, with the carriage house standing perpendicular to it.

"What is that building, Rhys?" Rose pointed to a small copse, where winter-dead vines twined up the structure's twin pillars.

"The chapel."

"How lovely," Rose said, gesturing toward a promontory far above the manor. "What about those stones up there?"

"The remains of an Iron Age fort. As a boy, I had great fun staging battles atop it."

"I am sure you did," she said with a laugh.

"It is amazing you have never been here. We so often brought you on our jaunts."

"I recall you invited me once, but Maman wanted to visit Scotland. Did we really have to bring Percy?"

Rhys barked a laugh. "Having finally caught the miscreant bird, Woodbine will be his new home. Thomasina is charmed by him and will enjoy his presence immensely."

"Good for Thomasina," she said with little enthusiasm. "Brinley will be most thankful for Percy's absence."

"As will most at Ravenscroft. That bird swears far too much for comfort."

Rose laughed. Everything would be all right.

CHAPTER

THIRTY-THREE

The manor enchanted Rose. Filled with light, the decor was horsey, the great hall done up in Ravenscroft's green-and-gold racing colors, with art by Stubbs and Gericault, and a maquette of Leonardo's Gran Cavallo. Yet it wasn't overdone. Built long before Fielding or Ravenscroft, the great hall was emblazoned with the royal arms of Elizabeth I. The L-shaped home contained striking fifteenth-century stencils, including a pattern of fleur-de-lys and a sacred sixteenth-century IHS monogram.

For all of that, the manor had a warm and welcoming feel—a book left beside a reading chair, a plaid throw on a sofa, scattered dog beds, obviously used. Rose found the casualness immensely appealing.

Anyone would admire Ravenscroft's grandeur, but Woodbine suited her better. She fit here, an odd sensation since they'd only just arrived.

"Would you enjoy sharing the master suite with me, or would you prefer your own rooms?" Rhys had asked.

She hadn't needed to think. "I wish to share your rooms."

"Then they will be ours."

272

They had begun sleeping together nightly, and before bed they would talk about horses, politics, art, all sorts of things. They read, too, played cards, and Rose even knit while enjoying other gentle evening pastimes. Most wonderful of all, they did lovely things with each other in bed—stroked, kissed, nibbled and more, though they had yet to make love in the strictest sense.

Lucy obviously approved as they put Rose's belongings away, while Porter did the same for Rhys', her husband having disappeared on an errand.

Rather than rest, Rose changed into one of her split-skirt habits, though she would've preferred her pantaloons. But it was too soon to shock the staff or her new sisters, intending to ease them into her unconventional attire. She needed a ride on Ace, that affectionate, silly, and wonderful Norwegian fjord with a sure-footedness few could match. Ace probably needed a jaunt, too.

She withdrew Bea's shawl from its bag and held it up—almost done.

A faint knock sounded at the door.

"Come in," she said, putting her knitting aside and standing.

Susannah breezed in wearing a lovely gown of pale blue that matched her eyes. She looked much like Rhys, far more so than Patrick, who had declined the invitation to visit Woodbine.

As a commissioned naval officer, he would soon depart on a new assignment, so they had left him at Ravenscroft.

Her new sister held out her hands and took Rosamund's, taking care with her wrapped wrist. "I am so glad you have come, sister. I am sorry for your loss."

A blush bloomed on her cheeks, given Rose wasn't the least sorry for the earl's demise. Regretful of her actions, true, but not sorry for the result. "Thank you, Susannah. I am thrilled to be here as well."

"Thomasina said your mare is soon to foal," Susannah said.

Rosamund grinned. "In three months or so. And I am beyond excited, but even more so to spend time with you and Thomasina."

"I intruded because the Duke of Devonshire has arrived,"

Susannah said. "Rhys has asked us to join them."

"Should I change into more formal attire?"

"I do not see the need. The duke never stands on ceremony. He is quite a comfortable man."

"Is that a glimmer in your eyes?" Rose was pleased Susannah wasn't shy when it was just the two of them.

Susannah chuckled as she walked clockwise around Rose. "This is one of those costumes you described in your letters. You can hardly tell when you're standing that the skirts are split."

"You can tell when I ride astride!"

"I would like to learn how."

"All these years, and you have never experimented?" Rose hooked an arm through Susannah's. "I am surprised."

Susannah dipped her head. "You know I have not the courage you possess to flout convention."

"Humm. Well, if you wish to learn, I shall teach you. Yes?"

"Yes," Susannah said with a shy smile. "We can flout convention together."

"I will get you in pantaloons yet!"

Susannah laughed as they walked downstairs.

The duke, Thomas, Angus, and Rhys sat in the family's informal parlor, the men talking as old friends do when they haven't seen one another for a time. Devonshire was a handsome man, very blond, and Rose would guess in his late thirties, a distinguished age which he carried off well.

When she and Susannah joined them, the three men executed lovely bows, to which Susannah and Rose responded with deep curtsies.

The duke raised Rose's hand. "My Lady Ravenscroft, I am delighted to meet you. Felicitations on your marriage."

"Thank you, Your Grace," Rose said. "I am pleased to meet you as well."

"Do call me Devonshire."

"And you must call me Rose."

Refreshments of biscuits, scones, bannocks, and other delights sat on a table, and Susannah poured the tea.

The conversation centered on horses, as the duke was in the market for a good hunter. Susannah was quiet, but Rose didn't miss the covert glances the duke cast upon her.

How very interesting.

Two months passed in a blink, with perhaps the most exciting event at Woodbine being the duke's first visit. Rose reveled in the calm, for there was a peace to the place that settled into her bones, the manor's scents of horse, lavender, and rosemary soothing.

She and Rhys rode daily, and Ace was a champ, his confident, stable gate much appreciated as they or her new sisters explored the hills and dales.

Firefly's belly had grown enormous—Enbarr was a very large horse—and she hoped that did not bode ill for the birthing. Thomasina assured her Firefly would do well, and the twinkle in her eye said Sina knew something she did not.

Both she and Rhys worked with the various horses, the flighty young thoroughbreds and the unflappable war horses, as they prepared for the breeding season soon to commence.

Mornings, evenings, and some afternoons, she and Rhys continued to love each other with their hands and mouths, giving and receiving great pleasure. As thrilling and satisfying as that was, they had yet to join in the full act.

Rose longed for more, even after orgasm, for making love would make them one. Yet at Rhys' insistence, she must initiate their joining. Rosamund always froze taking that final step.

Rhys must be impatient with her, though he had shown no sign of it. How could he not be?

On a chilly day early in March, she entered their suite through the sitting room to hear soft moans coming from their bedroom. She tiptoed to the half-open bedroom door. Rhys lay naked, face up on their bed...stroking his penis, eyes closed, face taut. She watched, fascinated, as he pumped faster and harder, until he brought himself to his peak. At that moment, her own body clenched with desire. He was so magnificent, it hurt.

She had given him that pleasure, which satisfied her enormously, but she wanted to bring him to completion while he was inside her.

And yet...

Later that day, Rose inspected the new raised bed where they would plant peppers, broccoli, and rhubarb, the latter a particular favorite. March in Devonshire was chilly and dry, and she tightened her shawl around her.

"Lady Rosie?" called Thomasina from the kitchen doorstep. "I want to show you something. I think you will like it."

Sina approached, grinning, and took Rose's hand, leading them toward the stables.

"Are we going for a jaunt?" Rose said.

"No."

"Is what you are showing me a secret?"

Sina pressed a finger to her cheek, deep in thought. "Not really, though I do not think anyone has paid me any mind, except maybe Susannah."

"I see." Rose didn't.

Sina peered up at Rose, her blue eyes wide. "Did you know I killed my mother?"

Thomasina killed her mother? *Heaven forfend*, what was Sina talking about? The girl had been what, three or four when she'd been taken from Ravenscroft. "Pardon?"

You said secret. Papa told me I killed Mama. That it was our secret. I did not understand, because I remember Mama was alive when I left."

"You remember everything, do you not, Sina?"

"Yes!" she said brightly. "I do not know why Papa would say that, but I must believe him. He said Rhys and Patrick and Susannah did *not* know, and that I must not tell them. If I did, they would hate me, he said. It was Papa's and my secret."

Thomasina's voice held no anger, though when she had spoken the words about killing her mother, her eyes had grown sad.

What a perfectly horrible thing for the old marquess to tell the girl. It wasn't true, of course, though Rhys had said his mother's decline began when their father ripped Thomasina away. "Have you never told your brothers or sister what your papa said?"

"No!" she said, her shock obvious. "I promised. And I want them to always love me."

Rose took Sina's hands. "They love you, Sina. They always will." Rose contemplated what to say next as they neared the far pasture where half-a-dozen mares and geldings grazed. Thomasina's mother had lived for several years after Sina's banishment.

Sina raced ahead, and Rose ran after her. "We must talk about this. Your papa was wrong. You did not kill your mama."

But she had lost Sina's attention, her sister focused on the horses.

Rose climbed through the paddock's fence as Sina had done, and they walked toward the center of the large enclosure.

"I taught them circus tricks," Sina said, pointing to the various horses, a mixture of gray, black, and bay.

"Did you?" Rose said. "From seeing them at the circus?"

Sina shook her head. "Patrick gave me a book. It showed all the different things horses could do. I told Susannah I wanted to teach them, and she got me another book, but that did not help much. Then Susannah got a man named Mr. Arctus to come. He helped me train them and taught me how to do it myself!" She clapped her hands in joy. "It is so much fun!"

"These are the horses you helped the stable master raise, are they not?"

"They are!" she said with her usual great enthusiasm. "They are my friends and like me a great deal. I like them a great deal, too."

"It must have been difficult teaching them."

Sina paused, biting her lip, eyes distant, and Rose wondered if she was picturing past events.

"Sometimes Prancer would *not* behave," Thomasina said, pointing to a large black horse. "Oofra could be bad, too. She is over there. The others mostly behaved, and soon Prancer and Oofra wanted to do what the other horses were doing. I cannot wait for you to see them!"

As expectant as Rose was to see the display, she couldn't help but be troubled by what Sina had said about her mother. Her father's words had been cruel. Time enough to find the truth after the performance.

"I'm very much looking forward to your show," Rose said.

Once at the pasture's center, Sina moistened her lips and let out a sharp two-note whistle.

The horses' ears perked. Sina whistled the same notes again.

To Rose's astonishment, all six horses galloped toward them at breakneck speed. Oh, my.

When they neared, they formed a circle around Sina and Rose, coming to a dead stop a mere three feet away. All six faced them at attention, ears straight up.

"That was amazing, Sina," Rose said.

Her sister grinned up at her. "There's more!"

Thomasina whistled again, different notes from the first. The horses' ears swiveled forward, and Sina whistled two more notes.

As one, they turned left and began to circle them, first at a trot, then a canter, finally a gallop, round and round and round. A thrilling sight.

Two more whistles, and as a unit, the horses reared, pawing the air, then thudded to the ground.

Thomasina walked to each horse, dispersing peppermints, then she made a brushing hand motion, and Rose watched goggle-eyed as the horses leaned back into a bow, their right legs extended forward.

Another whistle, and they rose and trotted away.

"That was astounding, Thomasina."

"Now the horses like doing it. It is a fun playtime for them. They always get treats after."

Rose shook her head, amazed at the incredible feat Thomasina had accomplished. Rose felt honored that Sina had shown her.

"Rhys and Susannah must see this."

"They will, but there is one more trick I wish them to learn first." Sina took Rose's hand once again. "Horses are wonderful."

"They truly are, and so are you, my dear Thomasina."

As they meandered back toward the house, Rose chose her words with care. "I'd like to tell you some things about your mama, things Rhys has told me."

"I like hearing stories about Mama."

They reached the fence and climbed through, Rose brushing off her skirts as she straightened.

"First of all." Rose squeezed Thomasina's hand. "She loved you very much."

"She did. I remember her very well."

"I am afraid your papa misstated things. You did not kill your mama, Thomasina."

"But Papa *said* I did."

"I know. But..."

A footman ran between the barns, and Rose quieted as he approached.

"Lady Ravenscroft, Lady Thomasina." He bowed. "His lordship desires your company in the formal drawing room, Lady Ravenscroft."

"Thank you," Rose said. "We will be there shortly."

The man cleared his throat. "He said to tell you it was urgent."

Rhys' interpretation of "urgent" was often far different from Rose's. "Thank you again. We will be there soon."

"Lady Ravenscroft!" came a bellow from the manor.

"Horse feathers!" Thomasina said. "Rhys never yells. We better go fast."

Frustrated by her unfinished talk with Sina, Rose nonetheless agreed, and they trotted for the manor, entering through the kitchens. Sina disappeared, and Rose found Rhys standing before a window in the great hall, hands clasped behind his back.

Rose peered outside to see a troop of horses drawing near, the light dragoons' brilliant uniforms caught in the rays of the sun. At their head rode the Duke of Wellington.

"The duke!" she said. "Why has he come?"

"I do not know," Rhys said, his voice flat.

"But you can guess."

"I can."

Wellington's party drew up to the portico, and Rhys turned to their butler to order a repast for themselves, as well as for Wellington's men and their horses.

He led her to the formal drawing room, and in minutes, its double doors swung wide, the butler announcing the great man.

"Your Grace," Rhys said, bowing.

Rose curtsied, and given Wellington's expression, he was shocked by her split skirts, his heavy-lidded stare down that long nose of his increasing both her curiosity and anxiety. She and Rhys sat, taking the sofa, and after a maid wheeled in the refreshment cart, and they waited until the doors closed to speak.

All the while, Rose prepared for battle, a covert one filled with nuance and innuendo. That man would not, *could* not have Rhys.

"What brings you to Woodbine, Your Grace?" Rhys said.

"We had maneuvers at the Royal Citadel. Having learned you were at Woodbine, I thought to pay a visit. I hope you do not mind."

"Rather the opposite, Your Grace," Rose said. "We are delighted. Forgive my appearance, but I was in the gardens and with the horses." Only a wee fabrication.

"Your reputation precedes you as a fabled horsewoman, my lady."

Putting it on too thick, yet Rosamund could not help her blush of pleasure. She poured their tea, and as they drank and ate, they talked horses for good long minutes, while Wellington's agenda hovered like an aphotic fog.

"My lady." Wellington's bedroom eyes hung at half-mast. "If you would excuse your husband and me, we must discuss some business."

"No need for her ladyship to leave, Your Grace," Rhys said. "My wife is privy to all my secrets."

Wellington chuckled, though his displeasure was obvious. "I want you back, Ravenscroft." He leaned forward, a hand fisted. "And I want you in India. Soon."

Rhys paused, and Rose forced herself not to break the silence.

"Your Grace," Rhys finally said. "I am deeply honored by your request, but I am afraid I must decline."

"His Royal Highness also desires that you rejoin my staff. None would be of higher military rank than you, Major General."

"Again, Your Grace, I am honored by both yours and His Royal Highness' faith in me. But I must refuse. The military is no longer my calling."

Wellington leaned forward. "You are exceptional, Ravenscroft. A farsighted man who sees beyond what is expected."

"I could not agree more, Your Grace," Rose said.

Wellington's eyes lit on her, she suspected with the hope of her supporting his request.

Lowering her gaze, Rose lay a hand on her belly and blushed. "Perhaps the time is not right, Your Grace.

The great man jerked, the room's currents thickening. He leaned back and sighed. "I see."

Rhys chuckled. "I fear you misunderstand, Your Grace."

Wellington rose. "I think not. We shall revisit this issue in several months."

The drawing room doors flew open, a stable hand rushing in. "Lady Sina says Firefly is foaling!"

"Do excuse us, Your Grace." Rhys rose and bowed, Rose fumbled a curtsy, and they raced from the room.

THIRTY-FOUR

irefly was early. A full month early.

Controlled chaos greeted them in the foaling barn. Firefly was down on her side and heaving, while Thomasina and the stable master orchestrated the two stable hands, much as a conductor would a symphony.

The huge stall felt crowded.

Sina nodded to them, and the stable master dismissed a man, muttering about too many cooks. A crotchety man, Mr. Grimes and his wife had raised Sina and regarded her as a daughter.

Rosamund took the stable hand's place, while Rhys stood behind to aid the foal if necessary.

Firefly's contractions sped up until hooves, then a nose appeared, and soon a tiny bay foal slipped out onto a clean bed of straw.

The little filly was perfect, and Rhys toweled her off while Firefly still labored with afterbirth contractions.

In a sudden move, Firefly heaved herself to a stand and began to pace.

Thomasina held up two fingers. "Two."

Rose was shocked. She hadn't seen the possibility, hadn't even imagined it. Twins.

Sina smiled.

Rose was terrified.

Twin foals rarely lived, and if both survived the birth, one was often so weak that it died within the first few hours. If they made it through the first day, Firefly might refuse to let one nurse or might not have enough milk for both. After the birth, the mare often sickened or died, as well.

"Do we have a milk mare?" Rhys said.

"Yes," chorused Thomasina and Rose.

Two front hooves began to emerge, ones much larger than the little bay's.

"Firefly is exhausted," Rose said.

Thomasina nodded.

Yet the mare labored on.

This second birth was daunting, Firefly in much pain, and Rose's worry deepened.

The foal's nose appeared between its front legs, and after Rose wiped the fetal membrane away so it could breathe, she grasped the foal's front legs to give the mare a little assistance.

"Thank God," Rhys said.

Firefly's labor stopped.

Rose sucked in a breath.

"We will see her through, Rose," Thomasina said with a bright smile.

"We will see *all* of them through this," growled Mr. Grimes.

Rose stared at Sina's calm, cheerful face. Over the months, she had come to love Rhys' eldest sister, for she was the kindest soul Rose had ever known. "Yes, we will."

A steadying hand on her back. Rhys. He was there for her. He always had been. Her lodestar.

Rhys smiled at Sina. "We will see them through."

Rose desperately wanted to believe that.

Rhys took charge of the little filly as Firefly paced, and they waited in anticipation. Thomasina massaged Firefly's belly, Grimes standing at Firefly's head, and as the foal's front legs again emerged, Rose gently tugged on the foal's front legs, causing traction.

With a huge rippling contraction, Firefly heaved, Rose gave a mighty pull, and the foal slid onto the straw.

"Heavens above!" Rose said, holding the little creature until the umbilical cord stopped pulsing and was snipped.

The colt was much larger than the little filly who preceded him, his conformation as perfect as perfect as hers. No, the surprise was his coat. For the colt was not a bay like his dam, nor all black like his sire, but splotched. His skin and coat were black, true, but large white splotches began on his sides and spread toward his back, neck, tail, and legs. His mane was also black, but his tail bore a comet streak of white, with a white blaze running from his forehead to his black nose, one white stocking completing the picture of an utterly original creature.

The stable hushed, and all stood back as Sina towel dried the little colt, while the filly nursed at her dam's teat. Rose went to Firefly's head, praising and stroking her for her mighty efforts. Then the mare lay down on her side and heaved a sigh.

Rose was speechless. Two foals, alive. The colt and filly touched noses, and everyone laughed. Yet the colt's coat continued to astonish.

A coat like his had happened before, where a solid dam and stud produced a multicolored foal. Rose had seen an oil painting of a similar horse, a racehorse belonging to King George III called "King of Trumps." But never in person.

Both colt and filly were magnificent.

Rose reached for Thomasina and drew her into a hug. "We saved them all, Sina!"

"We did!"

Now, the challenge remained for them to thrive.

• • •

Days and weeks passed, and they and the Woodbine staff gave round-the-clock attention to Firefly and her foals. No surprise that they needed the milk dam to supplement the colt's feedings, for he was a large boy, yet thinner than his petite sister. Each experienced rough patches, but now both had found their legs.

Firefly, on the other hand, fared poorly since the birth. She had gone off her feed and lost much weight. Too much weight.

Rose carried worry like a soggy blanket wrapped about her, each day a battle.

Grimes and one assistant, along with Rose, Sina, Rhys, Susannah, and Angus made sure Firefly had constant attention. They tried numerous remedies, yet had failed to discover why Firefly did not thrive.

As months passed, the foals grew healthier and stronger. The mare did not. Firefly was Rose's focus now, and she and Sina put all into their quest to save Firefly. Days turned to nights turned to days, and though her dread for Firefly persisted, Rose wished to remain forever at Woodbine. She had fallen in love with its animals and people, and its charm and peace.

Lucy thrived at Woodbine, as well. A stable hand hailed from India, as Lucy did, and though Lucy's and Arjuna's dialects were different, they bridged the gap via English to create a friendship.

The Duke of Devonshire visited often, even more so after the twins' birth, so Rose found nothing exceptional in his arrival on a rainy Thursday afternoon.

Rose was in the foaling barn, a pouring rain thrumming the rooftop, while she assisted in another birth, one far more conventional. Thomasina was there, and Susannah had also joined them. The mare lay on her side, the foal's birth proceeding normally when Rhys strode into the barn.

"Lady Ravenscroft," he said formally, as he often did with others present.

She rose from the stool where she had been resting. It had been a long night. "My lord?"

"Devonshire is here, and he wishes to see you."

How odd. Most often the duke and Rhys rose out, or the pair discussed guns or other subjects of interest.

"Of course." Her pantaloons were stained, her hair askew, and her shoulders ached. "I shall go change and be with you directly."

They raced through the downpour sheltered by Rhys' coat.

"Just wash up, Rosie," Rhys said when they arrived at the kitchen door. "This is important."

"All right, but I am a bit of a mess."

While the staff bustled about, he whispered, "But you are still adorable."

That surprised a laugh. "I am afraid, my love, at this moment you are the only one who would say that."

Rose scrubbed up, and she followed Rhys to the family parlor.

The duke stood as they entered, resplendent as usual. Even in a downpour, the man was perfectly attired, for he did not believe in dressing down. Yet he accepted Rose's use of men's clothing with equanimity. He approached Rose, taking her hand and bowing.

"No Lady Susannah?" he said as he straightened.

"She is with Thomasina, helping with a foaling."

"Ah," he said, his disappointment obvious. "How do you fare today, my lady?"

"Well, sir. And you?"

His lips pursed. "I have been better, Lady Rosamund." He glanced again at the door. Though Susannah liked the duke well enough, the duke's *tendre* for Rhys' sister was sadly not returned, and she had told Rose her heart was unengaged.

Given Rose's soiled clothing, she did not sit, the men remaining standing as well.

"Is there something special you wished to discuss with me, my lord?"

"As you know," Devonshire said. "I recently attended court for several weeks."

She hadn't known, nor did she see how that was germane.

"There have been..." The duke cleared his throat. "Murmurings about the late Earl Fielding's demise."

"Murmurings? At court?" Rose did not like Rhys' odd silence.

"Whispers that his death was not all it seemed, and this gossip is accompanied by finger-pointing. At you, I hesitate to say, my lady."

"It is widely known that I discovered the earl's...remains."

"True enough. But I found myself quite concerned about the innuendoes."

"Explain why, Devonshire," Rhys said.

"My lady, I liked neither the tenor nor tone of the words spoken and the implications made, and I worked to discover their source." He spared Rhys a glance. "I am afraid that your cousin, Fielding's new earl, is the source of these foul-play rumors, and I believe he has fanned them to flames."

"Foul play?" she said.

"Yes. That is what's being bandied about. So much so, I fear His Royal Highness will request your presence at court."

God forbid.

In the coming months, the conversation with Devonshire faded a hum, for Firefly was failing. The only good news—no rumors had reached them about Rose's cousin, Fielding's demise, or any foul play. Nor were any requests for her appearance at court issued.

Four months had passed since the foals' birth, the days softening into summer, ones that grew increasingly warm. Yet Firefly remained off her feed, her weight dropping further and further, and neither Grimes nor Thomasina nor even Rose could ferret out the cause of Firefly's decline.

Rose found Rhys standing in the mares' barn deep in conversation with Firefly and Rose watched from the shadows, listening. Though the mare's ribs stood out in horrid relief, her rump all bone, her ears were perked and her eyes alert, as if noting each word Rhys spoke.

"You see, you must get well, pretty girl. You are a fine, fine mare." He stroked Firefly's neck. "Think how sad my Rosie would be if something happened to you. How much she would miss you. She loves you greatly, and she has such a big heart, your loss would crush her."

Tears burned Rose's eyes, damnable tears, but the sweetness of Rhys' words staggered her. He had a big heart, too, one nearly crushed by war. But he was correct. She could not bear her sweet Firefly's loss.

The earl had taught her well—anything Rose loved, she would lose, for Fielding never wanted her attached to anything or anyone but him.

After a calming breath, Rose walked to Rhys' side, sliding an arm around his waist and resting her head on his shoulder.

"Firefly will come about," he said.

"She must."

He gave the mare a final scratch behind her ears. "Shall we go in?"

"I will stay here for a while, if you don't mind."

"All right, sweetheart. I am headed to the library if you need me."

Woodbine's library was a massive one, holding many dozens of books on the study and care of horses. Rhys had devoured them all in an effort to find some clue as to why Firefly failed to thrive.

God's blood, what was wrong with the beastie?

He leaned back in the wing chair, propped his feet on another one, and tossed a starry paperweight back and forth in his hands.

Firefly was not the only thing that nagged. Devonshire's words about Prinny continued to gnaw at him. That nasty gossip had taken hold at court was unsurprising, given the place was a circus of rumor and innuendo. But it was possible Prinny would conflate and heighten the intrigue to use his Rose against him. A low blow.

He dropped his feet to the floor, pulled a pad and charcoal from the table drawer, and began to sketch, the pastime often calming his mind. Not as well as his retreat, but serviceable.

Why the devil Prinny and Wellington insisted he alone could head off the impending Anglo-Maratha war, Rhys did not know.

For now, he had thwarted them both, but they were men who *always* got what they desired.

Anyone who had met Rose would give little credence to the rumors, though he and Rose knew the truth of them. Yet rumors were like a fungus that grew and expanded exponentially, ultimately handing the prince and Wellington the needed leverage for leveling an accusation against Rose. Which would give them power over Rhys.

The charcoal snapped. Furious at his lack of control, he tossed it aside. His assumptions could be wrong, of course, but Rose would be the perfect bargaining chip, her safety paramount to Rhys. Both men knew that well.

"Bollocks!" He pushed to his feet. Perhaps he should just yield, surrender to these powerful men who alleged he was indispensable. He loathed the practices of the East India Company, though Governor General Hastings was more than competent. The man was also a friend, and Rhys couldn't help but wonder if Hastings was behind all of this. He doubted it.

Power accompanied his marquessate, but that was ash on the wind compared to the desires of His Royal Highness and the commander of the armies. If he and Rose were summoned to court, a nasty political dance awaited them.

Hell, he was an expert strategist. *So, strategize, you fool!* Capitulation was unacceptable. He had never surrendered in the field, and he would not surrender now, especially with so much at stake.

CHAPTER

THIRTY-FIVE

On a Monday when the sun shined hot and a soothing breeze puffed the clouds along, Thomasina awakened Rose with a tap on her shoulder.

She sprang up. "Oh!" Everything ached, for Rose had once again fallen asleep in the chair by Firefly's stall. The mare nuzzled her over the door, and she scratched her jaw.

"Sina," she said, peering up at her sister through bleary eyes.

The young woman grinned, looking chipper and cheerful in her sprigged muslin gown, a spray of bluebells in her hand.

"Mr. Grimes and I have an idea, Rose!" Sina said. "These are for you!"

Rose thanked Sina and accepted the flowers, sniffing their lovely scent. "New ideas are good! I seem to have run out of them."

Sina stroked Firefly's neck in a way the mare obviously enjoyed. "You look bad, Rose."

"I agree, Sina." Rose had lost weight along with Firefly, the bruising beneath her eyes reflecting her lack of sleep, the barn an imperfect setting for a good night's rest. "I will survive, sister. Tell me this idea, please."

"First." She held up a finger. "Mr. Grimes believes while Firefly was thrashing during the birth, the sesamoid bone of her right rear fetlock was bruised or fractured."

"Those are Grimes' exact words, yes?" Rose said.

"Of course!" Thomasina knew horse anatomy, as did she, but Grimes had studied for a year at the Royal Veterinary College. Something Rose, as a woman, was not permitted to do.

"She has not been limping or favoring it," Rose said.

"I know." She nodded. "But Firefly is a horse too willing to please those she loves."

"You think she has been masking the injury?"

"Mr. Grimes does, and I think so, too. Out to the pasture yesterday, without the twins, we trotted her in circles. Her right rear leg began to hitch."

"Oh my," Rose said.

Thomasina held up a second finger. "The heat. It has been very hot. Mr. Grimes says too hot, and that is stressing Firefly."

"The heat... He may be right," Rose said.

Rose opened the stall door and explored the fetlock in question, taking great care. No reaction from Firefly, yet the area beneath her hand felt hot. The mare had much rest, true, but she was also turned out daily with her twins and the trio would race around the paddock like demons. "Cooling her down will help."

"It will!" Sina said. "She must rest for it to heal."

No more romping, with or without her foals. "That will allow the break or sprain to heal. She will not like it one bit, but she will survive her 'bedrest.'" Afterward, Firefly could race her heart out. "Let us bathe her with cool water. We can also lay cool sheets on her several times a day. I hope this heat breaks soon."

Thomasina wrapped her arms around Firefly's neck, hugging her tight. "She is a fine lady."

Rose caught Firefly's eye, bright with intelligence.

Their plan could work.

Hope was fragile and easily crushed. If Sina was correct, and she was seldom wrong when it came to horses, Firefly might thrive once more. But Rose believed her riding and birthing days were done.

She could accept that, for it meant Firefly would live.

A week later, after Rosamund and Sina followed Firefly's new regimen, the mare seemed to improve. That afternoon, Rose peered out the drawing-room window as the drizzle continued only to spot Patrick thundering down the drive on his pitch-black demon of a horse. She greeted him at the door, but he brushed by her with but a swift hello and headed for Rhys' study.

"Patrick?" Rose said, following after him. "What is wrong?"

"We have got problems, pipsqueak. Where is Rhys?"

"At Devonshire's estate. The duke purchased a new gun he wished to show him. I think they are on a shooting expedition or some such."

Patrick brushed some of the wet off his greatcoat and turned to leave.

"Hold up," she said, barring his exit. "Why are you acting as if the devil is chasing you?"

"An issue I must discuss with your husband."

"Rhys and I have no secrets."

"I am afraid it is not for—"

Rose smiled. "I will follow, you know."

"It is pouring!"

Did he think the rain would melt her? She gave him an acerbic grin. "I own a greatcoat, too."

"Damn you, woman!"

"Ah. There's the Patrick I know and love. Well?"

"His Royal Highness plans to request you attend him at court."

In the months since Devonshire's warning, the threat had hovered like a fat spider in the back of Rose's mind. She and Rhys had discussed how this ploy might be used to fold him back into Wellington's service. She had been waiting for it. Expecting it. Dreading it.

Rhys would *not* rejoin. But she knew her husband well. To save her, he would accede to their demands, which would destroy him.

Rosamund had spent hours considering how to address the problem, for she was not afraid for herself.

She and Rhys had talked of traveling to the continent, yet neither wanted to leave their family, their home, their horses, or their friends.

Only Lucy and Rhys knew the truth of that fateful day, both unbreachable vaults. No proof existed of her actions. But she was no fool. The prince, Cedric, and her accusers at court could embroider the situation and make her life hell.

Rose had told Rhys she did not need saving and he would respond, "Of course you don't." But he feared for her, a fear that might make him react in precipitous ways.

"Thank you, Patrick. As I said, Rhys is at Devonshire's. Do feel free to join them."

After Patrick left, Rose gathered Angus, Susannah, and Lucy in the family salon and explained the problem.

"Court is a viperous nest," Susannah said with disgust.

Her sister-in-law had come to Woodbine after her debut season, never to return to London or court, and though for years they had exchanged letters, Susannah had never once noted why she had abandoned London and the social scene. Nor did Rhys know the reason, as both he and Patrick had been away at war at the time. Susannah never mentioned it, and when Rhys had asked, Susannah declined to discuss the matter.

"For no discernible reason," Rose said. "My ridiculous cousin and his cronies have been fomenting this situation."

"I do not understand," Susannah said. "If Cedric claims foul play, what does he plan to do, disentomb the late earl?"

"I would not put it past him," Rose said. "Then again, he is not the most enterprising of men, preferring a languid existence to one of action. Spreading this vitriol feels out of character for him." While Cedric was a gossip, he had never been a cruel man.

Angus chimed in. "Under normal circumstances, the prince would ha' paid little heed to Cedric's nattering. But you may be right, lass. Wellington and the prince could use the earl's death as a bargaining chip for Rhys to return. He canna."

"The problem," Rose said. "is how to avoid this summons. We need to make it go away."

"I'm not sure we can, sister, but..." Susannah's eyes lit. "What if we steal a march on them?"

"And how shall we do that, Lady Susannah?" Angus said.

"A house party, of course!" Susannah said. "We shall throw a spectacular one at Woodbine, with a grand ball as its culmination. All the horse-mad peers will attend, for we have never opened the estate before, not in this way."

"A house party?" Rose said. "I am supposed to be in mourning for the earl."

Susannah took Rose's hands. "The earl has been dead these six months and more. It is not quite time, but at your home, it will do, or Thomasina and I can act as hostesses if you are discomfited. We can also circumvent gossip by inviting His Royal Highness. In truth, Rose, how much do you care what the *ton* thinks?"

Few knew her in London. Even fewer were friends, and Rose suspected she was a curiosity as the unknown who had wed the famous marquess. Party or no, she was fodder for gossip. She might as well meet the mess head-on. "How much do I care about the *ton*? Not one whit."

"The prince will attend, of course," Susannah continued. "Though he has quit the racing scene, he remains as horse mad as all the others. We will of course invite Wellington, your vile cousin, and Mrs. Fitzherbert."

"Who is this Mrs. Fitzherbert?" Lucy chimed in.

"The prince's mistress," Susannah said.

"I thought they were no longer a couple," Rose said.

Susannah's eyes twinkled. "That is what they wish all to believe, but they still meet in secret and often on weekends such as this. I have met her, and she is a fine lady with exceptional understanding and sensibility."

"I see," Rose said.

"I dinna ken," Angus said.

"Mrs. Fitzherbert is as horse-mad as the prince, Angus," Susannah said. "Especially racehorses, as is His Royal Highness. He might play the buffoon, but his taste in art, linguistics, and horse-flesh is unparalleled. Mrs. Fitzherbert's presence will put the prince in an amiable mood. He would do anything for her."

An idea bloomed in Rose's head, one that Rhys would oppose. One she must keep secret from all of them.

"I like the idea," Rose said. "The timing and the location will be ours. An advantage we cannot discount. You have come to know the staff here, Lucy. How soon can we organize a country weekend with a ball?"

Lucy plucked her lower lip. "Two weeks."

"From Patrick's urgency," Susannah said. "The summons could come any day now."

"One week," Angus announced with that commanding voice of his. "And we send out the invitations tomorrow."

"A week!" Lucy's eyes narrowed, then she began to silently tick off numbers on her fingers. She nodded. "It can be done. It *will* be done."

Patrick strode in looking disgruntled and soggy. "What the devil is going on?"

"We are having a house party," Susannah said.

Rose smiled. "Let us see how Cedric does on our turf, shall we?"

Rhys sailed in an hour later, muddied and pleased. Enbarr and he had a good gallop on the way home, and it had invigorated him. He'd left the stallion with a warm bucket of mash after a good rub-down, then greeted their little filly and colt.

Since the first Jockey Club's Derby, thirty-plus years earlier, interest in the sport had only increased. His hopes rested on these two foals, for if they possessed the same heart and speed as their sire and the sweet and determined nature of their dam, they could become the foundation stock of his and Rose's new line of race-horses. Each foal had survived and thrived, which indicated substantial will, and though their size greatly differed, their conformation was impeccable. Time would tell the story.

Rhys needed a bath and took the stairs two at a time, and after ridding himself of the mud and sweat, he went in search of his wife. How he loved the word "wife" when it came to Rosie. *His* Rosie.

What he found were servants bustling around the manor, and Rose and Patrick in his study poring over a schematic of Woodbine.

"Ho there, what's happening? The house is abuzz!" He embraced his brother with a hearty thump on the back. "I thought you were off to sea."

"Any day," Patrick said.

"Rosie?"

His wife grimaced, coming around the desk to give him a kiss, which he deepened, of course.

"That was a fine greeting, Rosie girl."

She flushed, fussing with her wedding ring. "Well, you see...um... we are hosting a house party, a country weekend, and a ball here, at Woodbine."

"What in heavens for?" Rhys said.

Rosamund sat on the sofa before the hearth and patted it. "Do sit, Rhys."

Instead, he turned to his brother. Whatever was happening, it wasn't good. He took in his brother, really took him in. The man was wearing a mud-stained uniform, exhaustion fanning lines from his eyes. This from a fellow who was meticulous in his dress. "Patrick?"

"After failing to find you at Devonshire's," Patrick said. "I returned here. I have news."

Rose twisted to face them, resting her arms on the back of the sofa. "The prince is about to call us to court."

"We have been expecting this," Rhys said. "Devonshire said as much months ago."

"Yes, well," she said. "We had a meeting and decided to move the playing field."

"We?"

Rose explained who'd made the decision and why.

"A week?" Rhys shook his head. That sounded like an impossibility.

"A week," Patrick said. "Susannah and Lucy, along with several staff, are working on the invitations. They will go out tomorrow. Sina and Grimes are in charge of making the stables presentable."

"They are always presentable," Rhys said.

"*More* presentable, then," Patrick said. "Our beloved Prinny, Wellington, and a host of others will be invited."

"You see?" Rose said. "We are moving the court here."

Rhys paced. "And what will this accomplish?"

"We've invited the new Earl Fielding, too," Patrick said. "Though needless to say, none of his cronies."

"Any confrontation will take place here." Rose grinned.

Rhys took long minutes examining their strategy from various angles. Rhys didn't love the idea, disliking Fielding's inclusion greatly, but he saw the advantages to the weekend.

He heaved a sigh. "All right. Though I do not see how this will greatly change the course of events."

His old uniforms were stored at Ravenscroft, and it would soon be time to ready them for the inevitable. For it was coming fast and hard.

THIRTY-SIX

Hours later, Rhys entered the first barn to find Rose brushing Lightning Rod, whom they called Roddy. There their little colt gleamed. He was an affectionate fellow, a surprise, and as mischievous as Enbarr had been at that age. Rose had already brushed Sparks of Fire, for the little filly's coat shined as well. She was as gentle and sweet as her dam, her nickname Dolce.

"I thought you were racing about as a madwoman in preparation for the weekend."

Rose whirled. "I didn't hear you come in." She offered him a bright smile, one that said she was planning secret mischief.

"You're up to something," he said, scratching Roddy behind the ears.

Rose laughed lightly. "Never. I am but a book you easily read."

"A book with much invisible text." Rhys strolled over to stroke Roddy. "How does he get on with his grandsire?"

This time, his wife's smile was genuine. "They have romped together in the pasture, and they're great friends, more so than with Dolce. I think Bug scares her."

"Where are Bram and Isla?" he said. "They are usually at your feet."

"Arjuna and Lucy have taken them for a constitutional."

He leaned his shoulder against the side of the stall, crossing a leg. "I wonder about that pair, the human one. Do you think Lucy and—"

"A certain attachment has formed, though how romantic it is, I cannot say."

Rose's smile widened at his soft laugh.

"They are very formal with one another," he said.

"That they are." She set down the dopp brush and wrapped her arms around his waist, resting her cheek on his chest.

"What is it, love?" Rhys held her tight.

"Am I?" she said.

"Are you what?" he said, confused.

"Your love? You have never voiced the words."

How strange. He'd said the words...hadn't he? "Do you not see my love in every—"

"Oh, drat!"

Lightning Rod had pranced from the stall dragging his lead line, the devil having somehow managed to undo the rope. And there he went, cantering down the aisle at a good pace.

"God's teeth," Rhys said. "Our colt will be the death of us."

Rose sighed, and then they tore after him.

Hiding in Roddy and Dolce's stall, Rose shoved away an annoying lock of hair that had somehow come loose. She sat on a pile of straw in her second-best morning gown and had even brought her treasured knitting to the stables, something she rarely did. She hoped the soothing rhythm would help her relax, for the upcoming house party might kill her.

At Fielding Manor, her parents never held house parties, even when Maman had been her social self. Though they had many a soiree at their London townhouse, the earl refused to give them at Fielding, saying it would be too much work and expense.

The earl had not been wrong in that instance.

Two days hence, their guests would descend upon Woodbine, and the manor was in a frenzy of preparation. Immense tubs of flowers arrived, dozens of champagne bottles appeared, and food by the cartload poured into the manor.

Games were chosen, including Blind Man's Bluff and Charades. They had set aside a room for chess and other board games, and the second drawing room was designated for the ladies after dinner, where parlor games could be played. The card room, billiards room, and library were all put in order.

Rose sighed and began another row. She was *so* close to finishing.

Susannah and Rose had planned tours of the manor and stables. The house would disappoint many, for it was not near so grand as Ravenscroft, and the only collections of note were the numerous horse sculptures and portraits. No, their home would not impress the high sticklers, but without a doubt, the stables would, along with the carriage house, with its extensive array of carriages, gigs, and phaetons.

The horse-mad folk would be in raptures over Woodbine's acres of fine horseflesh, which Rose resented because she would see nary a horse. No, she would be too busy orchestrating events or donning one of the many gowns essential for Woodbine's hostess.

For the men—and only the men—there would be hawking, swimming, and fishing activities from which ladies were banned. Ridiculous. But Susannah and Angus had insisted the event follow the lines of a traditional house party. Frustrating to Rose, but she had agreed. At least the women could take part in the archery contest. Rhys had also arranged a shooting party at the Duke of Devonshire's estate, and if the rain held off, they would have a picnic.

And that recitation of events, which seemed endless, did not include The Ball.

Her mother's facility in creating a convivial party atmosphere while appearing to float through life had always awed Rose.

She was not of Maman's ilk, had no desire to host the *haute ton*, and had little love of making chit-chat with vapid men and women who viewed status and wealth as the ultimate prize.

All she wanted was to spend time with Rhys, the family, Isla and Bram, and the horses.

Rose completed the final row and held up Bea's shawl to the light, its folds pooling on her lap. All that remained was binding off, weaving in the ends, and blocking the piece. She grinned and began binding off.

Susannah adding a musicale and a dreaded puppet show had spurred her retreat to the stables. When she was in the glums, it was the best place for her.

Thoughts of the cost alone nearly gave her the vapors.

Their servants had been outfitted with new livery, with additional help hired for the event, many of whom were at this moment cleaning and polishing Woodbine's best crystal, china, and silver. New sheet music was purchased for the pianoforte, as were fresh decks of cards, new games, and costumes for home theatricals. The ball itself required musicians, yet more food, and endless beeswax candles to light the long evening.

Fishing tackle, shooting supplies, and even a baccarat table had been purchased with seats for seven, a professional dealer hired from White's. All for Prinny, who loved nothing more than a game of chance.

The ladies, mostly separated from the men during the day, engaged in what Maman had loved—crafts. Lucy had even suggested a dedicated craft room, where the women could do needlework, paint watercolors, or even glue flowers to hats. While Rose was awful at many womanly arts, she enjoyed painting and knitting. She hoped Mrs. Fitzherbert would be inclined to take part, for it was imperative she spend time with the woman.

Rose had done her best to design country outings to popular

prospects and the area's local places of interest, as well as lawn bowls and shuttlecock, two pastimes permitted for a lady's "delicate" sensibilities.

Such hogwash.

If she were truthful, and Rose liked to think she was, none of that, not even her distasteful hostess duties, was what had brought her low.

Rhys was gone, and she missed him. He had disappeared two days earlier, along with Angus, on what he called a secret mission for the ball. He had been quite sly about his purpose, unlike his usual self, which only heightened her curiosity.

A dire thought intruded. Had their feverish preparations and the looming possibility of his reinstatement sent him into the woods? To a camp much like the one at Ravenscroft? To safety and solace where he could ease his mind and emotions?

Rose finished binding off, folded the shawl, and replaced it in her brocade bag, pleased she was nearly done.

Rhys had been doing so well of late and hadn't gone off since their arrival at Woodbine. Yet here they were, two days before the prince and Wellington's arrival, with Rhys on a "mission."

No time for worry. Between arranging flowers, ordering more wine, and having a new felt laid on the billiards table, Rose was full up. And yet she missed him terribly.

Roddy trotted over, pressing his cold nose to hers. She wrapped her arms around the colt's strong neck and pressed her cheek to his warm coat. The thought of Roddy's loss troubled her deeply.

Dolce nickered, and she reached out a hand to pet the filly.

Neither Susannah nor Lucy knew where Rhys had gone, and he had not taken Porter. Perhaps Rhys' valet knew his mission. She would speak with him.

Rose gave Roddy a final scratch, Dolce a last pat, and strode to the house in search of Porter.

Until she was waylaid.

And waylaid again.

And again.

Several hours later, about to descend the stairs, Rose found Susannah hovering at the bottom, requesting she take a final look at the archery bows. Rose was ready to scream, yet she smiled, and said, "Of course."

The bows gleamed. Made from red elm and maple, they shone on the wall, all in apparent good health. But Rose removed and inspected each one when her attention was drawn to a commotion in the front hall. Rose quickly replaced the final bow on its rack and bustled to address the latest disaster awaiting her.

Rhys! He stood in the entryway, wrestling a large piece of equipment comprising glass tubes, metal, and what looked like iron valves.

He was back and safe, and he looked none the worse for wear. Angus stood beside him, along with two men she did not recognize.

Rose wanted to run to the man, but she was still out of sorts with him.

Rhys spotted her, and his eyes lit. He took great care handing his burden off to Angus. Then he strode to her, wrapping her in a fierce hug.

"I have missed you, Rosie," he said. "Is all well with you?"

"Harrumph. You vanished for two days, and I have been frantic with worry."

"Worry? About what?" he said. "I did not vanish, but went on a very specific errand with Angus."

"Your *secret mission.*" Her eyes burned with those loathsome tears, a combination of anger and relief. She blinked them back, her worry dissipating.

"Sweetheart." He kissed the top of her head. "I am sorry you were concerned. I promise, no more secret missions."

"You'd best not!" Her chuckle sounded watery. "I am a pillock and apologize for my ill temper."

Then he kissed her with passion, and she answered. To be in his arms once again was heaven.

When they parted, his arm remained tight around her waist.

"Wait until you have seen what and who I brought!" he said with great enthusiasm.

Rhys left his hat and coat with the butler and drew Rose into his study, seating them on the sofa before the fireplace. They spent a few delightful moments sharing kisses, but when Rose went to take it further, her hand sliding across his thigh, Rhys pulled back.

"I shall explain all," he said, kissing her palm. "Our prince has interesting tastes, particularly for the unusual."

Rose sighed, resting her head on his shoulder. "Do I not know it? I recall when he personally opened the coffin of Charles I and had the head examined."

"I was overseas, but read about that strange occurrence. He's certainly prone to odd starts." He grinned. "His latest infatuation is called laughing gas."

"Laughing gas?" she said, snuggling closer.

"A gentleman named Humphry Davy discovered it."

"I have heard of Mr. Davy. A scientist, yes?"

"A serious one, but after the discovery of the gas, many in the *ton* have taken it up, inhaling it as a party sport."

"What does it do?" she said. "How does it work?"

"You fill a large silk bag with the gas and then inhale. It confounds your senses, similar to drink, but I was told it feels not quite the same. I have instructed the staff to set aside a room for its use."

"I guess that could be entertaining." Rose was most skeptical.

"Oddly enough, once you stop inhaling the stuff, your senses return to normal, your body yours once more. A silly party trick. Nothing more. The prince will be in raptures."

"We definitely want the prince in raptures."

A wisp of concern passed over his eyes. "We do. His favorable mood will work for us in the crises to come with your cousin."

Rose stroked his cheek. If he ever discovered her plan, he would not be so amenable. "Who was the other gentleman?

"Davy's great friend, Coleridge."

"Samuel Taylor? The poet?"

"The very same. He often assists Davy in his experiments."

"And Coleridge is *here*? The man who wrote *The Rime of the Ancient Mariner* and 'Frost at Midnight'?"

"Just so."

"Oh, my!"

"Would you like to meet them and see the device?"

"Very much!"

THIRTY-SEVEN

With Angus' and the staff's help, Rose scrambled to rearrange the breakfast room for Dr. Davy and his nitrous oxide contraption. Additional chairs, an assortment of drinks, and other needs requested by Davy were supplied. The whole idea seemed frivolous.

Then again, Prinny enjoyed frivolous entertainments.

So it surprised her on speaking to Davy and Coleridge that both men believed the gas expanded consciousness and was a metaphysical breakthrough. Rose may have caught Davy's, "The synthesis of the gas and its effect on animals and animal tissue is profound." Most of his subsequent words flew by her, as Rose was rather too fascinated with Coleridge and his work.

Both men were said to be geniuses, with Coleridge's erudition immense. Davy bore a more conventional mien, a man of exuberance and quick wit. The poet, wide-bodied with a light complexion, had large, soft eyes that commanded attention.

Neither talked down to her, impressing her further.

"Would you consider reciting something for me, Mr. Coleridge?" she said.

"I would be pleased to do so," he said with a smile.

"*In Xanadu did Kubla Khan*
A stately pleasure-dome decree:
Where Alph, the sacred river, ran
Through caverns measureless to man
Down to a sunless sea."

"Oh, my!" Rose said. "How beautiful and mysterious. Has it been published?"

"'Kubla Khan' will be published later this year," he said with a chuckle. "Though I wrote the thing decades ago."

"I shall purchase many copies, sir."

He smiled. "Good for me."

"And me!" Rose said.

"Tell her what you are working on, Humphrey," Coleridge said.

With a blush, Davy explained his idea for a lamp that would not ignite a fire in the mines.

"A light that will illuminate, but not catch fire?" she said.

"Yes," Davy said. "Thus, keeping miners safe from fire and explosions."

"I cannot imagine how that is possible."

Coleridge chimed in. "Humphry can. He is a wizard. He *will* accomplish it."

"Soon, I hope." Davy clapped a hand on his friend's shoulder.

Rhys went to the contraption, and, filling the silk bag with Coleridge's aid, inhaled. Rose had no desire to test it herself, but Angus looked as if he might.

Susannah entered, a smile wreathing her face, which surprised Rose, knowing her sister busy in the orangery. Even more surprising, both Coleridge and Davy moved to speak with her as if they were old friends.

Rose was gripped from behind and twirled. "Oh!"

A grinning Rhys stared back at her. The gas had obviously affected a change, as he pulled her close and initiated a sloppy kiss in front of Davy, Coleridge, Angus, and Susannah! When his firm hold finally loosened, his grin turned lopsided.

"Sorry, Rosie, but I simply had to. Your lips..." Her stoic husband blushed.

Angus's eye roll deepened Rhys' blush, and he shook his head, then released her, clearing his throat. Davy and Coleridge continued their animated chat with Susannah while Rhys peered at the machine.

"That," Rhys said to her after a pause, "was interesting."

"Indeed, my lord." Rose's effort to hide her smile failed. She giggled.

When Susannah left, Rose excused herself and surreptitiously followed her sister to the orangery, easing the door closed behind her.

"Susannah?"

"Rose?" Her sister donned her garden gloves.

"My curiosity has gotten the better of me." She lifted an orange and sniffed, feigning a casual demeanor. When she finally peered at Susannah, mirth lit her sister's eyes.

"You are wondering about Samuel and Humphry," Susannah said.

"Yes!" Rose said. "You seemed to know them well, and I confess I am curious."

"They are friends." Susannah bit her lip. "Though I should not have been so familiar with them, as I have given away the game."

"Come." Rose drew Susannah to the carved bench.

Her sister flopped down and grimaced. "I am pleased it was you who noticed, and not Rhys or Angus."

"So tell me, how did you come by a friendship with the poet and the doctor?"

Susannah fidgeted with her overskirt. "Oh, devil it, you will think me mad as a hatter."

"Possibly!" Rose laughed. "But I have a fondness for mad hatters."

"You see..." She clenched her hands. "I have written a novel."

"A novel? That is quite marvelous!"

"The idea came from an old tale about how a magical knife thrown by an ancient lord or laird, I am not sure which, always returned to him. The myth says the knife is here, at Woodbine."

"Could that be possible?" Rose said.

Susannah's eyes flashed. "I have been looking! So far, no luck."

"Fascinating. When did you begin to write?"

A peal of laughter. "Your question should be, when did I *not* write, for it feels as if I have always done so. Though I was only one, I became deeply distressed when Father banished Thomasina. My sadness did not abate, so as I grew, I began to write stories, tales that helped me ease my mind and heart. I never stopped, and several years ago, after I began my novel, I wrote to Ann Radcliffe and Maria Edgeworth, the latter introducing me via letter to Mr. Coleridge. He has been a great help, as has Mr. Walter Scott. Mrs. Radcliffe never answered, unfortunately."

"Mrs. Radcliffe's novels shine a light to so many social and personal ills, do you not think?" Rose took Susannah's hand and squeezed.

"I do, but I understand she has become a recluse, though I do not know why."

"What of the woman who wrote *Pride and Prejudice*? Have you corresponded with her as well?"

Susannah leaned close and whispered. "Yes. A bit. Her name is Jane Austen."

"I adore her novels."

"As do I," Susannah said. "But the lady is most retiring. You must tell no one."

"I shall seal my lips."

Susannah played with a fallen leaf, turning it this way and that. She dropped it, watching as it fluttered to the ground, then took

Rose's hand. "Writing is no longer a pastime, but has become essential to my life. I cannot explain it."

"Perhaps as horses are to mine?"

"Yes!" Susannah smiled. "Just like that."

"Do Rhys or Patr—"

"Lud, no. They would be horrified."

"Why?" Rose said. "Rhys would not object. I'm sure of it."

Susannah shrugged. "Perhaps. I rather fear exposing myself to the two of them. Both are great lovers of art and literature and, well, they might laugh."

"I take your point. I shall not laugh, for I want to read your manuscript."

Susannah grimaced, standing. "We shall see, sister."

Rose stood as well. "I hope so, for if so many literary lights enjoy your work, it must be fine indeed."

"Perhaps." Susannah sighed. "Or perhaps they are being kind to a marquess' sister."

"Humph. Did you tell these literary lights you were Rhys' sister when you first wrote to them?"

"Well, no, but..."

"All right, then," Rose said. "I understand your hesitation, and I will not press you. But I am a great admirer of Coleridge and Radcliffe. Please know your work will be in safe hands with me."

Susannah bussed her cheek. "I do. I am just..."

"It is all right, dear sister. Whenever you are ready, so am I."

After her brief respite with the laughing gas and Susannah, Rose returned to work, praying they would be ready in time.

A day later, the weekend had commenced and was progressing well, thank all the heavens. Rose managed to evade being alone with the prince, Wellington, or the odious Cedric, though she had no trouble chatting them up in a group. She wished it to stay that way until the ball.

At dinner that evening, Cedric was in fine form, passing gossipy *on dits* to anyone who would listen, his dinner companions seemingly entertained.

Now an earl, he sat near the table's head, only the Duke of Devonshire, Wellington, the prince, Mrs. Fitzherbert, and Rhys taking precedence, though they had broken convention by seating Rose to Rhys' left and Mrs. Fitzherbert across from the prince.

Unfortunate, as during the dessert course, Cedric brandished a bluebird handkerchief, flapping it for all to see.

Rose owned many, but she did not like the look in Cedric's eye when he grinned her way.

"See this handkerchief?" Cedric said to the table. "Beautiful white-diamond embroidery, quite obviously a lady's, and smeared with a dark-reddish substance that could be blood."

"Why are you waving it about, Lord Fielding?" Susannah leaned in to get a closer look.

Cedric raised a brow. "Because a maid at Fielding Manor handed it to me, saying she found it near the late earl's remains."

As his words were repeated down the line, the chatter died to silence.

"I find that quite shocking," Rose said in a steady voice. "I was the one who found the earl, and I do not recall seeing any handkerchief."

Cedric winked at her, of all things. "Perhaps it lay beneath him, and only came to light when he was moved."

Rose remembered using her handkerchief—was it a bluebird?—to wipe the earl's blood from his ear. She had stuffed it in her reticule and later burned it all. Hadn't she? She recalled tossing her reticule into the fire, but had she placed the soiled handkerchief inside? Or had she left the dratted linen at Fielding? She could not bring to mind those events, which were fuzzy in the extreme.

"Are there any identifiers, Fielding?" Rhys raised a brow.

"Hard to tell, Ravenscroft," Cedric said. "It is quite worn, the stitches fraying, and spattered with blood. Why would a lady's handkerchief be blood-spattered, for the earl was not bleeding?"

Those last words sent "oohs" and "ahhs" around the table.

Rose slipped a piece of cake into her mouth, forcing herself not to look at Rhys.

She was sure the handkerchief could not be hers. Almost sure. But if not, whose was it?

Bloody hell.

"I cannot remember," she said to Rhys later that evening as they prepared for bed. "I told you."

He was pacing the confines of their bedchamber, which only increased her worry.

Rhys halted before her and rested his hands at her waist. "I know. Forgive me."

"I simply do not see how it could be mine. And yet..."

"Nothing on the linen indicates that it was yours, correct?"

"I do not believe so. I most often embroider pansies and other flowers on them, rather than my initials." She chewed her lip. "Though I do own quite a few blue ones. I *think* I had a bluebird with me that day, but my memories are more like a dream, or rather a nightmare."

He pulled her close, running a soothing hand across her hair. "It will be all right. Knowing Cedric, he is using the thing to become the center of attention. Nothing more."

Rose prayed he was right.

The following day, with luncheon to be served in an hour, Rose escaped her guests to finalize her plan, then went in search of Mrs. Fitzherbert. According to Lucy, the lady often sat alone reading in the wildflower garden for the hour preceding the meal.

The sky was cloudy, the air biting her skin as Rose walked the garden path with its riot of blooming wildflowers. True summer's arrival. Most of the guests were resting before the meal, though some of the men were on a hunt in the far wood.

Around a bend, Rose spotted the elegant woman sitting on the cedar bench, a red leather-bound book in hand.

"Mrs. Fitzherbert." Rose approached and curtsied before the woman.

The prince's paramour looked up with a hint of a smile before putting her book aside. She stood and dipped a deep curtsy. "My lady."

"Please, sit," Rose said. "I hope you are enjoying the weekend."

"Very much so," Mrs. Fitzherbert said. "But I detect this is not a social visit?"

A canny soul, Rose decided, taking a seat beside the prince's mistress or wife, depending on whose story you believed. "Am I that transparent?"

Mrs. Fitzherbert chuckled, and it was a charming sound. "Oh, yes, I am afraid so, my dear."

Rose shook her head. "You are very discerning, and you are correct. I do wish a favor."

"You mean now, dear lady?" she said.

"Yes, soon. But not one without recompense."

Mrs. Fitzherbert lifted the book, smoothing her hands across the supple leather to peek at Rose beneath lowered lids. "Child, you intrigue me."

"I was hoping to do so," Rose said.

"I cannot imagine a single thing that would require a boon from me."

"We shall see," Rose said brightly, praying, hoping against hope her scheme met with success. "Arjuna!"

The imposing stable hand appeared holding Lightning Rod's lead line, the showman colt prancing as they halted before the two women. Arjuna bowed while Roddy sniffed the flowers on Mrs. Fitzherbert's bodice. The lady smiled.

The colt stretched his neck and nipped a pansy.

"Oh, dear!" Rose said.

Arjuna tugged Roddy's lead, moving him.

Mrs. Fitzherbert's eyes had gone wide at the site of the unique colt, and she now laughed uproariously, then tapped Roddy on the nose. "Those are not for your delectation, sir!"

Lightning Rod arched his neck and preened.

"He is quite the fellow," Mrs. Fitzherbert said, her eyes glued to the colt.

"That he is," Rose said. "High-spirited with a big heart, but sweet as pie. The marquess and I planned to raise him and race him, and hoped to use him as a foundation stud if he proved worthy. I have no doubt he will!"

"'Planned' in the past tense, Lady Ravenscroft?"

"Would you like to examine him more thoroughly?"

"Oh, no." The prince's consort stroked Roddy's neck, and he nickered. "I have seen enough."

"Thank you, Arjuna," Rose said.

The man bowed and led Lightning Rod away, the colt dancing down the path as if he were in the show ring. Or leaving on a great adventure, one in which Rose would not play a part. Emotion flooded her. He and Dolce were tied to both her and Rhys. They'd made a vow. A promise.

One she must break.

"You have shown me a powerful incentive, Lady Ravenscroft," said Mrs. Fitzherbert, her fingers moving over the book, the leather shiny with use. "What is it you wish to ask of me?"

Rose breathed deep and mentally crossed her fingers. "His Royal Highness and the Duke of Wellington wish for Lord Ravenscroft to return to the duke's staff and journey to India. I would like you to convince the prince to abandon his pressure on Rhys to rejoin."

Mrs. Fitzherbert's eyes narrowed. "You surprise me, my lady. I was sure you would ask me something regarding the rumors circulating about your father's death."

Rose shook her head. "No. They are baseless and my cousin Cedric is a blowhard. He can puff and huff, but there is nothing to indicate anything other than natural causes regarding my father's passing." Even as she said the word "father," a vile taste filled her mouth.

"What makes you think my words will hold sway with His Royal Highness?"

Now that was just absurd. "I believe they do, Mrs. Fitzherbert, and as such, I beg your help."

"Your major general is renowned, his work for England exceptional."

All true. Rose's emotions were getting the better of her, and she clasped her hands tight. All of this politeness and dissembling were exhausting. From everything Rose knew of the woman, she was a sincere and kind-hearted person who deeply loved the prince.

"I love my husband very much, ma'am," she said. "Were he to return to service, he would not fare well."

"Why do you say that, my dear?"

"I know him, as he knows me, and it would be deleterious to his health. I do not exaggerate."

"I can see you believe what you say," Mrs. Fitzherbert said.

Rose remained silent.

"And," Mrs. Fitzherbert continued. "Is that glorious colt meant to persuade me to your cause?"

"He would be a gift," Rose said. "A thank you, for aiding me in this. I do not embellish when I say that Lord Ravenscroft would fare poorly were he to rejoin Wellington's staff."

"If that is the case, what makes you think Lord Ravenscroft will agree to Wellington and the prince's request?"

Rose's eyes held Mrs. Fitzherbert's, allowing the woman to see her pain. "Me. His Royal Highness and the duke will threaten me, and Rhys will do anything to keep me safe."

"I see," Mrs. Fitzherbert said.

The bell for luncheon gonged.

Mrs. Fitzherbert stood. "I am quite famished from our discussion and reading *Emma*."

"*Emma!*" Rose said. "A wonderful book."

"It might be my favorite amongst our unknown woman's scribblings."

"Oh, I understand why, though *Sense and Sensibility* remains first in my heart."

"As does your husband, it appears. I will think on your proposal and you shall know my answer the night of the ball."

The ball. "But..."

"At the ball, Lady Ravenscroft."

THIRTY-EIGHT

The ball was still hours away, and Rose had not heard a peep from Mrs. Fitzherbert. She had hoped the lady would respond beforehand, but Rose was out of luck.

She was supposed to be resting, as were all the female guests. But a feeling nagged at her, a feeling that within the carnival surrounding Rhys' return to service, something didn't fit, as if she were trying to squeeze a puzzle piece into the wrong cutout.

Earlier this morning, Rhys had been closeted in his study with the prince and Wellington for a good two hours.

She could guess the outcome of said discussion and hoped Mrs. Fitzherbert would accept Rose's offer and solve the problem.

If not, perhaps she and Rhys should leave for the continent. Not a terrible solution.

But what was nagging her?

Of course. Cedric's odd behavior.

If her cousin spotted her walking down a hall, he would turn and go the opposite way. When the ladies were on the archery field, with Cedric escorting Lady Ellington in their direction, all appeared unexceptional. Until his eyes lit on Rose. Cedric bid the lady adieu, did an about face, and returned to the manor house at a swift pace. Finally, when he learned Rose planned to play croquet, he even passed on the match. And Ceddie loved croquet.

Cedric was avoiding her, which naturally made her curious. Was he ashamed for spreading tales about her?

The man seldom felt shame, no matter the gossip he recounted. Perhaps his avoidance had another cause, a more singular one.

Rose vowed to run him down, which, by happenstance, occurred far sooner than expected.

When there wasn't a birth, the mare's barn represented peace and calm, and where Rose had retreated for a few moments of relief from the chaos, for a burning fury had risen within her. Rhys had donned his stoic demeanor, and she knew exactly what that meant —Wellington and the prince had succeeded in getting Rhys to resume his military career.

Either she left the manor, or she would explode, her inappropriate outburst surely ending in disaster.

Roddy and Dolce's stall was large and abundant with fresh straw, and the mare's barn was prohibited to guests without a Woodbine escort. A perfect setting for a discussion with the foals. True, they did not contribute a great deal to the conversation, but she found their presence soothing as she chattered on.

A single set of footsteps sounded on the cobbles and Rose went silent. Most likely a stableboy. Ever wary, she crawled on hands and knees to peek through a knothole to see who was roaming the barn.

The footsteps were soft, unlike her nerves, her temper aflame at the prince and Wellington's machinations.

Ah. The feet came into view. Black shoes tied with silver bows, the legs covered with heavily clocked stockings, the breeches puce.

Of all the guests, only one person would wear such outlandish apparel in a barn or anywhere but a ballroom, for that matter.

Rose popped to her feet, opened the stall door, and stepped out to see the shocked face of Fielding's new Earl.

"Cousin!" Cedric said. "Eh, wot? You startled me."

She offered him a wide smile. "As was my intention, Cedric."

"Why, in blazes?"

Dolce and Roddy gamboled from their stall to prance around the disgruntled earl.

"Get them away from me!" he said. "They'll dirty my new breeches and stockings, ones I had specially made for this evening's ball."

"What are you doing in the barn in the first place?"

"Eh, wot? Lady Darlington has taken to following me. The widow is determined, and I need to avoid her attentions."

Rose laughed. "What a conundrum!"

Dolce butted her head against the puce satin.

"Stop it!" Cedric swatted at her, never touching her with his pristine white gloves.

"Yes, they will make a mess of you," she said with a faux sigh. "They are experts at it."

"Get them away!" He flailed at the foals.

To the foals, Cedric was playing a grand game, and the pair began to prance and rear, pawing the air with their tiny hooves.

"Answer my questions," she said. "And I will see you safe. Or should I say, your clothes safe?"

"Really, Rosamund!"

"I am serious."

"All right, damn you," he said, pushing at Roddy's rump, which had brushed his yellow tailcoat. "Ask away."

"Why did you voice those accusations to the *ton* about the late earl's death?" Rose said.

"Because I found it disturbing. As did his valet, who came to me with questions and concerns."

"Flummery!" Rose said. "Where did that handkerchief actually come from?"

"I told you."

"On the ground by the earl. What was the maid's name? I will speak with her."

"I don't know!" He shoved Roddy. "Florence. Jane. Mary."

"Do describe this maid," she said. "You must recall her, at least!"

"I do not!"

"You do not because you made it all up." His guilty look gave her hope. She'd seen it often enough as a child when the earl's late brother and Cedric came for a visit. "Tell me, what really lies behind your accusations, dear Ceddie."

"You daren't call me that. I am now an earl. How can you possibly have the effrontery to question my motives?" He fussed with his pink brocade waistcoat.

As if on cue, Dolce thumped a hoof onto his left shoe.

"Get them gone!" He shoved Dolce off him, then brushed away the dirt she'd left on his shoe.

"The truth, cousin," Rose said, crossing her arms. "I want the truth. You did not give a farthing about His Lordship when he lived, and even less about his valet. I do not believe a maid found that handkerchief, either. I want the truth." Rose suspected he made it all up.

"I distinctly remember carrying a white handkerchief that day," she continued. "One with daisies and violets embroidered on it." A lie, but he didn't know that. "I wonder to whom it belongs."

Roddy bumped into him, and Cedric teetered. Rose grabbed his arm and set him straight.

"That was close," she said as he huffed and puffed. "Well?"

"Yes. All right. Put these creatures in their stall and I will give you the truth."

Long minutes elapsed as she wrangled the two miscreants back into their stall, giving each a peppermint, then she returned her focus to Cedric. Who was exiting the barn at a rapid pace.

Leave it to him to skip out on an agreement. What a worm.

Rose caught up with him in a trice and grabbed the tails on his coat, hauling him to a stop.

She wanted to throttle him, say what a base creature he was, and how she hated her association with the name Fielding.

Reason prevailed, and she said none of those things. "Well?"

He fumed, but finally sighed. "Eh, wot? Don't you see, my dear, I needed the money."

"The *money*?"

"I am being paid a fat lot of pounds to perform the charade."

His chagrinned look infuriated her further. "You were *paid*? By *whom*?"

"A fine sum. Enough to allow me to purchase that pair of high-steppers I have longed for."

"You betrayed me? Rhys? For a pair of horses? How could you? "

He had the grace to look abashed. "I was doing it for the Great Man, or so I believed, the whole elaborate ploy intended to force Ravenscroft to bend to Prinny and Wellington's will."

"In truth, you do not believe Fielding wrongfully died?"

Cedric sat on a bench and scrubbed his face.

"Cedric!"

"Of course not. I care not one whit about the old earl's passing. I merely made a lucrative bargain with one of Wellington's aids. End of story."

"At the Duke's request?"

Cedric fussed with his cravat, plumping the linen. "I assumed so."

"*Assumed*? Who paid you, Ceddie?" she asked, though she believed she knew the answer.

"I cannot," he said. "Do you not see? He will... He made threats when I did not wish to continue."

What a coward. She snagged her cousin's eyes. "Rhys will do worse if I tell him of this refusal to answer. *I* will do worse!"

"Pennworth," he blurted out, swiping a handkerchief across his face. "You know, that top-lofty brigadier on Wellington's staff."

Rose should have expected the snake would rear his ugly head again. "I do not believe for one minute that either Wellington, or the prince, had anything to do with the scheme."

He tugged on his waistcoat, straightening it.

"You do not either, do you?" Rose loomed over him.

His nostrils flared. "Possibly not."

"Idiot! The viscount is no longer on the duke's staff." She waved her hands, furious. "In fact, he is not with the military *at all*."

Cedric cleared his throat. "Eh, wot?"

"Cedric!"

"I tried to renege. I *did*. He would hear none of it and insisted I continue or he would kill me! He is mad, I tell you. That light in his eyes. Insane."

"*Where* did you agree to this? On the Continent? In London? Where?"

"London."

Rhys must learn of this posthaste, with Cedric's confession adding yet another complexity to the weekend. To their lives. She damned Pennworth to hell.

Rhys stood by a potted palm as the ball swirled around him, an island of calm in a turbulent sea. Decision made. Problem solved.

Rose was safe.

He breathed deep. Having the inevitable arrive felt liberating.

His darling wife was an able hostess, and he watched her flit here and there, making sure the musicians had drinks, checking and relighting candles, and rectifying any disorder in the card or other designated rooms.

A smile twitched his lips at his brother as the ladies swarmed Patrick, buzzing in and out like bees to nectar. Thankfully, as a wed man, Rhys had not been plagued, though he'd signed several dance cards and twirled the ladies around the ballroom.

At present, Thomasina whirled the room with Angus, and his heart warmed. Sina was dancing, something he never thought to see in this lifetime. He would bet good money that Rose had taught her the steps.

Though in mourning, Beatrice visited for the weekend, but she did not attend the ball, while Charlotte and Claire mingled and danced, Claire's discomfort obvious at partnering with Wellington. The great man had that effect on women. But as the dance progressed, it pleased Rhys to see Claire relax. Charlotte needed no relaxing, for she laughed and smiled at all the men who partnered with her...with the exception of Patrick. Most likely his sharp tongue had put up her back.

Over by the refreshments, Rosie was chatting with Susannah, both women stunning in their gowns, though his Rose outshone them all.

The urge to flee roiled through him. Would that he could, for the last thing he wanted was to be surrounded by their guests' applause when the prince announced his return.

He might as well be a mummer, a mere silent player, the men with true power taking the primary roles in the charade.

He'd fought until the bitter end. But the threat to Rose—even a marchioness could be jailed and hanged for murder—was too much, with Cedric flapping that damned handkerchief that forced him to capitulate.

Notes signaled the conclusion of the country dance, and soon the orchestra began another waltz. Rhys approached Rose, bowing over her hand and kissing her white glove.

"Come dance with me, Rosie?" A poignant echo of that evening at Almack's when he'd first seen his love after eight long years.

Staring into that beloved face, Rhys found reenlisting was a minor price to pay for her safety. His lady was everything.

"I would be honored, my lord." Rose smiled, making him want to kiss her right here, right now. He did not, but, oh, how he wished to.

He winged out an arm, Rose laid her hand atop his forearm, and they proceeded to the dance floor, her skirts trailing behind. But her hand on his forearm clutched him in a death grip.

They glided into the waltz and he pulled her close, closer than was appropriate, but he cared not.

"What troubles you, Rose?" he said as he whirled her about the room.

She blinked several times. "Oh, just nerves, is all."

He chuckled, and she flushed. "I know you too well, my dear. What is it?"

"I hoped to have a surprise for you tonight, here, at the ball, but so far, it has not materialized."

"The night is far from over, love. Your surprise might yet appear."

"True!" she said brightly. "The night is young."

The prince and Mrs. Fitzherbert took to the floor. The man was a fine dancer, as was his lady—from whom he allegedly was estranged. Not by the looks of it, given the nibbles he gave her neck.

As the princely couple twirled by, Rose stiffened and it appeared she was trying to catch the prince or Mrs. Fitzherbert's eye.

The waltz ended. "Would you care for a turn around the balcony, love?"

"Yes!" Rose said. "No. No, I had better not."

"Greetings, friends!" The prince leapt onto the orchestra's dais. "I have an exciting announcement!"

Wellington stepped up beside the Prince, yet many eyes turned to Rhys. Word must have gotten out, and most were eager to see his reaction. Most, but not all.

Susannah looked severe, her brow furrowed. Angus was not so sanguine, his eyes burning with anger.

Rose paled, squeezing his arm. "You realize I will accompany you always, do you not? I have no intention of letting my husband gallivant around the world without me."

Her voice had wobbled, but her back was arrow straight, her head held high.

Hard to picture his Rosie quitting her beloved horses and following the drum. Neither of them wished to leave, and both knew it.

CHAPTER
THIRTY-NINE

Rose was devastated, but she refused, *refused*, to show her upset to the crowd or to the men flanking her, Rhys and Patrick, both standing stiff-spined, hands clasped behind steel-straight backs.

The prince, ever the dramatist, strutted upon the dais as he drew out the silence, and opened his mouth to speak.

A footman leapt upon the platform and whispered in the prince's ear.

All the while, with midnight fast approaching, the ballroom had grown increasingly crowded as guests entered from the various other rooms to hear the prince speak. Rose surveyed the sea of guests, as even more crowded inside, though she noted the absence of Thomasina and Mrs. Fitzherbert.

It mattered little, for soon all would be lost.

No. Her husband was a strong man, had survived battles, both mental and physical. With her joining him, she might soften the mental anguish he often experienced. Or so she hoped. As children, there was never a plan they concocted without the other's aid. Never a circumstance they failed to escape. Never a mood the other failed to lighten.

His posting to India could be like one of those romps, only darker and with higher stakes.

Why Wellington and Prinny discounted Rhys' reluctance was incomprehensible. His supposed friends were no friends whatsoever.

Murmurs rose from the arch near the grand hall, though she recalled nothing designated for the midnight hour. The whispers grew to an excited pitch, and then, like a calm before a thunderous storm, the ballroom hushed.

Patrick leaned close. "What devilry have you planned, Lady Ravenscroft?"

"None that I can think of." She could use some devilry right now.

A "clip-clop" resounded on the stairs—hooves on marble. She turned to her husband. "Rhys?"

"I have no idea, Rosie."

The mass of guests parted, revealing a sight that made her blink. With a thunk, Rose closed her open mouth.

Thomasina, accompanied by Mrs. Fitzherbert, led Lightning Rod into the ballroom and through the crowd.

That silly colt, draped in an embroidered HRH blanket, knew he was the focus of attention, for he pranced, head high, as the trio drew near the prince and Wellington.

Roddy, catching sight of Rose and Rhys, tried to beeline toward them. Sina restrained him, but not easily, the colt gaining muscle by the hour. What a magnificent stallion he would become.

Prinny dropped from the dais and walked toward the trio. "And what have we here, my dear Mrs. Fitzherbert?"

Mrs. Fitzherbert's smile grew, her eyes flashing with humor. "A gift. From our hosts."

Rhys did a double take, his forearm turning to iron.

Prinny petted the colt's neck to the accompaniment of Roddy's wickers, then circled the foal. "He *is* truly magnificent."

Mrs. Fitzherbert nodded. "I had to bring him to the ball so you could formally announce his arrival as a possible foundation stud in your stable."

Prinny's eyes widened.

His lady went on tiptoe to whisper in his ear. Prinny's eyes widened further. He shook his head, Mrs. Fitzherbert whispered another something, and after a lengthy pause, the prince nodded.

Thomasina held out the lead to the prince, and His Royal Highness walked the colt in a circle as the gasping crowd made way.

"Is he not stunning?" Prinny boomed to the guests.

Not to Wellington, or so it seemed, for his face was an odd mixture of fury and amusement. The duke knew exactly what had happened, and while it obviously angered him that Rhys would not be rejoining, his keen sense of humor found diversion in the turn of events.

The prince stopped parading before Rhys and Rose. "I thank you for this magnificent gift. Any chance of acquiring the filly?"

Through gritted teeth, Rhys said, "I am afraid we must keep her, Your Highness, for her exceptional qualities will be of great advantage to her foals here at Woodbine."

"Of course," the prince said, nodding sagely. "Two such gifts would be excessive."

The prince, Mrs. Fitzherbert, and Thomasina led Roddy from the ballroom, and the release of tension made Rose dizzy.

Rhys was safe. He would not go to war again.

Her husband banded an arm around her waist. "Shall we repair to the library, my lady?"

"But our guests, the ball."

His breath was warm on her ear as he leaned close. "*Now.*"

Rhys closed the door gently, turned the key, then whirled to face her, hands fisted at his side. "What have you done?"

Rose clutched the folds of her skirts to keep her hands from shaking. She notched her chin. "What I had to do to keep you safe."

"That colt means more to us than simply a horse."

"How so?" she said.

"He is…" Rhys frowned. "Or *was* ours. Both of ours. He was to be *our* stallion, perhaps for a new breeding line. Roddy and Dolce reflect our partnership as a man and a woman, as a husband and a wife. Our *bond*. You have broken my trust, Rosamund."

"Oh, rubbish." Rose flapped a hand. "All well and good, and I do not disagree, but you matter more to me than any vows or promises. You are everything, Rhys, and your return to war would kill your soul."

He crossed his arms. "My *soul* is in fine order, thank you, my lady. Do you think me such a weakling that I—"

"Of course not. You are not weak in any respect. But your kind and gentle heart has been gravely wounded."

Rhys snorted. "Do you recall your anger at my deception with trapping Pennworth? How is what you have done any different?"

She opened her mouth to reply, but he continued.

"No, this *is* different. It is more."

"It certainly is not!"

He raked a hand through his hair. "Think of what we went through birthing those foals. Of our love for them, and we *do* love them. You would blithely give one away without even showing me the courtesy of a discussion?"

"There was nothing blithe about what I did." Rose waved her arms. "You can huff and puff all you like, Rhys Lansdowne, but I made the right choice. One I would make again and again. Thomasina thought so, as well."

"And who else knew of this bargain you did not condescend to share with me?"

Rose was tired. From the ball preparations. From the fear of seeing Rhys dragged into war. And now from his anger, which clubbed her like an anvil. How could he not see?

"I regret you do not approve," she said. "But I would not undo my efforts. Not in a million years."

"You have sabotaged us, Rosie. Done us in."

"And you are being melodramatic!"

He stormed out, his words ringing in Rose's ears.

Rose awakened the following morning around noon with the suspicion that Rhys had flown. He certainly hadn't shared their bed —holding her close, nuzzling her, loving her—but had taken himself off to assuage his wounded pride and hurt feelings.

How could he not comprehend her choice had been a wise one?

She nuzzled Rhys' pillow, his scent drowning her in what ifs.

Rhys had most likely left for...somewhere. His camp, Ravenscroft, or perhaps Outer Mongolia.

She shouldn't care and punched his pillow. "Damn you for being such a prickly pear!"

"M'lady?"

The maid, come with her breakfast, was now tossing back the curtains to give sight to the gray day, the pelting rain a funereal dirge.

"Where is Lucy, Stella?" she said.

"She's taken them pups of yours for a walk, m'lady."

They would all get soaked. "His lordship?"

Stella finished with the curtains and curtsied. "I've not seen him this morning."

So he was off. Good for him. Rose had a house party to orchestrate...in the rain. Mother of heaven.

Rose was shocked. And after the events of the past six months, it took a great deal to shock her. But Rhys had accomplished it.

He had not fled.

At least his body hadn't left, but the man who walked beside her into dinner—other than his physical appearance—resembled her husband very little. Rhys was not a voluble man, true, but he had become positively sepulchral.

Rose *had* managed to tell him what she'd learned from Cedric about Pennworth's machinations, but even that had not initiated any genuine conversation.

The few times Rhys did speak to her, he uttered banalities about the delicious pheasant or that he was heading out to train a new gelding or he was taking Isla and Bram for a walk—unaccompanied by her, of course. Lifeless words absent of any warmth or laughter or even anger.

The man was broody, and Rose was heartily sick of it.

Because she missed him, damn her soul, missed his smiles and laughter, his quips and comments. Missed his touches and affection, both delicate and fierce.

Now, what was she going to do about it?

The house party had ended, and Rhys couldn't believe he continued to behave like a perfect arse. He strode beneath the trees of the Devonshire home wood with the duke, uncaring of the drizzle. Angus walked alongside him, while Devonshire trailed behind.

Someone should kick him for acting thus. In his soul, Rhys knew Rosie had not considered vows or promises when she'd traded Lightning Rod for Rhys' freedom. She was only thinking of *him*. Something she did with unfailing regularity.

He had to get over this pique caused by his infernal pride.

Yes, Rose had bruised his dignity. He snorted.

What a useless thing, pride. He'd puffed up like a blowhard to rail at her.

"I had a devilish good time at your house party, Ravenscroft." Devonshire came up beside him, his gun slung over a shoulder.

By all accounts, their weekend had been a success. A roaring one, where His Royal Highness had repeatedly gotten tipsy on Davy's gas, with Lightning Rod the weekend's climax. Prinny had hugged Rhys, for Christ's sake.

Wellington had departed early, and he could not blame the duke. A prancing pony had foiled his quest. The absurdity made Rhys grin.

The twinge at Roddy's loss hurt, but he'd made far too much out of Rose's grand gesture. And it had been grand, for she loved the colt as much or more than he did.

"That Davy contraption was quite remarkable," Devonshire said. "Did you try the thing?"

"I did," Rhys said. "Once was enough."

"More than a wee bit compelling," Angus said. "Unlike spirits, when you cease inhaling the gas, you're sober again."

"Near instantly, much to my disappointment," Devonshire said. "I say, shall we hit the far wood? The day is clearing and pheasants abound."

Devonshire was shooting mad, and they'd had another fine day, though Rhys was tired of plucking birds from the sky, given the birds were deliberately released for their sporting pleasure.

"I must decline a visit to the far wood, Devonshire," Rhys said. "I have a mission for Angus."

"A mission!" said Devonshire. "Sounds intriguing."

Angus arched a brow.

"A *secret* mission, Your Grace."

"Ha!" Devonshire said, bowing to both men. "I will see you on the morrow then."

"If at all possible," Rhys said. "And I thank you for the invitation." Once he and Angus remounted, he turned Enbarr toward Woodbine.

"A mission?" Angus said.

"I wish you to go to Ravenscroft."

"Yer aff yer heid!" Angus said.

"I am not out of my mind," Rhys said. "I wish you to retrieve an important something, that *something* to be kept between you and me."

Angus rolled his eyes, but nodded.

Having given Angus his instructions, Rhys headed for home. Time to make things right with Rosie.

CHAPTER

FORTY

Unlike yesterday's downpour, the morning's drizzle had transformed to blue skies with but a light breeze. Rose inhaled the crisp air, a welcome respite from her glums.

Maybe a good dunking in the pond would bring Rhys to his senses.

Rather than dunk Rhys—such an appealing idea—Rose went in search of Sina. They had unfinished business.

Thomasina wasn't in the stables, according to Arjuna, who had been promoted to assistant stable master. Not only was he good with the horses, he got along well with the stable hands, a key point. She would bet Lucy was pleased.

Back at the manor, Rose walked to the fourth floor, which housed Thomasina's art studio. Next to horses, Sina loved to paint. Though she used mostly watercolors, she had graduated to oils on a few of her paintings, mostly of flowers.

Rose knocked before entering.

"Come in!" came the musical voice.

Sina sat before her easel, the subject of her watercolor a bowl of floating lilies.

"Sina!" Rose said. "That's lovely."

"Thank you, Rosie!" Sina returned to painting, moving her brush to dapple light on a flower. "Not like my Mama's, though."

Rose had seen Lady Ravenscroft's paintings, and they were exquisite. "Your art is yours and your mother's is hers. Each beautiful in its own right and each unique."

"I like that, Rose," Sina said.

"Might I discuss something with you?" Rose said.

"All right." Thomasina continued to paint.

"I want to talk about your mama."

Sina's eyes narrowed, and she laid down the brush, while Rose pulled over another straight-backed chair to sit beside her.

"Thomasina," Rose said. "I remember what your papa told you, and I am sure he meant well."

"No, he did not, Rose." Sina shook her head. "I do not think he liked me very much."

"I see. Um." Rose took Sina's hand. "What I speak is truth. You did not kill your mother."

"But Papa..."

"He was wrong. I know this from Rhys, who is older than you. Your mama lived for several years after you were taken to Woodbine."

"She did?"

Rose wound an arm around Thomasina's shoulder. "Rhys said your mother loved you and missed you very much."

"Really?" Sina smiled beatifically. "I remember her. I can see her so clear. But I can't hear her voice."

"You were very young when you left, but Rhys remembers. And so do Patrick and even Susannah. They all tell the same story, Sina. That she loved you and longed for you after you went away."

"I really did not kill her?"

"No, you really did not."

"Truly?" Tears sprang to her eyes, though she continued to smile.

"When you went away, your mama was in fine health." Maybe

hanging would do for the late marquess. Too bad he was already dead.

Sina picked up her paintbrush and began working on the lilies again, while tears covered her cheeks. She stared intently at the painting. "I am glad."

"So am I. Rhys told me how she would speak of you to your brothers and sister."

"Did she?" Sina brushed a stroke of gold across a lily's stamen. "I wish I could see her paintings again. Do you know where they are?"

"I don't, but let us ask Rhys. What do you say we see them together?"

Sina set down her brush and hugged Rose, whispering in her ear, "I would like that very much."

"So would I."

Bea, Charlotte, and Claire were leaving for Halafair, and Rose would miss them.

"Come back soon," she said as they donned their spencers for the trip ahead.

"We will, my dear," Bea said, cupping her cheek.

"Wait. I have a gift for you, Bea." Rose retrieved her brocade bag and lifted the newly blocked shawl she'd folded and tied with a green ribbon. "Happy birthday, dear Bea."

Her stepmama's eyes melted as she undid the bow and unfolded the piece, all three oohing and aahing. Bea lifted the shawl to her cheek. "So soft, yet so hardy, just like you, dear Rose. A beautiful gift of the hand. Thank you, daughter of my heart."

A thrill went through Rose, and she hugged them all. "Safe travels and please return soon!"

Later that afternoon, Cook had an issue with the dinner menu, and Rose was discussing alternatives to the quail when a footman found her with a message from Thomasina. Rose was needed in the foaling barn.

She quickly changed into her pantaloons, boots, and an old shirt to assist. Breeze's foal was early, too early.

"Thomasina!" Rose said as she entered the foaling barn.

Odd. The place felt empty except for a stable hand mucking out stalls. If Breeze was in labor, the barn would be abustle.

After asking a stable hand about Sina, who hadn't seen her, Rose ran up the aisle, peering into stalls. No Thomasina.

Arjuna entered the barn at the opposite end, and Rose headed in his direction. "Do you know where Lady Thomasina is? She sent me a message that Breeze was foaling."

The man startled. "Breeze is in the mares' barn, m'lady, as far as I am aware."

"Let's check."

They strode through the covered passageway and into the barn, and Breeze nickered as they entered her stall. After treating her to a peppermint, Rose ran her hands across the mare's sides and belly. No contractions. She lifted the mare's tail to examine her genitals. No change since the previous day.

"I wish I understood," Rose said. "The note Thomasina sent me makes no sense. When did you last see her?"

Arjuna tilted his head. "Perhaps an hour ago, m'lady. She was speaking with a gentleman behind barn three. A footman was with her."

"A gentleman, you say?" Rose said. "Did you recognize him?"

"No, my lady. Is something wrong?"

"Probably nothing, but please show me."

Arjuna closed Breeze's stall door, and they walked the path between barn three and the one housing the stallions. "They were here, m'lady."

Given the previous day's rain, Rose saw numerous footprints, but nothing helpful. Inside the barn, where Enbarr and their two other stallions were housed, all looked calm and peaceful, the studs enjoying their late-day meal.

But at the end of the row, in an empty stall, a footman lay crumpled in the straw.

"Arjuna!" she hollered, rushing inside. Blood ran down the man's temple, but his chest rose and fell, easing her fear he was dead.

"My lady," Arjuna said as he ran into the stall and spotted the footman. "Son of a dog!"

"He is alive," she said. "Get help."

Arjuna ran, while Rose kept watch on the injured man, her worry for Thomasina heightening.

Three footmen returned with Arjuna, Lucy in their wake

"Lucy, have you seen Lady Sina?" Rose said.

Lucy shook her head as the footmen and Arjuna lifted the injured man and began carrying him toward the house.

Stable hands clustered as Billy Broad and Grimes tore down the aisle.

"What happened?" Grimes said.

"Lady Thomasina is missing," Arjuna said. "And this footman was accompanying her."

"I saw her," Billy said. "Maybe an hour gone. She was with a gentleman and the injured footman, who was saddling her horse. I found that strange. Why would a footman do that rather than have a groom saddle Firefly?"

Firefly. Rose no longer rode the mare. Nor should anyone else. Not merely her edict, but Grimes and Sina's as well. "What did the gentleman look like?"

"A tall man," Billy said. "His back was to me as he held the reins of another horse."

"Any other details?"

Billy shrugged. "Not much to see. He wore top-boots and one of those many-caped greatcoats. And tall, as tall as the marquess, but thinner."

"Mr. Grimes, marshal the men, saddle as many searchers as possible. We must find Lady Thomasina. Billy, you ride with me, but first I must get some things from the house and send a message to Rhys."

Rose raced to the study, and it took her a few minutes to find Rhys' small brass spyglass tucked in a bottom desk drawer. She then dashed off notes to Rhys and Devonshire, handing them to a footman for urgent delivery to the duke's estate.

Though her thoughts were a-whirl, she believed that by taking Firefly, Thomasina was sending them a message.

Hold on, Thomasina. We are coming.

Rose and Billy followed the signs, Billy noting the passage of two horses. The man was a decent tracker and after ten minutes, he paused.

"The horses we're following are traveling near side by side," Billy said in a whisper. "I'd almost guess one rider's holdin' the reins of t'other's horse."

"She took Firefly, Billy. I think Lady Thomasina was trying to alert us."

He nodded. "I thought the same, m'lady. We tiptoe around that mare as if she were made of spun glass."

They moved on, the trail leading into the home wood, whereupon the pair they followed took a side path, then another, as if they were on a meander through the forest. Perhaps the stranger was unfamiliar with the grounds, and Thomasina was buying time or leading him astray. Probably both.

The world was hushed, for the day had grown thick with humidity. Soon, the land began to rise, and they climbed a small hillock.

Billy's hand shot out for them to halt. "We should leave the horses here. We're close."

"What makes you say that?" Rose asked.

Billy shrugged. "My gut?"

"Good enough for me." Rose nodded.

They looped their reins over a maple tree branch and walked on, bending low as they ascended, and at the hill's crest, Billy dropped to his belly. Rose did the same, then she opened the spyglass and held it to her eye.

On the opposite ridge, at the edge of the woods, sat a small camp.

"There," she said, pointing.

A tent crouched on the opposing hill, one much like Rhys' at his camp in the woods, only larger. Tethered to nearby trees were four horses, including Firefly.

"Mighty odd," Billy said in hushed tones. "Why the hell... Excuse me, my lady, but I see no purpose for a tent."

"A trap, maybe?" Rose said, raising the spyglass again.

"No sense to it, ma'am, out here in the middle of nowhere. No, I'd guess it's concealin' somethin'."

A man in a baggy jacket, a flat blue cap, and thick boots exited the tent.

Rose poked Billy. "When the man raised the flap, I saw several barrels stacked inside. What could they be?"

"Were they straight up or on their sides?" Billy said, his voice harsh.

"Straight up."

"Not spirits, then," Billy said. "Gunpowder comes to mind, ma'am."

An awful thought, and she recalled Pennworth's shouted threats at Ravenscroft about blowing them up. If these men were planning destruction, that gunpowder destroy the manor. The barns. Both. She swallowed hard.

"See if you recognize the man who exited." Rose handed Billy the glass. "I don't."

Billy raised the glass. "Nor me, neither."

"You said the kidnapper was a gentleman," Rose said. "So did Arjuna. That one's no gentleman."

Billy nodded. "He looks more like a cutpurse or worse, if you get my meanin'. I seen plenty like him in London. Nasty fellas, them."

On the breeze, Rose caught a familiar lemongrass scent, then heard a slight rustle. She turned, knife in hand, in case she was mistaken. Lucy and Arjuna approached.

Lucy wore wide green pantaloons native to her country, with rust-colored wrappings around her chest and tied behind her waist. Arjuna's clothes, though not Indian, matched in color.

Rose tucked her knife away and skittered down the hill to meet them. "What are you two doing here?"

Arjuna frowned. "Miss Lucy insisted."

"She did, did she?" Rose's eyes narrowed.

"I was to meet Lady Sina for a driving lesson," Lucy said. "She did not appear, and when you and Billy left on horseback, I knew we must come. What is wrong? We are here for support."

Rose wasn't quite sure how the pair would be supporting them, but she never discounted Lucy. In India, Lucy had been a warrior with an arsenal of tricks. Rose suspected Arjuna had talents as well. Fine and good, but they could be injured or killed if it truly was Pennworth behind Sina's kidnapping.

Unacceptable. "Return to the manor, please. I have sent for Rhys, and many will accompany him."

Lucy shook her head. "We will be enough, *Minnu*."

Dear heavens, now she had Lucy and Arjuna to worry about.

The thought recalled Rhys' words. *You would be a distraction, Rosie. Split my focus.*

Rose finally understood.

Sounds came across the small valley, and their trio scrambled back up the hill to Billy, who held the spyglass to one eye.

She couldn't see Thomasina, but Rose caught her words' cadence and tone from within the tent. Her sister was furious.

A loud slap rang in the air.

"Damn them!" Billy said.

"Yes," Rose said.

A second man exited the tent, one equally disreputable looking.

The skies darkened and mist began to cloud the air, turning the world a soft gray.

She wished Rhys was here. He would have some clever way to rescue Sina from the ruffians.

Where was that damned gentleman kidnapper? If Pennworth was the perpetrator, he would be the one directing these ruffians.

Billy handed Rose the spyglass, and as if her wish were granted, Sina exited the tent, her pink habit in disarray, her blonde hair askew. A red mark blotched her sister's cheek, and was that blood on her lip?

Damn them to Hades. They had *hurt* Sina!

Behind Thomasina stood the man in the greatcoat, his pantaloons and bright Hessians saying he was the gentleman and the key to this whole hullabaloo.

Rose's gut clenched.

Though she hadn't wanted to believe, she had known. The man responsible was that maggoty curse named Pennworth.

The fool.

"He is a dead man," Billy said in a whisper. "Lord Ravenscroft will kill him. Or I will."

"Pennworth may be a fool, but he is also lethal, Billy," Rose said. "With Lady Thomasina in such danger, I shall cross the valley to their camp." She lifted the spyglass. If Pennworth was after Rose, he would save any pain or revenge for himself and not allow his men to hurt her. She could prove an excellent distraction.

"Your thoughts, Lucy?" Rose turned for an answer, but she stared at empty space. Both Arjuna and Lucy were gone.

"Look at them, ma'am!" Billy whispered.

Heaven above, they were headed down the slope toward the camp on the opposite rise.

A shot rang out and slammed into...nothing. Where were Lucy and Arjuna? They had disappeared. They were hard to miss, yet the shooter had.

The pair reappeared on her right.

Another shot.

Another miss.

A chorus of shouts. "Get them!"

"Where are they?"

"There!"

More shots, more misses.

Somehow, Lucy and Arjuna anticipated the shooters' aim and moved.

Her eyes had left the camp long enough for two horses to be saddled, and now Thomasina sat atop Firefly, her hands bound.

Pennworth mounted, then leaned in the saddle to speak with one of the men. When he straightened, his crop thwacked Firefly's rump. Sina didn't even have hold of the reins.

CHAPTER

FORTY-ONE

The mare tore off down the hill, Thomasina relaxed in the saddle even without the reins. That girl could ride!

Firefly veered sharply left toward the pastures and barns, obviously not Pennworth's intended direction as he rode hell-for-leather after her.

Rose and Billy scrambled to their horses in pursuit.

They cantered through the trees, halting just before the grassy strip that separated the wood from the fenced pastures. Rose glanced back to see a man on the hill aiming his musket at Billy.

Rose leapt, sending them both flying as a shot rang out.

"Bollocks and blazes!" Billy landed hard, taking the brunt of the fall. "Were they aiming at you or me?"

"I couldn't tell." Rose rolled off him. "Are you hurt?"

"Just my dignity, ma'am," Billy said.

"Then what's that on your arm?"

"Huh." Billy stared at the blood, then lifted his injured arm. Or tried to. "Damn, that's my shooting arm."

Rose used her knife to cut her shirttails, then wound the fabric around Billy's arm in a makeshift bandage. "I will return."

"But my lady…"

She mounted Ace and headed for the pastures, hunkering low over the saddle. No point in making herself an easy target.

Please come soon, Rhys. Please.

Rose prepared to jump the fence as Sina whistled two sharp notes.

Oh, clever girl.

Rose reined in and slid off Ace to crouch on the ground. She might carry a pistol, but was too far distant to shoot Pennworth with any accuracy. She could jump the fence and ride toward them, making herself a target. But rather than join the fray, Rose suspected Sina's plan and wanted to see it play out, a smile on her lips.

Billy crept up behind her. "What's happening?"

Rose explained about the whistles, then returned to the display at the pasture's center.

The horses' ears had perked, and Sina whistled the two notes again. The horses' ears swiveled forward, galloping full-out toward Thomasina and Pennworth, who was closing on her sister.

The viscount raised his crop to hit Sina, but the herd was close. Too close. He screamed at Thomasina, squeezed his horse's sides, and turned it away, preparing to run.

But there was nowhere *to* run, for the Woodbine horses had encircled them, racing faster and faster.

Sina's whistle changed pitch, sinking to lower notes. The circle widened, the horses slowing.

Two more unique notes and a white gelding cantered toward Pennworth, who was flailing his crop at the horses to no effect. He drew his gun as the gelding reared, its hooves on a downward arc barely brushing Pennworth and Thomasina.

Sina's thighs held on to Firefly, for she'd known what to expect. The hooves never touched her.

Pennworth tumbled from his mount like a tin soldier.

Distant shouts, men galloping toward them, with Rhys atop Enbarr in the forefront.

The horses' circle parted and Thomasina and Firefly trotted to meet Rhys, as the viscount staggered to his feet, his right arm limp.

He wobbled, then steadied himself, his left hand groping awkwardly for the pistol hanging from his right hip.

No!

Rose leapt onto Ace's back, reining him backward, then kicking him into a canter. He soared over the fence and galloped onward.

Pennworth fumbled, dropping his pistol.

Rhythm established, Rose leaned forward and raised her feet to the saddle, getting them beneath her as they neared.

When Ace drew close enough for her to leap, Pennworth again reached for his gun.

Rose leapt, spinning once, and kicking out her feet. Time slowed—the air thick, scents of new-mown grass, Pennworth aiming his pistol—as she arrowed toward him. Would she reach him in time?

She connected with Pennworth's back just as he fired.

Boom! Down they went in a jumble of limbs, Pennworth beneath her, her head slamming into a booted foot. She reeled.

"Cocksucking bitch!" Pennworth screeched, his hand rooting for his gun.

Rose blinked, dizzy and reeling.

Pennworth grasped his pistol, raising his double-barreled flintlock at Thomasina's back.

He might be out of range to hit her. Or he might not.

Rose's vision was blurry, the world still reeling. She *must* respond, and with a fierce jerk upward, she slammed the *adi* hand strike onto his temple.

Pennworth crumpled.

Rose was preparing for bed. Alone. Again.

The remainder of their day had been spent delivering Pennworth to the magistrate, rounding up his cohorts, and safely disposing of what indeed had been gunpowder.

Devonshire, having received her note, had followed Rhys to Woodbine. It was he who greased the wheels, given the legal ramifications of arresting the murderous Pennworth. The man was a viscount and a decorated officer, after all.

Thomasina, remarkably, was again her merry self. True, she had been frightened, but she also considered her kidnapping a grand adventure. Rose was thankful for that. Billy Broad's injury proved little more than a flesh wound and was properly bandaged, while Firefly was now ensconced in her stall, seeming no worse for wear. Another blessing.

Lucy and Arjuna resurfaced during the proceedings in the paddock, looking fit as fleas and quite pleased with themselves.

All of Woodbine was well and accounted for, thank the heavens.

Pennworth had gotten his just desserts. Finally.

A crease marred Rhys' abandoned pillow, and Rose smoothed it out.

After her spin and tumble, he had hugged her tight for long minutes, but had spent the rest of the day capturing Pennworth's felonious comrades. Hours had passed, and she ached everywhere. She wished Rhys were here beside her, in bed, safe and loving her.

Rose donned her nightrail. She should be happy, euphoric even, that the day's proceedings had turned out so fine when those she loved could have been injured or killed.

She lifted Bram from the bed to nuzzle his fur. "Is that stubborn man still in a pique or taking care of the day's business?"

Bram snored on.

Oh, bother!

She would hunt Rhys down. After pulling a wrapper around her, Rose entered her sitting room.

A knock at the door. Lucy, with her nightly delivery of chocolate.

"Come in."

The door swung open to reveal Rhys carrying a tray with cups, a pot, and biscuits, with Isla at his heels and Percy perched on his shoulder.

Rose froze, all the words she'd prepared flying like moths into the ether. Her beautiful man had come, though why he had that bird with him she couldn't imagine.

His smile twitched, and he shrugged. "Sina has been teaching him tricks. I thought he might make you smile."

But Rose couldn't smile because tears pressed against her eyes, so relieved that Rhys was teasing her once again.

"Do you wish your chocolate in bed or here?" he said.

"Here, if you please."

He set the tray on the small table and began removing its contents. "How are you feeling? After today's events, I mean."

"Tired." She walked to stand beside him. "Sore. But given today's events, that's to be expected, wouldn't you say?"

"I have seldom felt more terror." Rhys pulled out her chair, and she sat. "Thank God Enbarr is a tolerant fellow," he said. "For I pressed him hard, harder than I ever have to get to you, Rosie."

He took the opposite seat across from her, where she'd placed his cup of chocolate. Her chest hurt. "I..."

"I have been an arse, Rosie. A first-class arse."

No clever quip came to mind, so she lifted a biscuit and took a nibble.

He reached across the table and took her free hand. "I am sorry. I know you have been terribly unhappy with me, and I caused you pain, something I never wished to do."

She was too emotional, too overcome with a mixture of relief, joy, anger, and sadness.

"I will never again treat you thus," he continued. "I swear it."

That made her smile. "We will both get angry over the course of our marriage, and I suspect each of us will react poorly. We are human, husband. But thank you for your apology." She squeezed his hand.

"Pride can be a terrible thing." He rose and walked to open the door, lifting Percy from his shoulder. The bird flew into the hall, and Rhys shut the door behind him.

"Won't we need to recapture him?" she said.

"Not in the least. He adores Thomasina, which is why he will fly to find her. Sina claims Percy is brilliant. I have yet to see that aspect of the pest, but I will take Sina's word for it."

Returning to Rose, he moved his chair beside hers. "We were so far apart for so many days. I want to keep you close."

Rose rested her head on his shoulder. "I am sorry I did not tell you about Lightning Rod. But Rhys, I knew you would never agree to trade him for your freedom, you stubborn man."

Abandoning their repast, he lifted Rose from the chair and carried her into the bedroom.

"Love me, Rosie, any way you wish." He kissed her neck.

Rose wrapped her arms around him and kissed his lips, imbuing it with all the love and passion she felt for this man.

Rosie's kiss was an urgent one, one that told Rhys yes, now. A kiss that said this night would be different.

"I chose to marry you, Rhys. I will not cheat you out of a complete life. Nor will I permit the earl's actions to define my life." Rose smiled. "I am determined."

"Ah, darling Rosie," Rhys said. "I love you with all my heart."

Her eyes widened. "You said the words."

"What?"

"That you love me."

Christ, what was wrong with him? A thousand thousand times he'd said them in his mind. He'd meant to say them aloud, for words mattered. To Rose. To him. "I love you, Rose Lansdowne, and I will repeat it daily. Nay, hourly."

She was laughing now, and he was glad.

"I always have," he continued. "From the very first. You claimed my heart the day you brought Tessa. That has never changed. Nor will it."

Amidst the laughter, a tear spilled onto her cheek. "Oh Rhys, my most wonderful best friend. I do love you so very much. Tonight will be our new beginning."

When Rose threw off her nightrail, Rhys struggled, for he practically wept with desire. But no matter how fervently she had kissed him, no matter how much she wanted him, he must take care. Memories lurked within her, powerful ones that could catch her unawares if he moved too fast.

Finally naked—it seemed to take forever to undo his pantaloon buttons—he set Bram and Isla in their dog beds, lifted the covers, and lay down face up, emotions running riot inside him.

He donned a smile and opened his arms wide. "Do what you will, my lady."

Rose's eyes hungered as she climbed beside him onto the bed. She bit her lip.

"What is it?" he said

"A problem."

"Solvable?" Rhys arched his brow as he stroked her arm.

"I hope so." She looked everywhere but at him.

"We need not do anything. I can hold you in my arms while we sleep, as we have done many times. I have missed holding you, Rosie."

"As I have you. Terribly." She wove a hand through his hair, caressing its strands again and again. "You see, I fear I will panic."

"As I said, my love, we need not—"

"But I want to make love, you see? I... I desire you. Very much."

He grinned. "That is a blessing."

"Yes, and... I want children. Yours. And you need heirs, but I don't know if I can—"

"What need have I of heirs, at least not now? There is Patrick."

"I have another problem." Rose huffed. "I do not want you laid out like a fish to be gutted, with me..." Rose cleared her throat. "With me atop you."

He smiled. "Trust me, I feel nothing like a fish."

Her eyes sparkled. "Hum. You do not much resemble one, either. But...I want you to desire me."

Desire her? He was mad for her and becoming more deranged by the moment. His breath had quickened and sweat beaded his temples. Rhys gestured to his stiffened erection, near painfully hard. "I would say this is evidence. Would you not?"

She rested back on her heels, her hands wafting the air as if the words refused to come.

"Rose?" He pushed himself up on an elbow to get a better view of his complicated wife.

"I guess..." she said. "I guess it is that I do not wish you to lie back and think of England. I want you to show me your desire. To be yourself, Rhys. The man I love more than anything or anyone in this world."

Smiling, he quirked a brow. "Even Firefly?"

A watery giggle. "Even Firefly."

"What about Ace?" Rhys took her in his arms and down to the bed, lying face-to-face with his glorious Rosie.

"Ace, too." She laughed. "It is awkward, you see. If I am atop you, I am not sure how to proceed. But if you are atop me, I fear I shall panic. I do not know what to do, Rhys."

His smile widened, his eyes devouring her. "I do."

Rose nodded, and he lifted her thigh so it draped across hip, and stroked her with one hand, while kissing her lips, his fingers massaging her clitoris. Rose was busy too, her butterfly kisses everywhere, increasing his desire exponentially.

He paused. "Are you well?"

She nodded, whispering, "Exceedingly."

After long moments of pleasure, he moved his mouth to where his fingers had been so busy. His gorgeous girl climaxed just as he wondered how long he could hold off the volcano within demanding release. Easing away he gazed into those beautiful eyes.

"Now, Rhys," she said.

With great care, he slid an inch inside, then another, and another. Then he was home.

He paused, not simply for Rose to adjust, but to gather his tattered will. It felt as if he had wished for this union since he took his first breath. He did not wish to gallop.

At first, they struggled, their movements not quite in sync. But soon each caught the other's rhythm in beautiful harmony.

Rose's arms tightened around him, and she threw back her head, her glorious hair spilling across the pillow like liquid fire. Her eyes closed, her breaths quickened, and soft sighs of his name whispered from her lips.

His Rosie. Friend. Guiding star. Love. For as long as memory. Until forever.

They embraced side by side, sharing small touches and kisses in the warm, sweaty afterglow of their lovemaking.

"Oh, my." Rose raised Rhys' hand to her lips and kissed each finger. She had no words for the experience, had no comparison—dancing with the stars, perhaps—her heart more full than she could ever recall.

"My Rosie."

"That was so...lovely. Yes, perfectly lovely."

"*You* are perfectly lovely, my dear," he said.

She was full up with joy. Pure joy. "How unexpected."

"What?"

"The pleasure."

"That is what making love should be." Rhys kissed her nose. "God's teeth, that was grand."

"Um..." She grinned. "I do have one question."

"And what might that be, wife?"

"When shall we do it again?"

Rhys chuckled, which turned into a belly laugh, and he wrapped her in his arms and held her tight.

EPILOGUE

Their marital bliss continued the following week until Rhys received a message. He sought out Rose, finding her in the kitchen with Cook discussing the day's menus.

Taking Rosie's hand, he kissed her palm. God's breath, their nightly activities made him randy as a goat. "I must be off for a couple of days on business in London, my love."

Rose gave him a saucy grin. "Shall I join you?"

"I am afraid not. Sadly, I will be closeted with solicitors and thus have little free time. Unless you wish to shop."

"Shop?" Her smile was sly. "For a new horse, perhaps?"

Rhys chuckled. "Not this trip, I am sorry to say. But I may have a surprise for you on my return."

Her eyes widened. "Oh, do tell!"

"Sweetheart," he said. "What kind of surprise would that be?" He laughed, drawing her arm through his and walking out into the beautiful day.

"All right," she said with a moue of displeasure. "If you must keep secrets. Are you sure...?"

"Very," he said, affecting a commanding tone.

"I will miss you very much, Rhys."

He took her in an impassioned kiss, and when they drew apart, he smiled, shaking his head. "I will miss you more, my heart."

Rose was in the glums. "A couple of days" had turned to four, and she missed Rhys fiercely. Beyond the white fence where she leaned, Dolce gamboled in the pasture with Firefly and Bug. The little filly was growing at a rapid rate, her bay coat gleaming in the sunlight.

A scorching day, and she wished she'd carried her fan, for the air was humid and still.

This longing for her husband was a frightening thing. Rose shook her head as she pushed away from the fence and reached into her pocket. All three horses thundered toward her. She chuckled. They knew all about pockets, and upon their arrival, she handed each a peppermint, petting them, praising them, and telling Dolce how she was growing into a magnificent mare.

But the minute she left the horses, her glums returned. Ridiculous. Absurd. As a marquess, Rhys had many responsibilities, ones he took seriously. Often, he would include her in his excursions, asking her opinion, seeking her thoughts.

Yet he had not done so on this trip. Why? He might be busy during the day, but they would have had the nights.

A nasty thought occurred. If Rhys were in danger, he would move to keep her out of it. Or...

Trouble was, she failed to think of a single "or" and it nagged her. *Why had he not taken her with him?*

She crossed the pasture, stopped to check on Breeze and her new foal, then continued onto the manor.

Gravel crunching and much shouting in the drive signaled a vehicle's arrival. *Rhys!*

Her view obscured by the screen of crepe myrtles and blooming fuchsia, Rose picked up her skirts and ran.

At Woodbine's front entrance, a pair of shire horses driven by a stranger stood before a hitched wagon. The conveyance was unlike any she'd seen before, with a wooden bed and a high curved canvas top, its tailgate of wood rising to meet the canvas while the wagon shifted back and forth.

Then she saw him, Rhys, atop Enbarr, his white hair shining in the sun.

Rose ran faster. "Rhys!"

He leapt off Enbarr, and they met with a thump, him enveloping her in a near-painful grip.

Her world had regained its keel.

"It appears you are glad to see me, wife." He peered down at her.

"Very glad, my lord."

"As am I to see you."

His dear face filled her vision. "Was your business in London successful?"

Those blue eyes twinkled. "Very much so."

Ohhh. Rhys' surprise. "I must ask, what is in that strange wagon of yours?"

"The fruits of my success." Taking her hand, he led her toward the wagon's rear, where Angus stood wreathed in a knowing grin.

Rhys nodded, and Angus unfastened the locks on each side of the tailgate, then lowered it to the ground.

Rose peered inside, though she couldn't see much.

Angus strode up the ramp, then more stomping. And then a whinny.

"You *did* bring a new horse!" Rose said.

"Not exactly." His laugh was accompanied by the clopping of hooves.

"Rhys?"

A black nose peeked out and then...

Lightning Rod flew out of the wagon and began butting his head against her skirts.

Rose fell to her knees, arms encircling the colt's neck, her face pressed to his warm coat.

"How?" she said. "How did you do this?"

"Magic."

"Merciful heavens, you did not steal him, did you?"

"No, love." Rhys hunkered down beside them, chuckling. "I thought on what Mrs. Fitzherbert loves, pondered what she adores more than race horses. Jewels, my dear. The woman loves jewels. An amenable soul, one rather taken with our love story. We talked, and I liked her quite well. It seems Mrs. Fitzherbert acquires jewels to put them aside for a rainy day."

Rose sighed. "For when the prince leaves her for good." She inhaled Roddy's scent. He was here. He was home.

"I am afraid so," Rhys said. "She is a practical woman, and though she loves the prince, Mrs. Fitzherbert is not such a fool as to ignore her future security."

"I still cannot believe she would trade Roddy for jewels. She and the prince were so enthused."

"You gave Roddy to Mrs. Fitzherbert, if you recall, and the prince agreed the colt was hers. But I could not simply trade any gems. That would not suffice, love. Instead, I offered her the Ravenscroft emerald-and-diamond parure."

"The set I wore to our wedding ball?" Rose said. "You did not!"

"I did. Happily, in fact. The marquessate has abundant jewels, and I suspected you prize this little colt far more than cold stones."

"You know I do."

"Precious gems are replaceable," he said. "Roddy is not. *You* are not. I realized several things while I was away, and I know how much you love this little colt.

"So much," she said, rising to stand, Rhys rising with her. She held Roddy's lead, and Rhys took her elbow to steady her, the colt frisky after his travels.

Rhys brushed her knuckles with his thumb. "When I simmered down from my—"

"Pique?" she said.

"Unfortunately, yes, which was when I grasped my behavior was from my injured pride. The second thing that seeped into this thick skull of mine—"

"Harrumph!" she said. "You do not have a thick skull."

He whispered in her ear. "I finally understood that you loved me even more than this colt you adored."

"Well, of course I do." She wound a hand around his neck and gave him a proper kiss. At some point, Angus took Roddy's line and led him away.

Happier than she could recall, Rose leaned against Rhys.

"When do we return to Ravenscroft?" Rose said.

He squeezed her waist. "You prefer Woodbine, do you not?"

"I confess I do, and not just for the horses, but spending time with Susannah and Thomasina as well. I have even formed a small affection for the ridiculous Percy. He can say my name now!"

"Well, that decides it, then. We stay for as long as we wish."

"I am pleased. But no matter where we go—Woodbine, Ravenscroft, the moon—*you* are my polestar, my home."

"A colt or jewels does not define our bond," he said. "We do. You made a great sacrifice with Roddy, one I vowed to rectify."

"You have done that, darling, and so much more," she said.

He winged an arm, and Rose slipped her hand through it. "Shall we repair to the—"

"Bedroom." Rose grinned.

"Ah. I could not agree more, my lady."

Rose adopted a faux-serious demeanor. "Let us proceed in a dignified fashion, shall we?"

"Of course," Rhys said in a plummy voice. "That would only be proper."

"I am confident all Woodbine is watching."

"I see faces in the windows." He smiled and took her hand.

They ran.

ACKNOWLEDGMENTS

I'd like to thank my readers for giving me daily inspiration! You're the best!

Many thanks to those who helped shepherd *THE BOND* through to the finish line. Yet again, my incomparable editor, Aria Jones, worked her magic. No matter the genre, Aria is superb at what she does!

To the extraordinary Camille Cotton—this book wouldn't exist without you. To the amazing Rosemary Hill, whose friendship, aid, and insights are both invaluable and inspirational. To Monica—for your fantastic blurb help.

To my much-loved Betas: Ro, Camille, Joanie, Wayne, Meri, and Annette for their invaluable critiques and, most of all, their friendship. To Lorelai—who keeps me smiling through the sweat and tears.

To my exceptional cover artist, Blake Ricciardi, aided by Mike Le—you turned my dream cover into reality. Thank you!

MsPurdy's hats on Etsy are outstanding!

To the Illuterati and my Facebook pals who inspire me with warmth, humor, and truth-telling. To the Warrioresses, who soothe my heart, and to Parris Afton Bonds, who hugs my soul. To my yoga pals, Ren, Chris, Sheri, Franny, Annette, Edie, and Emma, who support me in so many ways.

To Let's Ride, and all its denizens both two- and four-hooved. To Andrea Urban, Suzanne Hendrich, Pat Murphy, Donna Cautilli, CJ Williams, Linda Windels—love you. To Cindy's Knitters for the many stitches we wove together. To Betsy Bair, Georgi Mueller, and Karen Waxman for your love and friendship. To Cynthia Michaels, for your friendship and giving Cranberry love.

To Peter, Kathleen, and Summer—your love and profound support make my world turn. Love you! Finally, to my beloved boys, Blake and Ben—for all that you are, for all that you have gifted me, and for your abiding love. I'm the luckiest mom in the world.

Any errors or screw-ups are mine alone.

THANK YOU! AND NEWSLETTER

Thank you for reading *The Bond*!

Reviews mean everything—they're an author's lifeblood as readers find us through your reviews. If you enjoyed Rose and Rhys' tale, leaving an honest review would be a kindness.

Would you like a free book? Do sign up for Vicki's newsletter (Sanna doesn't have one yet) and receive her bonus novel, *Body Parts*. Her monthly newsletter contains info on The Secret Tales, The Made Ones Saga, the Afterworld Chronicles, life in L.A., and lots more yummy stuff.

Come visit with me... VickiStiefel.net & SannaBrand.com
Facebook • Instagram • Twitter • BookBub

THE DECEPTION
THE SECRET TALES, BOOK 2

CHAPTER 1

The Duke of Devonshire's glittering ball was in full cry. Lord Patrick Ravenscroft Lansdowne, naval captain and recent viscount, had little use for it, his attendance for another purpose—to purchase a painting by the illustrious Reginald Pheland, the deceased Baron Halafair.

Though the baron was long dead, paintings by his hand came for a hefty price and were not often up for sale. While Patrick admired the artist's landscapes, his seascapes drew him like no other artist. The movement of the waves, the scudding of the clouds, the colors of the dawn and sunset at sea—Halafair's work compelled him.

This evening's purchase had come about through a circuitous route via factor and letters exchanged between himself and the seller.

The irony was not lost on him. He was acquainted with the late Halafair's former baroness, Beatrice, and their two daughters, Charlotte and Claire, stepmother and stepsisters to his sister-in-law, Rose. He ofttimes wondered what they would think of his passion, never wishing to raise the subject.

The factor insisted the seller wished to disguise his identity by wearing a mask and using the alias "Gumdrop."

The folly of the seller's nom de plume riled him, and he'd dashed off a note saying his purchase was no trifling business. Gumdrop indeed.

He had to confess, the seller's reply intrigued him. Gumdrop had written, "Life is a serious business, sir. This is commerce, and one cannot give a transaction too much weight."

The seller had a point.

Patrick chose to play along, calling himself Joseph Hart, a minor Baronet and friend who happened to be touring the continent. For Patrick lusted after the painting and would do just about anything to acquire it.

He stood on the manor's balcony, out the French doors where the ball was being held. The night was clear, stars spangling the sky, the same ones he charted at sea. He would return soon and was eager for it.

Unable to stop himself, Patrick checked his pocket watch yet again. The time for their meeting neared.

He slipped through the ballroom and made his way downstairs to the second floor and into Devonshire's library, as noted in the factor's missive. The vast room held stacks upon stacks of books, two sliding ladders, and a spiral staircase that wound upward to a second level.

Before him, a hearth large enough to fit a horse smoldered, with two wing chairs placed before its flames.

Patrick paced, for he was early by fifteen minutes, having planned to arrive before the seller did so. His nerves were aquiver, his adrenaline high, unusual feelings, far more so than standing on deck facing an enemy's brace of canon.

Midnight chimed from the mantel clock and behind him, a rustle.

Patrick whirled to see a woman in an elegant cobalt gown emerge from one of the wing chairs before the hearth. His shock yielded to an appreciation of her curvaceous form, a glittering mask shaped like an owl shading her eyes, much of her face, and her bound hair.

His "disguise" comprised a black mask and civilian clothes, as he most often wore his uniform.

"Have you brought the funds, sir?" the seller said.

Patrick froze, stunned.

Charlotte had been all nerves since the start of the ball. Even a dance with the handsome and skilled Duke of Devonshire failed to calm her.

As the appointed time neared, Lotte retrieved the small painting she had stored in an unused bedroom, the artwork now leaning against the chair from which she had risen.

The man before her wore a mask, yet struck a vaguely familiar cord that increased her caution.

Even wary, she must go through with the sale. Her mother and sister's well-being depended upon it. While their dear papa had been a warm and wonderful man and a lovely painter, he had not been wise when it came to funds. They had been destitute until her mother married Earl Fielding, and with the Earl's death, their comfort had reversed once again.

"Have you brought the funds, sir?"

The man stiffened and nodded, but he said not a word.

"Sir?"

He reached into an inner pocket of his tailcoat and withdrew a pouch.

Lotte crossed her arms. She would not release the painting to a man who did not utter a word, his silence suggesting deceit.

The absurdity of their face-off nearly made her laugh, and Lottie appreciated the situation's humor, as fit for a theatrical melodrama.

In a fit of pique, she lifted the wrapped painting from behind the chair. "I'm afraid we shall not begin with the sale, good sir, unless you speak." Lotte turned to leave.

The man's lips thinned, but she cared little for his anger.

She took a step toward the door. "If you do not speak to me, sir, I am afraid you will neither see nor leave with the painting you appeared to desire so very much."

If he overpowered her and stole the painting, she would scream the house down, the pistol in her pocket further insurance against any nefarious doings. Nonetheless, tension tightened her belly. Lottie forced a smile. "Well?"

"What do you wish me to say, Madame Gumdrop?"

Charlotte reeled. "Lord Patrick?"

He removed his mask. "Yes, Lady Charlotte, it is I."

She tossed her mask onto a chair and approached him.

Unbelievable. Patrick was a burr in her side, the nuisance who tweaked her and others with his sarcasm and quips.

"You admire my father's work?" she said.

The man's stiff back relaxed a fraction. "Admire is too weak a word for my regard for his paintings. His seascapes take me to the place I love most in this world."

He could not have surprised her more. Patrick Lansdowne was a sniping, caustic, hell-for-leather fellow whose set-downs were carved with a delicate but lethal knife. "That pleases me, for all this cloak-and-dagger wears on a person."

He let out a chuckle. "I agree, but the factor insisted upon it."

Lotte's cheeks heated. "I'm afraid that was my doing. Given that I am a woman, it makes it quite awkward to be selling one's own father's paintings."

"Why are you doing so?" he said.

"Shall we get on with it?" she said.

A rattle at the door, then it swung open, and a horde entered the library. Lotte's mother and sister, the Marquess and Marchioness of Ravenscroft, the Dukes of Devonshire and Wellington, and a dozen other ball attendees, including the very irritating Lady Ablethorp, a gossip with a nasty tongue.

Lady Ablethorp plowed her way forward to the front of the crowd. "What do we have here? An assignation?"

Ruination crashed upon Charlotte like an avalanche.

TO BE CONTINUED...

About the Author

BY VICKI STIEFEL

A fable~

Once upon a time...

When my great grandmother came to America from England, she carried only two items—her Bible and her great-grandmother's diaries. Great-nana Sanna Brand was an inveterate diarist and wrote daily. For years, I've been pouring through her journals, fascinated. Much she wrote was mundane—about family, fashion, food, and her beaus (until she met my great, great etc. grandfather).

I read and read until I came upon a peculiar journal— which turned out to be Sanna's novel!

(I also learned from her journals that her first name was actually Susannah, but her youngest brother couldn't pronounce the word and called her Sanna. Thus, forever-after, she used that name.)

So far, I've discovered four books penned by Sanna Brand.

What to do? Publish them, of course!

The first one, *THE BOND*, takes place in Regency England near Sanna's childhood home and is the first book in The Secret Tales.

Sanna's writing shocked me at first because *THE BOND* includes love, murder, adventure, some tender subjects, bits of naughty romance, numerous horses, a goat, dogs, and much more.

~In truth, that is how I imagine Sanna, my alter ego.~

Award-winning author Vicki Stiefel's romantic science-fantasy series, The Made Ones Saga, concluded with *Ascendant*. Vicki continues work on her Afterworld Chronicles, a five-book series begun with *Chest of Bone*. Her mystery/thrillers feature homicide counselor Tally Whyte, and Vicki's knitting love produced *Chest of Bone The Knit Collection* and *10 Secrets of the LaidBack Knitters*.

Having grown up in professional theater, Vicki planned to become an actress. Instead, she slung hamburgers, managed a scuba shop, and taught at Clark U. She's a mom to two wonderful humans and is currently playing with her pups, Penny and Sebastian, and her kitty, Sammy, while pounding the keys on *THE DECEPTION*, the second book in The Secret Tales.

Come visit with me...
vickistiefel.net or SannaBrand.com

PRAISE FOR VICKI STIEFEL

SANNA BRAND'S ALTER EGO

Ascendant, The Made Ones

"I really thought this was a fitting ending [to the Made Ones trilogy], and I bloody loved it!...A great series that I have no hesitation in recommending."—Archaeolibrarian

"The Made Ones Saga has been on my favorites list since I read *Altered* in 2019. This sci-fi/ fantasy/ romance mashup conclusion... is epic!"—Whiskey with My Book

Changed, The Made Ones Saga

"This was a fantastic second book. Absolutely recommended by me!"—Archaeolibrarian

"*Changed* is complex, captivating, dangerous and heartwarming. So if you are looking for fantasy, scifi, and/or romance you might want to check this one out."—Whiskey with My Book

Altered, The Made Ones Saga

"*Altered* contains romance, humor, flying horses, and a playfulness that any lover of fantasy or romance will want to spend their entire weekend devouring. This superbly written and well-edited book necessitates a rating of 4 out of 4 stars." —OnlineBookClub

"*Altered* is a delightfully different book. I loved the characters and

369

the world the author created. The whole subject of parallel universes is fascinating. It's a simple story but tugs at your heartstrings. Makes one wonder, how would I react if this happened to me?" —Cranky The Book Curmudgeon

THE AFTERWORLD CHRONICLES

"This third book in the Afterworld Chronicles, *Chest of Time*, sets quite the fast pace putting them all including Larrimer and their band of followers in even more dangerous, complex, and challenging situations...enjoy this wild and intense ride. — Lynn Latimer, reviewer

"*Chest of Stone* is a fast-paced urban fantasy with plenty of action and eclectic, vibrant world-building. Ms Stiefel's... writing is very original, it just flows, always in the moment, always unconstrained. There was nothing formulaic about *Chest of Stone*, and I thoroughly enjoyed that. — Nocturnal Book Reviews

"*Chest of Bone's* writing style is innovative, the world is very interesting and provocative. It's a great story! I's a bunch of crazy, but it's GOOD crazy, with some super vivid scenes and fascinating characters." —Nocturnal Book Reviews

THE TALLY WHYTE SERIES

"This is an amazing thriller with action on almost every page. The heroine is strong, independent and sees things nobody else does... Vicki Stiefel writes a brilliant psychological thriller." —Book Review.com

"Tally is a compelling protagonist—edgy, compassionate and vulnerable—with a clipped narrating style that keeps the tricky plot in focus. She can hold her own against genre heavyweights like John Sanford and Patricia Cornwell." —Publishers Weekly

"Compelling, touching, and a pleasure to read." —Robert Parker

"Three words describe the Tally Whyte series: Intense. Addictive. Chilling. Tally's personality will draw you in as surely as the mystery does in this series." —Fresh Fiction

Also by Vicki Stiefel

The Made Ones Saga

Altered

Changed

Ascendant

The Afterworld Chronicles

Chest of Bone— Also on Audible

Chest of Stone

Chest of Time

Chest of Fire (to come)

Tally Whyte/Homicide Counselor Series

Body Parts • *The Dead Stone* • *The Grief Shop* (Daphne duMaurier Award winner) • *The Bone Man* (Daphne duMaurier Award finalist)

Nonfiction

10 Secrets of the LaidBack Knitters

Chest of Bone The Knit Collection

Visit with Vicki:

Website • Facebook • Instagram • BookBub